"That can't happen! I can't be in at kind of danger."

eston tried to keep his voice as calm as possible. rd to do, though, with the emotions swirling e a tornado inside him. "I'm sorry. If there was ther way to stop him, then I wouldn't have e here. I know I don't have a right to ask, but ed your help."

an't."

u can't? You must want this killer off the et. It's the only way you'll ever be truly safe."

lie opened her mouth. Closed it. And she ed at him. "I'd planned on telling you. Not like

e was a new emotion in her voice and on her . One that W   nger 'Tell me wh

dragged in   her lders. "I   ight angler becau   ddie k another deep breath. "I'm three months gnant. And the baby is *yours*."

LONE WOLF LAWMAN

DELORES FOSSEN

Published in Great Britain 2015
by Mills & Boon, an imprint of Harlequin (UK) Limited,
Eton House, 18-24 Paradise Road, Richmond, Surrey, TW9 1SR

© 2015 Delores Fossen

ISBN: 978-0-263-25322-1

46-1115

Printed and bound in Spain
by CPI, Barcelona

Delores Fossen, a *USA TODAY* bestselling author, has sold over fifty novels with millions of copies of her books in print worldwide. She's received the Booksellers' Best Award and the RT Reviewers' Choice Best Book Award. She was also a finalist for a prestigious RITA® Award. You can contact the author through her webpage at www.dfossen.net.

Chapter One

Addie Crockett heard the footsteps behind her a split second too late.

Before she could even turn around and see who was in the hall outside her home office, someone grabbed her.

She managed a strangled sound, barely. But the person slapped a hand over her mouth to muffle the scream that bubbled up in her throat.

Oh, mercy.

What was going on?

This was obviously some kind of attack, but Addie wouldn't just let this person hurt her. Or worse. She rammed her elbow into her attacker's stomach, but it did nothing to break the grip he had on her.

"Stop," he snapped. "I won't hurt you."

Addie wasn't taking his word for it. She turned, using his own grip to shove him against the wall and into an angel Christmas wreath. The painted wooden angels went flying. But not the man.

Addie tried to get his hand off her mouth so she could call out for help. Then she remembered her brothers weren't at the ranch. Two were still at work, and the other was Christmas shopping in San Antonio. Only her mother was inside the house, and she had a sprained ankle. Addie didn't want her mother to come hobbling into the middle of this.

Whatever *this* was.

"Stop," he repeated when she kept struggling. His voice was a hoarse whisper, and he dragged her from the hall into her office.

Addie gave him another jab of her elbow and would have delivered a third one if the man hadn't cursed. She hadn't recognized his order for her to stop, but she certainly recognized his voice now.

Wes Martin.

The relief collided with the slam of adrenaline, and it took Addie a moment to force herself to stop fighting so she could turn around and face him. Even though the sun was already close to setting and the lights weren't on in her office, there was enough illumination from the hall to see his black hair. His face. His eyes.

Yes, it was Wes all right.

The relief she'd felt didn't last long at all.

"What are you doing here?" Addie demanded. "And how'd you get in the house?" Those were only the first of many questions, and how much else she told him depended on what he had to say in the next couple of seconds.

He didn't jump to start those answers. Wes stood there staring at her as if she were a stranger. Well, she wasn't. And he knew that better than anyone. He'd seen every last inch of her.

Ditto for her seeing every last inch of him.

And despite the fact that it was the last thing Addie wanted in her head at this moment, the memories came of Wes naked and of her in his arms. Thankfully, he wasn't naked now. He was wearing jeans, a button-up shirt and a tan cowboy hat.

But there was something different about this cowboy outfit.

Beneath his jacket, he was wearing a waist holster and a gun.

"I came in through the side door." He tipped his head toward the hall. "It wasn't locked."

That wasn't unusual. Because the ranch hands—and the family—were often coming and going. They rarely locked up the house until bedtime. Even then, that was hit-or-miss since security wasn't usually an issue.

Until now, that was.

"I didn't see your car," she said, and since she'd just come in from the main barn, Addie would have seen any unfamiliar vehicles in the circular driveway in front of the house.

"I parked just off the main road and walked up. I'm sorry," he added, following her gaze to his gun. "But I had to come."

That didn't answer her other question as to why he was there, and Addie wasn't sure if she just wanted to send him packing or try to figure out what the heck was going on.

She went with the first option.

Wes had crushed her heart six ways to Sunday, and there was no need for her to give him another chance to hurt her again.

"You're leaving," Addie insisted, and she turned around to head to the hall so she could usher him right back out the side door.

She didn't get far because he took hold of her arm again. Not the tight grip he'd had before, but it was enough to keep her in place. And enough to rile her even more. "Let go of me."

"I can't." Wes opened his mouth, but any explanation he was about to give her ground to a halt. "We have to talk," he added after a very long pause.

"And you had to sneak in here and grab me to do that? You could have called."

"I had to see you in person, and I grabbed you because I didn't want you shouting out for someone. I didn't want to get shot before you listen to what I have to tell you. And you have to listen."

It was partly her bruised ego reacting, but Addie huffed, folded her arms over her chest and glared at him. "You slept with me three months ago and then disappeared without so much as an email. Why should I listen to anything you have to say, huh?"

Still no quick answer. Probably because there wasn't one. Not one she'd want to hear anyway. But what she did want to hear was why he had on that gun holster that looked as if he'd been born to wear it. Also, why hadn't she been able to find out anything about him online?

Everything inside her went still.

"Who are you, *really*?" she asked.

Another long pause. "I'm not the man you think I am."

A burst of air left her mouth. Definitely not laughter. "Clearly. Now tell me something I don't know."

The hurt came hard and fast. Addie felt as if someone had put a vise around her heart. The tears quickly followed, too, and she tried hard to blink them away. No way did she want this man to see her cry.

"I'm sorry." He added more of that profanity and reached out as if he might pull her into his arms.

Addie put a stop to that. She batted his hands away. "You knew how vulnerable I was when you slept with me."

"Yes," he admitted. "You'd recently found out your birth father was a serial killer."

There it was, all wrapped up into one neat little summary. Stripped down to bare bones with no details. But the devil was in those details.

Well, one devil anyway.

Her biological father.

"Is everything you told me about your childhood the truth?" he asked.

She hadn't thought Wes could say anything that would surprise her, or stop her from forcing him to leave, but that did it. Addie just stared at him.

"When you were three, some ranch hands found you in the woods near here," Wes went on, obviously recapping details she already knew all too well. "You said you didn't remember your name, how you got there or anything about your past. You don't remember how you got *that*."

Before she could stop him, he brushed his fingers over her cheek. Over the small crescent-shaped scar that was there. It was faint now, just a thin whitish line next to her left eye, but Wes had obviously noticed it.

Addie flinched, backing away from him. What the heck was going on?

"Is all of that true?" he repeated.

Addie mustered up another huff and tried not to react to his touch. Wes didn't deserve a reaction. Too bad her body didn't understand that. Of course, her body was betraying her a lot lately.

"It's all true," she insisted.

For thirty years, Addie had tried not to think of herself as that wounded little girl in the woods with a cut on her face. Because she hadn't stayed there.

Thanks to Sheriff Sherman Crockett and his wife, Iris.

When no one had come forward to claim her after she'd been found, Sherman and Iris had adopted her, raised her along with their four sons on their Appaloosa Pass Ranch. They'd given her a name. A family. A wonderful life.

Until three months ago. Then, there'd been the DNA match that no one wanted. That's when her world was turned upside down.

"Why did your adoptive father put your DNA in the database when he found you?" Wes asked.

Again, it was another question she hadn't seen coming. Her adoptive father had been killed in the line of duty when she was just twelve, so she couldn't ask him directly, but Addie could guess why.

"Because he could have simply been looking to see if I matched anyone in the system. But I believe he wanted to find the birth parents who'd abandoned me and make them pay." That required a deep breath. "I'm positive he had no idea it'd lead to a killer."

And not just any old killer, either, but the Moonlight Strangler. He'd killed at least sixteen women, and fifteen of those crime scenes hadn't had a trace of his DNA. But three months ago number sixteen had. And while the DNA wasn't a match to any criminal already in the system, it had been a match to the killer's blood kin.

Addie.

Wes took her by the shoulders, forcing eye contact. "The Moonlight Strangler's really your father?"

It took Addie a moment to realize that it was actually a question. "Yes, according to the DNA match, he is. But Sherman Crockett was my father in the only way that will ever matter."

If only that were true.

Addie wanted it to be true. Desperately wanted it. But it was hard to push aside that she shared the blood and DNA of a serial killer.

"I need to hear it from you," Wes said. Not an order exactly. But it was close. "Is everything you said true? Do you have any memory whatsoever of why you were in those woods or who put you there?"

Addie threw up her hands. "Of course not. The FBI has questioned me over and over again. They even had me hypnotized, and I remembered exactly what I'd already told everyone. Nothing."

She had no idea why Wes was asking these things, but it was time for Addie to turn the tables on him.

"Who are you?" she demanded. "And why are you here?"

His grip melted off her shoulders, and now it was Wes who moved away from her. "My real name is Weston Cade, and I'm a Texas Ranger."

Addie had to replay that several times before it sank in. After learning she was the daughter of a serial killer and having Wes leave without so much as a goodbye, she hadn't exactly had a rosy outlook on life. She'd braced herself in case Wes was about to confess that he, too, was some kind of criminal. But this revelation wasn't nearly as bad as the ones she had imagined.

"A Texas Ranger," she repeated. Addie shook her head. "You told me your name was Wes Martin and that you were a rodeo rider."

"Martin is my middle name, and I was a rodeo rider. Before I became a Ranger."

Her mouth tightened. "And I was a child before I became an adult. That doesn't make me a child now. You lied to me."

"Yeah." He nodded. "I didn't want you to know who I was and that I was investigating the Moonlight Strangler."

She stared at him, waiting for more. More that he didn't

volunteer. "You were investigating him when you met me three months ago?"

No gaze-dodging this time. Wes, or rather *Weston*, looked her straight in the eyes. "I met you because I was looking for him. I followed you while you were in San Antonio, and after your interview with the FBI I followed you to the hotel where you were staying. I knew exactly who you were when I introduced myself at the bar."

That hit her like a heavyweight's punch, and Addie staggered back.

The memories of that first meeting were still so fresh in her mind. She'd been shaken to the core after the interview with the FBI, and even though her mother and one of her brothers had made the trip to San Antonio with her, she had asked for some alone time. And had ended up at the hotel bar.

Where she'd met Wes, a rodeo rider.

Or so she'd thought.

The attraction had been instant. Intense. Something Addie had never quite felt before. Of course, that intensity had dulled her instincts because she had believed with all her heart that this was a man who understood her. A man she could trust.

That was laughable now.

"Were you trying to get information from me?" she asked, recalling all the words—the lies, no doubt—he'd told her that night.

A muscle flickered in his jaw.

Then Weston nodded.

She groaned, and now Addie was the one who cursed. "And you came back to the bar again the next night, after I'd been through the hypnosis. You knew I was an emotional wreck. You knew I was hanging by a thread, and yet you took me to your room and had sex with me. Not just that night, either, but the following night, too."

"That was never part of the plan," he said.

"The plan?" she snapped. "Well, your *plan* had consequences." Addie had another battle with tears, but thankfully she still managed to speak. "Leave now!"

Of course he didn't budge. Weston stayed put and took hold of her arm when she tried to bolt from the office.

The phone on her desk rang, the sound shooting through the room. Addie gasped before she realized that it wasn't the threat that her body was preparing itself for. The *threat* was in her office and had hold of her.

"Ignore that call. There are things you need to know," he insisted. "Things that might save your life."

That stopped Addie in her tracks, and she did indeed ignore the call. "What are you talking about?"

He didn't get a chance to answer because she heard another sound. Her mother's voice.

"Addie?" her mother called out. It sounded as if she was in the kitchen at the back of the house. "I picked up the phone when you didn't answer. It's about those mares you wanted to buy."

It was a call that Addie had been waiting on. An important one. Since she helped manage the ranch and the livestock, it was her job. But she was afraid her job would have to wait.

"Tell her to take a message," Weston instructed.

Addie wanted to tell him a flat-out no. She didn't want to obey orders from this lying Texas Ranger who'd taken her to his bed with the notion of getting information she didn't even have.

"Why should I?" she snarled.

"Because you're in danger. Your mother could be, too."

Addie had been certain that there was nothing Weston could say that would make her agree to his order.

Nothing except that.

"Mom," Addie said after a serious debate with herself. "Take a message. I'll return the call soon."

She hoped.

"Start talking," Addie told Weston. "Tell me exactly what's going on."

But he didn't say anything. Instead, he started to unbutton his shirt.

Either he'd lost his mind, or…

It was *or*.

Addie saw the scar on his chest. The long jagged cut that wasn't nearly as faded and healed as the one on her face. It was one that she'd already noticed the night they'd landed in bed together. Weston had told her he'd been hooked by a bull's horn at a rodeo.

"The Moonlight Strangler did this to me," Weston said. "Your *father* nearly killed me."

Oh, God.

"You know who my birth father is?" She couldn't ask that fast enough.

"No. I didn't see his face. And I didn't have any leads to his identity until I found out the results of your DNA test."

Addie's heart was pounding now. Her breath thin. "You thought he'd come to me?"

Weston nodded. "I counted on it. I know your DNA match was supposed to be kept quiet, but I figured if I could find out about it, then so could the killer."

It took her a moment to gather her voice. "You leaked

my DNA results?" She shoved Weston away from her and would have bolted, but, like before, he held on.

"No," he insisted. "But someone might have. Maybe a dirty cop or someone in the crime lab who was paid off."

"Or it could have been you. And to think, I slept with you, not just that one night, either, but the following night, too. I…" Addie stopped because there was no way she would give him another emotional piece of herself. "You used me as bait."

Her voice hardly had sound now, but that didn't mean she wasn't feeling every inch of the proverbial knife he'd stuck in her back.

"No," Weston repeated. "But someone did. And it worked."

There went the rest of her breath. "Who? How?"

Weston shook his head. "I don't know the who or the how, but I know the results." He looked her straight in the eyes. "Addie, you're the Moonlight Strangler's next target."

Chapter Two

Weston waited for Addie's reaction, and he didn't have to wait long.

She shook her head, her bottom lip trembling just a little before she clamped her teeth over it. It only took a few seconds for Addie to process what Weston had just told her.

And to dismiss it.

"Why should I believe anything you say?" she asked.

Weston had no trouble hearing the hurt in her voice. No trouble hearing the anger, too. Yes, he was responsible for both, and while he'd never intended to hurt Addie, he also hadn't wanted a serial killer to have free rein to keep on killing. Too bad he'd failed.

Addie was indeed hurt.

And the killer was still out there.

Of course, Addie knew that better than anyone else: her own sister-in-law had been one of the Moonlight Strangler's victims.

"I'm sorry," Weston said, knowing his words wouldn't be worth much. "But it's true. I have proof the Midnight Strangler's coming after you, and we need to talk about that."

Judging from the way her eyes narrowed, he'd been right about that apology not meaning much.

Addie didn't jump to ask about his *proof*.

Her blond hair was gathered into a ponytail, but she

swiped away the strands that'd fallen onto her face during their scuffle, and she whirled around so that she was no longer facing him. At least she didn't try to make a run out of her office again, but she might do just that before this conversation was over.

Even though it had only been three months since Weston had seen her, she'd changed plenty. He had watched her for about a half hour before he'd gotten the chance to pull her into the office for a private chat. When she was in the barn earlier, Addie had been working with one of the horses, and she had actually smiled a time or two. She looked content. Happy, even.

Definitely something he hadn't seen when she was in San Antonio.

There, she'd been wearing dresses more suited for office work than the jeans and denim shirt she was wearing now. And she definitely hadn't been happy or smiling during their chats at the bar and in his hotel room.

No.

Most of the time, she'd been on the verge of losing it, and had been trying to come to terms with learning exactly who she was. Weston certainly hadn't helped with the situation by sleeping with her.

After several long moments, she turned back around to face him. In the same motion, she took out her phone from her jeans pocket. "I'm calling Jericho."

Jericho, her oldest adopted brother. He was also the sheriff in the nearby town of Appaloosa Pass, the job once held by her late father. Weston definitely didn't want to tangle with any of the Crockett lawmen, not just yet anyway, so that's why he reached for her phone.

"I want to find out who you really are," Addie snapped. "And you're *not* going to stop me from doing that."

It was a risk in case she tried to get her brother to

arrest him or something, but Weston decided to see how
this played out. Eventually, he'd have to deal with Jericho anyway. It was a meeting he wasn't exactly looking forward to since Jericho had a reputation for being
a badass, no-shades-of-gray kind of lawman.

"Jericho," Addie said when her brother answered. She
put the call on speaker. "I need a favor. Can you check
and see if there's a Texas Ranger by the name of Weston
Cade?"

Weston heard Jericho's brief silence. Was he suspicious? Definitely. But the question was—what would
Jericho do about it? If he came storming back to the
house, it might trigger something Weston didn't want
triggered.

"Why?" her brother asked her.

"Just do it," Addie insisted, "*please*." She sounded
more like an annoyed sister than a woman whose lip
had been trembling just moments earlier.

More silence from Jericho, followed by some mumblings, but Weston did hear the clicks of a computer
keyboard.

"Yeah, he's a Ranger in the San Antonio unit," her
brother verified. "Why?" Jericho repeated, but he didn't
wait for an answer. "And does he have anything to do
with that SOB scumbag you met in San Antonio, the
one who slept with you and—"

"I'll call you back," Addie interrupted, and she hung
up. She dodged his gaze when she slid her phone back
into her pocket.

Weston doubted she'd put a quick end to that call for
his sake, but it did give him a glimpse of what she'd been
going through for three months. She had obviously told
Jericho about her brief affair with a man who'd seem-

ingly disappeared from the face of the earth, and her brother clearly didn't have a high opinion of him.

SOB scumbag.

Well, the label fit. Weston didn't have a high opinion of himself, either, and he hadn't in a very long time.

Addie wouldn't believe that he had plenty of regrets when it came to her. After all his lies, she would never believe that he'd fallen in bed with her only because of the intense attraction he had felt for her.

An attraction he still felt.

Still, he shouldn't have acted on it. He should have just kept his distance and tailed her until her father made his move, no matter how long that took.

"Start from the beginning," Addie insisted, turning her attention back to Weston. "And so help me, every word coming out of your mouth had better be the truth, or I'll let Jericho have a go at you. I don't make a habit of letting my big brother fight my battles for me, but in your case I'll make an exception."

Weston figured that wasn't a bluff.

The *beginning* required him to take a deep breath. "Two years ago I went to my fiancée's office to see her. I'd just come off an undercover assignment and hadn't seen her in a few weeks. Her name was Collette, and I walked in on someone murdering her."

Hell, it hurt to say that aloud. It didn't set well with Addie, either, because she made a slight gasping sound.

"It was my birth father," she supplied. "I saw a list of his known victims. All sixteen of them, and Collette Metcalf was one of them."

Weston nodded, and it took him a moment to trust his voice again. "I didn't know it was him at the time, and I didn't get a look at his face because he knifed me and ran out. I obviously survived, but Collette wasn't so lucky. She died by the time the ambulance arrived."

She touched her fingers to her mouth. It was trembling again, and Addie leaned against the edge of her desk, no doubt for support. "Your name wasn't in the reports I read of the murders."

"No. The FBI and Rangers thought it best if they didn't make it public. They didn't want him coming after me to tie up loose ends. The killer hadn't gotten a good look at my face because I was still wearing my undercover disguise. But he must have found out who I was because letters from the Moonlight Strangler started arriving three months ago."

"Three months?" she repeated under her breath.

Addie no doubt picked up on the timing. Weston doubted it was a coincidence that the letters started arriving shortly after he met her.

"The killer mentions me in these letters?" she asked, and Weston had to nod.

That meant the Moonlight Strangler had perhaps already been watching Addie and had seen Weston with her. Or maybe the killer had been watching him. Either way, Weston figured the killer had started sending those letters because he knew about Addie and him sleeping together.

"All the letters and envelopes were typed," Weston continued, "so there's no handwriting to be analyzed. No fibers or trace on any of them. They were mailed from various locations all over the state."

Addie shook her head. "How can you be sure they're from the killer?"

"Because there are details in them that were withheld

from the press. Details that only the Moonlight Strangler would know."

She stayed quiet a moment. "The letters threatened you?"

"Taunted me," Weston corrected. With details of Collette's murder…and other things. I tried to draw the killer out. I made sure my address was public. I put out the word through criminal informants that I wanted to meet with him, but he wouldn't come after me."

"You made yourself bait," Addie corrected.

"Plenty of times."

Weston had failed at that, too.

"The killer's never contacted me," she said. "Of course I've been worried…scared," Addie corrected, "that he would. Or that he would do even more than just contact me." She paused. "How did you find out I was his biological daughter?"

"I was keeping tabs on anything to do with the Moonlight Strangler. As a Texas Ranger, I have access to the DNA databases, and I'd hoped there'd be a DNA match to someone."

Her next breath was mixed with a sigh. "And there was. Then, because you'd found out I was his biological daughter, you…what?" No more sighing. Her eyes narrowed. "You thought he'd want to connect with the child he abandoned in the woods nearly thirty years ago?"

Her anger was back. Good. It was actually easier for him to deal with than the fear and hurt. But unfortunately, he was going to have to tell her something that would bring the fear back with a vengeance.

"Yesterday, I got this." Weston took the paper from his pocket and turned on the light so she could better see it. "It's the eighth letter he's sent me. It's a copy, not the original, so it's okay for you to handle it."

She didn't take it at first. Addie just volleyed glances between him and the paper before she finally eased it out of his hand, taking it only by the corner as if she didn't want to touch too much of it.

Since Weston knew every word that was written there, he watched Addie's reaction. The shock.

And yes, the fear.

"'Tell Addie that it's time for me to end what I started thirty years ago,'" she read aloud. She paused. "'I can't have a little girl's memories coming back to haunt me.'"

Her gaze skirted over the words again. She cleared her throat before her gaze came back to his.

"This is why you asked if I remembered anything," Addie said. "I don't," she quickly added.

"And you don't remember that?" He tipped his head to the scar on her cheek.

"No." She handed him back the letter. "Did he cut the other women he killed like this?"

Weston settled for a nod. "That was kept out of the reports to the press, too. Only a handful of people know that he cut them first. Then strangled them."

"I see." Her mouth tightened a moment. "I'd always hoped I got the scar from a tree branch or something."

Yes, since that was far better than the alternative. Because that scar on her face meant the Moonlight Strangler had already gone after her once. When she was just three years old.

Now he was coming for her again.

"The killer could be worried that you remembered something in that hypnosis session," Weston said. "Or that you might remember something in the future. The FBI wants to do more sessions with you, right?"

She nodded, confirming what he already knew. Nearly every law enforcement agency in the state as well as the FBI wanted to keep pressing her to remember.

"We don't have much time," Weston continued. "He usually strikes on the night of a full or half moon. Like tonight."

Her attention drifted to the window where she could see that the sun was only minutes away from setting. Something else flashed through her eyes. Not fear this time. But major concern.

"My mother's in the house. And the ranch hands—"

Weston stepped in front of her to keep her from leaving. "They're okay. For now. It's you he wants, and, other than me, he hasn't attacked or hurt anyone else when he murdered his victims."

Of course, since Addie was his daughter, the killer might make a really big exception. That was what Weston had to guard against.

She frantically shook her head. "Has he ever named victims before he killed them?"

"Never."

"Then you have no way of knowing that he won't go after my mother. Heck, my entire family." A clipped sob tore from her throat. "I can't let him get to them."

"I've already arranged for someone to watch the road leading to the ranch. I won't let him hurt them." Weston hoped that was a promise he could keep. He didn't have a good track record when it came to stopping this vicious killer.

"Who?" she pressed.

"Friends I can trust. I didn't want to involve the Rangers in this because I'm trying to set a trap for the killer, and I didn't want him hearing about it. But these friends are armed, and they'll let me know if he tries to get to you."

That was part of the plan anyway.

But not all of it.

"I don't just want to scare off the Moonlight Strangler," Weston explained. "I want to catch him. *Tonight*."

Addie froze. Then her breath shivered. "You want to use me to draw him out."

"Yes." Hard for Weston to admit that, but it was the truth. "We know he'll probably come here, and since he doesn't know that I've contacted you—"

"What if the letter is a hoax?" she interrupted. "I mean, why tell you what he's going to do? He must know that as a Texas Ranger you'd try to warn me."

"That's not the only reason I would have warned you." Judging from the hard look she gave him, she didn't believe it.

He took out the copy of the second letter. "It came the same time as the other one, but it was a different envelope." Weston unfolded it, held it up for Addie to see. "If you try to save Addie, I'll kill Isabel and you," he read.

"Isabel?" she asked.

"My kid sister. She's in medical school. I've already had her put in protective custody. Now the next step is doing the same for you, but that's why I snuck onto the ranch. I didn't want the killer to know I'd come here. It might have provoked him or sent him into a rage."

Not that a serial killer didn't already have enough rage. Still, Weston had wanted to try to control the situation as much as he could.

The silence came. Addie, staring at him. Obviously trying to make sense of this. He wanted to tell her there was nothing about this that made sense because they were dealing with a very dangerous, very crazy man.

"Oh, God," she finally said.

Now her fear was sky-high, and Weston held his breath. He didn't expect Addie to go blindly along with a plan to stop her father. But she did want to stop the Moonlight Strangler from claiming another victim.

Weston was counting heavily on that.

However, Addie shook her head. "I can't help you."

That sure wasn't the reaction Weston had expected. He'd figured Addie was as desperate to end this as he was.

She squeezed her eyes shut a moment. "I'll get my mother, and we can go to the sheriff's office. Two of my brothers are there, and they can make sure this monster stays far away from us."

"You'll be safe at the sheriff's office," Weston agreed, "but you can't stay there forever. Neither can your family. Eventually, you'll have to leave, and the killer will come after you."

"That can't happen!" Addie groaned and looked up at the ceiling as if she expected some kind of divine help. "I can't be in that kind of danger."

Weston tried to keep his voice as calm as possible. Hard to do, though, with the emotions swirling like a tornado inside him. "I'm sorry. If there was another way to stop him, then I wouldn't have come here. I know I don't have a right to ask, but I need your help."

"I can't."

"You can't? Convince me why," Weston snapped. "Because I'm not getting this. You must want this killer off the street. It's the only way you'll ever be truly safe."

Addie opened her mouth. Closed it. And she stared at him. "I'd planned on telling you. Not like this. But if I ever saw you again, I intended to tell you."

There was a new emotion in her voice and on her

face. One that Weston couldn't quite put his finger on. "Tell me what?" he asked.

She dragged in a long breath and straightened her shoulders. "I can't be bait for the Moonlight Strangler because I can't risk being hurt." Addie took another deep breath. "I'm three months pregnant. And the baby is *yours*."

Chapter Three

Addie figured this was the worst way possible a man could find out that he'd fathered a child.

But she hadn't exactly had a choice about the timing of the news. Weston had come here to drop a bombshell that he wanted to use her to catch a killer, that the killer was actually after her, but she'd delivered her own bombshell.

And it had stunned him to silence.

Weston just stared at her for a very long time, and she could almost see the wheels turning in his head. This pregnancy changed everything.

At least it had for Addie.

Maybe it would for Weston, too.

Change him in a way that wouldn't put her in danger. Three months ago, she would have been willing to do whatever it took to catch the Moonlight Strangler. Weston obviously felt the same way. Especially since the killer had murdered a woman he loved. But even though the killer had murdered her brother's wife, Addie couldn't allow herself to be used in this justice net.

Unless…

"Can you guarantee me that the baby wouldn't be hurt?" However, she waved off the question as soon as she asked it. "You and I both know you can't. The Moonlight Strangler's smart. He's been killing and evading the law for three decades, maybe more, and he might have already figured out a way to get around you so he could come after me."

Heck, the killer might have figured out a way to use Weston. Too bad Addie couldn't think of how he'd done that, and she didn't want to find out the hard way, either. This had to end.

But how?

"You're pregnant," Weston said under his breath. He groaned, and this time he was the one to do the step-ping away.

She couldn't blame him for being stunned. The truth was, Addie had been pretty darn stunned herself when she'd first learned the news. She had always wanted children and figured that one day she would be a mom. She just hadn't thought it would happen like this, with her being unmarried and with the baby's father disap-pearing.

Weston shook his head. "But we used protection."

Ironic that she had said the exact same thing to the doctor when he'd confirmed the pregnancy test results. That day, she'd said a lot of things, including some pro-fanity in regards to Weston.

"Obviously, protection's not a hundred percent. Don't worry," Addie quickly added. "I was going to tell you if I ever managed to locate you, but I don't need anything from you, including child support. Or any other kind of support for that matter. As far as I'm concerned, you won't be a part of this."

The look he gave her could have blasted a giant hole through the moon. Weston's eyes went to slits, and the muscles in his face turned to iron. "It's my baby. I'll be a part of *this*."

"That's not necessary—"

"I'll be part of his or her life," he insisted.

All right. She hadn't exactly counted on that reaction. "After you ran out on me, I figured…"

Considering that his eyes narrowed even more, it was probably best not to finish spelling out that she didn't believe him to be the sort who stuck around. Even for his own child.

And then it hit her.

Addie really didn't know him. Didn't know anything real about his life because of all the lies he'd told her.

"Are you married?" she asked.

That didn't do much to help with those narrowed eyes. "No. I wouldn't have slept with you if I'd been married."

She let that hum between them, but hopefully he understood what she was thinking. A man who'd lie and then have sex with a troubled woman didn't exactly have a stellar moral compass.

"And no, I'm not involved with anyone," he went on. "Not now, and not when I was with you."

"Why did you sleep with me?" she demanded.

Mercy, she wanted to kick herself for blurting that out. Not because she didn't want to know the truth.

She did.

But Addie was a thousand percent certain that she wasn't up to hearing it spelled out now. Not with all the other news that Weston had just delivered.

Now he looked at her, and that wasn't a glare in his smoky brown eyes.

Nope.

It was a look he'd given her many times over the three days when they'd been together. It was something she felt right after she first met him.

Something she didn't want to feel, but Addie felt it again anyway.

The heat came like a touch. Barely a brush against her

skin. But it rippled through her. Gently. At first. Until the ripple became a tug and made her recall exactly why she'd landed in bed with Weston.

"Yeah," he said. "Remember now?"

Since a lie would stick in her throat, Addie settled for a nod. "But I slept with you only because of the attraction. Can you say the same?"

No quick answer. Not verbally anyway, but she got another glare from him. She'd always thought Jericho was the king of glares and surly expressions, but right now Weston had her brother beat by a mile.

"Like I said, that wasn't part of the plan," Weston finally repeated. "It just…happened."

She had the feeling he'd intended to say something else, but it was best if this part of the conversation ended. Addie didn't need any other reminders of the heat that'd been between them then.

And now.

"Sleeping with me wasn't part of this grand plan you keep mentioning," she said, trying to get her thoughts back on track. "But leaving was."

"I left because of the letters," Weston clarified, though she didn't know how he managed to speak through clenched teeth. "The killer warned me to stay away from you."

Addie hadn't thought there'd be any more surprises today, but she'd been wrong. Her heartbeat kicked up again, drumming in her ears. "Why did he give you a warning like that?"

"He didn't want us teaming up to find him," Weston readily answered. "He said he'd kill you if I stayed. That you'd live if I left."

That sent another rush of emotions through her. For

three months, Addie had dealt with the anger and hurt of having Weston walk out. In the past fifteen minutes, she'd had to deal with the news that her biological father was coming after her.

Now this.

If Weston had indeed left to try to save her, then that put him in a new light. One she wasn't ready to deal with just yet. After all, he had known who she was when he'd slept with her, and she wasn't ready to forgive him for that just yet.

Maybe not ever.

As raw as her emotions were and despite the fact Weston was still glaring at her, Addie had to push all that aside. Yes, she'd have to deal with it later, but for now they had a more immediate problem on their hands, and protecting the baby and her family had to come first. That meant making sure she was protected, as well.

Addie didn't intend to rely on Weston for that.

"I need to tell Jericho about the threatening letters you got," she said, thinking out loud.

However, she didn't even get a chance to reach for her phone before she heard the footsteps behind her in the hall. Weston obviously heard them, too, because he moved fast. A lot faster than Addie. He latched on to her arm, dragging her behind him, and in the same motion, he drew his gun.

Just like that, Addie's heart jumped to her throat, and the danger to her unborn child and family came at her like an avalanche. However, the threat that her body was preparing her for turned out not to be a threat after all.

"Put down that gun, and let go of my daughter," her mother demanded. She had something to back up that demand, too. Her mother aimed a double-barreled shotgun at Weston.

The relief hit Addie almost as hard as the slam of fear had, so it took her a moment to speak. It wasn't the killer, but her mother was limping her way toward them. "It's okay, Mom."

That wasn't exactly the truth. Everything was far from being okay, but Addie didn't want her mother pointing a gun at a Texas Ranger.

Even *this* Ranger.

Her mother obviously didn't buy her *it's okay* because she didn't lower the gun, and she continued to volley glances between Weston and Addie. Even though she wasn't a large woman, and her hair was completely silver-gray, she still managed to look tough as nails.

"Who is he?" her mother asked. But almost immediately her gaze dropped to Addie's stomach.

"Yes, he's the baby's father," Addie verified. "Mom, this is Weston Cade. Weston, this is my mom, Iris Crockett."

It seemed silly to make polite introductions at a time like this, but it did get her mother to lower the shotgun. What her mom didn't do was ease up on the glare she was giving Weston.

"You hurt my daughter," her mother said.

"I know," Weston readily admitted. "And I'm sorry." He, too, put away his gun, sliding it back into his holster.

Her mother didn't say the words, but her frosty blue eyes let Weston know that his apology alone wouldn't be nearly good enough. Maybe nothing would be. After all, her mother had no doubt heard Addie's crying jags and had seen the hurt and sadness.

"How did you get inside?" her mother asked Weston. "I didn't hear you ring the doorbell, and if you had, I wouldn't have let you in."

"He came in with me from the barn," Addie jumped to answer. Best if her mother didn't know she'd just been in a partial wrestling match with the man who'd fathered her child. "Weston has bad news. Well, maybe it's bad. If the letters he got are real, then it's bad."

"They're real," Weston insisted.

Again, her mother didn't say anything, but she grasped it right away. "This is about the Moonlight Strangler." Still limping, she moved protectively to Addie's side, slipping her left arm around her. "Is he coming after Addie?"

That was something both she and her mother had no doubt asked themselves dozens of times, but they'd never spoken of it.

Too frightening to consider aloud.

Of course, Addie had taken precautions. Always looking over her shoulder. Always on guard for her biological father to make some kind of contact. Or try to murder her. But after three months of the precautions, Addie had thought she was safe.

"I need to talk to Jericho," Addie said, taking out her phone. "I'll have him come home right away. Jax, too."

She almost explained to Weston that Jax was a deputy in Appaloosa Pass, but there was probably little about her and her family that he didn't already know. Well, with the exception of the pregnancy, but then there were only six people who'd known about that: her mother, her four brothers and the doctor.

"I'll alert the ranch hands so they can all get inside the bunkhouse," her mother added.

But Weston took hold of both their arms before either of them could make those calls. "If the Moonlight Strangler suspects you're on to him, he won't come here."

Her mother gave a crisp nod. "Good!"

"Not good." Addie groaned. "Because he might try to go after Weston's sister. Or he'll just wait to attack again."

Weston was right. They couldn't live at the sheriff's office or stay locked up in the house. They had a huge ranch to run. Plus, there was the baby. Addie didn't want her child to be a prisoner because they had had the bad luck to wind up in the wrong gene pool.

"So, what do we do?" Addie asked, hating that she didn't already have a plan. One that didn't involve Weston and that could ensure her baby wouldn't be hurt.

Weston opened his mouth to answer, but before he could say a word, Addie's phone rang. It wasn't Jericho's name she saw on the screen, however. It was Teddy McQueen, one of the ranch hands.

"If this is about those mares," Addie said the moment she answered, "we'll have to discuss it another time."

"Addie," the man said. His voice was barely a whisper.

"What's wrong?" she asked.

For several snail-crawling moments, all she heard was Teddy's ragged breath. That didn't help steady her nerves. Weston's either, because he took the phone from her and jabbed the speaker button.

"I was in the south pasture and spotted someone by the shed there," Teddy finally continued. "A man. I was about to ask him what he was doing, and he shot me with one of those guns fitted with a silencer. I didn't even see it until it was too late."

"Oh, God. Call nine-one-one and get an ambulance," Addie told her mother, and Iris immediately did that. "Teddy, how bad are you hurt?"

"Not sure. But the bullet's in my leg so I can't walk."

"Just hold on. We'll get someone out to you," Addie assured him.

"Tell whoever's coming to be careful. *Real* careful. You and Iris, too. I didn't get a look at the man's face, but I saw what direction he went."

Teddy took another long breath. "Addie, you need to watch out. He's headed straight for the house."

Chapter Four

Weston's first instinct was to curse. And to punch himself for not fixing this before the danger was right on Addie's doorstep.

Why the heck hadn't his *friends* warned him?

Later, he'd want an answer to that, but he had to focus on making sure this situation didn't go from bad to worse. For now, Weston settled for firing off a quick text to one of those friends to warn him that all hell had broken loose.

"How long do we have before the man gets here?" Addie asked the wounded ranch hand.

"He's on foot, but he's moving pretty quick. You got fifteen minutes, maybe less."

Weston figured with the way his luck had been running, it'd be *less*. That wasn't enough time for Jericho to make it out to the ranch, but maybe it was enough for Weston's friends to get onto the grounds and help.

The moment he finished the text, Weston slapped off the lights, pulled Addie's mom into the office with them and then closed the blinds. "Get down on the floor behind the desk. I'll go through the house and lock the doors."

"It'll go faster if I show you where all the doors are," Addie insisted.

"Or I could go," Iris volunteered.

Addie shook her head. "Not with your sore ankle. I

can move a lot faster than you can. You wait here and keep watch while I go with Weston."

Normally, he would have refused her help, but it was a big place even by Texas standards, and he didn't want to miss an entrance.

"All right." Iris shifted her shotgun so that it'd be easier for her to use. "I'll call Jericho. Just hurry and get back here."

Weston nodded. "Tell the other ranch hands, too, so they'll get inside and take cover. I also want you to stay away from the windows."

He wasn't sure the Moonlight Strangler was into shooting bystanders, but Weston didn't want to take any chances. Not with Iris. Not with Addie. Especially since she was pregnant with his child.

Later, he'd need to settle that with Addie.

And himself.

Weston figured he'd be asking himself a lot of "what the hell have I done?" questions.

"This way," Addie said, leading him not to the front of the house but rather the back.

She was focused on the task. Or rather trying to pretend she was. But Weston could still feel the fear coming from her. Could also feel her dodging his gaze. He couldn't blame her. She probably didn't want to trust him, but at the moment she had no choice.

"Your friends didn't see the killer when he shot Teddy," she said like the accusation that it was.

"Apparently not," he settled for saying.

"And you still trust them?" Again, an accusation.

"Yeah. With my life."

She glanced at him, a reminder that he'd trusted them with her life, too. And her mother's. The glance was well deserved. He had done just that. But both of his friends were former cops and had plenty of equipment that should have detected anyone in those woods surrounding the ranch.

It was obviously a precaution that'd failed big-time.

Addie and he threaded their way through a massive family room, turning off lights and locking two doors there before doing the same to yet three more off the kitchen and adjoining dining room. Even though Christmas was still three weeks away, everything was decorated for the holiday. Trees, wreaths and other decorations were in almost every room.

"My mother goes a little overboard. She loves Christmas," Addie said.

Maybe because Addie had been found nearly thirty years ago on Christmas Eve. From everything Weston had uncovered, Iris had always wanted a daughter, so this could be a dual celebration of sorts.

Next, there was another office. Jericho's no doubt, judging from the man-cave decor. And across the hall was a playroom filled with toys and books—a reminder that Addie had a nephew. Thank Heaven the little boy wasn't in the house, because it was more than enough just protecting Addie and her mother.

"The windows upstairs have child locks on them and are wired in case my nephew tries to open them," Addie explained. The words practically ran together, even faster than she was jetting around the house.

He doubted the Moonlight Strangler would climb a ladder to try to get inside. That would make him too visible, but he might try other ways. "Is there a security system for the rest of the house?"

Addie nodded, her breath still gusting. "Jericho had one installed after…well, just after."

It was the kind of security measure Weston would

have taken if he'd been in her brother's place, even if there'd been no hint of the killer coming after her.

"It's not armed," he reminded her. Weston knew that for a fact since he'd literally walked right into the house. Something he needed to stop the killer from doing.

"The keypad is by the front door." Addie led him in that direction, and while she set the system, Weston locked that door. He also checked the sidelight windows.

No one was out there. Yet. If a killer hadn't had a target on Addie, everything would have seemed normal. Well, everything outside anyway.

"Does the alarm cover all the windows and doors?" Weston asked.

She nodded. "But it won't go off if the glass breaks. Only if a window is actually lifted."

That was better than nothing.

Weston took Addie back to her office. Not ideal since there was a big window, but all the rooms on the bottom floor had them.

"Jericho's on the way," Iris informed them the moment they returned. "An ambulance, too. I called Teddy again and told him to hold on."

Maybe holding on would be enough and an ambulance could get to the ranch hand before he bled out. Of course, Jericho likely wouldn't let the ambulance onto the grounds unless he was certain it was safe for the medics.

And with a killer out there, it was far from safe.

"Get down," Weston reminded Addie when she hurried to a cabinet in the corner, where she took down a gun off the top shelf.

Good. He hated that she had to be armed, hated she was terrified to the point of shaking, but without backup, Weston wanted all the help he could get.

With his gun ready, he hurried to the window, staying to the side but still putting himself in a position so he could look out and keep watch. Weston lifted one of the blind slats, bracing himself for the worst. His heart nearly jumped from his chest when the lights flared on.

He cursed.

And it took him a second to realize it wasn't the glare of something from the killer. It was Christmas lights. Hundreds of them. They were strung out across the barns, shrubs, porch and fences, and they winked on and off, the little blasts of color slicing through the darkness.

"They're on a timer," Addie said. That's when he realized she had lifted her head and was looking out, as well. He motioned for her to get back down. "You want me to turn them off?"

"No."

They actually helped by lighting up the grounds, and it would make it harder for the killer to use the darkness to hide. Weston hoped. This wasn't the Moonlight Strangler's first rodeo, and he'd likely already cased the ranch to find the safest path for him to launch an attack.

Too bad there were plenty of places to do just that.

"Why is this monster doing this now, after all this time?" Iris asked.

While Addie filled her in on what they knew, Weston kept watch and took out his phone to call Cliff Romero, a former cop and one of the friends he'd positioned around the grounds surrounding the Crockett ranch.

"What went wrong?" Weston asked the moment Cliff answered.

"We're not sure. He didn't get past Dave and me."

Dave Roper. The other former cop out there. Both men had been armed with thermal equipment that should have detected anyone or anything with a pulse.

And that could mean only one thing.

That the killer had already been on the ranch grounds, maybe waiting in the shed for nightfall. He was also likely wearing some kind of clothing that would make it hard for the equipment to detect him.

"Hell," Weston said under his breath.

"My thoughts exactly. Dave and I are moving closer, hoping to pick up his trail. Make sure we're not hit with friendly fire."

"I'll try." He hung up and glanced back at Addie again. "Text Jericho and let him know there are two PIs headed in the direction of the house."

She did. But that didn't mean Dave and Cliff were safe. He only hoped the pair caught up with the killer before he could inflict more harm.

"Maybe he'll just leave if he knows we're onto him," Iris whispered.

Yeah, he probably would, and it was tempting to shout out something or fire a warning shot. But if Weston did that, it wouldn't end the threat. It would only postpone an attack to another place, another time. One when Weston might have a lesser chance of protecting Addie.

"Do you see him?" Addie asked.

Weston shook his head and tried to think of something reassuring to say. He failed. Addie no doubt saw the worry on his face and in his body language. And he was indeed worried. Even if the killer didn't attack, all of this stress couldn't be good for Addie and the baby.

The moments crawled by. Turning into minutes. Still no sign of the Moonlight Strangler. No sign of his friends or Jericho, either.

But Weston sensed something.

Exactly what, he wasn't sure, but he felt the knot tighten in his gut. Felt that warning slide down his spine.

A warning that'd saved his butt a time or two. And that's why he ducked back from the window.

Not a second too soon.

The bullet crashed through the glass in the exact spot where Weston had just been standing.

He'd braced himself for an attack, of course, but Weston doubted anyone could brace themselves for the roaring blast from the shot and the instant surge of adrenaline through their body.

"Stay down!" he warned Addie and her mother. He hoped the ranch hands were doing the same thing.

A second shot came. Then another.

Both went through what was left of the window and slammed into the wall behind him. They also helped him pinpoint the location of the shooter. All three shots had come from the area around the barn nearest the house.

The killer was way too close.

Not as close as he'd been when he had murdered Collette and left Weston for dead, but it was the first time Weston had been in a position to get a glimpse of him since that fateful night.

The rage roared through him. Not a good mix with the adrenaline and other things he was feeling, but Weston refused to let this snake go after anyone else. Especially Addie.

"Are there any ranch hands in the barn out there?" Weston tipped his head in that direction.

"There shouldn't be," Addie answered.

Good. That'd be fewer targets for this idiot to try to kill. And the man was definitely trying to kill them. Weston had no doubts about that as even more bullets crashed through the window.

It was always unnerving to have shots fired, but it

didn't help that knot in his stomach when the killer stopped shooting.

Did that mean he was on the move?

Probably. Because it was too much to hope that he'd run out of ammunition.

Weston ducked and hurried to the other side of the window. It was a better vantage point if the shooter was headed to the back of the house, but Weston still didn't see anything.

Not at first anyway.

Finally, the Christmas lights flickered over a shadowy spot by one of the trucks parked between the house and the barn. Yeah, someone was definitely there.

Weston took aim and fired.

And he got confirmation of the guy's location when he saw him scramble behind the truck. He also got another confirmation he'd been waiting for—the sound of sirens from a police cruiser. Jericho, no doubt.

But Weston obviously wasn't the only one who knew that backup was about to arrive. He saw the shooter dart out from the back of the truck. And the man took off running.

Hell.

Weston didn't want this monster to get away, and that's exactly what would happen if he waited for Jericho. It'd be a minute or more before Addie's brother could stop the cruiser and get into place.

A minute the killer would use to escape.

It was a risk. A huge one. Anything Weston did at this point would be.

He fired a glance at Addie. "Text Jericho and tell him where you are. Then stay down and shoot anyone who tries to come in through this window." He also tossed her his phone. "Text the first contact in there and let him know I'm out of the house."

She was shaking her head before he even finished. "You can't go out there," Addie insisted.

"I can't let him get away," he insisted right back. He knocked out the rest of the shards of glass from the window.

Weston wished he had the time to convince her that this was the only way, but he didn't. With Jericho so close now, he'd be able to protect Addie and their mother. But just in case the killer doubled back and tried to come through the window, Weston kept watch around him.

And he started running the moment his feet hit the ground.

For one thing, he wanted to get out of the line of fire in case Jericho mistook him for the killer. For another, he wanted to make up the distance between him and the guy he could see running flat-out ahead of him.

Weston could also see something else thanks to the Christmas lights.

The guy was dressed all in black and was wearing a ski mask, and he wasn't running in a straight line. He was darting in and out of whatever he could use for cover. In addition to a gun, he was also carrying something else.

Something that he tossed onto the ground after glancing back over his shoulder at Weston.

Weston darted around whatever he'd tossed, hoping like the devil that it wasn't a bomb or explosive device, but it wasn't.

It appeared to be a thermal scanner like the one Dave and Cliff had been using.

That was probably why the killer had managed to pinpoint them so quickly in the house. After all, he hadn't fired any shots except right into the office, where they'd been hiding.

Behind him, Weston could hear the cruiser approaching, and the slashing blue lights blended with those from the Christmas decorations. It didn't create the best setup for spotting a killer since it was playing havoc with his vision. But Weston kept on running. Kept looking over his shoulder to make sure this snake didn't have a partner who was trying to go after Addie.

The killer scurried out of cover, headed toward a second barn. Weston wasn't sure if there were vehicles inside or not, but he didn't want to chance it.

Weston stopped. And he took aim.

He didn't aim for the guy's head. Something he desperately wanted to do. Especially with all the rage he was feeling. He could avenge Collette's death right here, right now. No judge, no jury.

Just one executioner with really good aim.

However, if Weston did that, he wouldn't get answers, and there were a lot of families out there looking for missing loved ones that this piece of dirt could have murdered. Besides, Weston wanted to look this killer in the eyes and make him answer for what he'd done.

Weston fired.

The shot went exactly where he'd intended it to go. In the killer's right shoulder. It worked because the guy tumbled onto the ground.

"Move and the next bullets go in your kneecaps," Weston warned him.

Weston wasted no time going after him, and it wasn't long before he got close enough to see the killer's face. Or rather the ski mask he was wearing. He was bleeding, clutching his shoulder with his left hand.

But not his right.

Despite the injury, he was reaching for his gun that had fallen just inches away from him.

"You really want to die tonight?" Weston warned him, and he aimed his gun right at the killer's head.

The killer did move, though, but only to lift both his hands. Weston hurried to kick the gun aside so that the guy couldn't change his mind and reach for it.

Then, Weston did some reaching of his own.

He had to see the killer's face. Had to stare down the man who'd murdered Collette. He ripped off the ski mask, and he got a good look at him all right.

Weston cursed.

No.

Chapter Five

Addie wasn't sure who was more frustrated with this situation—Weston or her. At the moment, she thought she might be the winner.

Because they hadn't caught the Moonlight Strangler after all.

And that meant he was still out there. Maybe still plotting to kill her.

However, he hadn't tried to murder her tonight. Not yet anyway. The attacker who'd hurt Teddy and fired shots into the house wasn't old enough to be the Moonlight Strangler.

So, who was he?

Addie didn't know, but she was hoping to find out soon. The same was obviously true for Weston.

He had a death grip on the steering wheel of Addie's truck as they drove toward the hospital. She didn't miss the glares he was doling out to her, either. He clearly didn't want her on this trip with him into town. Didn't want her out in the open.

Well, Addie wasn't so thrilled about it herself, but she wouldn't have felt any safer at home than she would at the hospital, where she'd no doubt be surrounded by lawmen.

Maybe surrounded by answers, as well.

Since their attacker would soon be at the hospital, too. The injured man was just ahead of them in an ambulance. Jericho was inside with him and the medics. Her brother would also be doling out some glares when he learned she'd disobeyed his order for her to stay put at the ranch and had instead come to the hospital with Weston.

But before Addie had left the ranch, she'd first made sure her mother had plenty of protection, both from the ranch hands, Weston's two PI friends and her other brother Chase who'd hurried out to the scene. Only then, and only after the ambulance had driven away, had Addie demanded that Weston take her with him.

She'd deal with Jericho later.

Later, she'd have to deal with a lot of things.

Including Weston's arrival.

After three months of not hearing from him, she had written him out of her life. Out of her heart, as well. Addie wasn't certain what was going on in Weston's head, but she doubted he would just disappear again.

Well, not until he had caught the Moonlight Strangler anyway.

"I should have known," Addie heard Weston say.

It wasn't the first time in the past fifteen minutes he'd said something along those same lines. And maybe they should have known that the Moonlight Strangler would send a lackey to the ranch instead of risking a personal appearance.

Especially after the killer had let Weston know that she was his next target.

Still, a lackey could have killed her just as well as the Moonlight Strangler.

"He's way too young to be the killer," Weston grumbled. He was talking to himself now. Or rather berating himself, since the next mumblings had some profanity mixed in with them.

Yes, the guy was too young. Probably only in his late twenties, judging from the quick glimpse she'd gotten of him before Jericho had demanded that she go back inside. Since the Moonlight Strangler had been murdering women for at least thirty years, the shooter definitely fell into the lackey category.

Or worse.

He could be some kind of crazed groupie who had absolutely no knowledge of the Moonlight Strangler's identity. This could all have been some kind of a sick hoax.

One that could have gotten a lot of people killed.

They were lucky that hadn't happened, but they weren't out of the woods yet. Teddy was alive and was already en route to the hospital in an ambulance ahead of the one carrying their attacker, but Addie had no idea how serious his injuries were.

"Thank you for saving my mother and me," she told Weston.

He glanced at her, maybe wondering if she was sincere. She was. Despite the other stuff going on between Weston and her—the baby stuff—she was thankful he'd been there when the bullets had started flying.

She'd be even more thankful if she knew that was the last of the bullets. But Addie didn't think she would be that lucky.

"Is it possible this guy faked the threatening letters you got?" she asked.

"No." Weston didn't hesitate. "There were personal details in them. Like the cuts on the faces of the victims. That was never leaked to the press." But then he stopped, added more profanity. "I suppose, though, he could have sent the last two letters. The one that threatened you and my sister. Still…"

"What?" she pressed when he didn't continue.

"They felt real." His mouth tightened as if disgusted that he'd rely on something like feelings, but Addie didn't dismiss it.

"Maybe they felt real because my birth father told him exactly what to write." Now it was her turn to mumble some profanity. If that was the case, then they needed this slimebag lackey to talk, to tell them anything and everything he might know about the Moonlight Strangler.

"Are you okay?" Weston asked a moment later.

Addie didn't miss his glance that landed on her stomach. She wasn't okay, not by a long shot. She felt raw and bruised as if she'd gone through a physical attack instead of just the threat of one. The sound of those bullets would stay with her for the rest of her life.

"I'm fine," she settled for saying. And she hoped that was true. Her precious baby didn't deserve to go through this. No one did.

"You should see a doctor while you're at the hospital. Just to make sure," he added.

His tone made it sound like an order. Which made her rethink her notion that he'd just leave after catching her birth father.

No.

She really didn't want to have to deal with this on top of everything else.

"For the record, we barely know each other," Addie tossed out there. "And you won't exactly be welcome in my family."

Another glance at her stomach. "Is that supposed to send me running for the hills?"

"It might after you meet Jericho."

"I've already met Jericho," he countered.

"Barely." They'd exchanged brief introductions and

some testosterone-laced glares while waiting for the ambulance. "He's very protective of me."

Especially since he'd learned she was pregnant. Addie was thankful for his brotherly love. Thankful for all the other things he'd done for her, including offering her a shoulder when she'd been crying over her heart-crushing encounter with Weston. But Jericho wouldn't be showing much love to the man who'd slept with his kid sister and then dumped her.

"I'll deal with Jericho," Weston said as if it were gospel.

"Good luck with that," she said in the same tone he'd used.

Still behind the ambulance, he pulled her truck into the parking lot. The very truck that he'd insisted on driving from the ranch to the hospital. Normally, that wasn't a task Addie would have just surrendered, but the truth was, she was shaking, and the nerves were still there right at the surface.

Unlike Weston's nerves.

He just seemed riled that he hadn't been able to bring all of this to a close tonight. And it still might happen. If they could get some info from the shooter.

He took the parking space nearest the ER doors. "Stay close to me and move fast," he instructed.

She spotted the two night deputies already there. Both were positioned just outside the ER. Both with their hands over their guns. A reminder that this nightmare wasn't over.

"Search anyone who tries to get in," Weston told them, and he flashed his badge.

Weston used his own body to shelter her while they made the short trek into the hospital. They were just behind Jericho and the medics, who rushed in with their patient. She didn't hear what Jericho said to the nurse at the reception desk, but Addie didn't miss the scowl he gave her when he spotted her. He came toward her just as Weston pulled her away from the doors and to the far side of the room.

Maybe just to get her away from the glass doors.

Maybe so he could make this showdown with Jericho semiprivate.

"You should be home," Jericho insisted, and in the same breath he added to Weston, "And the two of us need to *talk*." Weston was on the receiving end of an even worse scowl than she'd gotten.

She seriously doubted Jericho had only talking on his mind, and that's why Addie stepped between them. "I can handle this myself."

All right, that didn't exactly cool the fire in Jericho's eyes. Nor did it stop Weston from moving her so that he was facing her brother head-on.

Jericho's index finger landed against Weston's chest. "You deserve to have your butt kicked for what you did to my sister. Now the question is—are you going to do something about it?"

"Yeah, I do deserve a butt-kicking," Weston readily admitted. "And Addie deserves some answers, but we can work that out later. Agreed?"

She wasn't sure Jericho would agree to anything right now, but he finally huffed, pulled her into his arms and brushed a kiss on Addie's forehead. "Are you okay? And I want the truth."

"I'll be fine," Addie assured him and stayed a moment in his arms. He might be the most stubborn brother in the universe, but he'd walk through fire for her. And vice versa.

"I already told her I want the doctor to check her out just in case," Weston insisted.

Jericho made a sound of agreement.

"I can think for myself," she reminded both of them.

But she was talking to the air because both of them ignored her. Jericho motioned for them to follow him, and he led them into a private waiting room just up the hall.

No windows, thank goodness. She figured it'd take a lifetime or two before she walked past one and didn't hear the sound of bullets shattering glass.

Weston tipped his head to the wallet her brother had in his left hand. "Does that belong to the shooter?"

It was clear her brother didn't want to drop the personal part of this conversation with Weston, but she saw the moment he shifted from big brother to lawman. "Yes. My brother Jax is running a background check on him, but we know his name is Lonny Ogden. He's thirty-one and lives in San Antonio."

Addie repeated it to see if it rang any bells. It didn't. "You're sure that's his real name?"

"The photo on the license matches the one at DMV. I'm running his prints just to verify, but on the drive over, I had Jax check on Ogden's rap sheet." Jericho paused, scrubbed his hand over his face and gave a weary sigh. "He doesn't have one. Ogden's never been arrested."

Hard to believe that the man who'd just tried to kill her had never been in trouble with the law.

"Ogden had a cell phone on him, and I had a ranch hand deliver it to Jax at the station. Jax'll examine the calls and any other phone records Ogden might have left."

"Did Ogden say why he did this?" Weston asked.

Another weary sigh from Jericho. "He rambled on a lot, not much of it making sense. When I asked him if he was working for the Moonlight Strangler, he said no, that he was working for a higher being that didn't live on this planet."

Now it was Addie's turn to sigh. "He's insane."

"Possibly. Or he could be faking it." Jericho's gaze came back to hers. "He said he couldn't have the Moonlight Strangler's blood live on and that you weren't doing all you could to help the cops catch the killer."

Good God. Addie had known right from the start that this attack was aimed at her, but it was sickening to hear the motive spelled out.

Well, if it was true.

"What exactly does Ogden believe I should be doing to help the cops?" Addie asked.

"It doesn't matter what he thinks. He's crazy," Weston reminded her.

That didn't make her feel any better. Mainly because it was coming from Weston. Yes, he'd saved her life, but Addie reminded herself that he'd also used her to find the Moonlight Strangler, the very monster at the heart of all of this.

"Ogden said you should try hypnosis and some drug therapy," Jericho finally answered.

"I've done both." A reminder that wasn't necessary since her brother and Weston already knew that. If she thought more hypnosis would help, she'd gladly repeat it. Ditto for another round of drug therapy once the baby was born.

"Ogden believes you know plenty of things you're not saying because you want to protect your birth father," Jericho added. "And remember that part about him being crazy."

Addie wanted to curse. Or scream. "I wouldn't protect him. Not ever." Of course, she hadn't needed to tell Jericho that. But it did make her wonder. "Is this personal for Ogden? Maybe the Moonlight Strangler killed someone he loved?"

Even though Weston wasn't touching her, she could almost feel his muscles tightening.

"We'll check all angles," Jericho assured her, but anything else he was about to say was cut off when they spotted a tall gray-haired man in scrubs making his ways toward him.

Addie instantly recognized him. It was Dr. Applewhite. There were only a handful of regular doctors at the small hospital, and she'd known Dr. Applewhite since she was in elementary school. However, she didn't usually see such a serious expression on his grandfatherly face.

"Teddy's in surgery," the doctor said right off. "He's lost a lot of blood. *A lot*," he emphasized. "But there doesn't seem to be any damage to his vital organs. He should pull through."

Addie hadn't even realized she was holding her breath until the air rushed from her throat. Like the doctor, she'd known Teddy most of her life, and it felt like a stab to the heart to know he'd been hurt because of her.

"Thanks for telling us," Addie said. "My mother's already called his family to let them know. They'll be here soon."

The doctor had no sooner stepped away when Jericho's phone buzzed, and she saw Jax's name on the screen. She also saw the debate Jericho had with himself before he finally put the call on speaker.

"I found something," Jax greeted.

Addie had braced herself for bad news, but the relief flooded through her. Guarded relief anyway.

"I'm looking at Lonny Ogden's phone records, and he's only been in contact with one person in the past twenty-four hours. Ira Canales."

Yet another name Addie didn't recognize, and apparently she wasn't the only one who didn't.

"Who is he?" Weston and Jericho asked in unison.

"He's the campaign manager for Alton Gregory Boggs."

Addie shook her head. "The attorney who's running for the state senate?"

"The very one," Jax confirmed.

She'd seen campaign ads. Everyone probably had. Pictures of a smiling Boggs and his equally smiling wife were plastered on billboards all over the area.

"It's not just a couple of calls to Canales," Jax went on. "Ogden phoned him six times today. All under a minute long so I can't be sure if Canales actually spoke with him. Ogden could have just left him messages."

True, but it was a start. Maybe Ogden had said something to Canales that would tell them if Ogden truly had a connection to the Moonlight Strangler. *Any* connection that would help them learn the killer's identity.

"I'll call Canales now and have him come in tomorrow," Jax continued. "Jericho, have you been able to question Ogden yet?"

But Jericho didn't get a chance to answer because of the shouts that were coming from the ER. One of the shouts she instantly recognized as coming from the night deputy, Dexter Conway.

"Stop!" Dexter yelled.

"Stay here," Jericho insisted. He drew his gun, then hesitated a split second so he could make eye contact with Weston. "Watch out for her."

Jericho rushed out, racing toward the sounds of Dexter's repeated shouts for someone or something to stop. Weston stepped in the doorway in front of her, and he, too, drew his gun.

Just like that her heart was right back in her throat. "What's happening?"

Weston shook his head.

But Addie heard something she definitely hadn't wanted to hear.

A gunshot.

The sound put her heart right back in her throat. "Another attack?" she managed to ask.

"Maybe." Weston didn't budge. He kept watch and then started a new round of profanity. "Yeah. It's a gunman. And Jericho's in pursuit."

Chapter Six

This day had gone about as bad as Weston could have imagined, and sadly it wasn't over yet.

Not with a hired gun on the loose.

And judging from the fact that Jericho hadn't called Addie and Weston yet, the sheriff and deputies had yet to apprehend the armed man who'd tried to get into the hospital. The same man who'd taken a shot at one of the deputies when he'd tried to question him.

With both Addie and Ogden in the hospital at that time, there was no way to know which one was the intended target.

But the thug had definitely had a target all right.

The deputy had reported that the man had been armed to the hilt and had tried to strong-arm his way into the hospital after the deputy stopped him for questioning. Too bad the guy had managed to run off before they could learn who he was after and who'd sent him.

That wasn't something Weston wanted to learn the hard way.

And that's why he'd insisted on bringing Addie back to her family's ranch. A plan heartily endorsed by her brothers. However, it was temporary. Well, it was unless they managed to figure out the identity of a killer who'd been eluding the police and FBI for three decades.

Yeah, this bad day definitely wasn't over yet.

Weston finished his latest call with one of his Ranger

friends, and he turned around knowing Addie would be right there in the ranch's kitchen. Waiting for news. What he hadn't figured was that *right there* was close enough that he bumped into her. He automatically reached for her.

Not a good idea.

Because she stepped back as if he'd scalded her.

Weston couldn't blame her. He'd gotten her pregnant, walked out on her, and here he'd been back in her life for only a couple of hours and someone had already tried to kill her. Worse, he couldn't even guarantee her that things would get better.

"Anything on the guy who got away?" she asked.

"No." But she might have already known the answer since she'd perhaps been standing close enough to hear his conversation. "I've asked the Rangers to assist with the search."

"Are you on good enough terms with them to ask that?"

Barely.

Weston kept that to himself and nodded. Most of his fellow officers thought he'd crossed a line between obsession and justice when it came to finding Collette's killer.

There were days, and nights, like this one when Weston had to agree with them.

"They'll find him," Weston assured her. At best that was wishful thinking. At worst, a lie. But he hated that look of worry on her face.

A face he could hardly see because all the overhead lights were off. But the Christmas lights were twinkling and shimmering outside the windows.

The lack of inside lights, even here in the kitchen, was a precaution in case a shooter managed to get past a wall of security that Weston had established with ranch hands, PIs and deputies—all on the ranch grounds to make sure Addie was safe.

She moved back to the counter, finished off a glass of milk and then studied him. "Would you still use me to draw out the killer?"

A reasonable question since several hours ago, that's exactly what he'd planned to do. "No. I'll have to think of another way."

One that didn't involve endangering the baby she was carrying.

Or her.

Yes, Addie herself was playing into this now. Weston could blame the blasted attraction for that. It was still there, just as it had been when he'd first laid eyes on her.

"So…that means you'll be leaving," she added. And it didn't exactly have a "please stay" tone attached to it.

"I'll stay until Jericho gets home." Whenever that would be. The sheriff was no doubt up to his ears in alligators.

"And then?" she pressed.

That was the million-dollar question. He didn't even have a fifty-cent answer. "Well, I won't be leaving for good. I'll be part of the baby's life."

"I don't expect that from you."

"You should." Weston tried to rein in the anger he heard in his voice. "Despite what you think of me, I'm not some dirtbag who'll run out on his own child. On any child for that matter."

"Oh." That was all Addie said for a long time. "So… you've always wanted children?"

"No." He didn't have to think about that, but he did have to consider how to explain it. "I always figured I wouldn't pass on my DNA to an innocent child. Let's just say my parents weren't stellar and leave it at that."

Her eyebrow lifted. "I think I've got you beat hands down in the bad DNA department. Were either of them notorious serial killers who wanted to murder you?"

He had to shake his head on that one.

She made a yeah-I-got-you-beat sound. "As far as I'm concerned, their DNA has nothing to do with this child." She slid her hand over her stomach. "After all, even with our bad blood, we didn't turn out so wrong."

The jury was still out on that when it came to him. Weston wasn't sure he could forgive himself for what he'd done to Addie.

Or Collette.

Nor was he sure he wanted their forgiveness.

He deserved this private hell he was living.

Addie paused again, glanced around. "Then I suppose we'll work out some kind of custody agreement. Something simple and nice that doesn't involve tempers flaring and such."

That was good, but it didn't ring true, and it felt as if someone had just scraped their nails on a chalkboard. Maybe it was that irritation or the events of the night. Heck, maybe he had indeed lost it, but Weston hooked his arm around her waist, pulled her to him and kissed her.

He'd meant for it to be a reminder that flaring tempers were the least of their worries. And that any agreement would be far from simple or nice. But one taste of her, and Weston got a lesson of his own.

Best not to play with fire.

And that's exactly what he was doing whenever he was within breathing distance of Addie.

It was a short-lived disaster. However, it still packed a wallop. Addie pushed herself away from him and looked ready to knock him into the middle of the next county.

"Don't," she managed to say. She even managed a glare before she cursed. "I won't make the mistake of sleeping with you again."

"Good." And he was reasonably sure he meant that. "Because right now, we don't need this kind of distraction."

"This kind of *distraction* isn't ever going to happen again," she clarified. And she was probably sure that she meant it, too.

Thankfully, they didn't have to deal with this mental foreplay any longer because Weston's phone dinged, and he spotted a text from Jax on the screen.

"Ogden's out of surgery," Weston read aloud so Addie wouldn't have to move closer to him to read it. "He lawyered up."

It was exactly what Weston had expected him to do since the idiot was facing multiple counts of attempted murder. Still, he might be willing to cut some kind of deal to give them info about anyone he might be working with.

Including Ira Canales.

Weston definitely wanted to be at the sheriff's office in the morning for that interview.

"Come on," Weston told her. "You need to get some rest." That wasn't just coming from him, either. The doctor had insisted on it when he'd examined her while they were at the hospital.

Addie stepped around him, careful not to brush against him. It didn't help. Weston could still feel her in his arms. Could still see images of her naked.

Yeah, that really didn't help.

It also didn't help that he was following her to her bedroom. He wouldn't go in the room with her, of course, but he would end up sleeping nearby. With Addie so close that he could remember that mistake of a kiss he'd just made.

"Jericho's going to insist on putting me in a safe house, isn't he?" she asked as they walked up the stairs.

"Probably. And if he doesn't, I will. And don't you dare say it's safe here, because the bullet holes in your office prove otherwise."

That earned him a huff. "Look, I'm not stupid. I want me and my baby to be safe. But I do a lot of things to help keep this ranch running, and I can't do those things if I'm locked away in a safe house."

"It's not permanent." Weston hoped.

She threw open the door to her bedroom and whirled around as if the argument might continue. It didn't. Addie just stared at him.

"You were in love with Collette?" she asked.

Well, that came out of the blue. And he was certain this wasn't a conversation he wanted to have. Weston settled for a nod.

"I'm trying to justify in my mind why you did what you did in San Antonio," Addie clarified.

"You can't justify that," he assured her.

"But you can." Those words hung in the air like knives over his head.

"I owed Collette. And I let her down." Weston figured that would be enough poking at old wounds tonight.

Apparently not.

"You owed her?" Addie's forehead bunched up. "What does that mean?"

Weston opened his mouth. Groaned. "It means you should climb into bed and get some rest."

As answers went, it sucked, but he was already too raw, too drained to take this bad trip down memory lane.

She stared at him several moments longer. Waiting

for something he wasn't going to give her. Addie must have finally realized that because she went into her room and shut the door. She even locked it.

Good.

He didn't want her to trust him, and if Collette were still alive, she would agree.

Weston looked up the hall to make sure Iris's door was still shut. It was. Addie's mom had gone there shortly after they'd gotten back from the hospital, and maybe she would stay put until morning. He doubted she'd get much sleep. None of them would. But he didn't want either Addie or her mom wandering around the house where they could be sniper targets.

With his back against the wall, Weston eased himself to a sitting position on the floor. No doubt where he'd end up spending the night, but that was okay.

A penance of sorts.

He'd been a fool to come here and think he could fix things, that he could make Addie feel safe. Instead, he'd flamed a fire—several of them in fact.

Weston closed his eyes, praying for a quick nap. Didn't happen. His phone rang, and he saw Jericho's name on the screen.

"Did you find the hired gun?" Weston greeted.

"Yeah."

It wasn't an answer Weston had been expecting. He figured on getting another dose of bad news. Then, he realized Jericho's silence probably meant that was still to come.

"I followed him to the old abandoned hospital outside of town," Jericho continued. "He drew on me, and I had to kill him."

Hell. They needed the guy alive so he could talk. "Did he have any ID?"

"No, but he had some pictures on him that made it pretty clear who he was targeting."

"He was sent to kill Ogden," Weston concluded, "before he could tell us anything."

"No. I wish." Jericho paused again, then cursed. "His target was Addie."

Chapter Seven

Addie thought a maximum security prison might have fewer safety measures than she had at the moment.

Weston, Jericho and three deputies. Plus the two PIs and two more armed ranch hands who'd followed Weston and her on the drive from the ranch to the sheriff's office. They were waiting outside as if they were about to be blasted to smithereens.

She didn't mind the protection. Not for her sake but for the baby's.

But there was something all of these lawmen weren't telling her.

Jax kept dodging her gaze. The other deputies, too. And more than usual, Jericho was scowling along with looking more intimidating. Of course, Jericho didn't just look intimating.

He was.

Yet, Weston seemed to match him in that department.

Maybe it had something to do with the fact that both had probably gotten very little sleep and were on edge. Jericho had spent the night at the sheriff's office, and Weston had stayed right outside her door. All night. She should probably be happy that he was showing such an interest in keeping her safe, but having him around was a reminder she didn't need.

Like that kiss.

Her brain was telling her this was a man she shouldn't

trust. Not with her heart anyway. He seemed to be doing a better than average job protecting her body. But that kiss was a reminder to guard her feelings. She wasn't sure she could survive another to have her heart broken by Weston a second time.

Worse, she wasn't sure if he had any immediate plans to leave anytime soon.

In the wee hours of the morning, he'd had someone deliver several changes of clothes to the ranch. And Weston had moved those things into the guest room across from hers. He'd also had several phone conversations with Jericho. About what, she didn't know, but Addie was about to find out.

"You're hardheaded," Jericho said to her the moment he finished a phone call. He came out from behind his desk and made a beeline toward her. "You should have stayed at the ranch."

"He's right," Weston agreed. Probably the only thing Weston and her brother actually agreed about. "There was no need for you to be here for Canales's and Boggs's interviews."

Oh, yes, there was. Especially for Canales, since the injured shooter had been in phone contact with the campaign manager. Of course, Weston had tried to talk her out of it. He'd failed.

"Boggs did say he wanted to see you," Jax volunteered.

It took Addie a moment to realize he was talking to her. "Me? Why? I don't know him."

Jax lifted his shoulder. "When I asked Boggs to come in for the interview, he wanted to know if you'd be here. I said no, probably not. And he said that was too bad because he wanted to meet you."

She hoped this wasn't another case of someone wanting to meet her because of her biological father. There were some strange people out there with fascinations about serial killers.

"What time are Canales and Boggs coming in?" Weston asked.

Jericho checked his watch. "Should be any minute now. After that, I want Addie back at the ranch."

Huffing, she got in her brother's face. "Tell me what's going on," Addie said, glancing first at Jericho then Weston.

Weston and Jericho did some glance-exchanges of their own. "The hit man who showed up at the hospital last night—he was after you."

All right. That was a truth that punched her a little harder than expected. Of course, she'd known Ogden had wanted her dead, but now this thug had wanted that, too.

"You're sure?" she asked, but immediately waved off the question. They were certain, and it explained all the extra security.

Jericho led her to his office. The first thing she spotted on his cluttered desk was a photo. A photo of *her*. It was a grainy shot that looked as if it'd been taken through a long-range lens.

"Did you know you'd been photographed?" Weston asked.

She shook her head. Hadn't had a clue. Which made this even more sickening. How long had this monster been following her? Or maybe it was more than one monster, since the person who'd taken that photo could have given it to the hit man so he'd be sure he was killing the right person.

Her stomach clenched.

"We got an ID on the dead guy around midnight," Jericho continued. "Curtis Nicks. Unlike Ogden, he's got a record, and the FBI got into his computer. There were more photos of you, but this appears to be the only one he printed out."

Because he only needed one.

But there was something else. She didn't ask Jericho what that was. Instead, she turned to Weston and motioned for him to continue. "I'm sure in one of those many conversations you had with Jericho, you know everything that's going on."

He made a sound to confirm that but took his time answering. "Nicks has a file on his computer with the address to the ranch and some other notes. The file was new, created just yesterday." Weston paused, met her eye-to-eye. "If Nicks hadn't been able to get to you, he planned to use your family to draw you out."

"Oh, God." Her knees buckled, and if Weston hadn't caught her, she would have fallen. He had her sit in the chair next to Jericho's desk. "Mom," she managed to say.

"I'm sending her to her sister's place," Jericho quickly volunteered. Addie's aunt had two sons, both cops, who lived with her, so that was a good first step.

"But what about you?" she asked. "And Jax, Chase?"

"All of us are taking precautions. We've even got someone on Teddy while he's recovering at the hospital. Ditto for Weston's sister. The Rangers have beefed up security for her, too."

Good. Addie didn't want anyone else hurt. Especially anyone connected to Weston. Her birth father had already cost him enough.

Jericho's phone buzzed, and he scowled when he looked at the screen. "I have to take this. Stay with her," he added to Weston.

"You heard what your brother said." Weston pulled

up the chair and sat so they were face-to-face. "Every-one's taking precautions."

Addie wasn't sure that'd be enough. "Is Nicks even connected to the Moonlight Strangler?"

"He appears to be. He mentions him in his notes. Not by name, just the initials MS."

Great. Now the Moonlight Strangler was hiring hit men to come after her.

"What about Ogden?" she asked. "Is he saying any-thing?"

"Not to any of us, but according to Jax, his lawyer was with him most of the night. Not a cheap attorney, either. This guy is top-shelf. Jax is following the money trail to see if anyone's paying for those round-the-clock legal services."

Good. Maybe that would lead to something.

"So, maybe Ogden wasn't connected to the other hit man who came to the hospital," Addie said, thinking out loud.

"Maybe. But two armed men in the same night prob-ably isn't a coincidence. That's why you'll need to go to a safe house," Weston added. "The marshals can set one up for you."

Twenty-four hours ago, she would have nixed the idea. Not now, though. Because Weston was right.

She was about to tell Weston to start the arrange-ments, but Addie got to her feet when she heard voices in the main squad room. She immediately saw Jericho greeting two men. One she recognized from the bill-boards.

Alton Boggs.

He wasn't a big man, only about five-eight, and he looked more like a 1940s film star than a former rancher. His black hair was slicked back. Teeth perfectly white and straight. His gaze shifted over the room until it landed on her. Only then did he smile, and it wasn't the sort of welcoming smile, either. It was as if he was trying to reassure her.

Or something.

The man with the salt-and-pepper hair who stepped in behind Boggs was at least half a foot taller. No smile for him. His mouth was pulled into what appeared to be a permanent frown. He barely spared her a glance. His attention instead went to Jericho.

"Sheriff Crockett," Canales said, the impatience dripping from his voice. "I hope to resolve this fast. Mr. Boggs has a fund-raising luncheon in San Antonio, and we need to get back on the road."

Boggs, however, showed no such impatience. He came closer to her, extending his hand for her to shake. "Addie Crockett. Your pictures don't do you justice."

She actually dropped back a step, and Weston moved in between Boggs and her. Only then did Boggs seem to realize he'd made her uncomfortable.

"Alton Boggs," he said, extending his hand to Weston.

"Weston Cade."

"Ah, yes, the Texas Ranger," Boggs provided.

Weston lifted his eyebrow, questioning how the man knew that.

"I see I need to explain," Boggs said. "Is there someplace we can all talk *privately*?" he asked Weston. "I'd like Addie to hear what I have to say, as well."

Jericho didn't jump to answer, but he finally tipped his head toward the hall and led them into an interview room.

"There's no need to get into all of this," Canales said to his boss. "The sheriff only wants me to explain why that idiot in the hospital called me."

"What do you mean by all of *this*?" Addie asked.

Boggs drew in a long breath and sank down into one of the chairs. He motioned for her to do the same and didn't continue until she had. "I've been trying to catch the Moonlight Strangler for years, and when I heard about your DNA connection, I'd hoped he would try to contact you. Has he?"

She groaned. "You're a groupie?"

"Hardly. Your father murdered one of my childhood friends, Cora McGee."

The name was familiar to Addie, as were all the victims. "*Birth* father. And I'm sorry."

"No need to apologize for anything he did. But you understand now why I was interested in you."

Weston and she exchanged uneasy glances. "Convince me why you were really interested." Weston insisted.

"You're obviously a skeptic. That probably comes with the badge. Well, I was interested in you as well since you, too, lost a loved one to the Moonlight Strangler," Boggs added.

"How did you know who I was?" Weston asked.

"I've made it a point to know anyone and everyone associated with the case. Clearly, so have you." Boggs stopped on the last syllable. "Or are you here in Appaloosa Pass because Addie and you are...*together*?"

Addie felt the goose bumps shiver over her skin. She had no intention of answering him, but Weston had a different notion.

"We're not together, not like that," Weston snapped.

Only then did she remember the killer's threat, that if she and Weston teamed up, he'd murder Weston's sister. Besides, they really weren't together.

And it would be dangerous to both of them if anyone thought they were.

"The only reason Weston is here," she said, "is because he wants to catch the Moonlight Strangler, too."

Boggs studied them a moment as if trying to figure out if that was true, and he finally nodded. "Of course. I just assumed it because you're two attractive people. But I can see I was wrong about that."

"There's no reason to get into any of this," Canales interrupted. He checked his watch again. "But to answer your question about this Lonny Ogden, I have no idea why he phoned me, because I didn't answer his calls. I'm sure the phone records will show that."

"They do," Jericho verified. "But that doesn't mean you don't know Ogden or know why he was calling."

"I don't know him." Canales's mouth tightened even more. "Plenty of people call me about the campaign. Heck, for all I know he could have been hired by one of Alton's opponents to sully his name."

"Maybe," Weston said, taking the seat next to Addie. "You still haven't convinced me. Maybe Ogden knew about your boss's connection to the Moonlight Strangler?"

"That's exactly the kind of talk I'm trying to stop," Canales snapped. "This will be a tight campaign race, and I don't want anyone using a smear tactic like this. We're running on a platform of traditional values. On family. Any mention of a serial killer could taint that."

Judging from his scowl, Weston wasn't pleased with that answer, and he turned back to Boggs. "Did Ogden try to contact you, too?"

"All my nonpersonal calls go through him these days." He aimed a glance at Canales. "So it's possible Ogden was actually trying to get in touch with me. It's also possible it was about the Moonlight Strangler." He paused, studied Addie again. "Has your father ever contacted you through a call or letters?"

Because Weston's arm was touching hers, she felt him tense. "No letters," she answered. And waited for Boggs to continue.

"Well, he might have sent me some," Boggs finally said.

It got very quiet in the room. For a couple of seconds anyway.

"Excuse me?" Jericho snarled. "What letters?"

Boggs held up his hands in a keep-calm gesture. "They might not even be real, but I started getting them a few months ago, and he said he was the Moonlight Strangler. Always signed them MS."

She looked at Weston to see if that matched the ones he'd received, and he nodded.

"What's in the letters?" she asked.

Boggs took another deep breath. "He doesn't say anything about the murders. He just keeps asking me if I remember him. I don't," he quickly volunteered. "But apparently he thinks we met years ago."

"Did you?" Weston sounded very much like a lawman right now. A riled one.

"No. Maybe," Boggs amended. "I'm sixty-one. I've met a lot of people, and it's my guess that he saw one of my campaign ads and latched on to me."

"He gets letters like that all the time," Canales added. "Some are nutcases who just want to be connected with someone famous. If we turned all of them over the police, the cops wouldn't have time to do their jobs."

"I want those letters," Weston insisted.

Boggs quickly nodded. "Of course. I'll have some-

one bring them here to the sheriff's office right away."
He took out his phone to make a call.

"I don't want them leaked to the press," Canales
snapped to Weston. "It could hurt the election if the
voters find out Boggs had any connection whatsoever
to the Moonlight Strangler."

"Yeah, yeah," Jericho grumbled.

Weston stood, faced Canales. "Your campaign isn't
even on my radar. I'll do whatever it takes to catch the
killer and keep Addie safe."

"I'll call you back," Boggs said to the person on the
other end of the line, and with his gaze fixed on Addie,
he put his phone away. "Are you in danger?"

The burst of air that left her mouth wasn't from laughter. "Yes. That's why it's important to know if you ever
met my birth father. I need to know who he is so he can
be stopped."

Boggs nodded. "You think those letters really could
be from him?"

"They could be," she settled for saying. No sense getting into the ones he'd sent Weston.

"The letters will be analyzed," Weston explained,
"and I'm sure the FBI will want you to go through hypnosis or something to see if you can remember if you
ever met this guy."

"Hypnosis?" Canales piped in. "That's not a good idea."

When Canales didn't explain, they all stared at him.

"I had a rough childhood," Boggs admitted. "Ira's just
worried that digging up old bones might be bad for my
mental state. And the campaign. People don't want to
hear about a poor kid who clawed his way out of abuse
and poverty. They want to see me with my beautiful
wife of nearly twenty-five years and know that I stand
for the same honest and upright values they stand for."

Weston added some profanity under his breath. "How bad do you think your mental state and the campaign will be if another woman is killed and you could have done something to prevent it?"

"Point taken," Boggs said, but it was clear from Canales's scowl that he didn't agree.

Boggs turned to Addie again. "I'd hoped by seeing you that I might remember if I'd ever met your father. Your *birth* father," Boggs corrected. "I thought maybe you'd look like him and that I'd recognize you or something."

"Do you?" she wanted to know.

Boggs glanced back at Canales, and for a moment she thought Canales would be able to silence his boss with the stern look he was giving him. He didn't.

"Ira, you remember I told you about the little girl that the daycare woman had for a while?" Boggs asked.

Canales didn't roll his eyes exactly, but it was close. "You don't think…" He cursed. "You think she's that kid?" He stabbed his index finger toward Addie.

That got her attention, and Addie slowly rose to her feet. Canales's question had her heart racing. Her breath, too.

"Over the years, I've talked to as many people as I could who lived within a fifty mile radius of where you were found. Because I figured your birth father had probably been in the area, too. A couple of months back, I met a woman named Daisy," Boggs explained. "She babysat a little girl for a while."

Addie jumped right on that. "Why would you think it was me?"

"Because the age and description are right. Blond hair, big blue eyes. Like yours. I figured if you truly were that little girl and if the killer was right about me having known him, then I might remember meeting you. Might remember meeting the killer, as well. But I don't recall running into any man who looked like that child. Or like you."

"But it's possible?" she pressed.

After several long moments, Boggs nodded.

That put her right back in the chair. They might have a link, though it was a slim one. What were the odds that Boggs would have seen her as a child?

Not likely.

But if Addie had indeed been with Daisy, then the woman might be able to answer a lot of questions.

"I'll get you some water," Weston insisted.

She must look as shaken as she felt for him to make that offer. More than anything she wanted answers, but Addie was afraid those answers weren't going to be ones she liked.

Nor would the answers necessarily make this danger disappear.

Weston left the room for just a minute and returned with three paper cups of water. He gave one to her and handed the others to Canales and Boggs. Canales drank his down without stopping. Not Boggs, though. He looked at Weston, his forehead bunching up, and he put the cup on the table.

"Thanks, but I'm not thirsty," Boggs said.

"Why didn't you tell the FBI about this Daisy?" Jericho asked.

Boggs shrugged. "I wasn't sure it was connected. I'm still not sure."

Jericho took out a notepad and pen and dropped it on the table. "I want Daisy's full name and any contact information you have."

"Daisy Vogel," Boggs provided, and he stood. "I don't remember her address, but I'm sure you can find it."

Weston looked at Canales, no doubt wondering if he had more info.

"Never met the woman. I knew Alton back then, but I never crossed paths with Daisy." Canales crushed his cup and tossed it into the trash can. "Just remember, I don't want any of this backwashing onto the campaign. Are we finished here?"

"For now," Jericho answered.

That was enough to get Canales moving. "Come on, Alton. We can't be late for that fund-raiser."

"Let me know if you find Daisy." Boggs reached out as if he might touch Addie's arm, but he must have remembered her earlier reaction because instead he mumbled a goodbye and left with Canales.

"I'll see what I can do about getting Daisy's number," Jericho said to Weston, and he tipped his head to the trash can. "I'll also bring back an evidence bag to take care of that. Too bad you couldn't get Boggs to take the bait."

"Bait?" Addie repeated, turning to Weston when her brother walked out.

Weston shrugged. "I wanted their DNA so we can compare it."

Addie felt her eyes widen. "You think one of them might be the Moonlight Strangler?"

"They fit the profile."

That stalled her breath in her throat.

"Are you okay?" Weston asked.

She nodded. She was getting good at lying. Or so she thought. Weston saw right through her.

"We just need to be sure," he added. He slid his arm around her waist. Not a hug exactly. But close.

All right, it was a hug.

And Addie couldn't help herself. She leaned against him.

Had she really just been face-to-face with her birth father?

"I thought maybe I'd feel something if I ever saw him," she said. "Maybe some kind of genetic memory connection."

"You're not like him. You probably won't feel anything like that at all."

But she would feel *something*. So would Weston. Especially since her birth father had murdered Collette.

"Will you ever be able to look at me, at the baby, and not think of Collette and her killer?" Addie wanted to snatch back the question as soon as she asked it. But it was too late.

"I don't think of them when I look at you," he said as if choosing his words carefully. "Trust me, that's not a good thing. Because it means I'm losing focus. And that might be dangerous for all of us."

Addie heard the footsteps in the hall, and she stepped away from Weston. But not before Jericho saw them. He scowled, of course. Probably because he thought she was on her way to another broken heart.

She wasn't.

Once the danger was over, she would put some emotional distance between herself and Weston.

"I got Daisy Vogel's home phone number," Jericho announced. "She has no record. Not even a parking ticket, and she's lived at the same place for the past forty years. I thought you'd want to listen in while I try to call her."

Addie nodded. "I do."

She held her breath, watching Jericho press in the numbers. He put the call on speaker and waited. They didn't have to wait long. A woman answered on the second ring.

"Daisy Vogel?" Jericho asked.

"Yes. And according to my caller ID, you're Jericho Crockett."

"That's right. I'm the sheriff in Appaloosa Pass. I wanted to ask you a few questions about a case I'm working on."

"Crockett," Daisy repeated, obviously ignoring Jericho's response. "You live on the Appaloosa Pass Ranch?"

"I do—"

"Is your adopted sister there with you?" Daisy interrupted.

Weston and Jericho looked as if they were debating the answer they'd give her, but Addie solved that for them.

"I'm here," Addie answered.

Silence. For a long time.

"Good." Though it didn't sound as if Daisy actually thought it was good. "The Crocketts named you Addie, right?"

"They did." And Addie waited through yet another long silence.

"I figured you'd eventually find your way to me," Daisy finally continued. "I knew sooner or later you'd find out."

Addie had to take a deep breath before she could ask the next question. "Find out what?"

Daisy took a deep breath, as well. "If you want some answers about your past, come and see me. Because I know who you really are."

Chapter Eight

As ideas went, this one was *bad*. Weston was sure of it.

But he couldn't see another way around it. Daisy had refused to say more on the phone, and after Jericho had called her back twice, the woman had hung up on him and hadn't answered any other calls.

Maybe Daisy had simply wanted to talk to Addie face-to-face, and this wasn't some kind of trap to lure Addie into the open. However, Weston had seen a lot of things as a lawman, and he wasn't about to trust some woman claiming to have information.

I know who you really are, Daisy had told Addie.

Well, he'd see about that.

Ditto for Jericho, who was behind the wheel of the cruiser. In the front seat with him, Jericho had brought along Mack Parkman, one of the other deputies, just in case this bad idea went even further south. The cruiser was bullet-resistant, and with three lawmen around her, Addie stood a good chance of being safe.

But a *chance* was far from being 100 percent.

According to the GPS, Daisy lived forty miles from Appaloosa Pass, and they were already halfway there. However, Daisy's place wasn't exactly on the beaten path. She lived on a farm road in an old house that'd belonged to her late husband, who'd been dead for nearly thirty years. About the same amount of time the Moonlight Strangler had been killing.

Weston hoped that wasn't some kind of weird coincidence.

"I don't remember any woman named Daisy," Addie insisted. She was leaning her head against the window, her eyes partly closed as if she were trying to coax those old memories into returning.

"You were three years old, maybe younger. Of course you won't remember her."

But the FBI would no doubt want to test that notion. The other times they'd hypnotized Addie and used drug therapy on her, they'd been specifically trying to get her to recall memories of the Moonlight Strangler. Now they would want to repeat that while pressing her about Daisy.

"This is a long shot anyway," Weston went on. "If Daisy really knew something about your past, then why hasn't she already come forward? Especially once it was leaked that you're the Moonlight Strangler's biological daughter."

Addie made a sound of agreement. Then she paused. "Unless she thought he would kill her. Which he might."

Weston couldn't dismiss that, and if Daisy turned out to be legit, the woman was in serious danger.

Jericho must have caught some part of that conversation because he glanced back at them using the rearview mirror. But it was just a glance, and he returned to the call he was on with the crime lab.

"Boggs or Canales might not keep quiet about Daisy," Addie added under her breath.

"Canales will." Weston couldn't say the same for Boggs, though. "Canales is more worried about the campaign than the investigation. Or your safety."

"Yes." She drew in a long breath, repeated her response. "And I might know soon if he's my birth father."

She lifted her head, looked at him. "But what about Boggs? You didn't get his DNA."

No, and Boggs had seemed pretty darn suspicious when Weston had brought that cup of water into the interview room. Not Canales, though. Maybe because Canales had nothing to hide. Or perhaps he just hadn't realized that Weston hadn't served him the water out of the goodness of his heart.

"There'll be other opportunities to get Boggs's DNA," Weston told her.

And maybe Daisy would tell them something—anything—that they could use to get a court order for the DNA test. Of course, with Boggs's connections, money and reputation, it was going to take a lot to force him to contribute his DNA for a murder investigation.

"Jericho's running Ogden's DNA, too," he added. "Ogden's too young to be the Moonlight Strangler, but Jericho thought maybe Ogden might have a record under an alias."

At least that's the explanation Jericho had given Weston. Maybe that's all there was to it. But it was possible Jericho had reasons he wasn't willing to share with him. With anybody just yet. It made Weston wonder—did Jericho believe Ogden had some kind of blood connection to the Moonlight Strangler?

"Jericho isn't scowling at you as much as he was," she whispered after glancing at her brother. Jericho was so involved in his conversation that he didn't seem to hear her. Neither did Deputy Parkman, who was making his own calls, trying to get more background info on Daisy.

"Should I be worried about Jericho's lack of scowls?" Weston was only partly serious.

They shared a very short, weary smile. "We both

should be. Does he know the Moonlight Strangler warned us about teaming up?"

"I told him. I arranged to have copies of all the letters sent to the sheriff's office. Just like Boggs. Maybe together they'll give us clues that we don't already have."

"Maybe," Addie said, not sounding very hopeful. "Jericho's convinced we'll find the killer soon. After that, don't be surprised if he tries to pressure you into marrying me."

Weston hadn't meant to hesitate, but he did, and that hesitation got Addie's attention.

She huffed. "He's already talked to you about it."

"It came up in conversation. But probably not like you think. Jericho doesn't believe I'm good enough for you. Because I lied to you about who I was. Because I left you."

Though he probably hadn't needed to clarify that for her.

"And there's that part about my being the target of a serial killer," she added. "One who murdered the woman you loved." Addie leaned forward, making eye contact with him. "For the record, I'm not getting married just because I'm pregnant." She shot a glare at her brother, who didn't seem to be listening. "I can raise this baby just fine without a wedding ring."

"Jericho said something along those same lines." Actually, it was exactly along those lines.

"Well, good." She sounded surprised that she and her brother were on the same page.

But they weren't on the same page with Weston.

"Your birth father might not even know you're pregnant," Weston explained. "And if he did, he might back off."

Addie stared at him with her mouth slightly open. "Is that some kind of argument for a big public announcement to tell everyone that in about six months we'll be parents?"

The parent label mentally threw him for a moment. So had the comment about her birth father killing the woman he loved.

That always felt like a twist of the knife.

But Weston pushed both aside and continued. "He wouldn't have to know the baby is mine. But I think your pregnancy should somehow make it to the press."

She stayed quiet a moment. "I don't want him to know. It makes me sick to think he has any connection whatsoever to this baby. Besides, he warned you about us teaming up."

"We won't present ourselves as a team. In fact, we can make sure everyone notices the tension between us. Which shouldn't be hard."

Since the tension was there for anyone to see.

She paused so long again that Weston was certain she was about to tell him no. But she finally nodded. "I don't suppose it could hurt. Besides, it won't be a secret for much longer. My jeans are already too tight."

Of course he had to look. Because he was stupid and male.

And, of course, he noticed her jeans were indeed tight. But not in a bad kind of way. Addie's curves had attracted him the first time he saw her, and they were still attracting him now.

Weston was thankful that the GPS interrupted his gawking with instructions to take the next road. The moment Jericho made the turn, the house came into view. No way could they miss it because it was literally sitting in the middle of some pecan trees and pasture and was the only house in sight.

As places went, it wasn't the worst for security. The tall

pecans weren't that wide, so a gunman couldn't use them to hide. He spotted only one vehicle, an old truck with blistered red paint. There was a barn, but it was a good fifty yards from the house. The barn doors were wide open, and he could see clear through to the other side. If a gunman was in there, then he was in the shadows.

Something Weston would be looking for.

In fact, Weston was looking so hard for possible security problems that he didn't immediately notice Addie's reaction. Addie pulled back her shoulders. Pulled in her breath, too.

"Are you okay?" he asked. "Did you remember something?"

She shook her head. "No." Addie tried to wave him off.

"What?" Weston pressed.

Another headshake. "I just thought I remembered a swing set. But not necessarily here. Nothing about this place looks familiar."

While he wasn't sure that was true, Weston decided he wouldn't pressure her. Not now anyway.

"I'm going to try to get Daisy's DNA," he explained. "So if you notice her drinking from a cup or glass, and you get the chance to take it, do it."

"Her DNA?" Weston saw the realization flash through her eyes. "You think she could be my birth mother?"

He lifted his shoulder. "I don't know what to think at this point. I just want to rule her out. Before we left the sheriff's office, I requested a background check on her late husband."

Judging from the way the color drained from her face, she had considered the possibility that her birth mother might factor into this investigation.

"We can postpone this visit," he offered.

"No." Addie didn't hesitate, either.

Good thing, too, because when Jericho pulled up in front of the house, the woman was in the doorway, clearly waiting for them. It was Daisy all right. She matched the photo from the DMV. Snow-white hair and with a face that showed every year of her age, but she had a sturdy build. A smile, too. But that smile did nothing to put Weston at ease.

"Don't get out yet," Weston said when Addie reached for the door handle.

Jericho confirmed that with a nod, and both the sheriff and deputy got out first. Weston followed them. All with their guns drawn. If Daisy was alarmed by that, she didn't show it. She stayed in the doorway, hugging her coat to her. A coat that could be used to conceal a weapon.

Deputy Parkman checked the left side of the house. Jericho, the right. Weston stayed put and kept an eye on Daisy and Addie.

"I got no plans to hurt anybody," Daisy volunteered.

But Weston didn't take her word for it. "Then you won't mind if I frisk you?"

"Wouldn't mind at all." She held open the coat and let him do just that. Since Daisy was almost as tall as he was, she looked him straight in the eyes while he searched her.

No weapon, and Weston didn't see one in the small living room just behind her.

"Nothing," Jericho announced, and the deputy agreed.

Only then did Weston motion for Addie to get out, and Daisy's gaze stayed on her as she made her way onto the porch.

"Come inside," Daisy offered, taking off her coat and hanging it on the hook by the door. "It's too cold to be standing out here gabbing."

It was. But since there might be hired guns inside, Weston stepped into the living room with Addie, and her brother and the deputy searched the house. It didn't take them long, just a couple of minutes, since the place wasn't that big.

"Take a seat," Daisy insisted.

Addie did, sitting on the sofa next to Daisy. The rest of them stood.

Daisy studied her. "Yep, you're that little girl that was here, all right. Faces age, they change, but eyes always stay the same."

Addie studied the woman as well, no doubt trying to figure out if she recognized her. Or if there was a family resemblance. There wasn't. Well, none that Weston could see anyway.

"You said you knew who I was," Addie prompted.

She nodded. "Me and my husband never did make money running this place so I use to do babysitting on the side. Folks came and went over the years, and one of those years, a man dropped by. Said he was a traveling salesman and that his wife had run off and that he needed somebody to watch his little girl for a week while he was looking for a new place to live. Her name was Gabrielle."

Addie repeated that name several times and then shook her head. "That doesn't sound familiar."

"The man called you Gabbie," Daisy added.

That still didn't seem to ring any bells with Addie.

"Gabbie," Daisy went on. "Didn't really fit because you said hardly more than a couple of words the whole week you were here."

"You remember the man's name?" Weston asked.

"Alton Boggs wanted to know the same thing when he came to visit. I couldn't recall it right off, but after Boggs left, I got to thinking, and I'm pretty sure the man's name was Steve Birchfield."

"I'm on it," Deputy Parkman said, taking out his phone. He stepped to the other side of the room.

Weston moved closer to Daisy. "What did this man look like?"

"Tall, lanky. Dark brown hair. Oh, and he was impatient," Daisy added after a long pause. "*Real* impatient. He didn't seem as interested in making sure his little girl was okay as he was getting out of here. Kept going on about how his wife running off was at the worst possible time and that it might cost him his job if he didn't get someone to watch the kid. The *kid*, that's what he kept calling her."

Addie looked up at Weston, and he could almost see what she was thinking. That sounded a lot like someone they'd recently met. Canales.

"Do you know Ira Canales, Boggs's campaign manager?" Weston asked.

Daisy thought about it a few seconds. "Can't say I do. He wasn't with Boggs when he came to visit a couple of months back." She paused, looked up at Weston. "Is there something creepy about Boggs, or is it just me?"

Yeah, but Weston wanted to know more about what Daisy thought. "Creepy how?"

"Well, he said he was here trying to track down anything about the little girl that the Moonlight Strangler fathered, that he was talking to lots of folks around here, but the thing is he didn't stop by any of my neighbors. Just here. I asked them, and none of them had laid eyes on him."

Interesting, and it contradicted what Boggs had told them. "So, why do you think he came to see you?"

She leaned closer as if about to tell a secret. "Well, I believe it's because he really wanted to find Steve Birchfield. That's who he was asking questions about. I figure that Birchfield fella might know something that Boggs wants to know."

"You mean like the identity of the Moonlight Strangler?" Addie asked.

Daisy shrugged. "I guess it coulda been that, but I just got the feeling that it might be, well, more."

More could be just Boggs's obsession with finding the person who'd murdered his childhood friend. But it could be something else. Something far more dangerous if Boggs had a more personal link to the killer.

Or if Boggs *was* the killer.

"How did Boggs know that Birchfield had been here thirty years ago?" Addie asked.

"Talk around town, I guess. Hadn't really kept it much of a secret."

Well, it hadn't been common knowledge because today was the first Weston had heard about it. Of course, there'd been plenty of leads just like this one that'd fizzled out.

"Is it possible that Steve Birchfield wasn't the little girl's father?" Weston continued.

Daisy's eyes widened. "You know, that is possible. I mean he didn't look a lick like her. And she didn't even give him so much as a goodbye when he left her here, much less a hug. When he would come by in the evenings to check on her, she'd just shy away from him."

That put a new spin on things. If Boggs turned out to be Addie's birth father, and the Moonlight Strangler, then maybe this Birchfield guy was trying to hide Addie.

"If the girl had been hurt or anything, bruises and such," Daisy went on, "I would have called somebody about that, but other than looking kinda sad and shy around her so-called daddy, she was fine the whole time she was here."

"Was there a swing set in the yard?" Addie asked.

Jericho looked surprised at the question. But not Daisy.

"Yes, there was. Honey, that was years ago. The thing rusted so bad that I had to have it hauled off to the dump. Why? You remember that?"

"No." Addie's answer was quick. "Not really. I'm probably thinking of one that used to be at the Appaloosa Pass Ranch."

A lie, but it was one Weston appreciated. Even if the swing set was a genuine memory, he didn't want her sharing it with Daisy. Not until they were certain they could trust the woman.

Deputy Parkman finished his call and walked back toward them. "There's no Steve Birchfield who matches the right age. There's also no birth record for Gabrielle or Gabbie Birchfield. You're certain that was his name?"

"That's the name he gave me," Daisy insisted. "But I got no way of knowing if he told me the truth or not. He paid in cash, and I didn't ask for an ID or anything. It didn't work that way thirty years ago. I just trusted him to be who he said he was and didn't give it a second thought until Alton Boggs came to visit."

Yes, and Weston wanted to question Boggs further about that visit. Boggs had made it seem random, but it was looking more and more like an intentional visit. First though, Weston had another question for Daisy.

"Why didn't you call the cops when you remembered this Birchfield and the little girl?"

"I did," Daisy answered. "I called the FBI tip line

number that I found in the phone book and said for them to look into it. I never heard back from them."

Probably because the FBI got hundreds of tips each day. Besides, until Addie had brought up that swing set, it really wasn't much of a connection. Forty miles was a lot of distance between here and the Crockett ranch.

"How much time was there between the little girl being dropped off here with you and Addie showing up near the Appaloosa Pass Ranch?" Jericho asked.

"I don't have any idea." Daisy's mouth trembled a little. "That was a bad time for me. My husband, Ernest— God rest his soul—was killed in an accident. It took me a while to pull myself together."

Jericho made a sound that could have meant anything, including some sympathy. "Is that why you didn't notice Addie's picture in the papers? After my dad found her, he had the newspapers run her picture for a month or more."

Daisy shook her head. "I didn't see it, sorry. Like I said, it was a bad time for me." Her gaze went back to Addie. "Guess it was a rough time for you, too."

"I don't remember any of it," Addie assured her.

"That's probably for the best." Daisy slid her hand over Addie's. "It don't matter what name that Steve Birchfield gave me. You're the little girl that was here. I'm sure of it."

Weston had no idea if it was true, and it didn't matter. If Daisy believed it and if the Moonlight Strangler learned she might have any information about him, then Daisy might become his target.

Even though Weston didn't say that to Jericho, it was obvious it had occurred to him, too.

"Daisy, why don't you follow us into town so we can talk with the county sheriff and he can take your statement?" Jericho suggested. Except it was more of an order. "It'll be a good idea if you didn't stay here by yourself for a while. Have you got some other place you can go, like maybe to a friend or relative?"

Weston expected her to show some concern. Maybe even fear. But Daisy got to her feet and hiked up her chin. "I'm not gonna let some pea-brained serial killer run me out of my home. I'll talk to the county sheriff. I'll do all the statements you want, but when I'm done, I'm coming right back here."

Good grief. He hardly knew her, but Weston doubted she would budge on this. That meant she'd need protection. Maybe something that could be arranged with the county sheriff.

"You can ride with Daisy," Jericho told his deputy. "I'll take Weston and Addie back to Appaloosa Pass and then meet you at the county sheriff's office."

That probably meant Jericho wanted to question Daisy further. But thankfully Addie wouldn't have to be around for that. She'd already had enough put on her shoulders today. Plus, she had to be stressed about what all of this was doing to the baby.

Weston sure was.

"The FBI will need to know about this," Addie said to him on their way out the door.

They would. It was the same for Daisy. She would have to recount her story to them and probably meet with a sketch artist to come up with a composite for Birchfield. "But this might be the break we've been looking for."

A break that would only come once Addie was put through yet more tests and questions to help jog her memory. Weston only hoped she could handle anything she might recall.

After all, she could have witnessed one or more of her father's murders.

"My truck's parked by the side of the house," Daisy said to the deputy. She grabbed her cell phone, put it in her purse and locked the door behind them. "No need for you to go with me, though. I can get there all by myself."

"I'm sure you can," the deputy said, "but I was hoping you could show me the way. I'm not familiar with this area."

It was the right thing to say. Daisy clearly wanted to stand on her own two feet, but she wouldn't refuse to help someone. Or at least she wanted them to believe she was cooperating.

Weston wasn't sure which.

He took Addie's arm as they headed out the door and then remembered he didn't want anyone, including Daisy, to think they were a couple. He backed away from Addie and went ahead of the others toward the cruiser. However, he'd only made it a few steps when all hell broke loose.

And the shots rang out.

Chapter Nine

The sounds of gunfire and Daisy's scream seemed to explode in Addie's head. The bullet had come close to her. Too close.

And before the fear and adrenaline could slam through her, Weston had his arm around her and dragged her to the ground on the side of the concrete steps that led up to the porch.

Not a second too soon.

Because another shot came her way and smashed into the dirt where she'd just been standing.

She was definitely the target, and the shots seemed to be coming from the old barn out in what was left of the pasture. There was another gunman. One who clearly wanted her dead.

Deputy Mack Parkman was on the porch, and he took hold of a still-screaming Daisy and pushed her behind some rocking chairs. Jericho took up cover behind the step railing. They were all out in the open.

All vulnerable.

Again.

Addie cursed the fact that once again her blood ties had put people in danger. Including her baby.

When was this going to stop?

At least Weston and she were semiprotected by the steps, but the railing and the rocking chairs weren't nearly enough to stop bullets. Mack and Daisy were especially vulnerable, but the shooter didn't take aim at them.

She hoped that wasn't because the shooter and Daisy were working together. But if they were, Daisy was putting up a good act because the woman seemed genuinely terrified.

Addie sure was.

The fear rose in her throat. Bitter and cold like the air. She had to fight to hold on to her breath, had to fight to keep it steady, too. It wouldn't do anyone any good if she hyperventilated or panicked.

More shots came, one right behind the other. Weston stayed down on the ground with her, sheltering her with his body. Jericho, however, lifted his head and gun, and he fired in the direction of the barn.

"You see him?" Weston asked.

Jericho shook his head. "Not yet. One of us needs to get into the cruiser and pull it closer."

Since it was bullet resistant, that's exactly where she wanted to be, but she wanted the others in there, too. However, the cruiser was a good fifteen feet away, and there was nothing but open space between it and the porch.

"Stay down," Weston told her.

But Weston didn't stay down. "Cover me," he told Jericho a split second before he moved off her. Only then did Addie realize he was heading for the cruiser.

Almost immediately, their attacker sent some shots Weston's way. Addie's heart pounded even harder, her throat tightened, and she could only watch, and pray, as Weston scrambled across the ground.

Jericho fired at the barn, and with the shots coming from the gunman, the sound was almost deafening. It seemed to take Weston an eternity to dive to the side of the cruiser, but she figured it was mere seconds.

"Keys," Jericho said, and he tossed them to Weston.

Weston didn't waste any time opening the cruiser door closest to him, and he climbed in. Started the engine.

The gunman was fixed on Weston now. Or rather on the cruiser tires. Addie had no idea if they, too, were bullet or puncture resistant. If they weren't and if the gunman managed to shoot them out, they'd be stuck. Yes, Daisy's truck was on the side of the house, but it would be dangerous to try to get to it.

Of course, staying put would be dangerous, as well.

One of the bullets slammed into the front tire, but that didn't stop Weston from driving forward. He maneuvered the cruiser so that the passenger's side door was aligned with the steps and so that the cruiser was literally blocking the path of the gunman's shots.

Weston threw open the passenger's side door for her. "Get in."

Addie moved as fast as she could, scurrying across the seat toward Weston. The gunman adjusted his shots, trying to shoot out the window. The glass webbed but thankfully held.

Weston threw the cruiser into reverse, backed up and maneuvered it again so that it was closer to Jericho. More shots came, some of them slicing across the porch. Her brother hurried down the steps and jumped into the front seat with them.

"I'll move into position so that Daisy and Mack can get in the backseat," Weston said.

And he had already started to do that when the shots stopped. They didn't just trail off, either. They stopped completely. It didn't take Addie long to figure out why. She saw the man running from the back of the barn.

"Hell, no," Weston grumbled. "He's not getting away. Stay with Addie," he added to Jericho.

Addie reached for him, but she wasn't nearly as fast as Weston was. He bolted from the cruiser and took off after the gunman.

It was a footrace now, and the shooter had a big head start on Weston. Plus, at any moment the man could turn around and fire. There weren't a lot of places that Weston could use for cover. Of course, Weston could fire, too, but they needed this man alive so he could tell them what the heck was going on.

"Go help Weston," she said to Jericho.

Her brother shook his head. "This could be a trap. There could be another gunman out here, waiting to get you alone."

Oh, God. She hadn't even considered that, but it was true. This was the second attempt to kill her, and it was obvious that whoever was behind this would do pretty much anything to make sure she was dead.

But why?

Addie kept going back to the initial threat from the Moonlight Strangler. He'd been afraid that she might remember something.

And maybe she had.

That swing set was becoming clearer and clearer in her mind. Did that mean she'd really been here all those years ago? Addie figured soon, very soon, she'd give that more thought, but for now she just watched Weston and prayed that they all got out of this alive.

Jericho kept watch, too, his gaze firing all around them. Mack did, as well. Daisy was no longer screaming, but she was sobbing and begging Mack to get her to the hospital.

That's when Addie spotted the blood on the woman's arm.

"I think Daisy's been shot," Addie let Jericho know.

Her brother cursed when he glanced up at the porch. "How bad is she hurt?" he called out to Mack.

Mack shook his head. "She was cut by some wood flying up off the porch. She'll need stitches."

That didn't sound life-threatening, thank goodness, but Daisy had to be terrified. Addie certainly was.

Unlike Weston.

He was charging forward, fast, closing the distance between him and the gunman.

"Watch out!" she shouted to Weston when she saw the man bring up his gun.

He fired.

But so did Weston.

And the gunman crumpled to the ground.

NORMALLY A DEAD hit man wouldn't give Weston a moment's pause, but he'd needed this one alive. Too bad Weston had been forced to kill or be killed.

"Maybe Jericho will find something when he checks the hit man's body," Addie said. "A phone. More photos. Something to tell us why he came after me again today."

Her words were right. Hopeful, even. However, Weston didn't see any of that hope in her eyes or body language. Of course, the adrenaline crash might have something to do with that. She looked past just being plain tired.

And probably was.

In addition to surviving two attacks, she was dealing with all the other stuff. The baby. The memories that might be returning.

Him.

All of that was taking a toll.

"I want you to get some rest," Weston insisted the moment they stepped into the ranch house. Her brother Jax had already searched it, and two armed ranch hands were standing guard at both the front and the back of the house. The alarm system was on, too.

Security was in place.

Now to make sure Addie didn't go into overload. She was already blinking back tears, and any little thing could push her over the edge.

His phone dinged, and while trying to brace himself for more bad news, Weston looked down at the screen. Nothing bad. Everything considered, it was actually good news.

"Your mom's settled at her sister's house, and Jericho hired a private bodyguard to stay with them," Weston said, reading the text. "And Jericho managed to get a DNA sample from Daisy."

"She volunteered it?"

"Not exactly. She refused when Jericho asked, but her blood was on Mack's shirt so we got it anyway."

"Oh." The disappointment was there now. "I didn't expect her to refuse. I thought maybe she'd want to help in any way possible."

Not judging from the woman's reaction when they'd gotten her to the hospital. She'd barely spoken a word to them, but Weston had heard her tell the doctor that she didn't want any of the Crocketts or Weston near her.

He couldn't blame Daisy if she was truly innocent in all of this, but the jury was still out on that, and he always found it suspicious when a suspect refused a DNA request. It usually meant they were hiding something.

Of course, she could have merely been reacting to the ordeal she'd just been through.

Weston slipped his arm around her waist to lead her to the sofa in the adjoining living room. He figured he stood a better chance of getting her to take a nap there than he did taking her upstairs.

Besides, it would be a really bad idea for him to try to put her to bed.

Addie's defenses were down. His, too. Added to the crash of emotions, and a bed would feel more like a powder keg. That's the reason Weston let go of her as soon as he had her seated. But Addie fixed that. She took his hand and pulled him down next to her.

"What if Daisy's a match?" Addie wasn't talking to him exactly but more to herself. "What if she's my birth mother?"

"Then, it'll soon put an end to this. Because if she is, she'll tell us the identity of your birth father, and we can arrest him."

Weston was certain of that. If Daisy knew who the Moonlight Strangler was, then he'd make sure she talked. Along with paying for anything that she'd done wrong. Including abandoning her child.

"Good. Maybe she'll be a match." Addie's breath was weary now. Like the rest of her. "I want to get on with my life. I want normal again."

"Good luck with that," Weston said before actually thinking about what he was saying. "I meant the pregnancy, the baby. That'll change things."

Not just for them but for her entire family.

She nodded. "Mom's already planning on turning one of the guest rooms into a nursery."

Of course she would want to raise the baby here. Her

home. A place where three generations of Crocketts had been raised.

But it wasn't Weston's home.

And even though Jericho and he had worked out a somewhat shaky peace agreement for the sake of the investigation, Weston doubted any of the Crockett lawmen would ever welcome him there.

His phone dinged again. Instant tightening in his chest, and it tightened even more when he read through the lengthy text.

"Bad news?" Addie asked.

"Ogden is being transferred to the hospital at the jail. His lawyer is going to use an insanity defense to try to get him moved to a mental facility."

She touched his forehead. "That didn't put the worry lines there. What else happened?"

"The safe house is ready."

Addie studied him. "How soon do I leave?"

"Soon. The marshals will be here in an hour or so."

"That is soon," she said under her breath. Then, the re-alization flashed through her eyes. "You won't be going with me?"

Weston decided to make this as light as possible. "No. Sounds like you'll miss me, though."

It was a dumber-than-dirt thing to say. She probably wouldn't miss him, but there were still those little flashes of fire between them, and that was creating this pull in-side him. Maybe inside her, too.

Definitely inside her, he decided, when their eyes met.

Those little flashes of fire were starting up again.

"I don't want to be attracted to you," she insisted.

That wasn't much of a surprise. But it was a surprise when her mouth suddenly came to his.

Everything inside him yelled that this was a mistake. It complicated an already complicated situation.

Did that stop him?

No.

In fact, Weston pushed his dumber-than-dirt actions to the limit. He slipped his hand around the back of her neck, pulled her to him and kissed her the way he'd been wanting to kiss her for months now. He figured if he was going to make a mistake, then it might as well be a good one.

And this one was *good*.

Yeah, that taste always got to him. The feel of her in his arms, too. It was obviously getting to Addie as well because she wiggled closer and closer until they were plastered against each other.

Great.

Now they weren't just kissing, they had advanced to a full-blown make-out session. While being alone in the house. And those little flashes of fire snapped high and hot when her hand landed on his chest.

She stopped, looked up at him, and a shivery breath left her mouth. *Finally.* She had come to her senses and was finally putting a stop to something they should have never started.

But no.

She pulled him back to her as if starved for him. Weston knew the feeling, and he also knew that kisses and touches were only going to skyrocket that need.

And they did.

He was clearly brainless when it came to Addie, and he proved it by lowering the kisses to her throat. She'd been his lover. For three whole days. Enough time for him to have learned how to pleasure her. Too bad she'd learned the same about him, because while

Weston was kissing the tops of her breasts, she put her hand on his stomach.

Oh, man.

He was in big trouble here, and while sleeping with her again would please every inch of his body, it would also distract him at the worst possible time.

Weston got instant proof of that when he heard one of the ranch hands shout his name.

Weston cursed himself, and he practically jumped off the sofa while drawing his gun. "Stay away from the windows," he warned Addie, and he rushed to the door.

"We got a visitor," the ranch hand called out to him. "A truck's coming up the road right now."

Well, at least it wasn't someone climbing over the fence. And it could be the marshals arriving a little earlier than planned. Weston disarmed the security system so he could open the door and stepped onto the porch.

The ranch hands and Weston all trained their guns on the truck as it pulled to a stop in front of the house. The windows were heavily tinted so Weston didn't get a look at their visitor until he threw open the truck door.

Definitely a stranger.

Tall, lanky with sandy brown hair. Jeans, cowboy boots and a Stetson hat. He looked like a cowboy. Until he flashed a badge when he stepped from the truck.

"I'm Special Agent Cord Granger, DEA," he said.

DEA? Not a marshal. He handed his badge to one of the ranch hands. "It looks real," the hand relayed to Weston.

"It *is* real," the man assured them. Not exactly a friendly sort, but then Weston wasn't in a friendly mood, either.

"Stay right there until I verify who you are," Weston insisted. "We've had some trouble lately."

"Yeah," Granger grumbled, but didn't come closer.

Without taking his eyes off the man, Weston called Jericho. "A DEA agent just showed up here. Cord Granger. Can you make sure this isn't another hit man?"

Jericho didn't say a word, but, as he'd done when Addie had asked him to verify Weston's identity, he got straight to work. "He's DEA. Records sealed. I'm texting you his photo."

Weston waited for the picture to load. Yes, it was Granger all right.

"I'll call you back after I find out why he's here," Weston said to Jericho, and he ended the call.

"I'm Weston Cade, Texas Ranger." And now that they'd gotten introductions out of the way, Weston went for the obvious. "What do you want?"

"To speak to Addie Crockett."

Now, why would a DEA agent want to see her? Unless her birth father was on the DEA's radar. If so, she wasn't exactly up to a round of questioning.

"Is this about the Moonlight Strangler?" Weston demanded.

He didn't jump to answer that, but finally mumbled another "Yeah."

Weston heard the movement behind him and cursed when he realized Addie hadn't stayed put.

"What about the Moonlight Strangler?" she asked.

Again, the agent didn't jump to answer. But his gaze fixed on Addie as he made his way toward them.

Weston glanced at her and saw that her attention was on the visitor, as well. "You know this guy?"

"No," Addie and the agent answered in unison.

He stepped onto the porch with them. Addie and the agent continued staring at each other.

"I don't remember you," Granger said almost in a whisper. "I thought, *hoped*, maybe I would."

"Who the hell are you?" Weston snapped.

It took Granger several more moments to look away from Addie. Then he extended his hand for Weston to shake. "The Moonlight Strangler is my biological father. I'm Addie's brother."

Chapter Ten

Addie's head was still spinning from the spent adrenaline and the kissing session with Weston. Spinning so much that she was certain she'd misunderstood what this DEA agent had just said.

"Her brother?" Weston challenged.

She was glad Weston had asked because it took Addie a moment to find her voice. "How?" Considering there was a whirlwind in her head, Addie was glad she could come up with a question.

Now she needed an answer.

One that Cord Granger didn't jump to give her. Instead, he glanced around. A lawman's glance, one that showed he was uneasy. And Addie didn't think that unease was all because of this bombshell of a meeting.

"We need to talk," he finally said to her. "And I'd rather not hang around on the porch with you standing there. Especially after what happened earlier."

Addie saw the fierce debate in Weston's eyes before he finally stepped back so that Cord could enter. Weston shut the door, but he kept himself between her and their visitor.

"Start talking," Weston told him. "And what you say had better make sense, or I'm tossing you out of here."

"None of this makes sense," Cord said. But then he huffed and put his hands on his hips, his gaze going to her, not Weston. "I compared my DNA to the Moonlight Strangler, and it was a match. A match to yours, too, Addie. We're fraternal twins."

A twin brother. *Her* brother. Addie had never lacked for siblings since she already had four brothers, but it'd been years since she'd considered the possibility of a biological one. "Why didn't you come forward sooner?" Weston snapped. "Addie's known for three months about the DNA match."

Cord shook his head. "I was on a deep cover assignment. No way for anyone to contact me. And because of what I do, my DNA isn't in the normal law enforcement databases so that's why there wasn't an immediate hit."

She looked at Weston to see if that was standard, and he nodded. He still didn't seem as if he was buying this, though.

"After I got off assignment," Cord continued, "I learned about Addie's DNA match, read about her background. It was too similar to mine so I had my DNA compared to hers and the Moonlight Strangler."

"Your background?" she questioned.

"When I was three, I was abandoned in the men's room of a gas station about a hundred miles from Appaloosa Pass. It was the same day you showed up here at the Crockett ranch. I don't have any memories of those things, but I learned about both later."

Cord's gaze slid around the foyer. Not exactly elegant, but Addie knew her family had a lot more than most. "You were lucky," he added.

Addie got the feeling that it hadn't been the same for him. She also got the feeling that it was something he didn't want to discuss with her. Not with anybody.

Almost frantically, she studied Cord's face and saw some features that were like hers. The eyes, mainly. And his mouth. Yes, a definite resemblance even though his hair was a lot darker than hers.

She didn't want to take a leap of faith and believe this man. But she did. There was something, maybe genetic memories or the weird bond between twins, but she knew in her heart that this was indeed her brother.

Weston's scowl, however, told her he didn't feel the same. "I want proof of what you're saying," he insisted.

"I figured you would. You have a reputation for being…driven. I had the DNA results couriered to Sheriff Crockett." He checked his watch. "He should have them by now."

While keeping himself in front of Addie, Weston took out his phone and called Jericho. He put it on speaker when Jericho answered, and he opened his mouth, no doubt ready to tell her brother what was going on, but Jericho beat him to it.

"I just got a classified DNA report on some federal agent. A Joe. What the hell do you know about this?"

"A Joe?" she questioned.

"Slang for deep cover," Weston explained. "What's in the report?" he asked Jericho.

Cord's gaze met hers while they waited, and Addie could have sworn a dozen things passed between them.

Memories, maybe?

Not of the swing set this time, but a toy. A stuffed brown bear. And a little boy handing it to her. It came like a flash and was gone before she could even try to hang on to it.

"According to this, Addie has a biological brother," Jericho snapped.

"Yeah, and the *brother* is here at the ranch," Weston supplied.

Jericho cursed. "And you let him in?"

"It's okay," Addie spoke up.

"Hell, no, it's not okay," Jericho fired back. "He might be a DEA agent, but we don't know if we can trust him."

"I trust him," she said. That earned her a scowl from Weston and more profanity from Jericho.

"I'm on my way out there," Jericho insisted, and he ended the call.

If Cord had a reaction to that, he didn't show it. In fact, he showed no emotion at all when his attention went back to Weston. "Why would I lie about this?"

"Because you could be a serial killer groupie, someone who wants to get close to Addie."

Cord held the stare between them. "It appears she already has enough people close to her."

Addie couldn't help it. She smiled, though heaven knew there was nothing to smile about.

"Do you remember anything about me?" Addie asked him. "About your childhood?"

"No." Unlike his other responses, it was fast. "When I found out about the DNA match, I went through hypnosis, therapy and lots of questioning. *Lots.* No memories before age four, but my handler pulled me from duty until they could get all of this sorted out."

That tightened his jaw.

She'd known this man only a few minutes, but Addie knew that had cut him to the core.

"The DEA is working on the case?" Weston asked.

"Plenty of people are working on it. Me included. Until the Moonlight Strangler is caught, killed or otherwise put out of circulation, the Justice Department believes I shouldn't be in the field doing a job that I'm damn good at."

Yes, a cut to the core.

"So that's why you came here?" Addie asked. "You

want to help us find him and vice versa so you can get back to work?"

He paused again. A long time. Then nodded. "And I wanted to meet you, to see if it spurred something."

She knew exactly how he felt.

"And?" Weston pressed.

"Nothing." Another pause. Cord's mouth tightened as if he'd tasted something bitter. "But there is some kind of connection. One I don't particularly want to feel because I don't want to worry about your safety. Is she safe?" he asked Weston.

"She soon will be."

Addie hoped that was true. Hoped it was true for her *brother*. But she doubted Cord would be going to a safe house. No. He wasn't the safe house type.

"What have you learned about the Moonlight Strangler?" Weston asked.

"I don't have a name. I'm guessing you don't, either, or there would have been an arrest. I just have a list of suspects, too many questions and nowhere near enough answers."

That got her attention. Weston's, too. "I want that list of suspects," Weston insisted.

Cord nodded. "And I want yours. Is Daisy Vogel on it?"

"Yeah," Weston confirmed. "Soon, I want to have a chat with her. What do you know about her?"

"Not as much as I want to know. She wasn't on my radar until the attack today. I've been monitoring what you've been doing, and when I saw you make the trip to her place, I ran a background check on her."

Weston took a step closer and got right in his face. "Did you know the attack was going to happen?"

"Of course not. I have no motive for you or Addie to be hurt. Or worse." He reached out, touched the scar on her cheek. "In fact, there's every reason for her to stay alive so we can catch this killer. What do you remember?" he asked her without even pausing for a breath.

For so long Addie's response had been nothing. And it'd been true. Until today. "A swing set. I think it was at Daisy's house, and she admitted that thirty years ago she babysat a little girl who might have been me."

"But I wasn't with you?"

She shook her head. "A man named Steve Birchfield took me to her and left me there for a week. Is he on your suspect list?"

"He is now." Cord took out his phone, fired off a quick text. "I'll see if there's anything on him."

"Jericho and I are already doing that," Weston snarled.

"Good. I'll take anything I can get." Cord's gaze shifted back to her. "You remember anything else?"

"I don't know. Everything's muddled, and I'm not sure if it's an actual memory from those days or something that happened after I arrived here at the ranch."

"Did you remember something?" Weston asked her. No snarling tone now, but he took her by the shoulders. "This is too much for you."

Addie had been about to assure him that she could handle it, but the truth was, her head was spinning, and she suddenly felt queasy. But not just queasy—she was about to throw up. She hadn't experienced any morning sickness yet, but she thought she might be getting a full dose of it now.

"Excuse me a minute." She didn't wait for Weston to agree. She hurried toward the powder room just up in the hall, and she got there in the nick of time.

Good grief.

She didn't need this now with everything else going on, but there was never a good time for morning sickness. As icky as it was, at least it was a reminder of the pregnancy. Of the baby. A reminder, too, that she needed to take better care of herself.

Weston and Cord must have agreed with that since they were both waiting for her in the hall when she opened the door.

"I'm not going to ask you if you're all right," Weston said, scooping her up in his arms, "because clearly you're not. I'm calling the doctor."

"Don't, please. I just need a cracker or something. There's some in the pantry in the kitchen."

Weston eased her onto the sofa, turned as if to go get the crackers, but then he no doubt remembered that would mean leaving her alone with Cord, a man he didn't trust.

"I'll get them," Cord volunteered, and he headed out of the room.

"How are you—really?" Weston asked her when they were alone.

Addie tried to give him a reassuring look. Failed miserably. Hard to look reassuring with her stomach lurching. "All the pregnancy books say this is normal."

"How long will it last?"

Addie lifted her hands. "A few months. Maybe longer. Some women have it the entire pregnancy."

He cursed and looked as if he wanted to continue the cursing for a long time. "I'm so sorry."

She managed another smile and took his hand. "I'll live." Except that was a reminder she might not if they didn't stop the Moonlight Strangler.

Weston tipped his head toward the kitchen and sat down next to her. "Do you believe him?"

"Yes," Addie said without hesitation.

A muscle flickered in his jaw. "Did you sense you had a biological brother?"

"No. Well, I used to think about it when I was a kid, but I wasn't really lacking in the brother and family department." Unlike Cord. "I guess those thoughts of sibling possibilities got overshadowed by the real ones."

"And what about the memories?" he asked.

But she didn't get a chance to answer because Cord came back in with a box of crackers and a glass of water. He set them on the coffee table in front of her.

"How far along are you in the pregnancy?" Cord asked. Obviously, he'd put two and two together.

"Three months." She took out a cracker, nibbled on it. Hoped it would help.

Cord glanced at their ring fingers. No rings, but since she still had hold of Weston's hands, Cord no doubt figured out the answer to a question he probably wouldn't have asked anyway—who was the baby's father?

The next look he gave Weston was more of a glare. One she recognized.

Mercy.

She didn't need another brother fighting her battles for her.

"Memories," she reminded both of them. That got their attention back on track. "I might have one. A stuffed bear. You handing it to me."

Cord took a deep breath, and he sank down into the chair across from them. He closed his eyes a moment as if to force that memory to the surface. "Were there Christmas lights?"

She hadn't remembered that. Only the little boy with the brown hair and eyes that were the same color as hers.

Like Cord's.

Addie closed her eyes as well, hoping for some other fragment of the memory. But nothing.

"We can both go back through hypnosis," Cord suggested. "In the meantime, we need to do something to draw out the killer."

"You're not using her as bait," Weston snapped.

Cord's gaze went to her stomach. "No. Not now, I won't. But I could be bait. I figure if he learns I'm remembering things, then he'll want me dead. He doesn't have to know that the memories are of Christmas lights and a brown stuffed bear."

Addie pulled back her shoulders. "I didn't mention the color of the bear."

Cord paused, nodded. "Yeah, we definitely need to be hypnotized again."

Weston didn't argue with that. "Who's on your suspect list?" he asked Cord.

"Alton Boggs," he readily answered. "I'm sure you've reached the same conclusion, that he's way too interested in the Moonlight Strangler for this not to be personal."

"Agreed," Weston said. "What about Canales?"

"He's on the list, too. Maybe one or both are the Moonlight Strangler."

That didn't help her queasy stomach. "You think they're killing together?"

"Could be. I found a criminal informant who said that Boggs and Canales used to be involved in a gun-running operation. There's nothing about it in any of their background checks," Cord added when Weston reached for his phone. "But the CI claims it was going on thirty years ago."

Weston stayed quiet a moment. "Did the CI think the murders were tied to the gunrunning?"

"The initial ones, yes. Then, he thought maybe the killer or killers got a taste for it."

It sickened her to think of it, but this could be the link they'd been searching for.

"I want the name of this CI," Weston insisted.

"She's dead." Cord glanced away from them. "I'm pretty sure I got her killed. I didn't think the Moonlight Strangler was watching me, but I was wrong. The SOB cut her on the cheek. Left his mark to make sure I'd see it."

"I'm sorry," Weston told him. Considering what her birth father had done to Collette, Addie was sure it was a sincere apology.

It didn't take Cord long to regain his composure. "I haven't had any luck connecting the first victims to either Canales or Boggs. Or to the Moonlight Strangler for that matter."

"I tried to get a DNA sample from Boggs. He didn't go for it," Weston said. "But we should have Canales's results back in a day or two. I told the lab to put a rush on it. We're also running DNA on the man who tried to kill Addie. Lonny Ogden. He's too young to be the Moonlight Strangler, but I want to make sure he's not connected to one of the victims."

"I'll see what I can do about getting DNA from Boggs." Cord opened his mouth to say more, but a sound stopped him.

A car approaching the house.

Weston hurried to the window and looked out. "It's Jericho."

The relief came—this wasn't the start of another attack. But the relief went just as fast. Addie stood to try to brace herself for what would no doubt turn into a testosterone contest, but when her brother came through the door, he wasn't focused on Cord. He was on the phone and was cursing at the person on the other end of the line.

"Find her," Jericho snapped, and at the same moment he ended the call, he aimed an expected glare at Cord. "You'd damn well better not be here to hurt Addie because I don't have time to deal with you."

"What's wrong?" Weston asked Jericho.

"Daisy's missing."

That got Addie on her feet. "What happened?"

Jericho had to get his teeth unclenched before he could speak. "I don't know yet, but I'm pretty sure her disappearance has something to do with *this*. It was left on the answering machine at Daisy's house, and I got the county deputy to play it for me."

Her brother lifted his phone and hit the play button on the recording.

Chapter Eleven

"Daisy, you need to disappear. *Fast.* Staying around here won't be good for your health. Leave and take this phone and answering machine with you."

Weston heard the message Jericho had just played for them, and he didn't know whether to groan or curse. So, he did both.

"That's Lonny Ogden's voice," Addie said.

Yes, it was. Weston had only heard the man speak a couple of times, but he was sure of it. What was that idiot up to now?

"First of all, how did Ogden get access to a phone?" Weston asked Jericho. "And how the heck does he know Daisy?"

"I don't have the answer to either of those things, but I'm about to find out." He made another call. "Jax," Jericho said when his brother answered, "set up a video chat with the dirtbag who left that threatening message for Daisy. Call me when you've got him on the line."

Jericho hit the end-call as his gaze snapped to Cord. "If you're here to try to talk Addie into doing something stupid, dangerous or otherwise, then there's the door." He hitched is thumb in that direction.

"I'm here to find a killer," Cord said, meeting him head-on.

Jericho tapped his badge. "Newsflash. We're all here for that, but you're not using my sister as bait."

Weston stepped to Jericho's side—despite the glare Jericho gave Weston to remind him that he'd wanted to do the same thing. Finally, here was something Jericho and he could agree on.

"I don't want Addie in danger, either," Cord said. He was probably telling the truth.

Probably.

However, Weston knew that kind of drive, that kind of hunger for justice, and a hunger like that just might override any feelings Cord had for a twin sister he hardly knew.

"I'm standing right here," Addie reminded them. "Last I checked, I could speak for myself."

"You aren't going to do or *say* anything to put yourself in further danger," Jericho argued.

Probably because Jericho looked ready to implode, she leaned in and kissed him on the cheek. "I won't be safe until the Moonlight Strangler is caught. Cord and I might have some new memories that could help."

"Fragments of memories," Weston corrected when Jericho stared at them.

A bear and a swing set. Childhood things that could have a huge impact if they were true and could be connected to other memories.

Too bad memories like that could make Addie even more of a target than she already was.

"I was about to call the FBI," Weston added. "I want them to go to the safe house and do the hypnosis once Addie's there."

Which shouldn't be long at all since the marshals were probably on their way. Of course, he'd gotten distracted from making that call because he'd been kissing Addie. Then Cord had arrived.

"So, that DEA agent's really your brother?" Jericho asked her.

She nodded. "I think so, yes."

Weston wasn't exactly sure what he saw in Jericho's eyes. Frustration.

Maybe a little jealousy.

He clearly loved Addie and had been a good brother to her all these years. But blood was blood. Or at least Jericho might see it that way. However, Weston figured blood would never come between the love Addie had for Jericho and the rest of her adoptive family.

Cord's phone buzzed at the same moment as Jericho's, and Cord stepped into the foyer once he saw the name of the caller on the screen. Weston kept an eye on him, but the bulk of his attention went to Jericho's phone. It was Jax, and he'd obviously managed to set up a video call. Judging from the background, he was at the hospital.

"Jax, put a camera on that weasel so I can see his face when he's talking to me," Jericho instructed. "If he lies, punch him."

Jax flexed his eyebrows in a *sure-whatever* gesture and turned the phone so they could see Ogden's face.

"Start talking," Jericho ordered the man. "Why'd you leave that message for Daisy Vogel?"

Ogden's eyes widened. "Because she didn't answer when I called her."

Weston moved in front of the phone screen so that Ogden could see his glare. "That's not helping your case. Why leave that message?"

"Because I had to."

That was it, apparently the only explanation Ogden intended to give them. Well, it wasn't enough.

"If you don't want to hurt more than you're hurting right now," Weston warned him, "then start talking."

Ogden glanced around the room as if looking for some kind of help, but since only Jax was there, he must have decided that he was on his own. "August McCain forced me to make the call. He even wrote down what I was to say."

Addie shook her head. "Who's August McCain?"

"His lawyer," Jericho growled. "Where is he?"

"He left. And he said he wouldn't be coming back. He also said I was to keep my mouth shut."

Jericho cursed, handed Weston his phone before he stepped away to use the land line in the foyer. "I'll get someone out looking for him. See what else you can get from this piece of work."

Gladly. "Why did McCain want you to scare Daisy, and did he do anything to her?"

"Do anything? Oh, man. You don't think he'd hurt her?"

"I don't know. You tell me."

Ogden frantically shook his head. "It was just supposed to be words. No violence. And it wasn't my idea. I was just the messenger."

Maybe. "Convince me of that."

Ogden no doubt heard that for the threat it was. He swallowed hard. "I've got no beef with Daisy. Heck, I don't even know her. Check my phone records. Today was the first time I'd ever called her."

Weston would indeed check those phone records. "Why'd McCain want her out of the picture?"

No eye widening this time, but Weston did see something he recognized. Ogden knew the answer to the question. "I can't tell you anything else." He leaned in closer to the phone screen. "McCain's dangerous."

"And you don't think I am? I'm the one who shot you.

There's a pecking order for dangerous, and I'm at the top of it. Now talk!"

Ogden did more of that glancing around until his attention came back to Weston. Weston made sure he was all lawman now. A lawman who'd do pretty much whatever it took to get to the truth. After all, Addie and the baby's safety were at stake here.

"I don't know all the details," Ogden finally said, "but it has something to do with a gunrunning mess. Not recent stuff but something that happened a real long time ago. Like maybe before I was even born."

Was it the same operation that might have involved Boggs and Canales? As much as Weston wanted to know, it wasn't a good idea to share that info with the likes of Ogden.

"Keep talking," Weston insisted.

"I don't know much more other than Daisy's husband might have been involved in it. I think that's what I heard McCain say anyway."

Since Cord had finished his call, Weston motioned for him to start checking on the woman's late husband. "Ernest Vogel," he mouthed to Cord.

Weston turned his attention back to Ogden. "Did this gunrunning have something to do with the Moonlight Strangler?" he asked.

Addie moved closer, no doubt wanting to hear the answer. Maybe dreading it, too, since Weston could see the pulse throbbing on her throat.

"I think so," Ogden finally said. "But I'm not sure what exactly. That's the truth," he quickly added when Weston scowled. "I think maybe all of this has something to do with the first victim."

"Leta Dooley," Addie provided.

Even though Cord was on the phone in the other room,

he obviously heard her and nodded. He also repeated the woman's name to the person he'd called.

Apparently, both Cord and Addie knew the list of victims as well as Weston. Leta was the first *known* victim anyway. The Moonlight Strangler's signature wasn't to hide bodies, but it was possible he'd done that early on when he'd started his killing spree. If so, there was no telling how many victims there were.

"You got what you need from Ogden?" Jax asked. "The jail guards are here to move him."

Weston nodded. "I got what I need *for now*. But, Ogden, if any of this is a lie, I'll be making a personal visit to the jail."

Weston ended the call and turned to Jericho. Both Cord and he were still on their phones while Addie volleyed attention among all three of them.

"Daisy has to be okay," she whispered.

Hell. Addie was shaky again. Looked ready for another round of morning sickness, too, so Weston had her sit back down on the sofa.

"It's possible Daisy was involved in the gunrunning operation," Weston reminded her.

Or involved with the murders.

Weston kept that to himself since Addie was already pale enough. Best not to remind her that her former babysitter could have been an accessory to murder. Or even more.

"My brother Chase is a marshal, but Jericho said Chase was tied up on an assignment and can't get here in time to go to the safe house. Will you go with me?" she asked.

That wasn't a question Weston expected to hear. He'd been sure Addie wanted to put some distance between them. Especially since distance seemed to be the only thing that would prevent his mouth from locating hers again for more of those mind-clouding kisses.

"For the marshals, I'll be just a job to them," she added, and she slid her hand over her stomach.

Yeah, she would be. But not for Weston. "I'll go with you."

And somehow figure out how to run his part of the investigation from the safe house.

He hadn't intended to do it, but he slipped his arm around her and pulled her closer. Along with brushing a kiss on her forehead. It didn't help. Well, didn't help with that jittery look in her eyes, and it earned him a really nasty glare from Jericho.

Then one from Cord.

Weston didn't budge, not even when the pair finished their calls and came toward them.

Jericho finally dropped the glare and cursed before he started talking. "According to his office, McCain's on a leave of absence. Family emergency that just popped up, his assistant said. I just put out a BOLO on him. On Daisy, too. The county sheriff is on the way to her house to see if she's gone back there."

Weston doubted she had. If Daisy was innocent, she was no doubt afraid for her life, especially since she'd already been injured in the latest attack. And if she was guilty, then she wouldn't want lawmen to find her, and her house was the first place they'd look.

"Did you freeze her bank accounts?" Weston asked.

Jericho nodded. "I'm trying to do the same to McCain, but it's a little trickier with him. He's well-connected, and he's trying to use those connections to stonewall us. It won't work. We'll find him."

Weston hoped that was true, but McCain had a head

start on them, and the lawyer could use those very connections and his resources to disappear.

Cord finally finished his call, and he made his way back toward them, as well. "Daisy's husband, Ernest, died in a tractor accident on or very near the same day Addie and I were abandoned."

That fit with what Daisy had told them.

"The coroner originally listed it as a suspicious death but then changed it to an accident," Cord explained. "The coroner was Alton Boggs's uncle."

Hell. That wasn't a good connection. Well, except that it might make it easier to get Boggs's DNA now if they could prove Boggs conspired with his uncle to cover up a crime.

"I've got my sources working on finding a link between the gunrunning, Daisy, her husband, Boggs and Canales," Cord added. "But the coroner died years ago, and his notes were destroyed in an office fire."

Convenient. But more likely a cover-up.

"I'll get my sources working on it, too," Jericho insisted. "I also want to find out who the heck Steve Birchfield is and if that was an alias. It could have been Boggs or Canales using that name."

Cord only nodded, and he glanced at the notes he'd made. "The first victim, Leta Dooley, lived about ten miles from Daisy, and her body was found three days after Ernest's tractor *accident*. She had a record for prostitution, and at the time of her murder, she was living with a lowlife who beat her on a regular basis. A few years later, he was arrested for—you probably guessed it—gunrunning."

Bingo. They were coming full circle now, all the players in place at the time of the gunrunning operation and

the start of the murders. Maybe Leta had learned the
wrong thing about the wrong person.

Like Boggs.

"Is Leta's old *heartthrob* still alive?" Jericho asked,
the sarcasm dripping from the term of endearment.

Cord shook his head. "Dead, too. Car accident. And
yes, the same coroner signed off on it."

And that meant Boggs had some explaining to do
about this uncle.

"There's more," Cord went on. "Leta had a son. The
kid disappeared into the foster care system after she was
murdered, but I've set tracers on him. He might know
something about what really happened to his mom."

Weston hoped all of this would lead to something.

The sound of a car engine had Weston, Jericho and
Cord all drawing their weapons, but when Weston hur-
ried to the window, he holstered his. That's because he
recognized the marshal who stepped from the car. It was
Daniel Seaver, and he and his partner were there to take
Addie, and him, to the safe house.

Jericho headed to the front door to let them in.

"You should get your things ready to go," Weston
told Addie.

She nodded. "My bag's upstairs, but I'd like to freshen
up before I leave."

Since Addie still didn't look too steady on her feet,
Weston took her arm to help her navigate the steps.
However, they didn't make it far before Jericho's phone
buzzed. He put it on speaker, and Weston stopped when
he heard Jax's frantic voice from the other end of the
line.

"Bad news," Jax said. "You need to shut down the
ranch now. Lonny Ogden just escaped."

Chapter Twelve

Addie figured she should feel panic over Ogden's escape, but maybe she was past that point. This seemed like just another setback in a string of setbacks.

"How did this happen?" she asked at the same moment Weston and Jericho voiced a similar version of the question. Hers, though, wasn't laced with profanity like theirs.

"I'm not sure," Jax answered. He seemed out of breath as if he were running. "But it appears someone ambushed the prison guards when they were leaving the hospital with Ogden."

Sweet heaven. "Jax, are you all right?"

"I'm fine. I wasn't there. I was on my way to the station when I got the news. I'm heading to the hospital now to see if I can pick up Ogden's trail."

"Be careful," she said, but she wasn't even sure if Jax heard her because he'd already ended the call.

"Is that there trouble?" one of the marshals asked as he walked up the steps to the porch.

At first, Addie thought he'd overheard the call from Jax, but the marshal's attention wasn't on them but rather on the black limo that was speeding up the road toward the house.

What now?

Weston didn't wait to find out. He pulled Addie away from the door and back into the family room. "Stay put," he insisted, drawing his gun again.

Jericho, Cord and both marshals did the same.

Since there was enough firepower to protect her, Addie went to the window and peeked out. And scowled. Boggs and Canales stepped out of the limo. She should have known, since there weren't many people who would arrive in a limo.

She caught a glimpse of the personalized license plate, and the first three letters were *AGB*, Boggs's initials.

"It's just me," Boggs said as if that was all that was necessary for them to put down their guns.

None of them did.

"Really? Are all those weapons necessary?" Canales snarled. "We're not criminals."

"The verdict's still out on that," Weston snarled right back. "Why are you two here?"

"Well, I tried the sheriff's office first," Boggs explained, "but the deputy said Addie, the sheriff and you were all at the ranch. We have to talk." Again, spoken like gospel, and he started toward the porch.

"Don't come any closer," Weston warned him. "And keep your hands where I can see them."

"See?" Canales said to Boggs as if proving a point. "These people think you're a criminal, and they're treating you like one. This is what you have to stop if you want to stand a chance winning the election."

Canales shifted his attention to them. Specifically to Weston and Jericho. "You need to back off with the mud-slinging. If not, you're both going to be facing defamation-of-character lawsuits. Addie, too. She's telling lies when she should be keeping her mouth shut."

That brought her out of hiding. Not to her brothers or Weston's approval, but Addie did step in the doorway.

"I haven't lied," she insisted. "Can you say the same?"

"Of course," Canales quickly answered. Boggs stayed

quiet. "I'm sure you told a boatload of lies to that Daisy Vogel. Now you've got her riled up. She called the newspaper, trying to get them to run a story about Boggs and me. Thankfully, the editor came to his senses."

More likely, the editor had been paid off by Canales, Boggs or both.

"You know where Daisy is?" Weston asked him. There wasn't a drop of friendliness in his tone. Nor was there in the look he gave her when he took up a protective stance in front of her.

"At her house, I assume," Boggs said.

"You assume wrong. She's missing," Cord provided.

"And who are you?" Canales asked, sparing him a glance.

"Agent Cord Granger. My biological father is the Moonlight Strangler."

Clearly, neither Canales nor Boggs had been expecting that. And Addie wasn't sure it was a good idea to let these two in on that information.

"How do you know he's your father?" Canales asked, stepping closer and studying Cord. However, he stopped moving when Cord aimed his gun at him.

"I had a DNA test done." Cord's voice was calm, a discussing-the-weather tone. "I'd like for that word to get around. I'd also like for it to get around that I'm fully cooperating with the FBI so they can help me remember anything about the killer. Like his identity, for instance," he said, staring at Boggs.

Great. Cord was making himself bait. Maybe to protect her. But she didn't want him hurt, and it didn't matter that she'd just met him.

"How long have you known about him?" Boggs asked Addie. He tipped his head to Cord.

"Not long," she settled for saying. "How long have *you* known about him?"

Boggs jerked back his head, obviously not expecting the accusation. "I didn't know."

She believed him. But Canales was a different story. He didn't seem nearly as surprised as his boss.

"You can handle these two clowns?" Cord asked Weston. "Because I've got errands to run."

Finding Daisy was no doubt part of those "errands." They needed that to happen fast. Ditto for finding Ogden.

Cord waited until Weston had nodded before he holstered his gun and headed down the steps. "I'll be in touch," Cord said. But he paused just long enough to glance at her. "Stay safe."

"You do the same." She doubted he'd take her advice, though, especially since Cord wasn't headed to a safe house and had just set up what he no doubt hoped would be a showdown with a serial killer.

"We should be going, too," Canales insisted when Cord got in his truck and drove away. "It's obvious the only way to settle this is to go ahead and file some lawsuits."

Without taking his attention off Cord's truck, Canales went back to the limo, got in and slammed the door.

Boggs stayed put. He gave an uneasy glance over his shoulder. "Sometimes, Ira can have a very narrow focus."

"What the hell does that mean?" Jericho snapped.

Another uneasy glance from Boggs. "He just wants to make sure that you know I'm innocent. Which I am. I wish you'd believe me so we don't have to go through with those lawsuits. That'll only keep tongues wagging."

"If you're as innocent as you claim, why don't you submit to a DNA test?" Weston asked.

Boggs looked just as surprised about that as he had Cord's revelation. "Why would I do that?"

"To prove you're not the Moonlight Strangler."

That seemed to tighten every muscle in Boggs's body. "I refuse to be a suspect in any of this."

"You can refuse all you want, but you're a suspect whether you call yourself one or not," Weston informed him. "Tell me about the gunrunning that was operating over in Comal County thirty years ago. When you're finished, convince me that your uncle wasn't a dirty coroner on the take."

Boggs cursed and his eyes narrowed. "You're making some very dangerous assumptions, Ranger Cade."

"That's not convincing me you're innocent," Weston told him. "How much do you know?"

The look Boggs gave him could have frozen the Sahara. "I know nothing," he insisted, and he stormed toward the limo and got inside.

Almost immediately, the driver took off. Addie and the others stayed there, watching until the car was away from the house.

Once it was out of sight, the marshals came onto the porch. "By the way, I'm Daniel Seaver," the bulkier man said. "This is Kirk Vance. And we should get going to the safe house before you get another round of visitors who shouldn't be here."

Weston introduced them to Addie, and then told her that he'd get her suitcase from her room upstairs.

Jericho looked back at her. "Your brother's either an idiot or he has a death wish."

Addie was thinking it was definitely the latter.

"You're my brother," she reminded Jericho. Something she wanted to clear up right away. "I'm not sure what Cord is to me yet, but I have room for one more if it comes down to it."

The corner of Jericho's mouth twitched. "You're sure about that? That's not what you used to tell Jax, Chase, Levi and me when you were a kid. You always said you had way too many brothers."

They shared a smile. Since Jericho was more of the scowling type, Addie took it as the rare gift that it was. From a brother she loved.

Weston came back downstairs, his bag in one hand. Hers in the other.

"You'll be okay?" Jericho asked her. "You won't take any stupid chances." That last one wasn't a question.

She nodded. But Jericho took his brotherly/sheriff duties one step further. "Take care of her," Jericho said like a warning to Weston.

"I will."

Normally, Addie would have balked at her brother taking charge of her. And of Weston accepting the hand-off. But after everything that'd happened, she was willing to take all the security she could get.

Like the other times they'd been outside, Weston got her moving as quickly as possible to the car, and they got in the backseat with the marshals in the front. Marshal Seaver didn't waste any time getting them on the road. When Addie looked back at the house, Jericho was already talking on the phone. No doubt trying to end this danger so she could come home.

Of course, that would be just the start of yet another hurdle.

With Weston.

The baby was still months from being born, but they

would need to make arrangements and set some ground rules. Too bad she had no idea what kind of ground rules to put in place. Or if they'd even do any good. Her body seemed to have its own rules when it came to Weston.

"You know the drill," Seaver said to Weston. "I'll have to drive around until I'm sure we aren't being followed. You might want to grab a nap," he added to her.

Addie thanked him, but no way would that happen. She was exhausted, but her mind was whirling with everything she'd just learned. Still, she closed her eyes and hoped to settle down the nerves. It didn't work until Weston slid his arm around her and eased her against him so she could use his shoulder as a pillow.

Yes, her body definitely had its own notions when it came to Weston.

She could almost feel the tension drain from her. It didn't last, though. They'd only been on the road for fifteen minutes or so when Weston's phone buzzed, jarring her nerves right back to the surface.

"Sorry." Weston moved away from her so he could take his phone from his pocket.

"Put it on speaker," she insisted when she saw Jax's name on the screen.

"I decided to make this a conference call with Jericho," Jax greeted, "so I could update you all at the same time."

While Addie was all for getting updates, she knew from her brother's tone that he was about to deliver more bad news. She tried to brace herself for it and prayed that Cord's challenge to the killer hadn't led to some kind of violent confrontation.

"The cops went to McCain's house, and he wasn't there," Jax explained. "There were signs of a struggle. Some blood, too."

No. She'd been sure if they could find the lawyer that he'd eventually give them some info that would lead them to the Moonlight Strangler. Or at least to the person who'd actually hired him.

"Someone's tying up loose ends," Weston grumbled. "Unless the scene was staged."

"Not likely on the staged part. Too much blood for that, and there were some expensive paintings and such that had been damaged. But SAPD did manage to get something from McCain's computer records."

SAPD. San Antonio Police Department. "What did they find?" she asked her brother.

"McCain has done legal work for both Canales and Boggs."

That didn't surprise her at all, and it gave them a connection between them and Ogden since McCain was Ogden's lawyer, too.

"Any idea which one of them hired McCain to represent Ogden?" Weston pressed, taking the question right out of her mouth.

"It's hard to tell. The payment for representing Ogden came from an offshore account. There are layers and layers of cover so it might be impossible to find out who actually owns that account. The FBI is on it, so maybe they'll get something."

Maybe, but that seemed like a long shot. If either Canales or Boggs had set this up in advance, then they'd no doubt make sure it couldn't be linked back to them.

"We need to find Ogden," Jericho snapped. "He's the key to sorting this out. Hell, he could be the owner of that offshore account."

"Could be, but there's a problem with that." Jax huffed. "It appears Ogden didn't cooperate with the escape. I used the word *appears* because he could have been faking it, but he was yelling for help when the men took him. And one of the guys punched him."

That caused Jericho to curse. Addie wanted to do the same. If Ogden was a loose end that was about to be *tied up*, then there went one of their best chances of linking him to the killer.

"There's more," Jax said.

"Good news, I hope," Addie mumbled.

"Not really. Well, it's good news for Canales. We did a rush on his DNA test, and he's not the Moonlight Strangler."

"You're sure?" she asked.

"I'm sure unless Canales somehow managed to tamper with the test. That would mean he has an insider at the lab. Possible, I suppose. That's why I'm having another test run at a different lab."

Good. Addie figured a man like Canales could—and would—tamper with potential evidence.

"Wait a sec," Jericho said, "I got another call coming in. It's from Cord."

That instantly put a knot in her stomach. From the sound of Jericho's voice, he had a similar reaction. But his reaction probably wasn't because he was afraid for Cord's life.

Unlike the conference call, Addie couldn't hear what Cord was saying because Jericho had put them on hold. Jax, Weston and she just waited. And waited. With that knot tightening even more.

"If Cord's calling," Weston reminded her, "then he's all right."

True. That was something at least. But she doubted he'd stay all right if he continued to taunt a killer.

It seemed to take an eternity for Jericho to come back

on the line, and even when he did, he didn't jump right into an explanation about Cord's call.

"What's wrong?" she asked.

"It's Daisy," Jericho finally said. "The cops found her. Addie, I'm sorry, but she's dead."

Chapter Thirteen

Daisy was dead. *Murdered.* According to Jax, she'd been strangled and had that obscene, too familiar crescent-shaped cut on her cheek.

The signature of the Moonlight Strangler.

Definitely not the way Weston had wanted this to go. Even if it turned out Daisy was involved in the attacks against Addie, Weston had wanted her alive so she could talk. Now they'd lost that chance along with perhaps an innocent woman losing her life.

That meant the danger to Addie was just as great as it had been two days earlier. And worse, she was beyond shaken. The moment they'd arrived at the safe house, she had gone to her room. Probably not to rest, but Weston had pretended that was happening so she could have some time to try to come to terms with all of this.

If that was possible.

Maybe the shower she was taking now would help. Since she'd been in there a good half hour, Weston figured she was in there crying. Or cursing their situation.

Maybe both.

Even though he was across the hall in another bedroom, they'd left their doors open, and he heard her phone ding. Not her usual phone but a safe, untraceable one that the marshals had given her to use. The only people who had the number were members of her family.

Since the phone was on the nightstand, he went in her room to have a look. It was from Jericho.

You okay? her brother texted. Just checking.

Too bad Jericho hadn't texted with good news. That might improve Addie's mood.

Or not.

She stepped out of the bathroom, her attention going right to him. For just a second he saw the emotions and the hurt in her eyes before she did her best to shut down. She failed.

Yeah, there wasn't much that was going to help with her mood.

She was dressed, thank goodness, in jeans and a dark green top. Weston figured his mind was already in a bad place, and it sure wouldn't have helped if a naked Addie had come walking out of the bathroom. Of course, she likely wouldn't have done that since there were two other marshals in the house.

Addie went to the window and glanced outside. Not that there was much for her to see. The safe house was located in the middle of nowhere with no other houses around for miles.

Once, it'd been a small working ranch, but now the barn and pastures were empty. Ditto for the road leading to the place. There'd been no traffic the entire week prior to their arrivals, and the marshals knew that because a motion-activated security sensor had been fitted to one of the trees right off the road. If anyone tried to get to the place on foot or by car, Daniel and Kirk would be alerted.

"I hope we don't have to be here for Christmas," she said under her breath.

Heck, he hoped so, too, since Christmas was nearly

three weeks away. He wanted the danger over and done with well before that.

"Jericho just texted you." Weston tipped his head to the phone and sank down on the edge of her bed. "He wants to know if you're okay."

She made a soft as-if sound, but she did send a text with their now routine lie, to say that yes, she was okay.

"It's my fault Daisy's dead," Addie said as soon as she finished the text.

Weston huffed. "And how do you figure that?"

Her hair was wet, her face rosy and damp from the shower, and when she walked closer to him, he caught the scent of a floral shampoo.

And her own scent, too, swirling beneath it.

Hard to miss those scents when she sat down next to him. Much too close. Of course, maybe a mile was too close when it came to Addie.

"I should have made Daisy understand the danger she was in," Addie finally answered.

"Because of your ESP, right?"

She frowned at his attempted humor.

"Daisy knew the risks when she sneaked out of the hospital," Weston added. "She could have just stayed in protective custody with one of your brothers. She didn't. She ran. And in my experience, innocent people don't run from the law."

"Maybe…"

She was no doubt about to launch into stage two of a guilt fest that wouldn't do her or the baby any good. So Weston put a stop to it.

By kissing her.

Of course, that didn't fix anything. Addie pulled back, looking surprised, confused and maybe a couple of other emotions he didn't want to identify.

"Bad idea, I know," he said before she could say it.

But Addie didn't say it. She just stared at him for a few seconds, then slid her hand around his neck to pull him back to her.

And she kissed him.

Okay, so maybe not such a bad idea after all. Or perhaps they were both making a mistake. One touch of his mouth to hers though, and Weston didn't care how many mistakes they made.

This was the heat he'd felt with her in that San Antonio hotel.

The instant fire mixed with the slam of sensations. Her mouth, her touch.

Her.

And just like those others times, Weston felt himself falling. Touching, too. Because obviously his crazy body thought he hadn't screwed this up enough so he hauled her closer and closer. Until she was practically in his lap.

There was a serious problem with kisses this good. They only upped an already too hot heat. Ditto for the touching. His hand landed on her breasts. Then under her top so that bare skin was on bare skin.

The heat went up a notch.

Weston quit thinking about notches, however, when he lowered his head, shoved down her bra and kissed her there. Actually, he quit thinking about everything and just kept taking.

Addie was taking, too. Fumbling with his buttons. Putting her hand inside his shirt and on his chest.

Then lower.

That's when Weston took hold of the tiny grain of sanity he had left. He didn't let go of her, but he got them to their feet, and, without breaking the kisses and touches, he maneuvered them to the door so he could close it.

They didn't make it back to the bed, though.

Addie pushed him against the door, pinning him in place. Not that he needed to be pinned. Weston had no plans to go anywhere unless it was to drag her to the floor.

So that's what he did.

More sanity returned when she reached for his zipper. Oh, man. He really wanted what she clearly had in mind, but talk about bad timing. Bad everything. This was probably some kind of adrenaline crash reaction that Addie would regret later.

Weston doubted he could talk any part of his body into regret.

Still, he had to think of her. Had to give her a breather so she could try to consider all of this with a clear head.

Or not.

She cursed him when he tried to stop her, and that's when Weston realized they'd taken this past the point of no return. Well, for her anyway.

He shoved down her zipper and slipped his hand inside her panties. All right. He had to grind his teeth together to keep himself from saying something stupid.

Like—*let's do this now.*

They would do something, but he had to keep some shred of sanity. If he was inside her, no sanity.

She was still struggling with him, to make this a round of old-fashioned sex. Good sex, no doubt. But Addie stopped when he sank his fingers inside her.

Clamping her teeth over her bottom lip, she didn't make a sound. Didn't look at him. But, man, the pleasure was there all over her face.

Pleasure for him, too.

It didn't take much for him to finish things for her. Probably because those kisses had put her right at the brink. It only took a few strokes, and Weston saw—and felt—her shatter.

Now she made a sound. A sharp moan that tugged at him. Well, it tugged at one very hard part of him anyway, and that idiot part of him started to suggest some bad things.

"Everything okay in there, Addie?" Seaver called out a split second before Weston heard the marshal's footsteps making their way down the hall toward them.

Addie gasped and scrambled away from him. Not easily. Especially since she was trying to fix her top and jeans.

"We're fine," Weston lied for her. "Any news?"

"Jericho might have a lead on Lonny Ogden. If anything comes of it, I'll let you know." The marshal reversed his steps and went back toward the front of the house.

"Good grief," Addie said under her breath.

Weston hated that she looked embarrassed. "I've seen you stark naked, and I've kissed nearly every inch of you, remember? This was like second base."

"Third," she corrected, making him chuckle.

There was a hint of that humor he missed. Addie hadn't exactly been cracking jokes during their time in San Antonio, but there'd been moments when she had managed to keep things light.

She didn't move closer to him but glanced at his very noticeable zipper region. "Should I do something about that?"

Weston gave her a blank stare. "I'm a man. The answer to that question is usually a yes. *Usually,*" he emphasized.

"But I'm thinking you've got five minutes tops before the climax wears off and you come to your senses."

It didn't take her anywhere near five minutes. More like five seconds. "You're right. Sorry." She finished fixing her clothes. "Sex is a complication I don't need right now."

It hit him then. The baby. Something that hadn't been on his mind when his hand had been in her panties. "Is what we did okay? I mean for the baby?"

Now she was the one giving the flat look. "The baby is fine. Pregnant women can and obviously do have climaxes. As you just proved." She actually blushed. "Maybe talking is safer," she grumbled.

No doubt, but he figured that meant Addie would go back to discussing Daisy, the attacks or the killer.

She stared at him. "Are you ever going to tell me why you never wanted to have children?"

Okay, not a question he especially wanted on the conversation table. Still, maybe it was better than talking about sex or murder.

Maybe.

Or maybe he was just playing with a different kind of fire.

Addie was clearly waiting for an answer, but it took Weston a while to find one he could manage. "My father didn't abandon me the way yours did, but I wish he had."

She stayed quiet a moment. "Did he have something to do with the scars on your back?" The flat look returned when he just stared at her. "I've seen every inch of you naked, too. You have at least a dozen scars on your back."

Yeah, those. He always lied about them, saying they were rodeo injuries, but it didn't seem right to lie to Addie. "My dad was a mean drunk, and my mother did whatever she could to make sure she wasn't the one on the receiving end of his fists and his belt."

Addie glanced away, swallowed hard. "My father gave you the other scar. The one on your chest." She touched her cheek. "Both of us have lots of scars. Some visible, some not."

Weston leaned toward her. "I gave you one of those invisible scars. A broken heart." He touched her heart. At least that was his intention, but it also meant touching her breast.

She didn't exactly skitter away from him. "Who gave you your broken heart?" She leaned over, brushed her fingers over his chest and sent a nice trickle of heat through him.

"Amy Wilkins. Tenth grade."

But he knew that wasn't what she wanted to hear. No. This was the talk. *The* one he'd never had with anyone.

"I wasn't in love with Collette," he said. There, it was like ripping off a bandage. It hurt like hell, but the wound was there for Addie to see.

"W-what?" Obviously, it wasn't a confession she'd expected.

"I tried to love her," Weston explained, "but I knew I couldn't give her the life she wanted. So I went to her office that night to break things off with her. Instead, I walked in on her being murdered."

"Oh, God," she whispered.

Weston had repeated that a couple of thousand times since her murder. Along with wanting to punish himself.

"Did she know you didn't love her?" Addie asked.

"Considering I'd never said those words to her, I'm pretty sure she knew."

Addie made a sound of surprise. "You never told her you loved her?"

"Before I met you in San Antonio, I didn't make it a habit of lying to people." He let that hang in the air between them. "Obviously, lying didn't work out so well."

She didn't argue with that and probably wouldn't have even if her phone hadn't rung. "It's likely one of my brothers checking on me." She got up and went to the nightstand.

Then, she froze.

"It says unknown caller on the screen," Addie said, her gaze flying back to him.

Weston couldn't get to the phone fast enough. He hit the answer button and put it on speaker.

"Hello, Addie," the caller said. It was a man, and Weston didn't recognize his voice. "We need to talk."

"Who is this?" she asked. "And how did you get my number?"

"I got it from your brother Chase. Rather, I got it from his phone. Don't worry. He's all right. Or at least he will be once the effects of the stun gun have worn off. Funny thing about brothers. Even adopted ones. They don't like to share information about their kid sister."

Hell. Weston hurried to door, threw it open and called out for the marshals. "Make sure Addie's brother Chase is all right and try to trace the call she just got."

Daniel nodded and took out his own phone. The other marshal did the same.

"Who is this?" Addie repeated, her voice shaking now.

"You don't know? Well, let's just keep it formal, okay? You can call me the Moonlight Strangler."

Addie froze. Her eyes, widened. Her breath stalled in her throat.

"How do we know you're who you say you are?" Weston demanded.

"Ahh, Ranger Cade. You're one of those devil-in-the-details kind of people. Well, here's my proof. I cut all my ladies on their cheeks. That's not in any of the reports, is it, Ranger Cade?

No, it wasn't. But it wasn't enough. "Convince me. Give me something else."

"No wonder you and Addie have a thing for each other. Like minds and all that. All right. Here's your something else. I took Leta's necklace. A little gold angel. I'm sure in the reports her brother said she wore it all the time and that it was the only thing missing when her body turned up."

Weston nodded when Addie looked at him. None of the other victims had been missing any jewelry or items of clothing.

"Chase is okay," Daniel relayed to them. "His phone was stolen, but I reached him through a fellow marshal who's on the scene with him now." Then he shook his head. "We can't trace the killer's call. He's using a prepaid cell."

Of course he was. This snake had avoided capture for thirty years or more. However, he'd taken a huge risk going after Chase. Addie's brother was a marshal and might have seen or heard something that could help them identify him.

Addie took a short breath of relief before turning her attention back to the phone. "Who are you?" Addie demanded. "And by that, I mean what's your name?"

He made a *tsk-tsk* sound. "Wouldn't do to tell you that. Jail's no place for me."

"Then tell me about my birth mother."

Weston hadn't expected the question, but the Moonlight Strangler obviously had. "She's dead," he answered without hesitation.

Addie put her hand over her heart, no doubt to try to steady it. "Did you kill her?"

"Yes." Another quick admission. "But she won't be on your list of victims. Sometimes, it's best if I don't show off my work."

Her bottom lip started to tremble, and she had to clamp her teeth over it for a few seconds. "You're insane."

"Possibly. But I do have my own personal code of conduct, and I'm not the one after you."

Like Weston, he could see Addie replaying that in her head. Did she believe him? Not a chance. But anything this guy could tell them might help them catch him.

"Then who is after me?" she asked.

"Secrets, secrets," the man taunted.

Hell. Weston wanted to reach through the phone and strangle this idiot. Since he couldn't do that and because punching walls wouldn't be very productive, he went in another direction.

"Did you send me a letter that threatened my sister?" Weston asked him.

"Not me. Your sister is of no interest to me."

"You're sure about that? I've been working damn hard to find you, and you could want to get back at me."

"I wouldn't have expected anything less from you. It's the reason I don't go after lawmen. Too persistent. Persistence got Addie's sister-in-law in trouble, didn't it? By the way, how's your brother doing?"

That didn't help the color in Addie's cheeks. "Paige," she said under her breath. "And how do you think my brother's doing?" She had a lot more volume in her voice when she asked that. "You murdered his wife."

"His ex-wife," the man corrected.

Weston knew the details of Paige's murder. Too many details. The kind that made it hard for him to sleep at night. The kind that'd no doubt given Addie and especially her brother Jax plenty of nightmares. This monster had taken way too much from the Crocketts.

"Paige's death couldn't be helped," he said as if that excused everything. "If it makes you feel better, she's the only one I regret. Tell your brother that."

"Jax won't ever hear that from me," she snapped. "Because I don't believe it for a minute. I doubt you're even capable of feeling regret."

"You're wrong." He paused again. "But we're getting off topic again, and I need to end this call soon."

"Not until you give us some answers," Weston insisted.

"All right. Here's an answer, Ranger Cade. You're of no interest to me. Addie, well, she's of interest only because we're family."

The anger fired through her eyes. "You're not my family."

He chuckled. "A sensitive topic, I see."

Weston was tired of dealing with this. "Tell us who's after Addie and why."

"Secrets, secrets," he repeated. "There's a big surprise planned for you."

"Quit playing games." Weston added some profanity to that.

"But games are *so* much fun. But I will say this—if you want to stop him, then make sure Addie remembers all about her time with Daisy. I'm not the only one with secrets."

"Daisy's dead. Your doing?" Weston asked.

"Hardly. Not my type. Not like Collette and the others."

"I wasn't your type," Weston reminded him after he got past the mental punch to the gut at hearing the killer say Collette's name, "and you left me for dead."

"You got in the way. If you're not careful, the same will happen when he comes after Addie."

"He?" Addie and Weston questioned together. "Give me a name," Weston demanded.

A very long silence.

"All right. Here's a name. Lonny Ogden. I'm pretty sure he's trying to pull a copycat."

Finally. But Weston had no idea if it was the truth or if the Moonlight Strangler was just playing more games.

"Did you put Ogden up to coming after me?" Addie asked.

"No way. I take pride in what I do, and Lonny-boy's a sloppy mess. My own fault, though."

Weston didn't like the sound of that. "What do you mean?"

"I mean…" The killer didn't jump to finish that until he'd made them wait several moments. "I'm responsible for creating Lonny-boy. It's my blood running through his veins."

And with that, he laughed and ended the call.

Chapter Fourteen

Addie hadn't realized just how weak her legs had gotten until she felt Weston hook his arm around her waist. He had her sit on the bed, his attention immediately going to Daniel.

Her mind was whirling. As if a tornado had gotten inside her head. She'd actually heard the voice of the Moonlight Strangler. Chase had been attacked. Her birth mother was dead.

If the killer was telling the truth.

"Is there any chance the Moonlight Strangler can use that phone number to find the location of the safe house?" Weston asked the marshals.

Oh, God. That put her heart right back in her throat. She hadn't even considered that.

"No," Daniel assured them. "Each of Addie's family members was given the phone number but not the address."

Good. That was something at least, but it didn't get her heart out of her throat. Mercy, when was this going to end?

"We had DNA tests run on Ogden, and they should be back in a day or two," Weston explained to Daniel. "Jericho and the FBI will need to know about this, too."

"And Chase," Addie added. "I need to talk to Chase."

Daniel had already said that Chase was all right, but she wanted to hear her brother's voice, to make sure he wasn't trying to shield her. Things were already bad enough, but if her brother had been hurt…well, she didn't want to go there.

The marshals both stepped out in the hall to make the calls, but they didn't go far. Definitely not letting her out their sight. Of course, Weston wasn't leaving, either. He sat next to her, pulling her into his arms.

"Ogden is my brother?" she asked.

"The killer could have been lying about that," Weston reminded her.

True. But why would he do that?

It's my blood running through his veins.

And that meant it was the same blood running through hers.

"I didn't feel any kind of connection to him," she added. "Unlike Cord. I felt something there." Plus, there'd been the memory of the brown bear.

"Ogden's probably crazy," Weston went on. "And I don't mean he just acts crazy. He might truly be insane along with being a Moonlight Strangler groupie. Ogden maybe somehow convinced the killer that he was his son so he could deepen whatever connection he thinks is between them."

Perhaps. But the killer didn't seem to be someone who could easily be convinced of anything, especially a lie.

Weston caught her chin, lifted it, forcing eye contact with her. "The good news is the killer said he wasn't the one after you. If that's true—and I think it might be—then all of this makes a lot more sense."

She had to shake her head. "None of this makes sense."

"But it does. You've known for three months that the Moonlight Strangler is your biological father. I kept going back to the question—if he wanted you silenced, then why hadn't he come after you sooner? If I could just walk onto the ranch, then he could have, too. He didn't."

Addie couldn't argue with that, but she did see a problem. "The same could be said of a copycat. Why now?"

"Maybe it has to do with Cord."

All right. That got her attention.

"Cord found out he was a DNA match about the same time the attacks on you started," Weston continued. "Someone might not want you teaming up with your brother and recalling any shared memories."

Since that'd already happened, then it was a valid fear. But the problem was neither Cord nor she had remembered anything incriminating about anyone.

"I've got your brother Chase on the line," Daniel interrupted.

Addie couldn't get to his phone fast enough. "Are you okay?" she asked Chase right away.

"I'm fine. How about you?"

Her brother didn't sound fine. He sounded shaken up. And riled. Addie knew exactly how he felt. "I'm worried about you."

"Don't be. I was just zapped when I got out of my car to interview a witness. Nothing to do with the Moonlight Strangler. This is all my fault, really. I was distracted, and I didn't see the stun gun in the woman's hand until it was too late."

"A woman?" Weston asked.

"Yeah. She looked as if she'd been attacked. Clothes torn. Hair a mess. She staggered toward me, and when I reached for her, she hit me with a stun gun. When I came to, I was facedown in the parking lot and my phone was missing."

Addie felt the chill snake down her spine. Chase could have been killed, and she was betting the reason he was distracted was because he was worried about her. "Any idea who the woman was?"

"None. I'll check for any surveillance cameras, but I figure she was just a lackey. Maybe even a homeless person hired to do the job. Don't worry. I'll be more careful. You do the same."

There was an alert that another call was coming in, so Addie told her brother goodbye and handed the phone back to Daniel. Daniel cursed as soon as he saw the screen.

"It's an unknown caller again," Daniel told them.

At the same moment, there was a text from Jericho on Weston's phone.

Ogden is about to call you, Jericho texted Weston. Call me after you've talked to him.

Addie was actually relieved it was Ogden. She wasn't sure she was up for another round with the Moonlight Strangler when she hadn't recovered from their initial conversation. But, of course, talking to Ogden wouldn't exactly be a picnic.

Especially after what she'd just learned.

It's my blood running through his veins.

"Marshal Seaver, don't hang up," Ogden greeted. "I've been calling all over the place, and that rude sheriff in Appaloosa Pass finally gave me your number. I need to speak to Ranger Cade right now. He's not answering his phone, and I'm betting you know how to get in touch with him."

Weston wasn't answering his phone because, like Addie's, his had been left at the ranch and swapped out with ones that couldn't be tracked. They certainly hadn't given Ogden their new numbers.

"I'm listening," Weston said, moving closer to the phone. "Where the hell are you?"

"As if I'd tell you. The sheriff kept asking me the same thing, and I'll say to you what I said to him. You won't find me unless I want to be found. And I don't want to be found right now."

"Really?" Weston fired back. "Because I heard you were kicking and screaming when those men took you from the hospital. Was that all an act?"

"No!" His voice was a screech. "I have no idea who they were, and I got away as soon as I could."

"You managed to escape with that injury?" Weston sounded as skeptical as Addie felt. Because Ogden could be lying, not only about this but anything else he told them.

"Yes, I did. I'm resourceful when I have to be. But there's a problem. I managed to get to a computer to access the security feed I set up around my apartment."

Daniel looked at Weston, silently asking if he knew about the feed, and Weston shook his head. If Weston and the other lawmen hadn't seen cameras, then they were well hidden.

"There are cops in my apartment," Ogden went on, "and I want you to tell them to get out. I can't hear what they're saying, but I can see them going through everything. I don't want them touching my things."

Good grief. That was his biggest concern right now? Maybe Weston was right about Ogden being insane. Or else this was Ogden's way of trying to make them believe he was. That way, if he was caught, he could be looking at time in a mental hospital instead of jail.

"There's an easy fix to this problem," Weston snarled. "If you want the cops out, just turn yourself in, and give them whatever it is they're looking for."

"You know I can't do that. You'll arrest me."

"Yeah, I will, but the alternative is you dying while

on the run. I take it your kidnapper didn't have friendly intentions toward you?"

"No." For one word, it carried a lot of emotion. Mainly anger. "They wanted me to do things I didn't want to do."

"Like what?" Weston pressed when Ogden didn't continue.

"I'm not after Addie. Not anymore. I don't want her dead, and I didn't have anything to do with that stuff that went on at that old lady's house."

"Really? You're not after Addie? Convince me."

That was Weston's favorite order. *Convince me.* Something she doubted Ogden could do.

Ogden made a sound of disapproval, clearly not pleased with Weston's sarcasm. "I can't, not over the phone. But if you get those cops out of my place, I'll turn myself in so we can talk face-to-face. I'll be able to convince Addie and you."

She wasn't holding her breath about that.

"Give me some time," Weston finally said. "I'll see if I can help."

"You don't believe he'd turn himself in," Addie protested when Weston ended the call and reached for his own phone.

"No. But obviously there's something in that apartment that Ogden doesn't want them to find."

While the marshals were busy with their own calls, Weston worked his way through several people in SAPD before he was finally connected to an officer, Detective Riley Jenkins, on the scene of the search of Ogden's apartment.

"Just got a call from Ogden, and he claims to be watching you via remote camera access," Weston told the detective. "He also says he'll turn himself in if you and your team leave the apartment. He won't, of course, but he might be stupid enough to try to get into his place to retrieve whatever it is he's worried about you finding."

"I think we've already found it," Jenkins answered in a whisper.

Addie felt a too familiar punch of dread. She doubted there was anything in Ogden's apartment that would put her at ease.

"Hold on while I step outside," the detective added. It only took a few moments for him to come back on the line. "I'm not sure if Ogden has audio, but I didn't want to risk it. We found the cameras shortly after we got in."

"Does Ogden know that?" Weston asked.

"Oh, yes. We've blocked the one we found in the bedroom. I'm sure that's got him running scared. He's been calling all over, looking for someone who can get us out of here, and I'm hoping he'll panic and try to move us out of here himself. We're ready for an attack. Ready to catch him and put him back in jail where he belongs."

Good. Because Ogden sounded as if he was at a breaking point.

"What'd you find?" Weston asked.

"Plenty. I'm texting you a picture of something we saw in his bedroom."

Addie pressed her fingers to her mouth and prayed that it wasn't another dead body. But it wasn't. As the picture loaded, it took her a while to figure out exactly what she was seeing. There were newspaper clippings taped to the walls. Dozens, maybe even hundreds of them. And from what she could tell, all the clippings were articles about the Moonlight Strangler.

"It's like a shrine," the detective went on. "In addition to the stuff on the walls, he has folders from where he's printed out blog posts and anything that mentions the killer. That's where we found the letters from the Moonlight Strangler."

Letters. Ogden hadn't mentioned those.

"You think they're real?" Weston asked.

"At least one of them is. It's typed, no envelope so we don't have a postmark, but there's a detail in it that only the killer would know. It has to do with a necklace and one of the victims."

Leta's necklace.

But that immediately gave Addie an uneasy feeling.

That was the same item the Moonlight Strangler had offered them as proof of his identity. Was it possible that someone like Canales or Boggs had gotten access to that detail and was using it to manipulate Ogden?

If so, had that really been the Moonlight Strangler who'd just called her? Or maybe someone was just playing sick games with her.

"The letter's an apology, and it's dated about three months ago," Jenkins explained. "The Strangler tells Ogden he's sorry for not being there for him, that he knows Ogden had a tough life. And he did. When Ogden was three, he was adopted by a couple who used him as a punching bag. Lots of trips to the ER for broken bones and such."

Addie hadn't known that about Ogden, and it almost made her feel sorry for him. *Almost*.

"His adoptive parents were both killed in a car accident and left him a nice trust fund," Jenkins added, "but I'm sure that doesn't make up for the abuse."

No. Nothing could make up for something like that. But a trust fund meant Ogden had access to money that he could have used to hire the hit man who tried to kill her.

"Did the Moonlight Strangler say anything about

being Ogden's biological father?" Weston asked. It was the exact question on Addie's mind.

"Not outright, but he implied it," the detective said without hesitating. "Apparently, you'd already put in a DNA test on Ogden so I just called about fifteen minutes ago and got the results."

"The test is back?" Weston said, giving her a long look. He also put his arm around her. "And?"

"It's a match."

Addie felt the air swoosh out of her. This wouldn't have been easy no matter what, but it was a hard pill to swallow that her own brother had wanted her dead.

"The lab compared Ogden's DNA to the Moonlight Strangler's biological daughter, Addie Crockett, and although it's not a full sibling match, the DNA does prove that Ogden is her half-brother. Same paternal DNA, different mother, though."

Weston jumped right on that. "Any idea who that mother is?"

"No. Her DNA's not in the system."

Which meant she didn't have a criminal record. It was also possible that she was still alive.

Unlike Addie's own birth mother.

If she was to believe the killer, then her birth mother had been one of his victims. But maybe not Ogden's mother. And if the woman was alive, she might be able to give them the identity of the Moonlight Strangler. Of course, that would mean finding her, but maybe Ogden could help with that.

"Thanks," Weston told Jenkins. "If Ogden shows up or if you find anything else, let me know. Addie Crockett's life could depend on it."

The detective assured him that he would, and they ended the call.

"He's really my brother," Addie managed to say.

Weston stared at her. "No. Don't go there. Ogden's DNA didn't make him the way he is. You heard what the detective said about the abuse."

She had, and Addie had no choice but to latch on to it. But there was something else bothering her about this.

"Ogden's thirty-one. Cord and I are thirty-three," she explained. "Jenkins said Ogden wasn't adopted until he was three, and that means he was a year old when Cord and I were abandoned. So where was Ogden during those two years before he was adopted? With his birth mother or with our sick excuse for a father?"

Weston shook his head and took out his phone again. "I don't know, but I'll see what I can find out. If the adoption was legal, then maybe I can get the records unsealed and go from there."

However, Weston didn't get a chance to make the call because another one came in, and Addie saw Jericho's name on the screen.

"I just heard about Ogden's test results," Jericho said the moment Weston answered the phone. "Is Addie okay?"

She opened her mouth to tell him yes, but the lie stuck in her throat. "I'm dealing with it," she settled for saying.

Jericho cursed. "I'm sorry. If there's anything I could do to make this go away, I'd do it."

"I know you would." Weston would, too. The only bright spot in all of this was the lawmen who would protect both her baby and her with their lives.

But Addie prayed it didn't come down to that.

"I just got off the phone with the FBI," Jericho continued a moment later. "I'm not sure I like their idea, but they're insisting this is the best way to try to recover your lost memories."

"The best way?" she asked at the same moment that Weston said, "What are you talking about?"

"More hypnosis," Jericho said after taking a long breath. "But this time, they want to do the session at Daisy's house. Addie, they want you there tomorrow."

Chapter Fifteen

A dead woman's house was one of the last places Weston wanted Addie to be.

But he could see the rationale behind bringing her here. The place had triggered the memory of the swing set, and maybe it would trigger something else.

Especially since they were practically at a dead end in the investigation.

Ogden was still on the loose, and there were no adoption records for him. No birth certificate, either. Added to that, there was no concrete evidence to get search warrants for Canales and Boggs. In fact, Boggs was still fighting the request for his DNA on the grounds that he didn't want to be any part of the investigation into the Moonlight Strangler.

Of course, Boggs was also claiming that he was still looking for the killer, but Weston wasn't buying Boggs's claim that it was all to avenge a childhood friend's murder. There was something else going on.

Something Addie might remember.

However, at the moment she didn't look any more comfortable with this than Weston was. Her nerves had been sky-high on the drive over, and seeing the house hadn't helped, either. Probably because someone had tried to murder her there just the day before.

Weston had to make sure that didn't happen again.

There were five lawmen at Daisy's house—including

her brother Jericho the two marshals and Appaloosa Pass deputy Dexter Conway. Addie had been escorted in while wearing a Kevlar vest, and she'd leave the same way.

But it was this middle part of the visit that was no doubt causing the most alarm in her eyes.

"It'll be okay," Weston tried to assure her.

The assurance sucked, and the kiss he brushed on her forehead earned him a glare from Jericho. Weston ignored him and gave her a quick kiss on the mouth before stepping away so the therapist, Dr. Melissa Grinstead, could get to work.

Since the pregnancy prevented the doctor from administering any drugs, she had Addie lying on the bed in the guest room. The door, both windows and the blinds were closed, and while the room wasn't exactly pitch-dark, it was close thanks to the room being on the east side of the house. The late afternoon sun wasn't threading much light inside.

Dr. Grinstead had already warned Jericho and Weston that while they could remain in the room, they weren't allowed to say anything.

No matter what.

Weston figured that meant Addie might remember some things she didn't exactly want to remember. The stuff of nightmares.

The doctor's voice was soft and soothing, and for several minutes she just talked to Addie, telling her how to breathe and to think of relaxing things, like a running creek and warm sunlight.

Addie's eyes drifted down, and Weston finally saw the tension ease from her body. Surprisingly, it stayed that way even though the therapist began to ask her questions about her childhood, and she didn't use Addie's name but rather called her Gabrielle.

"Think back," the therapist prompted. "Do you remember being in this house when you were a little girl?"

"There's a swing set outside," Addie readily answered.

"Did you play on it?"

Addie smiled. A child's smile. "Lots."

"Were you alone?" the doctor asked.

No smile this time. "Sometimes. Davy's not with me."

The therapist glanced back at Weston and Jericho to see if they knew who that was, but they shook their heads.

"Who's Davy?" Dr. Grinstead continued.

"My brother. He didn't come to the lady's house with me. I wanted him to come so he could push me in the swing."

Addie was likely talking about Cord since Ogden would have been too young.

"Do you remember your whole name?" the doctor continued.

"Gabby-elle." She said it the way a child might, and that was it. No surname. Of course, these were the memories of a three-year-old.

"What about your parents? Do you know their names?" The therapist was obviously trying a different angle.

One that didn't work. "Mama and Daddy," Addie answered. "But Mama's gone."

"Gone where?"

Good question. Especially since the person claiming to be the Moonlight Strangler had said he'd killed her birth mother.

"Don't know," Addie finally said, and Weston didn't think it was his imagination that there was sadness in her voice. Maybe that meant she'd loved her mother. Didn't all kids?

Well, except for him.

"Where's your daddy?" the doctor tried again.

"Don't know. The man brought me to the lady and said I was to stay until Daddy came back."

"And did he come back?"

Addie squeezed her eyes shut even tighter. Hell, Weston hoped she wasn't remembering something god-awful.

"Don't know," she repeated.

It was both a relief and frustrating. If she had remembered her father returning, then she might have been able to give them a description, but she might have also remembered a murder or two.

"Tell me about the lady you stayed with," Dr. Grinstead continued. "Was she here alone with you, or were there other people in the house?"

"Sometimes, we were alone." Addie's forehead bunched up again. "Sometimes, the man who stayed with the lady was there."

The man who stayed with the lady. Likely Daisy's husband since he was still alive then.

"But sometimes," Addie said, her voice small now, "there were other men. They didn't come when the lady was there. Only when she was gone."

"Did you know them?" the doctor asked.

Addie frantically shook her head and pulled her hands in a tight pose against her chest. "They were scary. They had guns."

All right. That hit Weston like a punch to the gut, and it darn sure didn't help when Addie's mouth started to tremble. "I don't like those men. They yell at the lady's man."

And Addie started to cry.

Not an ordinary cry. Sobs of a terrified little girl. It cut Weston to the core, and if Jericho hadn't caught onto him, he might have bolted forward to pull her into his arms. Weston soon realized, however, that Jericho had likely grabbed him to stop himself from doing the same thing.

"Did those men hurt you?" the doctor pressed.

"No. Just scary."

The relief hit Weston almost as hard as the anger. He hated that Addie had been through this, but he also knew it could have been a heck of a lot worse.

"I don't want to think about them anymore," Addie murmured.

"Okay. Then, let's talk about the other man, the one that brought you to the lady. Was he nice to you?"

Addie lifted her shoulder. "He gave me a donut. With sprinkles."

"Do you remember anything else about him? Like maybe his name? Or what he looked like?"

Another shake of her head. "No. Don't remember. I don't want to be here anymore. I want to go home." The sobs returned. "Please, let me go home. *Please.*"

The doctor looked back at them, not exactly asking permission to stop the session, because that's exactly what she did a few seconds later.

The moment Addie opened her eyes, her gaze went straight to Weston. And he went straight to her. He didn't even attempt to comfort her with words. Because there weren't any that'd help. But getting her out of there just might.

"I remember everything I said," she whispered to him.

A good lawman would have pressed to learn if there was something else. Something she hadn't talked about remembering. But Weston decided this wasn't the time to be a good lawman.

"Let's get her back to the safe house," he told Jericho, and her brother certainly didn't argue with that.

Since she didn't look too steady on her feet, Weston put the Kevlar vest back on her and scooped her up in his arms. There was no need to tell Jericho they were moving fast once they were outside. Jericho knew the possible dangers out there as well as Weston did.

"I'm okay, really," Addie said, not convincing him in the least.

Weston put her in the backseat of the marshals' car. Jericho, the doctor and the deputy followed along behind them as they drove away from the house and back onto the road. Eventually, when they were sure it was safe, Jericho would head back to the sheriff's office so that the doctor could write up her report. Addie, Weston and the marshals would spend yet another night in the safe house.

Addie looked up at Weston. "I didn't give you or the FBI anything you can use to find the killer."

"Not true. Thanks to you, we know several other men visited Daisy's house. We can question everyone in the area to see if they remember them."

Yes, it was a long shot, but that was true of this entire investigation.

"I kept thinking there was something else," she continued. "Something right at the edge of my memory."

"It might come to you." And if it did, Weston hoped like the devil that it didn't make her cry.

"Hell," Daniel snapped.

Weston looked up, following Daniel's gaze. There, ahead of them was a herd of cows ambling across the road. It wasn't that rare of a sight in rural Texas, but there was something about it that put Weston on full alert.

He soon figured out what.

When there was a break in the herd, he got a glimpse of a car on the other side of the cows. A black limo.

One that Weston instantly recognized.

Hell.

IT TOOK ADDIE a moment to realize why Daniel had cursed. And why Weston had drawn his gun.

Canales and Boggs. Again.

This couldn't be a coincidence, and she was certain it was their limo since she'd caught a glimpse of the front license plate with the *AGB*.

"Get down," Weston told her, and he made sure she did just that by pushing her onto the seat.

The fear came, churning and twisting inside her. So did the anger. She was so tired of feeling this way.

"You see anything?" Weston asked the marshals.

"Just the limo and the cows," Daniel grumbled. "No one's getting out of the limo."

Addie could no longer see the limo. Just the cows that were meandering past the marshals' car. The cows were taking their time even though Kirk was honking the horn at them. Because of the noise from that and the cows themselves, it took her a moment to hear another sound.

One she definitely didn't want to hear.

A gunshot.

Addie wasn't sure where the bullet landed, but it caused Weston to push her even farther down on the seat.

"The windows are bullet resistant," Daniel reminded them. "But I don't want to test that. Put the car in Reverse," he told Kirk, and he motioned out the back window, no doubt at Jericho.

Because of her position on the seat, she couldn't see Jericho's cruiser behind them, but Addie heard the squeal of the tires. Her brother was no doubt doing the same thing, trying to get the heck out of there.

"Hell," Kirk spat out. "An SUV just came up behind Jericho, and it's blocking the road."

And that meant they were trapped.

More shots came.

This time, Addie had no trouble figuring out where they landed because they smashed into the window right next to where Weston was seated.

Oh, mercy.

Someone was trying to kill them again. And it wasn't just a few shots. The barrage came, one bullet after another until the sound was deafening, and the windows on the right side of the car were webbed with the direct hits.

She tried to pull Weston down with her, but he stayed put, his gaze firing all around them. He couldn't lower what was left of the window to return fire, but if the shooters kept up, they'd have to figure out a way to return fire.

"You see the shooter?" Daniel asked.

"No," Kirk and Weston answered in unison. "The shots are coming from both sides."

That stopped her breath for a moment.

Addie wasn't familiar with this part of the county, but she remembered there were a lot of patches of thick trees and underbrush along the country road. Not many houses, either. Gunmen could have taken up position in those trees and then used the cows to stop them so they'd be easier targets.

And they'd succeeded.

"They're shooting at the limo, too," Kirk volunteered. "Their windows aren't stopping the bullets. And there's an SUV behind them as well, pinning them in."

Addie certainly hadn't expected that. Did it mean

that Canales and Boggs weren't behind this attack? If they were, they were taking a huge chance with all those shots being fired.

"Can you see who's in the limo?" Weston asked him.

"No," Kirk readily answered.

So, maybe it wasn't Boggs and Canales inside, after all. But if they weren't there, then who was?

Behind them, Addie heard a horrible crash, the sound of metal ripping into metal. "Jericho," she said on a rise of breath.

Had he been hurt?

Addie lifted her head and managed to get a glimpse of her brother's cruiser crashing into the SUV that'd trapped them. But only a glimpse before Weston cursed and pushed her right back down.

"Don't get up again," Weston ordered her. He moved sideways in the seat, his attention volleying between the front and rear of the car. "Jericho's using his cruiser as a battering ram to get the SUV out of the way."

Addie wasn't sure if that would work. Or if it was the safe thing to do. But at this point, nothing was safe.

And it got worse.

She heard the shift in the direction of the gunfire. The shots no longer seemed to be aimed at the limo but rather at Jericho's cruiser. Whoever was out there had now made her brother a target.

"Hold on," Kirk warned them a split second before he gunned the engine.

Kirk didn't go straight ahead, however. He jerked the steering wheel to the right, and that's when Addie realized he was darting around what remained of the herd of cows still on the road. There had finally been a big enough opening for them to try to escape.

Good thing, too, because the bullets were coming even faster.

Almost immediately, Kirk jerked the car to the right. No doubt so that he wouldn't crash right into the limo.

"My brother," she said. "We can't leave him here."

"Jericho's right behind us," Weston told her.

Addie believed him, but she lifted her head just a fraction to make sure Jericho was okay. She tried to take in everything at once.

Jericho's cruiser was there.

Just as Weston had said, it was behind them, weaving around the handful of cows still on the road. The limo was on the move, too, but it wasn't coming after them. It was speeding away in the opposite direction.

And then Addie saw something else.

A blur of motion at first.

A man.

And even though Weston tried to push her back down, Addie stayed put and motioned toward the person who was ducking behind one of the trees. The man didn't duck nearly fast enough, though, because Addie got a good look at his face.

Oh, God.

What was *he* doing there?

Chapter Sixteen

Ogden.

Weston didn't like that the man kept turning up in bad situations. Like the latest attack near Daisy's house.

But Ogden had been there all right.

Weston had managed to get only a glimpse of him, but there was no mistaking that it was Ogden.

"Any luck finding Ogden?" Addie asked him.

Weston had to shake his head. For the past two hours, while the marshals were making their way back to the safe house, he'd been on the phone, trying to locate the man. But no one knew where he was. Jericho had sent several deputies to comb the woods near the attack, and they hadn't had any better luck finding him than Weston had.

"What about Canales and Boggs?" she pressed. "Anything else on them?"

She already knew parts of their update, that one of the deputies had found Canales and Boggs. Or rather just Canales and his driver.

"We verified that Boggs wasn't within fifty miles of the attack," Weston explained. "He was at a fundraiser. That doesn't make him innocent," he quickly added. "Because Boggs could have hired someone to fire those shots."

That someone could have been Ogden.

Though Weston had to admit he hadn't seen a gun

in Ogden's hand, and since those shots had come from a rifle, a weapon of that size would have been hard to miss. Of course, Ogden could have discarded the gun when he realized his targets were getting away.

And one of those targets appeared to be Canales.

Appeared being the key word. Canales had escaped without so much as a scratch, so maybe he only wanted them to think he'd been in danger.

When Kirk took the final turn to the safe house, Daniel and Weston glanced around to make sure no one was following them. No one was. They had the road to themselves, just as they had for the bulk of the drive away from that nightmare of an attack. Eventually, they'd have to do reports and such, but for now Weston just wanted Addie off the road and someplace safe.

"Jericho hasn't had a chance to fully question Canales yet," Weston continued, talking to her. "But Canales claims he was out there because he got a phone call from Ogden asking him to meet him."

"And he went?" There was plenty of skepticism in her voice. Weston felt the same way.

"Canales says that Ogden was threatening to derail the campaign by claiming to have proof that Boggs is the Moonlight Strangler. Canales said he wanted to get that so-called proof from Ogden."

"Yes, I'll bet he did. If the proof exists." She paused. "You think maybe Ogden managed to get a DNA sample from Boggs?"

"It's possible." Anything was at this point, but if Ogden did indeed have proof that Boggs was the Moonlight Strangler, then Ogden had a huge target on him. No way would Boggs let him live.

From the front seat, Daniel finished his latest call and turned to look back at them. "We found the owner of those cows. A small-time rancher not far from the road. Someone tore down his fence and herded the cows out of there. The guy doesn't have a record, or a connection to any of our suspects."

So it was another dead end.

Kirk pulled to a stop in front of the safe house, and Daniel got them inside while Kirk put the car in the detached garage. Probably so that the vehicle wouldn't be out in the open. The place was in the middle of the sticks, but if someone happened to drive by, those shot-out windows might cause them to get suspicious. Soon, the marshals would have to swap out vehicles, but since it was nearly sunset, that probably wouldn't happen until morning.

"You should try to eat something," Weston reminded Addie once they were inside.

"Maybe later. I need to catch my breath first," Addie added and headed for her bedroom.

Weston didn't get overly concerned until she shut the door. Oh, man. She was probably on the verge of a meltdown.

"You think she's okay?" Daniel asked while he set the security system.

"Probably not." Weston went after her. He gave one knock on the door before he opened it.

And his jaw dropped to the floor.

She sure wasn't falling apart but rather undressing. Addie already had her jeans unzipped and off her hips.

"They're too tight," she said, slipping them all the way off. Her short top gave him a nice view of her panties. Blue with little flowers. "It was making me queasy."

He doubted that was the only thing making her queasy. Unlike him. He suddenly felt a lot of things, but queasy wasn't on the list. Seeing Addie half-naked gave him all sorts of bad ideas.

And memories.

After all, they'd had a steamy kissing session in this very room the day before. A session his body reminded him of right now.

She glanced out into the hall. No marshals nearby but Weston closed it just in case they came by and got a glimpse of Addie searching for something to wear in the bag she'd packed. She finally pulled out a pair of gray flannel pajama bottoms. Hardly hot. Well, on anyone else, they wouldn't be.

But this was Addie.

With those curves, she could make a brown paper bag look hot.

"You're staring at me," she pointed out.

"Yeah," he admitted. "I'm trying to convince myself that it'd be a good idea to go in another room. Away from you. Away from the memory of just seeing you nearly naked."

Her eyebrow rose. "And?"

"I'm failing."

Addie managed a very short-lived smile. "I do a lot of failing when it comes to you."

Weston didn't like the sound of that. "What do you mean?"

"I didn't remember what needed to be remembered while I was with the therapist."

Hell. Not that. "Well, it might help if I could stop people from shooting at you. Nearly dying every day can put a damper on lots of things—memory included."

"Some memories," she whispered.

And just like that, they weren't talking about the hypnosis anymore. At least he didn't think they were. Addie wasn't falling apart as he'd predicted, but she was obviously beating herself up over something that wasn't her fault.

Addie took a deep breath, sank down on the foot of the bed. "What did you think the first time you saw me?"

All right. That didn't clear up much for him. Weston had never considered himself a pro at figuring out a woman's mind, but this was more confusing than usual.

"And it's okay to lie," she quickly added. "I'd rather not hear that you saw me and your first thought was 'she'll be good bait for a killer.'"

Weston wasn't confused at all about this answer. "That wasn't my first thought. And that isn't a lie. Truth is, when I first saw you, it was pure attraction."

But that was a partial lie. It didn't tell the whole story.

"I felt as if I'd been hit with a sack of bricks. *Good* bricks," he clarified. Though it hadn't exactly felt good at the time. "You were so beautiful that I had to remind myself to breathe."

Tears watered her eyes. The little smile returned. "Now, that's romantic."

"I'm not sure it was all romance I was feeling. Parts of me were just thinking sex. Well, one part of me anyway."

"That's okay." She stood, rubbing her hands on the sides of the pajama bottoms. "Parts of me were thinking the same thing about you."

"Really?" That gave him another hit of the fiery hot heat that he needed to start cooling down. "You were sort of an emotional mess. I figured sex was the last thing on your mind."

"Not sort of. I *was* an emotional mess. But seeing you seemed to cut right through all of that. The first time you kissed me, I could have sworn everything stopped. My heart. Any thoughts in my head."

Yeah. For him, it'd been like more bricks. Bad ones, that time. Because he'd known she was the only woman he'd ever want to kiss again.

Not exactly a comforting thought for a lawman living a lie.

She blinked away the tears, and her chin came up. He could see her steeling up for the next set of memories. The post-sex ones where he'd crushed her into a million little pieces.

What she didn't know was that he'd crushed himself, too.

"Will you ever forgive me?" he asked.

She didn't answer him. Not right away. "I'll forgive you if you'll give me something."

Before he jumped to say anything, Weston tried to think this through. "What do you want?"

Addie came to him. Put her arms around him. First one, then the other. "I need you to help me forget. Even if it's for a few minutes, I just need this noise in my head to stop."

Well, it wasn't a big declaration of feelings. Something Weston wasn't sure he wanted anyway.

"So...you want sex?' he clarified.

She shook her head. Kissed him. "I want sex *with you*. You're the only one who can get me through this."

Flattering, yes. Could he do it?

Oh, yeah.

But that nagging feeling in the back of his head shouted out one big question. Was this the right thing to do for Addie?

"If it's too much to ask..." she started.

"Sex with you isn't a chore," Weston interrupted. "But I want to make sure something else won't work just as well. Something that won't mess with your mind afterward."

She closed her eyes a moment, and when she opened them, he saw pretty much all he needed to see. The need. It went bone-deep in her.

"I don't want anyone or anything else," she whispered. "Just you. Right here, right now. We'll deal with any mind-messing later."

Addie stared at him, clearly waiting.

"Did I convince you?" she asked.

Hearing one of his favorite lines aimed at him nearly made him smile. Nearly. However, it was hard to smile when her body brushed against his.

Weston took that as the move of a woman who was certain of what she wanted. And yes, it convinced him.

He didn't deserve, but he'd take it. Not just the kiss, either. He took her. Into his arms, pulling her close to him.

His body instantly geared up for sex. And he knew it'd be good. But gearing up for sex was just the start. There was no way he could get Addie into bed again and not have it change their lives forever.

The question was—*how* would it change things?

Weston mentally repeated that, tried to come up with the consequences, but those thoughts flew right out of his head when he deepened the kiss.

This was wrong on so many levels. The danger breathing down their necks. The emotional complications from the pregnancy. Addie should be resting, but judging from the way she was kissing him, there'd be no rest for either of them.

Part of him wanted to stop, but there wasn't much common sense left for him. Just more of that feeling he'd just been hit with more bricks.

"Three months is long time to go without you," she whispered, her breath hitting his mouth. "And I don't count the third base yesterday."

That was enough of a green light. Of course, with his erection testing the limits of his boxers, almost anything she would have said to him—other than stop—would have been a green light.

Well, she wasn't saying stop.

And Weston didn't, either.

He caught onto her top and slipped it off her so he could kiss the tops of her breasts. She helped with that, too, by unhooking her bra so he could taste her the way he wanted. She was warm, her skin like silk but she tasted like something forbidden.

Which she was in some ways.

That's probably why it only fired them hotter, and it didn't take many of those breast kisses before Weston wanted a whole lot more. Addie clearly wanted more, too, because the battle started to get them each undressed.

He had the easy part, and while Addie was still grabbling with his shirt, Weston reached over and locked the door. In the same motion, he pulled off her pajama bottoms and her panties. In just a couple of moves, he had her naked and back on the bed. Where he kissed her.

On her stomach.

And lower.

He really liked going lower, and the kiss must have been right where Addie wanted it because she froze. For a couple of seconds. Then she made that sound. That moan of pleasure that went through every inch of him.

"No. You're not finishing things that way," she insisted, latching onto his hair. "No third base this time."

Well, that only left one thing, and Addie was working hard to make sure that happened. She hauled him away from the *lower* kisses, all the while battling with his jeans. Since she just wasn't very good at the whole

undressing-a-man thing, Weston helped her. He managed to get all the necessary clothes kicked or pulled off.
He'd have bruises, but they'd be worth it.

Their bodies were in a frenzy by the time Weston
made it back up to her mouth, and even though that
brainless part of him was pushing him to take her now,
he took a moment just to look at her.

Oh, man.

Would he ever be able to see her like this and not feel
as if someone had sucked all the air from the room? He
hoped not.

"Homerun time," she murmured.

It was. And it darn nearly felt like a homerun when he
pushed inside her. That kick was more of a punch from
a heavyweight's fist now, and it took him a moment to
rein himself in enough to find the rhythm Addie needed.

Not that she needed much.

Maybe because of the three months without, or maybe
the adrenaline and nerves was playing into this. Either
way, it didn't last nearly long enough. Addie slipped her
legs around him. Her arms, too.

And she flew into a million little pieces.

"Do this with me," she begged.

That was the plan.

Again, it didn't take much of an effort. Addie had done
the hard part by taking him to the brink, and Weston let
her climax finish him off.

Chapter Seventeen

Addie woke up in Weston's arms.

He was naked. So was she. And she had settled against him as if she belonged there. Even more, she'd actually slept, something she hadn't managed to do for a while. Not since the attacks had started.

Apparently, Weston had a cure for insomnia.

A cure for a lot of other things, too, since now even hours later, she could still feel the slack pleasure sliding through her. Of course, that pleasure was already starting to slip away as the questions came. Well, one big question anyway.

What was next?

In just six short months they'd be parents. Forever bonded by the child they'd created. But that didn't mean that bond would extend to more of this.

Addie glanced at his bare chest and got another dose of the heat that only Weston could dole out. If they stayed around each other, there'd definitely be *more of this*.

And that's why she had to be careful.

Sex could cloud things, especially her judgment, and she didn't want to jump into a relationship with Weston until she was sure that was what he wanted.

"Go back to sleep," he whispered. He never even opened his eyes but idly brushed a kiss on her forehead, pulled her closer to him.

"Do I snore?" she asked. "Is that how you knew I was awake?"

Probably not the best question after sex, but it bothered her that he could tell without even looking at her that she hadn't been sleeping.

He laughed. A low and smoky sound that fanned more of those flames inside her. Of course, anything at this point would have fanned her flames.

"No snoring. The rhythm of your breathing changed."

She thought about that for a second. "You were tuned in to that?"

He lifted one eyelid, peeked out at her. "I'm tuned in to a lot of things when it comes to you."

Mercy, the man knew just what to say to turn her to mush. And to make her even more confused.

"Want to talk about it?" he asked. Apparently, he also had the tune-in ability to read her mind.

Addie didn't want to talk about it, not until she'd sorted out her feelings for him. That might take a while. She didn't even get a chance to tell him that, though, because his phone buzzed.

She groaned, checked the time. It was only ten o'clock at night, but she figured anyone calling now wouldn't be delivering good news.

Weston groaned, too, and maneuvered himself to a sitting position so he could grab his phone from the nightstand. He groaned again when he saw the name on the screen.

"Boggs, what the hell do you want?" Weston snapped when he answered the call. He put it on speaker, but Addie was so close she would have had no trouble hearing whatever the man had to say.

"We need to talk," Boggs insisted. "*Now.* I have something to tell Addie. And it's important."

All right. That got her attention, and Addie sat up, as well. Weston seemed more riled than curious. Probably because he knew they couldn't trust anything Boggs had to say.

"What do you need to tell her?" Weston demanded.

"I'll only say it to Addie and you face-to-face."

Of course Boggs would want something like that. Since he was a top suspect not just for the attacks but also for being the Moonlight Strangler, Addie didn't want to get anywhere near him unless he was behind bars.

"Is this a joke?" Weston cursed. "It has to be because you know a meeting with Addie isn't going to happen."

"It has to happen." Now it was Boggs who groaned, but it didn't sound like it was out of frustration. Was he upset about something? Maybe over the fact they were close to catching him?

"If it has to happen," Weston continued, "then it'll happen over the phone. If you've got something to say to Addie, then start talking."

But Boggs didn't do that. He hesitated. A long time. "It's too late. Everything has been set in motion."

Weston looked at her, no doubt to see if she knew what he was talking about, but Addie had to shake her head. Still, this sounded like the start of an admission of some kind of guilt. Weston must have thought so, too, because he hit the function on his phone to record the conversation.

"What the hell are you talking about?" Weston pressed when Boggs didn't continue.

"I'm talking about Addie. And those memories she had from childhood."

That rid her of any remnants of the heat she'd been feeling just minutes earlier. "What memories?" she asked.

Weston frowned at her, probably because he hadn't wanted her to be part of this conversation. But Addie was part of it. Heck, she was the reason for it, and Boggs might say more to her than he would to Weston.

"What memories?" she repeated when Boggs gave them the silent treatment again.

"You tell me." Boggs no longer sounded upset. The anger crept into his voice. "The FBI is scrambling to listen to the recording of your session from earlier today, the one you did at Daisy's house. And I can't get a single person to tell me what's on those recordings."

Good grief. That's what this is about? But Addie rethought that. Maybe this meant Boggs believed she'd remembered exactly who he was.

Her birth father and a serial killer.

"You expect us to be torn up that you don't have a rat in the FBI who'll leak secrets to you?" Weston challenged. "Or is this some kind of confession? If so, spit it out."

"No confession. Not about that anyway. I just know that childhood memories can be planted." Boggs paused again. "And I think that's exactly what happened with Addie."

Since she hadn't remembered much, Addie doubted the planted-memory theory. If someone had gone to the trouble to do that, they would have planted details that would have led to her identifying something or someone. But it did lead her to another question.

"Do you really think someone would have tried to plant memories about you?" she asked.

"Of course." No hesitation that time. "I'm a powerful man in the middle of a campaign, and what better way to discredit me than to try to smear my name with the false memories planted in your head."

"Who would have done that?" Weston snapped.

"I'm not sure."

But Addie got the feeling that Boggs did know. Was he trying to protect Ogden because he was Boggs's own son? Or was this about his old friend, Canales?

"You know," Weston continued, "there's one way for you to discredit what Addie remembered. You could have a DNA test done to prove you're not the Moonlight Strangler."

"What did she remember?" Boggs shouted.

So Weston had hit a big nerve with the hint, or rather the lie, that she'd witnessed something as a child, something to indicate that Boggs was indeed the serial killer.

"I'll tell you what she remembered when I have your DNA results," Weston countered.

"No." Boggs shouted that, too. And he repeated it. "I'm not the Moonlight Strangler. I'm not!"

"Then prove it." Weston put that challenge out there. And they waited. And waited.

"A DNA test could be a problem for me," Boggs finally said. "Not because it would prove I'm a killer. It wouldn't. But I have a secret that needs to stay hidden."

"Excuse me?" Weston cursed again. "This is a murder investigation, Boggs. You're a suspect, and that's about to be all over the news. So what secret is worse than that?"

"I fathered a child." Boggs sounded as if he were choosing his words carefully. "Not Addie."

"Ogden?" Addie asked.

"No. Not him, either. A son who was born twenty years ago. A lowlife. And his DNA's in the system because of multiple arrests. He has nothing to do with the Moonlight Strangler, nothing to do with the attacks or your investigation."

It didn't take Addie long to fill in the blanks. "But if people found out that you fathered this *lowlife* while cheating on your wife, it wouldn't mesh with the family values you're spouting about in your campaign."

Boggs's silence confirmed that. However, that wasn't the only question Addie had.

"'It's too late,' you said earlier. 'Everything has been set into motion.' What did you mean?"

Yet another long hesitation. "I'm sorry, Addie. Really sorry."

Boggs ended the call, and, still cursing, Weston hit redial. The man didn't answer, but there was a knock at the bedroom door. Addie was still reeling from Boggs's call so it took her a moment to realize something had to be wrong for one of the marshals to come to her door at night.

"You need to get up right now," Daniel said from the other side of the door.

Weston did, and while he pulled on his boxers, he hurried to throw open the door. "What happened?"

"Our location's been compromised," Daniel said, already hurrying back up the hall. "We need to move Addie right now."

WESTON FOUGHT THROUGH that punch of dread and began to throw on his clothes. Addie did the same.

One glance at her and, even in the dim light, he could see the fear on her face. He hated that it was there. Hated that once again they might be on the verge of another attack.

"Compromised? How?" Weston called out to Daniel.

"We're not sure yet. But someone just triggered the sensor on the road."

"Maybe a deer or something?" Weston hoped. Prayed,

actually. Anything was better than another hired gun.
Or worse—the Moonlight Strangler.

"No," Daniel answered. "It's someone in a car."

Hell. Weston doubted this was someone out for an
evening drive.

"Maybe it's nothing," she whispered.

"Maybe." But Weston figured Addie didn't believe
that any more than he did.

He finished dressing, fast, and with Addie right behind him, they went into the hall. The lights had already
all been turned off, and Kirk was at the front window, his
gun drawn and a pair of night scope binoculars pressed
to his eyes.

"See anything?" Weston asked. Beside him, Daniel
slipped on a Kevlar vest and handed one to Weston and
another to Addie. Kirk was already wearing one.

"I'm not seeing nearly enough." Kirk handed the binoculars to Weston so he could have a look. Before he
did, however, Weston motioned for Addie to stay away
from the windows.

It took Weston a moment to spot the dark-colored
SUV. It wasn't moving but it was parked about thirty
yards from the house. He couldn't see the driver through
the tinted windshield, but the exhaust from the engine
was mixing with the cold air and was creating a mist
around the vehicle.

"I've already called for backup," Daniel explained,
"but we're looking at thirty minutes or more before it
arrives."

That was way too long. Weston doubted whoever
was in that SUV would wait a half hour before doing
whatever he was planning on doing. But it did make him
wonder—why was the driver just sitting there? Maybe

because whoever arrived for backup would be walking into a trap.

"I'm going out the back door," Kirk said, already heading to the door off the kitchen. "I need to check the car and see if someone managed to put a tracking device on it."

Well, that would explain how the place had been compromised, since Weston was certain they hadn't been followed. However, it wouldn't explain how someone had managed to put a tracker on the car in the first place.

Unless...

Weston cursed. "Someone could have been hiding in the ditch during that last attack."

With all the chaos going on—the cows and the shots being fired—they wouldn't have easily noticed something like that. Especially since the side windows had been cracked and webbed from the bullets.

Daniel made a sound of agreement and hurried to the side window. No doubt so he could cover Kirk. The detached garage wasn't far, only about five feet from the house, but Kirk would be out in the open for a few critical moments where he could be gunned down.

"Get on the floor behind the sofa," Weston told Addie, and he kept his attention on the SUV.

The vehicle still wasn't moving. It was just sitting there like a dangerous animal stalking them.

There was a swooshing sound. Not a gunshot, though. A moment later, Daniel cursed and ran toward the back door.

Weston saw it then. The blaze in the garage. Someone had launched a firebomb into the building.

"What's wrong?" Addie asked.

Weston wanted to assure her that everything was okay,

but it wasn't. Far from it. "Did Kirk get out?" Weston called to Daniel.

A moment later, though, he had his answer when Kirk practically came crashing through the back door. "We need to get out of the house," Kirk insisted, his words rushed. His breath gusting.

Addie's was gusting, too, and even though she couldn't see the fire in the garage, she could no doubt smell the smoke that was already starting to make its way to the house.

"Who's out there?" Weston asked.

But Kirk shook his head and motioned for them to hurry to the door. "Someone with darn good aim—on the road near that SUV. The car's destroyed, and I'm thinking the house will be the next target."

It would be.

That meant they had to get out now. No choice about that. But it also meant that person with *darn good aim* could pick them off the moment they stepped outside.

Weston grabbed a coat from the sofa and handed it to Addie. In the same motion, he took hold of her arm and got her moving.

When they'd arrived at the safe house, he'd familiarized himself with the grounds, and there wasn't much out there they could use for cover. Still, there were a few things that might work especially since it was dark.

Might.

They headed for a woodpile about three feet high on the side of the house, and they ducked behind it while Addie put on the coat. It was freezing, literally, but they might not have a choice about being outside until backup arrived. Maybe the coat would help. Maybe the Kevlar vest would, too, though Kevlar wouldn't stop a fatal bullet to the head.

Weston positioned Addie between himself and the woodpile so he could give her at least some protection. His gaze fired all around them. The marshals did the same. And Weston got his first real look at the garage.

Or rather what was left of it.

The fire was already eating its way through the wooden building, and soon it would be nothing but ash. But why had their attackers gone after the car instead of the house?

Obviously, the person behind this hadn't wanted them to use the car to escape, but if that firebomb had gone into the house, then they probably wouldn't have been in any shape to get out of there. And it was possible they'd all be dead.

Did that mean the person didn't want to kill them?

That question was still repeating in his head when he heard another of those swishing sounds. Weston pushed Addie to the ground.

Just in time.

Judging from the sound of breaking glass, the firebomb crashed through one of the windows in the front of the house, and within seconds, the flames and the smoke started to shoot out.

"The idiot who fired that is somewhere on the road near the car," Daniel told them.

Yeah, Weston had already come to the same conclusion. He'd come to another conclusion, too.

A bad one.

If the shooter could launch a firebomb at the house and the garage, then he could also hit the woodpile.

"We need to warn the backup," Weston insisted. "And we need to move."

Kirk took care of a text to warn whoever was responding as backup so Weston glanced around for a possible escape route. They didn't exactly have a lot of options, though. Basically, everything in the line of sight of the shooter was off-limits.

That left the old barn.

And it was a good thirty yards away.

Thankfully, the darkness, fire and the smoke had created a semicover that would hopefully conceal them enough, and the barn was probably out of range from their attacker. If the guy tried to get closer to deliver a firebomb into the barn, then he'd face the same problem they had.

Very little cover.

Weston would be able to see him and maybe take him out.

"Are you thinking what I'm thinking?" Daniel asked him, tipping his head to the barn.

Weston nodded. There were two trees between the barn and them and an old bathtub that'd likely been used as a watering trough. It's wasn't much but it'd have to do.

"Stay low and move fast," Weston told Addie, and helped her to her feet.

The marshals took up cover on either side of her while Weston stayed in front. They started to run the moment they came out from behind the woodpile and headed for the tub.

Not a second too soon.

Because the third firebomb came flying through the air.

Chapter Eighteen

Addie didn't look back, but she heard the now-familiar sound of the firebomb crashing into something. The woodpile, no doubt, and she had that confirmed when the four of them scrambled behind the old cast-iron tub.

Sweet heaven.

If they'd stayed just another second or two, they would have been caught in that tinderbox. Her heart was already in her throat. Already pounding too hard. She tried to steady it for the baby's sake, but she failed.

The ground was frozen, and it didn't take long for the cold to seep through her jeans and shoes. Weston was practically on top of her, the front of his body pressing against her back. She could feel the thud of his heartbeat and the tightness of his muscles.

"It'll be okay," Weston told her.

At best that was wishful thinking, but Addie figured it was closer to a lie than anything else. They were far from okay, and if backup didn't arrive soon, they could all die.

Because the Moonlight Strangler or someone else wanted to kill her.

That broke her heart, not only for her precious baby. But also for Weston and the marshals who'd gotten caught up in this mess.

Addie looked back, and her gaze connected with Weston's. Thanks to the watery moonlight, she could actually see him. Despite his attempt to reassure her, the worry and the fear were right there, all over his face. But she also saw something else.

Determination.

"He's not getting to you," Weston said like an oath.

Even though there was no way he could guarantee that, it gave her hope and was a reminder that she couldn't give in to the fear. The stakes were too high for that.

"We have to move fast again," Weston added a moment later.

She'd already spotted the pair of trees between them and the barn, and that's where they headed. Addie held her breath, bracing herself for another firebomb or even gunfire.

But nothing happened.

They made it to the trees, ducking behind them. Immediately, the marshals and Weston surveyed the area. No doubt looking for anyone trying to sneak closer. But it was impossible to see the road now because of the smoke and fire.

"Come on," Daniel said, and they all took off again.

Even though Weston was keeping watch, he was also glancing at her. And cursing. Probably because he was afraid that all of this running wouldn't be good for the baby. That didn't concern her so much since she'd been physically active on the ranch, but Addie was terrified about what the stress was doing. And that thought brought on the anger.

She hated that monster out there. Hated that he was trying to take everything away from her.

They moved behind another tree. Not nearly wide enough to cover them all, and that's likely why they only stayed there a few seconds. Just long enough for Addie to catch her breath.

They started for the barn. Such as it was. It appeared to be falling apart, and the door was literally hanging on by a hinge. It was swaying back and forth with the gusting night air.

Her lungs were burning now from the cold and exertion. And she was shivering despite the jacket. Every step they took was a reminder that it could be her last.

But no more firebombs.

No shots of any kind.

They finally made it to the rickety barn, and Weston pulled her behind the back of it. There was no door there, only the one in the front, but he soon took care of that problem. He bashed his shoulder against some of the boards. It didn't take much for several of them to give way, and he pushed them aside to make an opening.

"Wait here," Daniel insisted, and he stooped down to maneuver himself through the makeshift opening.

Daniel kept his gun lifted, but he didn't go far. Just a few steps inside. "Can't see a thing," he grumbled.

Too bad. Because someone could be hiding in there. Yes, there was a sensor on the road, but that didn't mean their attacker hadn't managed to get a hired thug in through the pasture and into the barn.

Daniel moved deeper into the barn while the rest of them waited. Addie forced herself to slow down her breathing and tried to stay calm. Hard to do with every nerve in her body on full alert.

That full alert went even higher when she heard a sound. Not from inside the barn but from the area in front of the burning house.

A gunshot.

And it came right at them.

Weston cursed, sheltering her with his body. Or at

least he was trying to do that. The shooter clearly had them in his line of sight.

"Get inside," Weston insisted, and he pushed her through the opening of the barn, following right in behind her.

Kirk stepped in as well, the three lawmen instantly pivoting in all directions. No doubt looking for anyone who was about to attack them.

The barn was indeed dark, but there was some moonlight filtering in through the front door. There were also holes in the roof, and the light came through like needles hitting on the hay-strewn floor. Not nearly enough illumination, though, to see much beyond where they were standing in the middle of the barn.

There were shadows.

Plenty of them. And plenty of places for a gunman to hide, too.

It was also cold. So cold that Addie could see her own breath, and she started to shiver.

None of them said a word. They all stood there, just listening. And thankfully the shots outside stopped so that made it a little easier to hear what was going on. Well, it would have if the wind hadn't been causing that door to creak or if her own heartbeat hadn't been crashing in her ears.

Weston maneuvered her away from the opening. Away from the door, too, and about five feet away into what was left of a stall. Daniel stayed in front of her while Kirk went to the left. Weston, to the right.

Both searching the area.

Both also keeping watch on the front door in case the shooter tried to make his way inside.

Her breath froze when Weston came to an abrupt

stop, and he whipped his gun toward the far right front corner. Not too far from that creaking door.

Daniel was a big man, but Addie came up on her toes so she could see what had captured Weston's attention. And she soon saw it.

Something, or maybe some*one*, in the shadows.

"Get down!" Weston shouted, and he did the same, diving to the side of some crumbling hay bales.

At that moment, a gust of wind caught the barn door and slapped it fully open so that the shadow was no longer a shadow. It was a man, and Addie saw his face.

And she also saw the gun he held in his hand.

OGDEN.

Of course.

Weston figured Ogden had some part in this, and that gun in his hand proved he was up to his old tricks. He was there to try to kill Addie again, but Weston had no intention of letting him do that.

"Addie, stay down," Weston warned her, and he took aim at Ogden.

Weston expected the man to fire or at least try to duck behind something. But he didn't. Ogden just stood there, staring at him.

"Why are you here?" Ogden asked.

Not only was it a strange question, Ogden's body language was strange, too. He had his left hand bracketed on the barn wall, using it to support himself.

The barn door shut again, but Weston's eyes had adjusted enough to the darkness that he could see that Ogden wasn't pointing the gun at them. It was aimed at the floor.

"What are you doing here?" Weston fired back.

Ogden shook his head and looked around. Not the

kind of look of a man trying to escape or decide what to do. He was looking at the place as if seeing it for the first time.

"Why did you bring me here?" Ogden said.

Weston cursed. Then he groaned. Either Ogden was high or drunk, or else he wanted to make it seem that way. It wouldn't matter which. Weston didn't trust this fool for a minute. Nor would he let Ogden distract him so that the hired guns could come in for the kill.

He motioned for Kirk to keep watch at the back. Weston did the same at the front, but he doubted he'd actually be able to see anyone sneaking up on them. The darkness would work in favor of their attackers, and there were plenty of ways to get to the barn. Of course, a shooter wouldn't have to get too close to send another firebomb their way.

"I didn't bring you here," Weston said to Ogden, "but you're going to tell me why you're holding that gun."

Ogden glanced at the gun then. And he dropped it. He frantically shook his head again. "That's not my gun." He touched his fingers to his temple. "Did you give me pills or something to get me here?"

"I didn't give you anything."

Weston went closer to Ogden to kick the gun out of his reach. He also patted the man down. Ogden wasn't carrying any other weapons. Nor did he smell of alcohol. However, he was wobbly, and if Weston hadn't helped Ogden lean against the wall, he probably would have fallen.

Heck, maybe someone had drugged him, or he could have drugged himself. Once backup arrived, Ogden could be taken and tested. Too bad backup was still probably fifteen minutes out.

"Now it's your turn to answer some questions," Weston demanded. "Did you hire those shooters out there?"

Ogden's eyes widened. "No. Why would I do something like that?"

"You tell me. But my guess is you wanted to try to have another go at Addie. Especially since that attack on the road failed big-time."

"Attack?"

"Yeah, you know—the one where you blocked the road with the cows and then tried to kill Addie."

No headshaking this time. "That wasn't me."

"I saw you," Addie insisted. "You were in the woods near Daisy's house."

Ogden made a sound of disbelief. "But I wasn't there to kill you. I was running for my life."

Weston made his own sound. One of skepticism to let Ogden know he wasn't buying any of it. "And you just happened to be in the same area when bullets started flying?"

"Yes, because I escaped from a car. Someone kidnapped me again. Like this time. Someone must have kidnapped me and brought me here."

"Who would do that?"

Ogden didn't answer Weston for a long time, and the already distressed look on his face got a whole lot worse. "My father maybe."

"The Moonlight Strangler brought you here?" Weston was fishing for info and hoped he didn't get a yes from Ogden. Not on this anyway.

Ogden turned toward the stall where he'd heard Addie's voice. "Addie, you have to believe me. I don't want you dead. Not anymore. I was confused. I thought my father was telling me to kill you. But I don't think it was my father doing that."

"Then who was it?" Weston asked.

Ogden opened his mouth to answer, but the sound of the blast stopped him. Not from a firebomb this time but from another bullet. And this shot sounded a whole lot closer than the other ones.

Weston kept an eye on Ogden, but he pivoted in the direction of the barn door. Just as another shot came.

This one slammed into the rotting wood at the front of the barn. And it wasn't a single shot. More came. One right after another, and Weston had no choice but to dive back to the ground with Addie. He also heard something else he didn't want to hear.

A thud.

And Daniel started cursing.

Kirk had fallen and was clutching his chest.

Hell, the marshal had been shot.

Except he hadn't been, Weston quickly realized. No blood. The gunman had fired a shot into the Kevlar vest that Kirk was wearing. It wouldn't be deadly, but Weston knew from experience that it hurt like the devil, and it'd clearly knocked the breath from Kirk because he was gasping for air.

Gasping in pain, too.

Daniel pulled Kirk to the side, away from the door, and began to unstrap the vest so he could get the scalding hot bullet off Kirk's skin.

The shots didn't stop. They continued to tear their way through the barn.

"Get down!" Weston yelled to Ogden when the man just stood there in a daze.

Ogden seemed to freeze. For a second or two. And then he got down all right.

But not the way Weston had figured he would.

Ogden, too, clutched his chest. No Kevlar vest for him. So, this time, there was indeed some blood.

He'd been shot.

"Help me," Ogden groaned before collapsing to the ground.

Weston didn't go to Ogden because he heard something behind him. Not Kirk or Daniel. But something else.

Something that got his complete attention.

Addie made a strangled sound.

And that's when Weston saw the man come through the back opening and put the gun to Addie's head.

Chapter Nineteen

Addie didn't move fast enough. She'd heard the footsteps behind her a split second too late and hadn't scrambled out of the way in time.

It could turn out to be a deadly mistake.

Because someone now had her at gunpoint and was using her as a human shield to stop Weston and the marshals from shooting him.

The fear slammed through her, but she tried not to panic. Hard to do, though, when her baby was right back in danger again.

She couldn't see her attacker's face. But Weston could. And judging from his profanity and glare, he knew the man. So this probably wasn't just another hired gun but rather the person behind all these attacks.

"Canales," she said without having to look back at him.

Boggs wasn't much taller than she was, and this man was stooping, trying to keep his body hidden behind hers. It had to be Canales.

"Put down that gun and move away from Addie," Weston ordered him.

"You really think that'll work?" Canales asked, the sarcasm dripping from his voice. "I'll put it down when I'm done here. Which shouldn't be long. I just need a few answers."

"So do we," Weston fired back.

Daniel made a sound of agreement about that and moved protectively in front of Kirk, who was still on the ground trying to regain his breath.

"Is he dead?" Canales asked tipping his head to Ogden.

Weston didn't even look back at Ogden. He kept his attention focused on Canales and her. "Probably. Why, are you all torn up about that?"

"No. But he would have made such a good scapegoat. I'd planned on pinning all of this on him. Copycatting his daddy will make good press. The reporters will gobble it up."

They would. *If* Canales got away with this. Addie had to figure out a way to make sure he didn't.

"Now all of you toss your guns into the center of the barn," Canales demanded. "If you don't do it right now, I'll shoot Addie. I won't kill her yet, but I will hurt her."

She believed him, and any shot could cause her to miscarry. Still, it sickened her when the marshals and Weston threw their guns onto the floor near Canales. She wasn't sure if Weston had a backup weapon on him or not. They'd run from the house in such a hurry that it was possible none of them had another gun they could use to try to put a stop to this.

"I'm surprised you didn't send one of your hired lackeys to do your dirty work," Weston said to Canales.

"My *lackeys* have failed, time and time again. And because they didn't do their jobs, Addie got yet another round with that therapist." Canales put his mouth against her ear. "I just need to know what you remembered during the hypnosis session."

So that's what this was about. Or at least part of it. She knew from the DNA test that Canales wasn't the Moonlight Strangler, but it didn't mean he wasn't working for him.

"Is Boggs the Moonlight Strangler?" she asked.

"Answer my question!" Canales shouted.

She jumped from the sheer volume of his voice, but Addie steeled herself. Or rather tried to do that. "You answer mine first, and then I'll tell you what you want to know. Is Boggs the Moonlight Strangler?"

"Not a chance." Canales mumbled some raw profanity. "The man can barely tie his own shoes. Hardly the serial killer type. He's much better suited to being a politician. Or at least the front for a politician, and that was our arrangement."

It was possible Boggs could be lured into a deal like that. But did that mean Boggs was innocent? Or maybe he was in on this plan. If so, backup might be able to capture him if he was out there somewhere. Of course, her first hope was that backup would be able to save Weston, the marshals and her.

"So who's the Moonlight Strangler?" Weston snapped.

"Wouldn't have a clue," Canales answered, "but I'll soon find out. He's not pleased with me. I got some nasty letters telling me to back off. Or else. I went with the *or else* and decided to set a trap for him. If all went well, that trap is being sprung as we speak."

A trap? She wondered what it was. Or if Canales was even telling the truth. After all, he didn't need the Moonlight Strangler around if he wanted to pin their deaths on him and Ogden.

"You decided to let everyone believe the Moonlight Strangler was behind this," she concluded. And Canales sure didn't deny it.

"We're getting off track, and I don't have a lot of time." Canales jammed the gun even harder against Addie's head. "What did you remember?" he repeated.

Addie winced, hoping her sound of pain didn't send

Weston charging at the man. He certainly looked ready to tear Canales limb from limb.

"I didn't remember anything," she said.

"Liar! The FBI's doing all kinds of checks on gun-running operations in the area thirty years ago."

So, they were back to that. "I didn't remember any gunrunning, only men with guns."

"Tell me everything you said to that FBI shrink." Even though she still couldn't see his face, Addie knew he was speaking through clenched teeth.

Anything she said to him right now was a risk. A huge one. But there was no way he would allow any of them to live anyway. No. His plan was likely to learn whatever information she had and then he'd kill them all. Canales couldn't leave them as witnesses. After that, he'd work on trying to cover everything up.

"I remembered you." Addie let that hang between them for several moments. "Of course, I didn't know your name at the time, but I was able to describe the guns. And Boggs and you. The two of you came once when Daisy wasn't there. You met with her husband."

She held her breath, waiting and praying that her lie wouldn't get her killed right here, right now.

Addie had no idea if Canales had actually ever been to Daisy's house, much less with Boggs and a gun shipment. The only thing she had remembered were several armed men. She had no clear images of their faces.

But Canales didn't know that.

"You don't have to worry, though," she continued, "the statute of limitations is up on the gunrunning."

She left it at that, though Canales no doubt knew that the gunrunning was the least of his problems. The conspiracy. The cover-up. All of that would send him to jail for the rest of his life.

A feral sound tore from his throat. "Everything I've worked for could be gone. And all because of you!"

He dug the gun barrel so hard into her temple that she felt the skin break. Addie clamped her teeth over her bottom lip to stop herself from crying out in pain, but she hadn't needed Weston to hear anything for him to react. He charged toward Canales.

Canales reacted, too. Fast.

He turned the gun on Weston. And Canales fired.

The shot was deafening, and it drowned out Addie's own scream. Everything was one big blur of shouts and movement, but the only thing she could think of was Weston.

Mercy, had he been shot? Or worse. Was he dead?

It took her several painful moments to focus on what had actually happened. Weston had scrambled to the side of the barn, and even though she couldn't see all of him, he was alive. He lifted his head from behind one of the hay bales.

"Try that again," Canales warned him, "and I'll have the privilege of killing you myself. The same goes for you two," he added to the other marshals.

Her ears were roaring from the blast, and the shock of nearly losing Weston had put her in panic mode. But she finally heard something she'd wanted to hear since this latest nightmare had started.

Sirens.

Backup was finally here.

Of course, that didn't mean they were all safe. She was betting Canales had hired thugs stashed out there somewhere. Judging from the threat he'd just made, he planned on using those thugs to finish them off.

"This isn't over," Canales insisted. "I can do damage control with the FBI. And I can discredit the memories of a brat-kid, especially one with killer blood running through her veins."

As it usually did, the killer blood comment turned her stomach. But from the corner of the barn, she heard a loud groan. Not one of pain, either.

It was the sound of outrage.

At first she thought it'd come from Weston. But then Addie saw Ogden come off the ground. He snatched up his gun.

And pulled the trigger.

WESTON CURSED HIMSELF.

He'd been so focused on stopping Canales that he hadn't noticed Ogden. Weston moved as fast as he could and prayed it was fast enough to stop a bullet from hitting Addie.

But it was already too late.

Except the shot hadn't gone toward Addie, Weston quickly realized.

Ogden had shot into the back opening of the barn. At first Weston thought the man just had bad aim, but then he heard someone groan. The ski-mask wearing gunman who'd been waiting outside crumpled to the ground. Weston hadn't had the right angle so he hadn't even known the guy was out there.

Canales cursed and moved, too, dragging Addie to the side of the barn.

Or rather that's what he was trying to do.

Addie wasn't making it easy for him. She was fighting to get away, and she rammed her elbow into the man's stomach. It didn't stop him, but Canales did bash his gun against the side of Addie's head.

The rage went through him, so strong that Weston could have sworn he saw red.

Weston grabbed his gun from the floor and raced toward Canales. The man still didn't have control of Addie, though he tried to put the gun to her head. Not that he would need a head shot to kill her. With all the struggling going on, the gun could accidentally go off, and he could lose both Addie and the baby.

He had to make sure that didn't happen.

Weston immediately tossed his gun aside so he could dive into the fray. He hit the ground, hard, and it nearly knocked the breath out of him. Still, that didn't stop him. Weston latched onto Canales's hand while he tried to push Addie out of the way.

From the corner of his eye, Weston saw Daniel run in Ogden's direction. Good. Yes, Ogden had shot that ski-mask-wearing thug, but there was no telling what else he would do.

Canales kicked Weston, the blow landing right in his stomach. It dazed him for a second. Just enough for Canales to grab Addie by the hair and drag her a few inches away.

Weston went after him again.

No way was he letting Canales hurt her. But that's exactly what Canales was trying to do. Addie had hold of his right wrist and she was obviously trying to wrestle the gun away from him, but Canales was a lot stronger and bigger than she was, and he got the barrel aimed at her head again.

"Back off," Canales growled to Weston.

With Addie still struggling, Canales managed to get into the corner with her. Hell. She was his hostage again.

Outside, the sirens stopped, and Weston couldn't hear the sounds of anyone about to burst in and rescue them.

It was entirely possible that Canales's hired guns had overpowered the backup, too.

"You want her to die?" Canales taunted. "Then, make a move toward me. She won't have time to draw another breath."

Weston believed him, and that's the only reason he didn't lunge at the man. For now anyway. But when he got the chance, he was going to make Canales pay, and pay hard, for this.

In the darkness, Weston's gaze met Addie's. She no longer looked terrified, and that wasn't a look of surrender in her eyes.

"I'm sorry," she said.

Weston shook his head. "Don't." He didn't know exactly what she had in mind, but he didn't want her trying to fight her way out of this. "Think of the baby," Weston added.

Yeah, it was dirty, but it worked. He saw that in her eyes, too.

"A baby? Oh, that's touching," Canales snapped. "And it works in my favor. You want your kid to live?"

It took Weston a moment to realize that Canales was talking to him. "Of course I want my baby and Addie to live. How can I make that happen?"

"Easy. I take Addie with me, and you'll help me undo all the damage she's done. It might include taking out a few FBI agents who can't be bribed. That idiot therapist, too."

Hell. Canales wanted him to murder to tie up all these loose ends.

"I can't trust you," Weston insisted. "How do I know you won't kill Addie the moment you leave here with her?"

"You don't. That's a chance you'll just have to take."

Addie was shaking her head, but it wasn't necessary. No way would Weston agree to a deal like that, because if Canales managed to get Addie out of here, there's no way he'd keep her alive.

"I'm Sheriff Lawton," someone called out. Backup. He was the sheriff from a neighboring town, and apparently Canales's thugs hadn't gotten to him.

Not yet anyway.

Weston hoped the sheriff had brought plenty of men with him.

"Marshal Seaver?" the sheriff added. "We got a problem out here."

"Yeah, we got a problem in here, too," Daniel answered. "A gunman with a hostage. What's going on out there?"

"There's a guy behind a tree, and he's armed with some kind of grenade-launcher-looking thing. He's got it aimed at the barn."

Not a grenade but a firebomb.

Daniel cursed. "Tell him not to pull the trigger. Tell him his boss is still alive in here."

That might stop the idiot from killing them all. But if he managed to shoot that firebomb into the rickety barn, their chances of surviving wouldn't be very good.

"Hank?" Canales called out, obviously speaking to his hired gun. "If I'm not out in one minute, launch that firebomb."

"But, boss, you'll die." It was easy to hear the hesitation in the man's voice.

"Yeah, but so will everybody else in here." Canales glared at Weston.

"You're bluffing," Weston snarled.

Canales laughed. "Either let me leave with Addie…" He stopped, shook his head in disgust. "You're not going to let me leave."

It wasn't a question, and in the same breath, Canales shouted out to his hired gun. "Go ahead, Hank. Fire!"

There was no time to react. None. Weston heard the ominous sound. A split second later, the metal canister crashed through the front of the barn.

ADDIE TRIED TO shout for everyone to run, but she didn't get the chance to do or say anything.

Canales hooked his arm around her and, with her in tow, he leaped through the makeshift opening in the back of the barn. They immediately fell onto the ground, but thankfully, she didn't land on her stomach. Instead, she landed on the dead guy Ogden had shot just minutes earlier.

"Weston!" she yelled.

But she saw him before she even finished calling his name. He hurdled through the opening, landing right next to her.

Not a second too soon.

The flames and smoke swooshed out at them. The heat was blistering hot, but Weston saved her from being burned by scooping her up. He took off running. However, they weren't running alone.

Canales was right behind them.

The man came bolting out of the smoky cloud, his arms and legs pumping as fast as they could go.

"What about the marshals and Ogden?" she managed to ask, though Addie wasn't sure how she could speak with so little breath.

"I think they got out through the front," Weston said.

Think. But he wasn't sure.

She prayed it was true, that they'd managed to get out in time. Even though Ogden had attempted to kill her several days ago, he'd also tried to save them tonight by shooting that hired gun Canales had brought with him.

Or at least he'd appeared to save them. It was still possible Ogden was in on this.

Weston ran, but they'd only made it ten yards or so from the burning barn when Addie heard the gunshot. For one terrifying moment she thought Canales had shot Weston in the back, but then she realized that the sound had come from the front of the barn.

Had that hired thug managed to shoot Kirk or Daniel?

Addie didn't have time to figure that out, though, because she looked back and saw Canales had quit running.

He still had his gun.

"Stop or you die," Canales warned them. Not a shout, just a cold-blooded order that Addie knew they had no choice but to obey.

Weston pulled up, immediately releasing her from his arms so that she was standing. And so that he was in front of her.

Protecting her again.

The problem was that Weston no longer had his gun. He'd likely dropped it in the earlier scuffle with Canales. And there really was no place for them to take cover. They were literally out in the open where Canales or one of his henchmen could gun them down.

"This is over," Weston told Canales. "Killing us now won't do anything except maybe add the death penalty to the charges you'll face."

"I'm already facing the death penalty," he admitted.

That was it, the only thing Canales said before he lifted his gun and took aim at them. He was no doubt about to pull the trigger when there was another sound.

A loud crash.

Behind him, the barn collapsed and sent a spray of smoke, debris and fire right at him. Canales glanced over his shoulder, cursed and started running again.

This time, right toward them.

And Weston was waiting for him.

"Get down," Weston told her.

He lunged right at Canales, tackling him, and like in the barn they went to the ground.

Weston didn't get hold of the gun, but he did managed to grab Canales's right wrist, and he tried to wrench the gun away from him.

Canales held on.

Even when Weston bashed his hand against the ground.

Addie immediately looked around for something she could use to help. A rock or anything. But there was nothing. Just bits of the fiery debris from the barn, and Canales and Weston were rolling around, both of them jockeying for position.

The jockeying stopped with a gunshot.

The sound jolted through her and nearly brought her to her knees. Oh, God. Had Weston been hurt?

She couldn't tell, especially when the fight started again. Weston drew back his fist and punched Canales in the face, but the man must have been fueled with pure adrenaline because he was fighting like a wild animal.

Addie hurried closer to see if she could help, but she didn't get far when she saw Canales bring up his hand again. He still had hold of the gun, and he was trying to aim it at her.

She dropped back down to the ground.

Just as the shot blasted past her.

Weston glanced back at her. Cursing. And he punched Canales again. And again. Canales finally moved the gun so that it was no longer aimed at her.

But rather at Weston.

"Watch out," she warned Weston.

Though it was already too late for a warning. The sound of the shot tore through the night.

And the fight stopped.

Addie thought maybe her heart had, too.

She could only stay there for several terrifying moments. Moments where she didn't know if Weston was dead or alive. He wasn't moving. But then, neither was Canales.

"Weston?" she finally got out, and she forced her legs to move.

Addie went to Weston, caught him by the shoulder and moved him off Canales. That's when she saw the blood.

"I'm okay," Weston said to her.

It took her several more heart-stopping moments to realize it wasn't Weston's blood. It belonged to Canales, and it had covered the front of his shirt. Weston had hold of the man's gun.

Despite his injury, Canales laughed. "It's time for a deal."

"You're bleeding out," Weston told him. "Besides, you've got nothing I want."

"Maybe. But if I were you, I'd do everything possible to keep me alive."

"And why would I do that?" Weston asked.

Canales laughed again, but it was followed by a weak, shallow cough. "Because I know where the Moonlight Strangler is. I trapped him. And if you want him, then you'll make sure I'm a free man."

Chapter Twenty

This ordeal wasn't over, but Weston hoped that it soon would be.

No thanks to Canales.

The man hadn't budged on telling them about the Moonlight Strangler before the ambulance had taken him away, but with some luck—or rather Jericho's interrogation skills—they might get the information from Canales's injured gunman, the one Daniel had shot. They'd gotten lucky that it wasn't a serious injury, so Jericho was with him at the hospital where he was being stitched up.

Weston didn't know the hired gun's name or what had caused him to get involved with a snake like Canales, but it didn't matter now. The only thing that mattered was his telling Jericho the location of the Moonlight Strangler. If there was a location to tell, that is. And if the thug wouldn't or couldn't tell them, then maybe Canales would do that when and if he came out of surgery.

The other thing that mattered, and it mattered most, was that Addie and the baby were okay. For now. She still had that stunned look in her eyes. Still didn't seem too steady on her feet, which was why Weston had his arm around her.

That was one of the reasons anyway.

The other reason was because having her close stead-ied his own raw nerves.

"Canales could have been lying," Addie repeated, something both Weston and she had been reminding themselves of since they'd arrived at the sheriff's of-fice to wait on news from Jericho. "We should be at the hospital to see if we can pressure the thug into talking."

Yes, that was tempting, and if Addie hadn't been in the picture, that's exactly where Weston would be. But it was still too big of a risk for Addie to be in the open. Actually, it was a risk for her to be anywhere, but at least he had Jax, Kirk and Daniel at the Appaloosa Pass sher-iff's office to help guard her. Plus, the three lawmen were all working to track down some info on what was left of the investigation.

"I wish you'd sit down," Weston said to her—some-thing else he'd been repeating for the past hour.

She looked up at him, their gazes connecting. "I'm still too wired."

It was the same for him. So, Weston tried a kiss in-stead. Just a quick brush of his mouth to hers. Or at least that was the plan. But the kiss didn't stay quick. Weston added some pressure, pulled her closer to him until it fi-nally helped. He felt Addie practically sag against him.

The kiss and the hug garnered Jax's attention, but her brother only gave a half smile and continued his phone conversation.

"Maybe we'll hear something about Ogden soon," she said.

Addie didn't have to add that she was worried about him. She was. So was Weston, but probably not worried in the same way as Addie. After all, the man had tried to kill Addie a few days ago, and he was no doubt insane.

Even if he made a full recovery from his injuries, he'd spend the rest of his life in a mental hospital.

"Ogden did try to save us in the barn," Addie whispered.

He had indeed, and that was the only reason Weston didn't want to tear the man's head completely off. That and the fact that he was Addie's half-brother. However, that shared blood bond didn't extend to the Moonlight Strangler. Weston would kill him if he got the chance.

"SAPD picked up Boggs about a half hour ago," Jax said when he finished his latest call. "There won't be an arrest."

Not exactly a surprise. "Because of the statute of limitations on the gunrunning allegations," Weston said.

Jax nodded. "But at least Boggs is talking. He claims he only gave Canales money to fund the gunrunning, that he wasn't actually a part of it and that he wasn't part of the attacks, either."

"The cops believe him?" Addie asked.

Another nod from Jax. "There's nothing to link him to the attacks. Nothing to link him to anything that Canales did to get to Addie."

And Canales had done a lot. All because he'd been afraid that she might remember seeing him all those years ago.

"Boggs is ruined," Jax went on. "Even though he can't be charged with assorted felonies like Canales, if it's leaked to the press about his old connections to gunrunning, it'll cost him the campaign."

Good. That was something at least. Even if Boggs wasn't responsible for murder and attempted murder, he didn't deserve to hold political office.

"You okay?" Jax asked, his gaze nailed to Addie.

"No, she's not," Weston answered for her. "I'm taking her to the break room." There was a cot back there, and maybe she could get some rest.

"I'm okay, really," she insisted.

That was partly true. The medic had checked her out right after they'd arrived at the sheriff's office, and at least she hadn't physically been harmed. Mentally was a whole different story, but she dug in her heels to stay put.

"Convince me you're okay," Weston challenged.

She kissed him. Since he'd done the same to her just seconds earlier, he figured she'd gotten the idea from him. It was a nice distraction. Nice for his body, too, to feel that heat slide through him.

"Not very convincing," he grumbled.

Addie lifted her eyebrow. "Really?"

"The kiss doesn't prove you're okay. It just proves we're attracted to each other. We already knew that."

The eyebrow lift continued.

"Okay, more than just attracted," Weston admitted.

A whole lot more that he would have told her if Jax's phone hadn't rang.

"Jericho," Jax greeted when he answered the call.

That stopped Weston, and both Addie and he went back to Jax's desk so they could hear what Jericho had to say. Jax put the call on speaker for them.

"Canales died in surgery," Jericho started. "But the rat he hired started talking when I mentioned the death penalty was on the table. According to the rat, Canales lured the Moonlight Strangler to Daisy's house. I've got the county sheriff on his way there now, and yeah, he's taking plenty of backup with him. They'll be out there any minute now."

The county sheriff would need all the help he could get if he did indeed come face-to-face with the killer.

"Why lure him to Daisy's place?" Weston wanted to know.

"Apparently, Canales persuaded the killer that there was a photo at Daisy's that he needed to retrieve. A photo that would reveal his identity."

Addie pulled in a sharp breath. "We need to find that photo."

"Doesn't exist," Jericho explained. "According to the rat, it was just a lure to get the Strangler there so two more of Canales's hired guns could capture him. That way, Canales would look like the big hero, and that in turn would be some good publicity for the campaign."

Weston thought about that for a moment. Not a bad plan, but things had clearly gone to hell in a hand basket. However, he had the feeling this was more than just a campaign ploy. "If there was a connection between Canales, the Moonlight Strangler and the gunrunning, then Canales would want the Strangler dead so the connection couldn't come back to bite him."

"That's my best guess, too," Jericho agreed. "I can't think of another reason Canales would go to all that trouble to lure a killer there."

Neither could Weston. "Call me when you hear anything from the county sheriff."

"Will do. And you'd better take good care of my sister," Jericho added before he ended the call.

It wasn't a surprising request, but there was something in Jericho's voice. Not exactly a warning but more like a strong suggestion.

Or maybe Weston was reading what he wanted to read into it.

And what he wanted to read into it was that he did indeed want to take care of Addie. Not just because of the danger. And not just for tonight.

Weston realized he wanted a whole lot more.

"What?" Addie asked, staring at him.

Probably because he had a strange look on his face. The look of a man who'd just been thunderstruck.

Well, heck.

"When did this happen?" Weston had intended to keep that question in his head, but it somehow made it out of his mouth.

Addie kept staring. "When did what happen?" The last word sort of died on her lips though, and she shook her head. "No, you're not going to ask me to marry you."

Since that's exactly what he'd planned to do, Weston was sure he looked even more thunderstruck than before. He was also a little riled that Addie seemed riled.

"Why not?" Weston demanded.

Then he realized something else. The three lawmen in the squad room were no longer on their phones. They were listening to him fumbling around. And they were somewhat amused by it. Even Jax. Of course, he could be amused because Addie had just shot Weston down.

Or not.

"You giving up that easy?" Jax asked. "My advice, don't. You two belong together. More advice—finish this conversation in the break room." He tipped his head in that direction.

It seemed to be an endorsement from her brother. One that Weston didn't need, but was still thankful for. He couldn't say the same for Addie.

"Stay out of this," she warned Jax, and she no longer sounded exhausted and shaky.

"No," Addie continued once they made it to the break room. She whirled around to face him. "You're not going to propose to me simply because you're blaming yourself for the danger I was in. Or because you're relieved we're alive. Or because I'm pregnant with—"

Weston kissed her again. It was meant to distract her. And it worked.

Of course, it distracted him, too. Addie's mouth had a way of doing that to him. Ditto for the rest of her.

When they were both good and breathless, Weston broke the kiss and looked down at her. "What if I'm not asking for any of those reasons?"

She blinked, probably because she hadn't been expecting that. Or the knock that caused her to gasp. The door wasn't closed, but Jax had knocked on the frame to get their attention.

"Sorry to interrupt." Jax held up his phone.

Weston cursed but then remembered Jax wouldn't have come back here if it weren't important.

"Two things." Jax paused as if debating which news to give them first.

"Something happened?" Addie asked, touching her fingers to her mouth.

"Everyone's okay," her brother reassured her. "Well, everyone who counts. Ogden is out of surgery and will soon be on the way to a state mental hospital. He wanted to give you a message, though. He says he's sorry."

While that seemed to soothe Addie a little, both Weston and she were waiting for the other boot to drop.

"The county sheriff didn't catch the Moonlight Strangler," Weston tossed out.

"No, he didn't," Jax verified. "But the killer was at

Daisy's house. At least it looks that way. Both of Canales's hired guns are dead. Both strangled and their faces cut."

The same MO as the Moonlight Strangler.

Since the face cut wasn't common knowledge, it was their proof that her birth father had indeed been there.

Jax came closer and held his phone out for Addie to see. "The Strangler left you a handwritten message."

Weston's instinct was to step in front of her, to protect her from reading whatever the killer had left for her. She'd already been through way too much tonight to have more added to her burden. But there was no way he could stop her, of course.

"Addie, I was never after you and yours," she read aloud. "Never will be. That was Canales playing games, and he paid for it. Blood ties are worth something to me. Be happy."

It wasn't a scrawled message but rather neatly written on a plain piece of paper.

"You all right?" Jax asked her.

Addie nodded. Cleared her throat and nodded again. "It's really from him. He means it. He won't be coming after us."

"Maybe. It could be a fake," Jax argued.

"No," she argued back. Though she didn't elaborate, Weston could tell she felt, in her gut, that she was safe from her birth father.

He felt it, too.

"The note will be processed for prints and trace," Jax added.

Weston doubted they'd find anything. The Moonlight Strangler had almost certainly taken precautions. And while Weston still hated the man to his core, he was thankful that he'd given Addie this small measure of peace.

Weston felt that same sense of peace. Finally. Addie and his baby would be safe.

"Guess there's no reason for you two to hang around here," Jax said. He shifted his gaze to Weston. "Why don't you go ahead and take Addie home...after you've finished your proposal."

Jax was probably attempting to lighten things up a little. He failed. Well, kind of. The somber mood was still there, hanging over them, but for the first time in days there was the hope of something good. Something right.

"Will you marry me?" Weston asked, and he kissed her again, hoping it would cloud her mind enough for her to jump right into saying yes.

It didn't work.

Another "no" left her mouth when they broke for air. "There's only one reason I'll ever marry, and it's not because I'm pregnant."

Oh.

That.

Well, shoot. Weston regrouped. "I thought it was obvious. I'm in love with you."

"Obvious, yes. But you still have to say it."

Weston smiled. "I love you." And just in case she hadn't caught it, he repeated it a couple more times in between kisses. "And now I want the words, too. Give them to me, Addie."

She pulled back, ran her tongue over her bottom lip. A little gesture that had his body begging for a yes and a whole lot more. But first, he wanted that yes.

"Well?" he prompted.

Addie fought a smile. "Convince me that this is exactly what you want, that you're really in love with me."

"Convince you?" he repeated. "I think I've heard that expression somewhere before."

"The man I love says it a lot. But this time, I want more than words. Convince me, Weston."

He did exactly that. He convinced Addie the best way he knew how. Weston pulled Addie to him and kissed her.

* * * * *

USA TODAY *bestselling author Delores Fossen's* *brand-new series,* **APPALOOSA PASS RANCH,** *is just getting started.* *Don't miss TAKING AIM AT THE SHERIFF*

Every muscle in his body stiffened as he thought he heard a faint cry coming from the hole in the ground.

He turned on his flashlight and shone it down, seeing nothing but earth.

Had he heard her crying? Weeping because she knew this was the end of her walks? Should he go down and console her? Or let her cry in private? He had a feeling that if she was crying, she wouldn't welcome his presence.

He heard her again, only this time instead of weeping, it sounded like a scream of terror. With his gun in one hand, his flashlight in the other and adrenaline pumping through his body, he dropped down into the hole.

The first thing he saw was the penlight beam, shining at him from the floor in the distance. What he didn't see was any sign of Savannah.

"Savannah!" He yelled her name, and it echoed in the air.

He quickly walked forward, his gun leading the way and his heart pounding a million beats a minute. Where was Savannah? Why was her flashlight on the ground? What in the hell was happening?

He didn't know, but he wouldn't give up until he found her.

SCENE OF THE CRIME: THE DEPUTY'S PROOF

CARLA CASSIDY

MILLS & BOON

Published in Great Britain 2015
by Mills & Boon, an imprint of Harlequin (UK) Limited,
Eton House, 18-24 Paradise Road, Richmond, Surrey, TW9 1SR

© 2015 Carla Bracale

ISBN: 978-0-263-25322-1

46-1115

Printed and bound in Spain
by CPI, Barcelona

Carla Cassidy is a *New York Times* bestselling author who has written more than one hundred books for Mills & Boon. Carla believes the only thing better than curling up with a good book to read is sitting down at the computer with a good story to write. She's looking forward to writing many more books and bringing hours of pleasure to readers.

Chapter One

It was a perfect night for a ghost walk. The Mississippi moon was nearly hidden from view by the low-lying fog that seeped across the land and invaded the streets of the small town of Lost Lagoon.

Savannah Sinclair retied the double-beamed flashlight that hung at her waist beneath a white, gauzy, floor-length gown. She used talcum powder to lighten her face and knew that most people would think her actions were more than a little crazy.

Maybe she'd been a little crazy for the past two years, since the night her older sister, her best friend, Shelly, had been murdered and found floating in the lagoon.

From that night forward, Savannah's life had been forever changed. *She* had been forever changed, and what she planned to do at midnight tonight just proved that Shelly's death still haunted her in a profound way she couldn't get past.

She stared at her ghostly countenance in the bathroom mirror and wondered, if Shelly's murder had been solved and her killer arrested, would things be different?

She whirled away from the mirror and left the bathroom. The clock on the nightstand in the bedroom indicated that it was eleven thirty. Time to move.

She turned off all the lights in the four-bedroom house that had once been home to her family, grabbed a palm-sized penlight and then slipped out the back door.

The dark night closed in around her, and she glanced at her nearest neighbor's house, satisfied that all the lights were off and her neighbor, Jeffrey Allen, was surely in bed. She used the penlight in her hand to guide her toward a large bush at the back of the yard.

Shoving several of the leafy branches aside, she revealed a hole big enough for a person to drop into. She knew there were earthen steps to aid in the three-foot drop, and she easily accomplished it, finding herself at the beginning of a narrow earthen tunnel.

She'd discovered the tunnel last summer when she'd been working in the yard. Initially she had to crouch for several feet before the tunnel descended deep enough that she could stand in an upright position and walk.

Half the town already thought she was crazy, gone around the bend because of her parents' abandonment, her brother's rages and the murder of her sister.

If they only knew what she did on moonless nights when she wasn't working the night shift at the Pirate's Inn, they'd probably have her locked up in an insane asylum for the rest of her life. But there was a rhyme and reason to her madness.

The tunnel system was like a spider web running under the town, although Savannah had only explored one corridor, the one that would take her directly to the place where her sister had been murdered.

She moved confidently with the aid of the bright but tiny beam of her penlight leading the way. It had been rumored that Lost Lagoon had once been home to a band of pirates, and she suspected these tunnels had been made by them years and years ago.

She occasionally moved by dark passageways she had never explored and wondered if anyone had been in them in the last hundred years or so.

She hadn't told anyone of her discovery of the tunnels. They were her secret, her voyage to the last link to her sister. It took her a little over fifteen minutes to reach her destination, a set of six old wooden planks embedded into the ground that led up to another hole beneath a bush at the base of a cypress tree.

She shut off her penlight, climbed up the planks and crouched behind the tree trunk. At this time on a Friday night, most of the town would be at Jimmy's Place, a popular bar and grill on Main Street.

But moonless Friday nights when the fog rolled in— the teenagers in town knew those were the nights that Shelly's ghost walked the night.

Savannah could hear them, a small group of teenage girls giggling behind a row of bushes that separated the swampy lagoon from the edge of town. Set in the center of the row of bushes was a stone bench where her sister and her boyfriend, Bo McBride, used to sit at night and talk about their future, but Shelly had never gotten a future.

Between the bushes and the swamp was just enough solid ground for a "ghost" to walk in front of the bushes and the bench and disappear into the wooded, swampy area on the other side.

She remained hidden for several minutes until she thought it was just about midnight, and then she turned on the flashlight strapped around her waist beneath the gauzy white gown. The double-sided beam produced an otherworldly glow from her head to her toes.

Performance time, she thought. Her role as Shelly's ghost required very little of her, an appropriate costume but no script to memorize. She started to walk across the "stage." She walked slowly, her head half-turned away and her long dark hair hiding her features from her audience.

"There she is!" A young female voice squealed.

"It's Shelly. It's really Shelly," another voice cried out.

Savannah embraced the sound of her sister's name into her heart as she continued her walk. Tears burned in her eyes, but she swallowed against them. Shelly's ghost didn't cry. She just walked across the place where she'd been murdered and then disappeared almost as quickly as she'd appeared.

To the continuing squeals of her sister's name, Savannah reached the woods on the other side of the "stage." She shut off the flashlight at her waist and headed for a tangled growth of vines behind which was the small entrance of a cave. The opening of the cave was hidden and couldn't be seen unless you knew what you were looking for.

She quickly moved the concealing vines aside and clicked on her little penlight, using it after she'd entered the fairly large cave that led downhill. The cave narrowed somewhat as it continued but remained wide enough that a pirate could push trunks of treasure or buckets of jewels through it.

This passageway eventually intersected with the one that would take her to her backyard, a perfect escape route for the ghost of the dead.

She moved quickly, eager now to get back to the house where she lived. It was the house she'd grown up in, but it hadn't felt like home since two months after Shelly's murder, when her parents had left town and moved to a small retirement community in Florida.

They'd left the house for Savannah and her older brother, Mac, to live in. Mac had married and moved out months before, leaving Savannah in the house that contained far too many haunting memories.

She felt a cathartic relief and a little bit of guilt as she reached the earthen steps that would bring her up into her backyard.

Everyone in Lost Lagoon loved a good ghost story, she told herself. The town was steeped in stories of the walking dead. The ghosts of dead pirates were rumored to walk the hallways of Pirate's Inn.

Savannah had been working there as night manager for a little over a year, and while she occasionally heard odd bumps and thumps in the night, she'd never seen a ghost.

But the rumors of sightings of apparitions were repeated again and again by thrilled townspeople and occasional tourists. The ghost of an old, toothless hag supposedly appeared in the alley beside the Lost Lagoon Cafe, and several people had sworn they'd seen the faint wisp of ghostly figures around Mama Baptiste's Apothecary Shop.

She turned off her penlight, stepped up out of the tunnel and squeaked in surprise as she saw a tall, dark figure standing before her. She fumbled to turn on her penlight once again and found herself face-to-face with Deputy Josh Griffin.

"Hi, Savannah. Busy night?" he asked.

Her heart sank as she realized she'd been busted.

Josh shone his own flashlight on the slender, dark-haired woman. Her doe-like brown eyes were huge in a face that was unnaturally pale. Her lower lip trembled even as she raised her chin and glared at him defiantly.

"If you're going to arrest me, then just get on with it," she exclaimed.

"How about we get out of the dark and go inside and talk about my options," he replied.

Savannah Sinclair and the murder of her sister, Shelly, had haunted Josh for a long time. Before the murder Savannah had been a lively, charming twenty-seven-year-old who was often seen out and about town.

"Okay," she replied. Despite her initial upthrust

of her chin, as he walked just behind her he saw her shoulders slump forward and felt the energy that had momentarily radiated from her disappear.

Despite the ridiculous outfit she wore, he noticed the slight sway of her slender hips beneath the gauzy material, could smell the faint scent of a fresh floral perfume that emanated from her.

The few times he'd seen her since her sister's murder, he'd been filled with guilt. The consensus at the time had been that Shelly had been murdered by her then-boyfriend, Bo McBride, and that law enforcement simply hadn't found the evidence to make an arrest. Josh knew how little had actually been done in the investigation.

But that was then and this was now, and it had taken him weeks to figure out the mystery of "Shelly's ghost." He now had questions for Savannah that he wanted answered.

She opened the back door that led into the kitchen. She turned on the overhead light and gestured him toward a chair at the round wooden table.

"If you don't mind, I'd like to change clothes before you decide to take me in," she said. She didn't give him a chance to reply but instead left the room.

Josh sat in a chair at the table and looked around. Red roosters danced across the bottoms of beige curtains at the window, and a hen and rooster salt and pepper shaker set perched on the pristine stove top. Other than a coffeemaker, the countertops were bare.

There was an emptiness, a void of life in the room,

as if it were a designer home where nobody really lived. He heard water running in another room, and a few minutes later, Savannah returned.

She'd changed out of the gauzy gown and into a pair of jeans that hugged her long slender legs and a blue-and-gold T-shirt advertising the Pirate's Inn. She sat across from him at the table. She'd obviously washed her face, for her color was more natural. Her cheeks were faintly pink.

"So, are you going to arrest me?" she asked. Gone was the defiance, leaving behind only a weary resignation in her voice.

"What would I arrest you for? Impersonating a ghost?" he asked with a touch of amusement. "I don't want to arrest you, Savannah. I want to talk to you. What are you doing? Why are you pretending to be Shelly's ghost?"

Her long-lashed brown eyes gazed at him, and she tucked a strand of the long, silky-looking dark hair behind one ear. "How did you know that I'd appear out of the bush in my backyard?"

"I've been tracking the sightings of Shelly's ghost for about a month," he replied. "I saw your performance a couple of weeks ago and instantly realized it was you, but I couldn't figure out how you appeared and disappeared and got back here without anyone seeing you. So, I've been staking out your house and watching your movements."

Her face paled slightly. "You've been stalking me?"

"Basically, yeah," he admitted. "But I have to say, you aren't an exciting person to stalk."

Her cheeks grew pink again. "Sorry if I bored you with my life. Aren't there other people you should be stalking? Don't you have any real crime fighting to do?"

"Things have been pretty quiet since we managed to get Roger Cantor arrested," he replied. The affable coach of the high school had been exposed as a deadly stalker and was now behind bars. "And you didn't answer my question. What are you doing pretending to be Shelly's ghost?"

"Entertaining the locals," she replied airily, but her dark eyes simmered with a depth of emotion that belied her words. "And you didn't answer mine. How exactly did you figure out that I'd appear by the bush in the backyard after one of my ghostly walks?"

"The last time you pulled your stunt, I was here, watching the backyard to see if you'd sneak across the lawn. To my surprise, you came up from under the ground."

Josh had always been attracted to Savannah's high spirits, her beauty and more than a touch of sexy flirtation that had always lit her eyes when they happened to encounter each other. But that had been before her sister's murder, and the woman who sat across from him now appeared achingly fragile, a mere shell of what she'd once been.

A touch of guilt swept through him again. As a lawman, his job was to solve crimes and get the guilty behind bars. But officially Shelly's case remained an open one, without resolution.

"There's a tunnel," she finally said. Her finger traced

an indecipherable pattern on the top of the wooden table, and her gaze followed her finger's movements.

"A tunnel?" Josh felt like he was attempting to pull a confession from a hardened criminal.

She stopped the movement of her hand and looked at him once again. "There's a tunnel that runs from the backyard to a tree near the lagoon where Shelly was murdered. I discovered it about a year ago."

"What would a tunnel be doing in your backyard?" he asked.

Her slender shoulders moved up and down in a shrug. "I guess you'd have to ask the person who dug it, but it looks like it was made a long, long time ago. Maybe it was used to transport goods from the lagoon to here by the pirates who once lived around here."

Josh frowned thoughtfully. Lost Lagoon had a history rich in pirate lore. He supposed it was possible that pirates could have unloaded their treasures onto little boats to navigate the small lagoon and then bring them here, where they might have had an inland camp.

He focused his attention back on her. "You haven't answered my question. Why, Savannah? Why are you doing this?"

He studied her intently, wanting her to explain, to tell him what the payoff was for pretending to be her sister's ghost. She frowned and looked out the darkened window.

Josh was a patient man. It was one of his strengths as a deputy. He leaned back in his chair, not willing to go anywhere until he had the answer he needed from her.

Was she crazy, as many people thought? Had the murder of her sister, the destruction of her family and her own isolation from everything and everyone caused mental illness of some sort?

She finally looked back at him and leaned forward. Her hair came untucked from the back of her ear, the long dark strands shining beneath the hanging light over the table.

"A month after Shelly's murder, my parents forbade us ever to speak her name again," she began. Her dark gaze went over his shoulder to the bare wall behind him. "They packed all of her things away in the storage shed out back and pretended she had never existed."

She looked back at him, her eyes filled with a depth of simmering emotion. "I wasn't ready to say goodbye to my sister, my best friend and the person I'd shared a bedroom with since I was born. As time passed and Bo left town, everyone stopped talking about Shelly. It was as if she had never existed anywhere at any time. Even after my parents left town and I tried to talk to Mac about Shelly, he shut me down. He was so angry, still is so angry. He definitely didn't want to hear Shelly's name or anything I had to say about her."

Josh understood her pain. He'd lost a twin brother when he'd been fifteen years old, and he knew for the rest of his life he'd feel as if an integral piece of himself was missing.

"I found the tunnel a year ago," Savannah continued. "It took me weeks to get up the nerve to go down inside and explore where it went. When I finally did and realized it came up next to the place where Shelly had been murdered, I came up with the ghost plan."

"But why? What do you get out of pretending to be her ghost?"

"I get to hear squealing teenagers say her name. I make sure nobody forgets about her. I keep her alive by pretending to be her apparition in death." She shook her head. "I know it sounds crazy and you probably can't understand it, but for those few moments when people are crying out Shelly's name, I feel better. I feel as if she's still with me."

"It's dangerous," Josh replied. "You're sneaking out of your house alone in the middle of the night to go down into a tunnel that you don't even know is safe. There could be a cave-in, or somebody could come after you while you're doing your little show."

A whisper of a smile curved her lips, and for a moment Josh saw the semblance of the young woman she'd once been. "Actually, a couple of weeks ago Bo McBride did come after me. Apparently his new girlfriend, Claire Silver, told him about Shelly's ghost and encouraged him to see the spectacle. I'd just finished my walk when he jumped over the bushes and chased me into the woods. I jumped into my rabbit hole and disappeared."

"But that's my point," Josh protested. "You disappear down that tunnel, and if anything happened to you, nobody would know you were in trouble." He leaned forward. "I want to check out this tunnel."

Her eyes widened, and her gaze slid away from his.

"I don't think that's necessary. I've been using it for almost a year, and it's perfectly safe."

"I'd still like to check it out for myself," he countered. She looked at him again, and he knew in his gut that she was hiding something. "I figure you've got two choices."

"And I figure I'm not going to like either one of them," she retorted.

"You can take me down through that tunnel and I can see for myself that it's safe and secure, or I can get a backhoe in here to fill in the entrance in your backyard."

She sat up straighter in her chair, a flash of anger in her eyes. "You can't do that. My backyard is private property."

"I can do it," he replied calmly. "That hole is a danger. A small child could fall down it. I can make a case to have it filled in without your permission for the safety of the community."

She glared at him. It was the most emotion he'd seen from her since her sister's death. "Fine, I'll take you down into the tunnel."

Josh nodded and stood. "Why don't we plan on around noon tomorrow? I'll come here and we can check it out."

She stood as well, her body vibrating with tension. "Don't take this away from me, Josh. It's all I have in my life."

He had a ridiculous impulse to step forward and pull her into his arms. Instead he stepped toward the back door. "I'm just trying to keep you safe, Savannah. That's my job."

"If I felt unsafe, I would have called Sheriff Walker," she replied.

"Maybe you aren't in a mental state to know what's safe and what isn't."

He knew he'd spoken the wrong words by the flash of unbridled annoyance that filled her eyes and stiffened her stance.

"Contrary to popular belief, I'm perfectly sane. I know people think I've become a weird recluse who only comes out at night to work at the local haunted hotel, but that's my choice. The way I live my life is nobody's business but my own."

"Point taken," Josh replied. He opened the back door. "I'll see you at noon tomorrow. Good night, Savannah."

She shut the door behind him with more force than was necessary, and he headed for his patrol car parked at the curb in front of her house.

He got into the car and started the engine but didn't immediately drive away. Instead he sat and stared at her house. No lights shone from the front windows just as very little light had shone from her eyes on the occasional times he'd seen her in the last two years.

Despite his intense attraction to her two years ago, since that time he'd tried not to think about her. It was only curiosity about Shelly's "ghost" that had brought him here tonight.

Guilt was a terrible thing, he thought as he finally pulled away from the curb. Savannah was broken.

She'd been broken since Shelly's murder…a murder that had never been investigated as vigorously as it should have been.

As a deputy, Josh had followed orders, but as a decent man, he had known nobody was doing enough to close the case. Closure might have made a difference to Savannah.

Yes, she was broken, but he had no hero complex. He wasn't the man to fix her, but what he could do was make sure she was safe if she insisted on doing her ghostly walks.

He couldn't go back in time and do things differently in the case of her sister, but he could see to it that if Savannah insisted on continuing her haunting ghostly walks, at least the tunnel she used was safe.

Chapter Two

Savannah awoke with the unaccustomed emotion of anger tightening her chest. It had been so long since she hadn't awakened with the familiar grief that it took her a moment to recognize the new feeling that pressed so tight inside her.

Then she remembered the night before and Deputy Josh Griffin and knew immediately he was the source of her unusual anger. He was going to be here at noon and insist he go down into the tunnel with her, and when he did, he'd ruin everything.

He'd see that it wasn't just a single tunnel but rather a network of tunnels. Word would get out, people would start to explore and her nights of ghost walking would be over forever. She'd never hear Shelly's name again except in the deepest recesses of her broken heart.

She rolled over in bed and stared at the opposite side of the bedroom. The wall was covered with pictures of Shelly and Savannah, hugging each other when they were ten and eleven, Shelly dressed for prom at sixteen with Savannah posing with her, moments captured in time of the closeness of the two.

A desk held items that had been special to Shelly—the dried flower corsage that Bo McBride had given to her on prom night, a framed picture of the Manhattan skyline at twilight, a ceramic frog and a variety of other knickknacks.

Savannah had unpacked the items from the shed after Mac had moved out, comforted by the little pieces of Shelly that now remained in the room the two had shared for so many years of their lives.

She glanced at the clock on the nightstand. Just after ten. Normally she'd sleep until at least noon or one due to her overnight work hours at the Pirate's Inn. She'd be sucking wind tonight if she didn't get a nap in sometime during the afternoon or early evening.

Minutes later, as she stood beneath the shower spray, her thoughts turned to Josh Griffin. Before Shelly's death, she'd thought him one of the most handsome, hot single men in town.

He'd only grown more handsome in the past two years. As he'd sat at the table the night before, she couldn't help but notice on some level how his dark hair enhanced the crystal blue of his eyes.

It had been impossible not to notice how his broad shoulders had filled out his khaki deputy shirt and that he'd smelled of spicy cologne that had stirred her senses on some primal level.

She didn't want to like Josh Griffin. As far as she

was concerned, he was just part of the law enforcement in town that had botched her sister's murder case. And now he was going to ruin the only thing that made her feel just a little bit alive.

She dressed in a pair of denim shorts and a light blue T-shirt and then made a pot of coffee. The silence of the house was comfortable to her. When she and Mac had shared the house, there had always been shouting and cursing. Now the silence was like an old familiar friend.

Mac had been one of the loudest voices proclaiming the guilt of Bo McBride in Shelly's murder. But he'd always thought Bo wasn't good enough for her. Sometimes Savannah wondered about her brother...but she never allowed the perverse thought to take hold.

She sat at the table to drink her coffee and stared out the window that gave her not only a view of her own backyard but also a partial view of her neighbor's.

Jeffrey Allen was out there now, weeding a flower bed, his bald head covered against the July sun by a large straw hat. Jeffrey wasn't a pleasant man. In his midfifties, he worked as a mechanic at the local car repair shop and for the past five years or so had had a contentious relationship with the Sinclair family.

She only hoped he finished his lawn work before Josh arrived to check out the tunnel. The last thing she wanted to do was give Jeffrey any ammunition to work with to get her out of this house.

He'd made it clear that he wanted to buy her house

for some of his family members to move into, but Savannah had no plans ever to sell.

By eleven forty-five, Jeffrey had disappeared from his yard and gone back into his house, and a nervous energy flooded through Savannah's veins. Within a few minutes, Josh would arrive and destroy the one thing that had kept Shelly relevant beyond her death.

Savannah was still seated at the kitchen table when Josh appeared at the back door. She wanted to pretend he wasn't there, ignore the soft knock he delivered, but she knew he wasn't going to just go away, especially since he could see her through the window.

Reluctantly she got up to let him inside. Josh worked the night shift, like Savannah, and so instead of his uniform, he was clad in a pair of jeans and a black T-shirt.

With his slightly unruly black hair and his usual sexy grin curving sensual lips, he looked like the proverbial irresistible bad boy. He was a bad boy. He was about to rock her world in a very adverse way.

"Good afternoon," he said when she opened the door.

"Not particularly," she replied, embracing the alien emotion of the anger she'd awakened with. It felt so fresh, so different from the pervasive grief that had possessed her for so long. "It would be a good day if you'd kept your nose out of my business."

He frowned, the expression doing nothing to distract from his handsome, chiseled features. "Savannah, I'm not the enemy here."

Yes, he was. He just didn't realize it yet. Right now

he was the beginning of the end of her world. With even Shelly's ghost gone, Savannah didn't know who she was or where she belonged.

"Let's just get this over with," she replied. She noticed that he carried a high-beam flashlight, and she walked to the cabinet under the kitchen sink and grabbed a flashlight for herself.

As she followed Josh out the back door, she hoped his shoulders got stuck in the hole, then realized he would probably somehow manage to get out anyway and bring in that backhoe he'd talked about the night before.

She just had to come to terms with the fact that he was about to discover not just her secret, but a secret that had been hidden from the entire town for who knew how long.

As they reached the bush, she stepped in front of him and caught a scent of the sexy cologne she'd noticed the night before. It only aggravated her more. "I'll go first," she said and bent down to shove aside the branches to reveal the hole.

She used the narrow earthen steps to go down. "Okay, your turn," she said and moved away so that he could drop in.

He didn't use the steps but landed gracefully on the ground. Apparently a three-foot drop wasn't a big deal for a tall man with long legs.

He clicked on his flashlight and shone it straight ahead. "Wow, who would have thought?" he exclaimed in shock.

From this vantage point, the other passageway entrances weren't visible. "See, it's safe as can be," she said. "The earth is hard-packed and solid."

He shone his light beyond her. "I want you to take me to where you come up to do your nightly walks by the swamp."

This was what she'd been hoping to avoid, but she knew there was no way to stop him. "Follow me," she said in resignation. It would take only about three minutes for him to know that "her" tunnel wasn't the only one down here.

"Did it ever occur to you that the person who murdered Shelly might have used this tunnel to escape the scene of the crime?" he asked after only a step or two.

"You mean the murderer you all never caught?" The anger was back. She stopped and turned to face him, her light shining in his eyes.

He winced. "You don't believe that Bo McBride was responsible?"

"No, even though nearly everyone else in town, including all of you lawmen, believed him guilty. I never believed in my heart that he'd hurt Shelly. He loved her more than he loved himself."

"Did you know he's back in town to stay?" Josh asked. "And turn that light away," he added with an edge of irritation.

She lowered the beam to the center of his chest. "He's been back for over a month. I know he's living with Claire Silver because the creepy stalker that was after her burned Bo's family house down. I also know he and Claire are trying to find the truth about who murdered Shelly. When he chased me that night, I already suspected he was back in Lost Lagoon to stay."

"Look, I'm not down in this dungeon to reinvestigate your sister's murder. I'm sorry how things turned out and that nobody was ever arrested, but that's not why we're down here."

"You were the one who brought it up," she replied.

Suddenly she just wanted to get this over with, get back into her silent house where she lived with just memories of the family who had once filled the quiet with life.

She turned around and continued walking, and when she came to the first passageway that shot off the main tunnel, she heard Josh gasp in surprise.

"I thought you said this was just one tunnel, from your backyard directly to the edge of the swamp." He shone his light down the new tunnel.

Once again she turned to face him. "I lied. There are tons of tunnels down here. I think they run under the entire town, and now that you know that, everything is going to be ruined for me. You'll feel obligated to tell somebody, and word will get out, and there will be tons of people down here exploring everywhere."

To her horror, she burst into tears…the first tears she had shed since the day they had buried her sister.

JOSH WASN'T SURE what shocked him more, the discovery of the other tunnels or Savannah's unexpected tears. No, they weren't just simple tears. She leaned against the earthen wall and sobbed as if her heart was breaking.

"Savannah," he said softly, and he touched her arm. She jerked away and cried harder. "Savannah, please don't cry." Not knowing what to do, unaccustomed to sobbing females, he tucked his flashlight into the back of the waist of his pants and pulled her into his arms.

She stiffened against him and then melted into him, crying into the hollow of his throat. Although she was tall, she felt small and fragile in his arms. Her hair smelled of wildflowers, and she fit neatly against him.

It lasted only a couple of heartbeats, and then she twirled out of his embrace and swiped at her tears as if angry at herself for the display of emotion. "I'm sorry. I didn't mean for that to happen."

She faced him, the eerie illumination of their flashlights casting dancing shadows on her features. "You just have no idea what you're taking away from me."

"Why don't we continue on, and we can talk about it all when we're above ground again," he suggested and pulled his flashlight out of his waistband.

She nodded and turned to lead the way once again. Josh tried to keep pace with her, but he slowed each time he passed yet another tunnel that branched off the one they followed. And there were plenty of branches.

Throughout the walk, he could tell they were descending, although it was impossible to tell just how deep they were beneath the ground.

He counted at least seven branches of darkened tunnels by the time they reached the end of the main one.

Plank steps led upward. They hadn't spoken a word to each other as they'd travelled forward.

He'd been too amazed by the subterranean world he'd been introduced to by Savannah. Where did the other tunnels lead? How big was the network? Who knew about it besides Savannah?

He was fairly sure the answer to the question was that nobody except Savannah and now him knew about the underground network. Otherwise he would have heard about it before now. Lost Lagoon was a small town, and a secret this big would have been revealed.

He followed her up the plank steps that led them next to a large cypress tree surrounded by thick brush. The ground was spongy beneath his feet, although not wet enough to cover his shoes. There was nobody in the area, and he was glad that nobody was around to see them ascend from the ground.

Directly in front of them was the swath of land where Shelly's "ghost" walked. He looked at Savannah, whose features were void of emotion. "So, you walk across here and then what? How do you get back to this same entrance to get back home?"

"I don't. On the other side of the path is a hidden cave that leads back to the tunnel we were just in." She didn't wait for his response but quickly walked across the path that was her "stage" on nights she performed her ghost routine.

Josh hurried after her, his mind still reeling from where he'd been and what he'd seen. When they reached the other side, he followed her up a small hill through thick woods.

She stopped and pulled a tangle of vines and brush aside to reveal the mouth of a cave. Once again a sense of shock swept through him.

He'd been a deputy in Lost Lagoon for the past ten years. He'd moved to the small town from Georgia when he was twenty-one to take the position of deputy. Ten years and he hadn't heard a whisper of the presence of the underground network.

He followed her into the mouth of the cave and found himself again in a tunnel that merged into the one they'd used from Savannah's backyard.

They were silent as they returned the way they had come. The initial excitement and surprise of what he'd seen had passed. Instead he was acutely attuned to the air of defeat that emanated from Savannah while she walked slowly in front of him.

He dreaded the conversation to come. There was no way he could keep this information to himself. Who knew what might be found in the other tunnels? Who knew where they led? It was a historical find that should be made public to the appropriate authorities.

What surprised him was that Savannah had possessed the nerve to go down there and explore on her own. It must have been frightening the first time she'd decided to drop down that hole and follow the tunnel.

When they came back up in her backyard, the July sun and humidity were relentless. He hadn't realized how much cooler the tunnels had been until now.

"Come on inside and I'll get us something cold to drink," she said without enthusiasm.

It wasn't the best invitation he'd ever gotten from a woman, but he was hot and thirsty, and they weren't finished with their business yet.

Once inside, he sat in the same chair at the table where he'd sat the night before. She went to the cabinet and pulled down two glasses.

She turned to look at him, her eyes dull and lifeless. "Sweet tea okay?"

"Anything cold is fine," he replied.

She opened the refrigerator and poured the tea. She then carried the glasses to the table and sat across from him. Her eyes were now dark pools of aching sadness, so aching that he couldn't stand to look at them.

He took a sip of the cold tea and then stared down into the glass. "You know I can't keep this a secret," he finally said.

"I know you can't keep it a secret forever," she replied.

He gazed at her, and this time in her eyes he saw a tiny spark of life, of hope. He steeled himself for the argument he had a feeling was about to happen.

God, it just took that single spark in her eyes for him to remember the woman she'd been, and he couldn't help the swift curl of heat that warmed his belly. It was a heat of the visceral attraction he'd forgotten had once existed where she was concerned.

"Give me one more night," she said. "Just let me have one more walk before you tell anyone about the tunnels." She leaned forward, her eyes now positively glowing with focus. "One final walk, Josh. At least let me have that before it all blows up."

"Savannah…"

"Those tunnels have been a secret for who knows how long," she said, interrupting him. "Can't you just keep them a secret for another week or so?"

He told himself it was too big, that he should report on what he'd found out immediately. He sat up straighter in his chair, determined to do the right thing, and then she surprised him. She reached across the table and covered one of his hands with hers.

"Please, Josh, all I'm asking for is a week. I can do a final ghost walk next Friday night, and then you can tell whoever you want about the tunnels."

Her hand was warm, almost fevered over his, and for just a moment, as he stared into the dark pools of her eyes, he forgot what they'd been talking about.

He mentally shook himself and pulled his hand from beneath hers. Duty battled with the desire to do something for her, something to make up for letting her down two years before when he should have chosen real justice over his job.

He took another drink of tea and then stood. He needed to think, and at the moment he was finding it difficult to think rationally.

"I assume you're working your usual shift tonight at the inn?" He moved toward the back door. He needed to get away from her winsome eyes, the floral scent of her that filled his head.

"Eleven to seven," she replied. "Why?"

"I need to think about everything. I won't say any-thing to anyone today, and I'll stop by the Pirate's Inn tonight sometime during my shift and let you know what I've decided to do."

She opened her mouth as if to make one more plea, but closed it and nodded. "Then I guess I'll see you sometime tonight."

He left her house and walked around to his car. No patrol car today, just a nice red convertible sports car that most women would definitely consider a boy toy.

He'd bought the car a year ago, and the day he signed the ownership papers, his head had been filled with the memory of his twin brother, Jacob.

When the two boys had been growing up, they'd dreamed of owning a car like this…flashy and fast and nothing like the old family car their parents had driven. That old car had been held together by string and hope because new cars cost money the Griffin family didn't have.

Driving to his house, he once again thought about the surprising discovery of the tunnels. The presence of them had been such a shock. Had they been made by pirates who were rumored to have used the Lost La-goon town as a base camp? Would there be treasures and artifacts in one of those passageways that would identify who had made them and why?

It was much easier to think about the tunnels than about the woman he'd just left. But thoughts of Savannah intruded. Of the two sisters, he'd always thought she was the prettiest. She was softer, a little bit shyer than Shelly, but she'd drawn Josh to her.

She'd had a smile that lit up her face and made it impossible not to smile back at her. He wondered if she had smiled at all in the last two years.

He pulled into the driveway of his three-bedroom ranch house. He'd bought the house when it was just a shell and had added amenities like an extra-long whirl-pool tub for a tall man to relax in and a walkout door from the bedroom to a private patio. He'd also put in all the bells and whistles in the kitchen area. He'd been told by the builder that it would be good for resale value.

The cost of living in Lost Lagoon was relatively low, and his salary was good, as few lawmen would choose to spend their careers in a small swamp town.

When he got inside, he sat at his kitchen table with a bottle of cold beer, and once again his head filled with visions of Savannah.

One week. That was all she'd asked for. Just seven days. But was it even right for him to indulge her in one more ghost walk? Wasn't it better just to end it all now and hope that she got some sort of help for the grief that had obviously held her in its grip for far too long?

And what if Sheriff Trey Walker found out that he'd known about the tunnels and hadn't come forward immediately? Trey was a tough guy who demanded

100 percent loyalty from his men. Would Josh be putting his job on the line to give Savannah what she'd asked for?

He took a long sip of his beer and reviewed his options—none of which he liked.

Chapter Three

Savannah stood behind the reception desk in the large quiet lobby of the Pirate's Inn. The inn had two stories, and the centerpiece of the lobby was a huge, tacky treasure chest that the inn's owner, Donnie Albright, had been repainting for the last couple of weeks.

He'd finished the six-foot-tall chest itself, painting it a bright gold, but he still had to spruce up the oversized papier-mâché and Styrofoam jewels and strings of pearls that filled the chest.

He was also in the process of re-carpeting the guest rooms, all in anticipation of the amusement park that had bought land and was building on a ridge above the small city.

Most of the businesses were eager for the park to be done, knowing that it would bring in tourists who would shop and spend their money in town. There were plenty of people in town who wanted Lost Lagoon to be "found" and hoped that would happen with the large amusement park under construction nearby.

At the moment, the last thing on Savannah's mind

was the new pirate-themed park. It was a little after 2:00 a.m., and Josh hadn't come in yet to tell her his decision about giving her one final walk before telling other people about the tunnels.

She sat in a raised chair and began to doodle on a notepad. There was only one couple staying in the inn tonight. Beth and Greg Hemming stayed in a room at the inn once a month. They had four children, all under the age of six, and Savannah suspected the night out was not so much about romance, but more about a good night of uninterrupted sleep.

For years the inn had mostly catered to occasional people who came to Lost Lagoon to visit with family members. It was rare that real tourists stopped in for a room for the night unless they were lost and desperate to spend the night someplace before returning to their journey.

Shelly had worked as the night manager before her murder. Savannah had taken on the same job a year ago. She was certain it was the most boring job in town.

She had a degree from a culinary school and had at one time entertained the idea of opening a restaurant in town. Lost Lagoon had a pizza place, George's Diner, which was just a cheap hamburger joint, and the café. There was no place for anyone in town to have a real fine dining experience.

That was why she had been living at home, working at the café and saving her money before Shelly's murder. But the loss of her sister had also stolen Savannah's dreams.

A rap on the front door drew her attention, and she grabbed the ring of keys that would unlock the front door. The inn was always locked up for security purposes when she arrived for her shift at eleven.

She rounded the monstrous, gaudy treasure chest to see Josh standing outside. Her heart fluttered unexpectedly at the sight of him, so tall and handsome in his khaki uniform.

It was impossible to tell what news he brought by the lack of expression on his face. She fumbled with the key and finally got the door unlocked to allow him inside.

"Busy night?" she asked as she led him back to the reception area where, in front of the desk, two sofas faced each other and were separated by a large square wooden coffee table.

"Probably no busier than yours," he replied. He sat on one end of a sofa, and she sat on the other. "Any guests in the house?"

"Beth and Greg Hemming are in room 202."

"No sightings of old Peg Leg or his drunken friend?" There was a touch of amusement in his eyes as he mentioned the most popular "ghosts" in town.

"Donnie probably made up that story about pirate ghosts haunting the hallways when he first bought this place years ago," she replied and wished he'd just get to the point.

"With the new pirate theme park going up, I imagine Donnie is anticipating lots of guests in the future."

"There are certainly going to be big changes around

here when the park is finished next summer," she replied.

"Whoever thought Lost Lagoon, Mississippi, would become a family vacation destination? I expect we'll see some new businesses popping up in the near future."

"Josh," she said impatiently.

"Okay, you don't want small talk. You want to know what I've decided to do about the tunnels." The blue of his eyes darkened slightly.

She had a sinking feeling in the pit of her stomach. If eyes were the windows to the soul, then she was about to be bitterly disappointed.

"I stewed about it all day. You know I have to tell, but I'm willing to wait until next Saturday on one condition. Friday night, when you do your final walk, I go with you."

"I've been making these walks alone for the last year. It isn't necessary for you to come with me," she protested. He threatened her just a little bit. He was too sexy, his smile was too warm. He radiated a vibrant energy that felt dangerous to her.

"That's the deal, Savannah. I go with you next Friday night, or tomorrow I tell Trey about the tunnels."

She could tell by his firm tone that he meant it. She should be grateful that he had given her as much as he had. "All right," she said. "I appreciate you giving me one last walk. I go down into the tunnel about eleven thirty or so. If you aren't by the bush at that time next Friday, I won't wait for you."

"Don't worry. I'll be there," he assured her and stood.

She got up as well and followed him back to the door. "So, we have a date next Friday night," he said, the charming amusement back in his eyes.

"A date under duress," she replied coyly.

He pushed open the door to leave but turned back to look at her. "You know, you might try walking in the sunshine sometime. It's so much better than walking in the shadows."

He didn't wait for a reply but turned and walked away. She locked the door after him and returned to the chair behind the desk.

She didn't even want to contemplate his parting words. He knew nothing about her, nothing about her life…her loss. All she had to do was see him one last time, next Friday night, and then she wouldn't have to see Deputy Josh Griffin again.

The night passed uneventfully, and by seven, when owner Donnie Albright showed up to relieve her, she was exhausted. She'd spent most of the quiet night as she usually did, sitting and trying not to think, not to feel.

Once at home, she changed out of the tailored blouse and black slacks she wore to work and into a sleeveless cotton nightgown and then fell into bed. The dark shades at her bedroom window kept out the sunlight, and she didn't have to worry about phone calls or unexpected guests interrupting her sleep.

Since Mac had moved out, the only person who ever came by the house was Chad Wilson, who delivered groceries to her once a week on Thursday afternoons.

Because she was off Thursdays and Fridays, she always got special items to cook on those days, meals she might have served customers in her own restaurant if her world hadn't fallen apart.

She finally fell asleep and dreamed of days gone by, when Shelly and Bo were a couple and she often spent time with them. Bo often teased that he was the luckiest guy in the world, with two beautiful women on his arms. He'd been like a brother to her, and she'd grieved the loss of his friendship almost as deeply as she did Shelly.

Her dream transformed, and a vision of Josh filled her mind. He held her in his arms, his body fitting close against her own as his lips covered hers in a kiss that seared fire through her.

She awakened irritated that the sexy lawman had held any place at all in her dreams.

For the next four days, she went to work each night and came home each morning and slept. In the late afternoons, when she was awake, she vegged out in front of the television, trying not to think about the fact that Friday night would be her final tribute to her sister.

She was almost grateful on Thursday afternoon when Chad showed up with the bags of groceries she'd ordered the day before from the grocery store.

Although she'd always found the thirtysomething deliveryman a bit odd, he brought her not only the things she wanted to cook but also a wealth of gossip.

If Josh hadn't held up his end of their bargain, she would know about it from Chad. He'd tell her all about the discovery of the tunnels and the exploration that was taking place.

She answered his knock on the back door and allowed him and his grocery bags inside the kitchen. "How are you doing today, Savannah?" he asked with his usual good cheer. As always, his dark brown hair stood up in spikes, and his caramel-colored eyes danced around the room as if unable to focus on any one spot.

"Good. How about you?" she asked. He placed the bags on the table, and she began to unload them.

"I've been busy today. Old Ethel Rogers fell and broke her hip last week, so I made a delivery to her earlier. You look pretty in that sundress. You should get out of this house more often."

"Thank you for the compliment," she replied. "What else is going on around town?"

He sat at the table as she continued to unpack and put away the food. "Mayor Jim Burns is pressuring all the businesses on Main Street to update and renovate their shops, and some people aren't happy about it. Former mayor Frank Kean is buzzing around between town and the construction site for the new park, and Claire Silver and Bo McBride got engaged."

He slapped his hand over his mouth, his eyes wide. "Maybe I shouldn't have told you that last part."

Savannah smiled. "No, it's okay. I hope he and Claire will be very happy together." She wasn't surprised they had found love together, and she wanted love for Bo. He would always hold a special place in her heart as the man who had once loved Shelly.

"You know, maybe we could go out some time," Chad said. "Maybe have dinner at the café. You know, just casual-like." His gaze moved from her to the stove and then back to her.

"I'm sorry, Chad. It's nothing personal, but I don't go out."

He frowned. "Are you sure it's nothing personal? I know I don't have a great job, and I'm not as smart as a lot of people."

"It has nothing to do with that, and I think you're very smart," she quickly replied. "I think you're very nice. It has nothing to do with you, Chad. I just don't go out with anyone."

Chad appeared satisfied with her answer. He stayed until the last food item had been put away, and then he left. She'd had a feeling that he had a crush on her, but she never played to it.

All she really knew about him was that he worked for his mother, Sharon, at the grocery store and lived in a small apartment in the back of the store. He was a pleasant-looking man, but he was a bit slow.

Today had been the first time he'd actually asked her out. She hoped she hadn't hurt his feelings by turning him down.

Dismissing those thoughts, she focused all her attention on pulling out the ingredients she needed to make Cajun skillet fillets. There was nothing better than beef fillets and shrimp paired with a special blend of blackening spices and lobster stock. She decided to cook a side of fresh asparagus in garlic and butter.

The only time she allowed any happiness to fill her heart, to seep into her soul, was when she cooked. All of her thoughts, all of her energy went into the food.

There were many times Sharon special-ordered items for her because the local store didn't carry much in the way of specialty foods.

It didn't take long for the kitchen to fill with a variety of wonderful scents. It brought back the times that Savannah's mother had cooked delicious meals for the family. She was always experimenting and tweaking recipes and was responsible for Savannah's love of cooking.

She cooked two steaks and a dozen shrimp, deciding that she'd eat the second portion the next night… the night she walked for the last time as Shelly's ghost.

It was six o'clock and everything was ready for plating when the doorbell rang. She nearly jumped out of her skin. She couldn't remember the last time she'd heard the chime indicating somebody was at the front door.

She looked out the peephole to see Josh on the front porch. Had he changed his mind about giving her tomorrow night? She opened the door, and he greeted her with the sexy smile that twisted her heart in an uncomfortable way.

"What a surprise," she said as she opened the door to allow him inside.

"Since it was one of my nights off, I just thought I'd

stop by and check in before tomorrow night," he said. "Hmm, something smells terrific."

"It's dinner. I was just about to put it on a plate."

"Smells like a lucky plate," he replied.

She thought of the two steaks and the dozen shrimp. "Are you hungry? I have plenty if you'd like to join me."

His eyes lit with pleasure. "I'd love to join you."

As he followed her into the kitchen, she wondered what in the world had possessed her to invite him to dinner. She told herself the reason was that she had to play nice with him until after tomorrow night, and then she wouldn't have to play with him at all.

She gestured him to a seat at the table as she moved to the cabinet to get down another plate. She didn't know what to say. She'd forgotten how to make small talk. It was a surprising revelation.

"I assume you've had a quiet week," he finally said, breaking what had grown into an awkward silence.

"I always have quiet weeks." She filled two glasses with iced tea and added them and silverware to the table, then returned to the stove to put the food on the plates. "What about you?"

He leaned back in the chair, looking relaxed, as if he belonged there. "Let's see. On Monday night I got a call of an intruder in the attic of Mildred Samps's house. It turned out to be a raccoon that had gotten in through a hole in the eaves. I called out Chase Marshall from Fish and Game, and he managed to get the creature out."

"Tell me more," she said as she focused on plating

the food in a visually pleasing way. She'd much rather listen to him talk than have to talk herself.

"On Tuesday night I was called out to Jimmy's Place to break up a fight between two drunks."

She glanced at him in surprise. "Jimmy doesn't usually let things get out of control like that, and I still think of it as Bo's Place."

"Bo definitely had a flair for bringing in a crowd when he owned it. Jimmy doesn't have Bo's natural charisma. Anyway, that brings us to last night, when there were no calls and I just drove up and down the streets for hours. Working the night shift in this town isn't all that challenging."

"I'm sure there are times when a good deputy is necessary after dark. Isn't that when bad things happen?" She delivered the plates to the table.

"Jeez, it all looks too pretty to eat. Do you cook like this every night?"

She sat at the table across from him and shook her head. "Usually just on my nights off."

"That's right. I just remembered that you went to culinary school in Jackson. Didn't I hear somewhere that you were going to open a restaurant at one time?"

"That was another lifetime," she replied. "Dig in while it's warm."

He cut into the steak and took a bite. "This is amazingly delicious. You should put opening that restaurant in this lifetime."

She felt the warmth of a blush creep into her cheeks, along with a flush of pleasure that swept over her at his words, but it lasted only a moment. "I don't have the passion I once had for cooking for other people."

He popped a shrimp in his mouth and chased it with a drink of tea. He gazed at her curiously. "So, what do you have a passion for these days?"

"Keeping Shelly's memory alive." The one thing he was taking away from her. "Besides, as far as I'm concerned, passion is vastly overrated," she added. "What about you? What do you feel passionate about?"

"My job, this town and the people I serve," he answered easily.

"What about a girlfriend?" She was just curious. She certainly didn't care one way or the other whether he had a girlfriend or not.

"Nobody special. Although I'm ready to find the woman who will be by my side for the rest of my life, the woman who will give me some kids, and we'll all live happily ever after." He laughed. "I sound like a woman whose biological clock is ticking."

His words brought a smile to Savannah's lips. "You sound like a man ready to move into a new phase of life."

He stared at her. "You should do that more often. I'd forgotten how you look when you smile."

"Eat your dinner," she replied as a new warmth filled her. She was ready for him to leave. He confused her. He made her feel uncomfortable. He had no place at her table, and she had been impulsive in inviting him in.

He seemed attuned to her discomfort. He ate quickly and didn't ask her any more questions but rather kept up an easy monologue about his work, the new amusement park and the changes that were already happening in the town.

When they'd finished eating, she insisted he not help with the cleanup but instead hurried him toward the front door. "Thanks for the unexpected meal," he said. His eyes had gone dark blue like deep, unfathomable waters.

"No problem," she replied. Away from the kitchen with all its cooking scents, she could smell his cologne and remembered the brief moment of being held in his arms while she wept in the tunnel.

"Then we're still on for tomorrow night?" he asked.

"Definitely. We'll meet at the bush in the backyard at around eleven thirty or so tomorrow night."

"Then I'll see you tomorrow night."

She breathed a sigh of relief as she closed and locked the door behind him. She sank into a nearby chair, the scent of him still filling her head.

There had been a time when she'd been certain he was going to ask her out, and there had been a time when she'd desperately hoped he would. He'd been the one man in town who had managed to quicken her heartbeat at the mere sight of him.

They had flirted outrageously with each other whenever they were together in a group. Shelly had teased her unmercifully about her crush on Josh.

But that had been before life had kicked her so hard she didn't want to play anymore. She'd picked up her marbles and crawled into a cave where she felt safe and secure, a place where no more hurt could touch her again.

She got up from the chair and went back into the kitchen to clear the dishes from the table and clean up the rest of her cooking mess, dismissing any more thoughts of Josh.

She slept late the next morning, as was her custom with her night job, and spent most of the afternoon and evening restlessly pacing the floor, cleaning things that were already clean, both anticipating and dreading the night to come.

By eleven o'clock she was in the bathroom, using powder to whiten her face and already clad in her "ghost" costume for the last time.

Tonight she would hear Shelly's name shouted, and after tonight she didn't know if she would ever hear anyone speak of her sister again. It was as if Shelly was dying a second time, and this time it would be final.

By eleven thirty, she was at the bush, waiting for Josh to arrive. She couldn't ignore the aching sadness in her heart and yet also knew that these Shelly walks were a part of her that wasn't quite rational.

She waited impatiently, expecting Josh to show up any moment. But minutes passed, and when she'd waited fifteen minutes, she had to move. She'd warned him that if he wasn't here on time, she'd go it alone, as she had so many times in the past year.

With a final glance around the backyard and no sign of Josh in sight, she slipped down the rabbit hole and turned on her penlight.

Everyone knew that Shelly's "ghost" usually showed up on Friday nights around midnight. She couldn't let down her "fans" by being late. She'd even heard from Chad one time that young teenagers planned slumber parties and included coming to watch for Shelly's ghost as part of the night's activities.

She moved through the tunnel more quickly than usual, all the while listening for the sound of Josh coming down to join her.

Tomorrow this place would probably be crawling with people. Experts of one sort or another would explore all the passageways, try to date the network, and eventually there might even be tours set up by the town, eager to make money off the unexpected find.

She reached the planks that would take her up, surprised that she'd heard nothing to indicate that Josh was somewhere behind her. He'd obviously been held up by something.

She went up the steps and crouched by the trunk of the tree. For a moment the only things she heard were the croak of frogs and the splash of water from the nearby lagoon.

Wouldn't it be ironic if there was nobody hiding behind the bushes tonight, nobody to witness this final tribute to her dead sister? Then she heard them…the giggling and whispering of her audience. Thank goodness she wouldn't make this last walk without anyone to watch.

When she thought it was just around midnight, she turned on the flashlight that gave her the otherworldly glow. She made her walk as cries of her sister's name filled the air.

Shelly. Savannah missed her so badly. Without these walks, Shelly would eventually become completely irrelevant and forgotten. The fact ached in Savannah's heart.

When she reached the other side, she turned off the light and hurried to the opening of the cave. She disappeared inside and leaned weakly against the earthen wall of the tunnel.

It was done. It was over. Now the memory of Shelly would remain only in her mind. Perhaps for several weeks, maybe even a month or so, teenagers would gather behind the bushes to see her "ghost," but when no more appearances occurred, eventually they'd find something else to do on their Friday nights.

Turning on her penlight, she then began the trek back to where she'd begun. Weary sadness moved her feet slowly. Her parents rarely spoke to her. She had no relationship with Mac. Now her last link to Shelly had been broken.

She'd been alone for the past two years, but now she felt an emptiness, a depth of loneliness she'd never felt before. *You'll be fine*, a little voice whispered in her head. And she would be okay. She still had her work at the inn and her nights of cooking, and that was all she really needed.

She had three more dark offshoot passageways to go by, and then she'd be home. As she started past the first one, a hand reached out and grabbed her by the arm.

She shrieked in shock and yanked backward. She crashed to the ground, the penlight falling just out of her reach. Panic and terror shot through her as somebody or something grabbed her by the foot and began to drag her into the dark tunnel.

She kicked and clawed the ground in an effort to get away, but whoever had her was strong, and she felt herself being slowly pulled into the blackness of the unknown corridor.

Chapter Four

"You both need to stop this cycle," Josh said impatiently. He glared at the couple seated on a sagging sofa in one of the shanties that stood near the swamp on the west side of town.

Daisy Wilcox sported a split lip, and her husband, Judd, had scratch marks down his cheek. This wasn't the first time Josh had been called here for a domestic situation.

"I should just take you both in, let you spend some time in jail," Josh said, aware that time was ticking by and it was just a few minutes before he was supposed to meet Savannah in her backyard.

"It was just a little lover's spat," Daisy protested and grabbed Judd's hand. "I overreacted and shouldn't have called the sheriff's office. We're fine now. There's no reason to arrest us."

"Yeah, we're cool," Judd said and patted his wife's ample thigh.

The small room reeked of alcohol and pot. Daisy's words were slurred and Judd's pupils were huge. Josh had cause to take them in, but they weren't bad people. They were part of the poor of Lost Lagoon, swamp people who had little hope and tried to escape that hopelessness by masking their pain with whatever was available.

Besides, if he ran them in, there would be paperwork to fill out, processes that needed to be followed. It all took time, and he was aware of every minute that ticked by. In any case, each of them would refuse to press charges against the other, and it would all be a waste of time.

"If I'm called out here again tonight, then you're both going to be arrested," he warned them as he had a dozen times before. "Put the booze and whatever else you're using away and stop this nonsense."

"We will," Daisy replied and leaned into her husband. She smiled up at Judd. "You know I love you, baby."

Judd returned her smile. "Back at you, babe."

Minutes later, as Josh drove to Savannah's house, he thought about the couple he'd just left. About once a month one officer or another was called to the address to respond to a fight.

Usually by the time the officer got there, the fight was over and the two were lovebirds once again. Their injuries were usually superficial and always sported by both. Josh swore to himself that the next time he was called out there, he would make arrests and let the both of them cool their heels in jail and hopefully make them think about abuse and love. Some people just didn't get it. Love wasn't supposed to hurt.

His thoughts quickly shifted to Savannah as he looked at the clock on his dashboard and cursed inwardly. It was midnight. She was probably already making her ghostly walk.

By the time he parked in her driveway and ran to the backyard, he figured he might as well just wait. She should be coming back up at any moment.

Dammit, he'd wanted to take this final walk with her. Even though he thought what she was doing was more than a little bit crazy, he knew tonight's walk would be emotionally difficult for her.

He'd wanted to be by her side. The darkness of her eyes and the obvious emptiness in her life haunted him. He felt partially responsible for how isolated she'd become, for the obvious grief that still ate at her.

He had so many memories of the laughing, flirting Savannah who had stirred his senses, a woman he'd wanted desperately. He wanted to find that woman again, to help her heal not just for herself, but for him. Time hadn't erased his desire for her.

Would things have been different for her if he'd pushed Sheriff Trey Walker in the investigation of Shelly's murder? If the case had been closed and the killer was behind bars, would that have given Savannah the closure she needed to move forward in a meaningful way?

The problem was, she had nobody to offer her support and encouragement. Her parents had left town, and she apparently wasn't close to her brother. Whatever friends she'd possessed had either drifted away or been shoved away by her, leaving her alone to cope… and she hadn't coped.

Every muscle in his body stiffened as he thought he heard a faint cry coming from the hole in the ground. He turned on his flashlight and shone it down, seeing nothing but earth.

Had he heard her crying? Weeping because she knew this was the end of her walks? Should he go down and console her? Or let her cry in private? He had a feeling that if she was crying, she wouldn't welcome his presence.

He heard her again, only this time instead of weeping, it sounded like a scream of terror. With his gun in one hand, his flashlight in the other and adrenaline pumping through his body, he dropped down into the hole.

The first thing he saw was the penlight beam, shining at him from the floor in the distance. What he didn't see was any sign of Savannah.

"Savannah!" He yelled her name and it echoed in the air.

He quickly walked forward, his gun leading the way and his heart pounding a million beats a minute. Where was Savannah? Why was her flashlight on the ground? What in the hell was happening?

"Josh, help!" Her cry seemed to come from all sides of him. He moved faster, and when he came to the first entrance of an offshoot tunnel, he spun to shine his flashlight and gun down into the darkness.

"Savannah," he shouted again.

"I'm here." Her voice came again. He shone his light back up the main tunnel and saw her crawling out of one of the offshoot passageways ahead of him.

He ran toward her, his heart still beating at a dizzying speed. She crawled toward him and began to cry. Before he reached her, she got to her feet and raced toward him, slamming into his chest and holding tightly to him. "Somebody grabbed me," she managed to gasp between sobs. "He tried to drag me down the tunnel."

Josh peeled her away from him. "Get out of here and get into your house. I need to check it out."

She grabbed his arm. "Be careful." She quickly turned and hurried toward the exit. Josh shone his light on her until he saw her leave the tunnel. Then he turned around and headed forward.

Every nerve, every sense he possessed tingled with hyperawareness as he approached the passageway where, according to Savannah, somebody had jumped out and grabbed her.

He didn't even want to think about how frightened she'd been, how filthy she'd looked and how helpless she'd appeared crawling along the floor out of the unexplored tunnel.

When he reached the place she'd crawled out of, he shone his light to illuminate the utter blackness of the underground. Nothing. He couldn't see anything as far as his flashlight beam could reach.

Tightening his grip on his gun, he walked down the unfamiliar tunnel. There was nothing to distinguish it from the one he'd just left. He followed it until he came to a fork and didn't know which way to go. Uncertain whether he could find his way back if he ventured too far, he gave up the hunt. Besides, he imagined Savannah's attacker was long gone by now.

He turned back, eager to get to her and find out everything that had happened. Who had been down here? Who would have attacked her? Hopefully she had managed to get a glimpse of whoever had grabbed her.

As he headed toward her house, he checked the yard but saw nothing amiss, nobody hiding in the shadows of night. When he reached the back door, he saw her seated at the table. She got up and unlocked the door to allow him in.

"I didn't see anyone," he said as they both sat down. She looked like hell. Dirt covered her white gown, and the absence of the white makeup she used showed in the tiny trails of her tears. Her eyes still held the haunting vestiges of horror.

He reached across the table for one of her hands. She grasped onto him, hers trembling. "Tell me exactly what happened," he said.

"I waited for you." There was no censure in her slightly breathy voice.

He squeezed her hand a little tighter. "I'm so sorry I wasn't here. I had a domestic call I had to respond to." How he wished he had been by her side. Nobody would have touched her if he'd been down there with her.

She nodded. "I finally went and did my walk, and when I was coming back, somebody from that connecting tunnel reached out and grabbed me by the arm.

I managed to jerk away, but I fell down and lost my penlight."

She paused a moment and drew a deep, tremulous breath. "Then whoever it was grabbed my foot and started to drag me." She looked down at her fingernails. He noticed the dirt beneath them. "I desperately clawed at the ground and kicked as hard as I could, but whoever it was, was strong...too strong for me to get away. As soon as you called my name, he let go of me. Thank goodness you showed up when you did."

"Did you see anything? Get a glimpse of his face?" Josh asked hopefully, but she shook her head.

"He had a bright light shining in my face." She frowned thoughtfully. "I think the light was on a hat."

"You mean like a miner's hat?"

"Yes, like that." She pulled her hand from his and instead wrapped her arms around herself as if chilled to the bone. "I thought he was going to drag me off before you could find me, and nobody would ever know what happened to me. I thought I was the only one who knew about those tunnels, besides you. Why would anyone else be down there? Why would they want to attack me?"

So many questions, and he had no answers for her. "We need to call Trey," he finally said. "It's time he knew not only about the tunnels but also about somebody being down there and assaulting you."

He pulled out his cell phone and made the call to the sheriff, who indicated he'd be there in the next twenty minutes or so.

"He'll think I'm crazy," she said and uncrossed her arms from around herself. "He'll have to know about my ghost walks, and he'll write me off as a nut."

"I won't let that happen, Savannah. I'm not going to let anyone write you off as a nut. I'm on your side." As he should have been two years before.

"I think for the first time in a long time I need somebody on my side," she replied, and as she held his gaze, he swore to himself that he would do whatever possible to find the person responsible for the fear that still shadowed her eyes.

SHE DESPERATELY WANTED to shower. She needed to get the dirt off her body and out from under her fingernails and the last of the white makeup off her face. But Josh insisted she wait until after Sheriff Walker arrived and she spoke with him.

When the doorbell rang, Savannah remained seated at the kitchen table while Josh went to answer the door. She was still shaken to the core. If Josh hadn't heard her scream, if he'd been five minutes later, who knew what might have happened to her? Any thoughts in that direction terrified her.

She sat up a little straighter when Josh came back into the kitchen, followed by Sheriff Walker. Trey Walker was a nice-looking man in his early forties, but she'd always believed he'd let down her entire family by not doing a thorough enough investigation when Shelly had been murdered. He'd been so certain that

Bo McBride had killed Shelly. She believed he'd never really looked at anyone else.

"Are you dressed up for Halloween already?" Trey asked as he entered the kitchen and looked at her. Josh sat next to her, and Trey took the chair across from her.

"No, I'm dressed like Shelly's ghost who walks the night for the amusement of silly teenagers," she replied. She explained to him about pretending to be Shelly's ghost for the last year.

"I've heard about the ghost rumors, but I'm afraid I never caught one of your performances," Trey replied with a touch of amusement. "So, why am I here tonight when I should be at home and in bed?"

"Savannah was attacked," Josh said. "There are tunnels under the town, and she was down there when somebody attacked her."

"Whoa." Trey held up both his hands to stop Josh from saying anything more. "Tunnels under the town? What are you talking about?"

"There's a whole network of tunnels," Savannah said. "I used one to go from my backyard to the edge of the lagoon where Shelly was murdered, but there are a bunch of them down there."

Trey stared at her as if she'd spoken a foreign language. "What are the tunnels for? Where do they go?" he finally asked.

Savannah explained to him that she only knew the one she used and had no idea where the others went. "I thought I was the only one who knew about them until

I told Josh, but obviously I was wrong. Somebody else was down there tonight."

Trey scratched his head as if that might help him absorb the information. "I've never even heard a rumor about tunnels under the ground, and I've lived here all my life."

"I think they're old…really old," Savannah said.

"The whole point of calling you is that somebody attacked Savannah when she was coming back in one of the tunnels from her ghost walk," Josh said, as if impatient that Trey was preoccupied with the tunnels and not focused on the attack that had taken place.

"Okay, let's hear what happened," Trey said.

As Savannah recounted the attack, a cold core built up inside her as she remembered her horror, the shock of realizing not only she was not alone down there, but also somebody had intended to drag her off to some-place unknown.

When she was finished, Trey frowned. "You haven't given me much to go on. You didn't see the person, so you can't identify anyone. Have either of you told anyone about the tunnels besides me?"

"No," they said in unison.

"I intended to tell you about them in the morning, but then things went crazy tonight," Josh said.

"Don't tell anyone else," Trey said. "I need to talk to Mayor Burns, and I don't want a bunch of yahoos going down there before we've had a chance to discuss how to proceed responsibly."

"I'd just like to get my hands around the throat of the person who grabbed Savannah," Josh said with a touch of fervor in his voice.

"Maybe she surprised whoever was down there and he just reacted," Trey offered.

"All he had to do was back away deeper into that tunnel and I would never have seen him," Savannah replied.

"First thing tomorrow morning I'll be here, and you're going to show me exactly where the entrance to the tunnel is," Trey said to Savannah. "Maybe by figuring out where the other tunnels go, we can also figure out who attacked you."

"I want to be here in the morning, too," Josh said.

"You can't work all night and work all day as well," Trey replied.

"I'll be off the clock at seven. If I decide to be here when you go down, it's on my own time and it's my own choice," Josh countered. "I can always catch a nap before my shift tomorrow night."

Trey shrugged. "It's your call." He turned to look at Savannah. "Why don't I plan on meeting you here at nine?"

"That's fine," she replied. It was now out of her hands. The secret had been told, and she was vaguely surprised to realize she was a bit relieved that she had little or no control over what happened next.

Once the sheriff had left, Savannah also realized she wasn't quite ready to be alone. "Would you mind hanging around long enough for me to take a shower?" she asked.

"Of course. I'll hang around as long as you need me," he replied.

"Feel free to make some coffee or get anything else you want to drink." She got up from the table, eager to get beneath a spray of hot water. She felt as if the tunnel dirt had burrowed into her very soul. The touch of a stranger who meant her harm clung to her and needed to be washed away.

"I'm good. I usually meet Daniel Carson at George's Diner around three thirty, and we grab a cup of coffee together," he said, speaking of a fellow officer who worked the night shift as well.

"You should be able to meet him as usual," she replied. "I shouldn't be long." She got up from the table and headed for the master bedroom with its adjoining bath. The bedroom was empty of furniture, but she often used the bathroom because it was bigger than the one in the hallway.

She set the water in the shower to hot and then climbed out of the filthy gown, untied the flashlight at her waist and took off the white slip she wore beneath.

All the clothing would go into the garbage. Shelly's ghost would walk no more. She adjusted the water so she wouldn't scald herself and then stepped beneath the spray.

She used a small bath brush to scrub the dirt from beneath her nails and then shampooed her hair twice. Each time the horror of those moments in the tunnel tried to take hold, she shoved it back, telling herself it was over now. Josh had gotten to her in time, and there was no reason to be afraid anymore.

And yet the fear didn't seem to get the message that she was now safe. There was no reason to believe the person in the tunnel was specifically after her, no reason to think she was in any more danger.

By the time she finished her shower, she'd managed to distill some of the fear. She noted on the nightstand clock that it was three in the morning. She pulled on her nightgown and a pink cotton robe and then combed her long wet hair and pulled it back with a clip at the nape of her neck.

She found Josh still seated at the table. His eyes lit up at the sight of her. "Feel better?"

"Tons better," she replied.

"Savannah, I'm sorry I wasn't here when you went down into the tunnel."

She offered him a small smile. "Josh, you're a deputy. Trust me, I don't blame you for not being here. You have other responsibilities that come first."

"Still, I should have been here for you." His features displayed his irritation at himself.

"I'd just like to know who was down there and what they were doing."

"Hopefully over the next couple of days we can figure that out." He gazed at her curiously. "How do you feel about no longer doing the ghost walks?"

"Conflicted," she answered honestly. "Someplace in the back of my mind, I knew it had become an unhealthy compulsion, but it helped me keep Shelly relevant…alive. But I meant it when I said tonight was my last walk."

"If you got out more, you'd realize that she's still very relevant. Since Bo has returned to town, he and Claire are asking questions about the night of her death, trying to figure out the truth about what happened that night."

"And what do you think the truth of that night is?" she asked.

"I don't know." He said the words flatly, as if he didn't want to talk about it.

She looked at the clock on the wall. "You'd better get going if you're to meet Daniel at three thirty."

"Are you okay to be here alone?"

"I'm fine now. I'm just ready to go to bed and get a short but good night's sleep before Trey shows up here in the morning." She stood, a deep exhaustion hitting her out of nowhere.

He got up as well, and together they walked to the front door. Before opening it, he turned to face her. "I was just thinking, you gave me a great gourmet meal last night. How about next Thursday night you let me cook for you?"

"Oh, that's not necessary."

"Come on, Savannah. It wouldn't be nice of you not to let me return the favor."

She stared at him. He was so handsome, and there was no question she was drawn to him in a way that was both exciting and frightening. *It's just dinner, for crying out loud*, a little voice whispered in her head.

"Okay," she heard herself agree.

"Great. Why don't we say around six thirty at my place? In the meantime, I'll see you in the morning."

He opened the door, but before he stepped out, he turned back to face her. "You know, tonight wasn't necessarily the end of anything. If you let it, it could be the beginning of a new phase in your life. You don't have to be alone, Savannah."

"I know. Good night, Josh, and thank you for being there when I needed you."

In the back of her mind she wanted to be in his arms. She wanted him to kiss her until she was mindless and no longer had the lingering taste of fear in her mouth. She took a step backward, shocked by her desire.

"Anytime." He hesitated a moment, as if he sensed her desire. His eyes darkened and her breath caught in the back of her throat, but then he turned and went out the door.

She watched him until he reached his car in the driveway, and then she closed and locked the door. She checked the back door to make sure it was secured and then headed for bed.

It was only when she was curled up on her side that she thought of Josh's parting words. What he didn't understand was that she didn't want a new phase in her life. She didn't want a new life at all.

What he didn't understand was that she'd been

blessedly numb in her isolation. What she feared most was that if she stepped out of that isolation, she might feel again, and those feelings would truly drive her into madness.

Chapter Five

It was a restless night for Savannah. She tossed and turned with thoughts of the horrifying attack, her confused feelings about Josh and the knowledge that she would never make a ghost walk again.

She didn't want to, not now that she knew somebody else was also using the tunnels, somebody who had presented a danger to her. In fact, she wouldn't mind a bit if Josh brought in that backhoe and filled in the entrance to the tunnel in her backyard.

As she dressed for the day, she thought about the dinner invitation she'd accepted from Josh. She shouldn't go. She should find some reason to cancel. It was just a bad idea, and yet when she thought of how his features had lit up when she'd finally agreed, she knew she wasn't going to cancel on him.

She'd get through the meal, and then that would be the end of any interaction with Josh. She wasn't interested in a romantic flirtation. She wasn't interested in finding love.

She'd loved her parents, and they had deserted her. She'd loved her brother despite his flaws, but he wanted nothing to do with her. Finally, she'd loved Shelly, and Shelly had been stolen from her. She would never use her heart again. She would never allow her emotions to return to life again.

Dinner and done, she thought as she worked her hair into a single braid down her back. As an afterthought, she slid a pale pink lip gloss over her lips and then left the bathroom.

Josh, Trey and Mayor Burns should be arriving within the next fifteen minutes or so. She poured herself a cup of coffee and sat at the kitchen table to wait for them.

She was going down that tunnel one last time with the men. She had to show Trey Walker exactly where she had been dragged and into what tunnel she might have disappeared if not for Josh's fortuitous appearance.

She was unsurprised when Josh was the first of the men to arrive. He appeared at the back door. His night of work showed in his tired eyes and in the slightly deepened lines on his face.

"Coffee?" she asked in greeting.

"Please," he replied and plopped down in the same chair where he'd always sat before, as if he'd claimed it as his own.

He'd obviously gone home from work and changed clothes before coming here, for he wore a pair of jeans and a dark blue T-shirt that did dazzling things to his eyes.

"You look like you need some sleep," she said as she set the coffee before him and then resumed her seat.

"I'll be all right. I'll get a second wind going, and then later this afternoon I'll catch a nap before heading back in to work at eleven." He took a sip of the coffee and set the cup back on the table.

"I checked in with Trey a little while ago, and he and Mayor Burns are eager to get down into the tunnels. They're bringing ropes and colored chalk to mark the passageways so that none of us gets lost down there."

"I think it would be easy to get lost down there," Savannah replied. "That's why I never veered from the tunnel that took me to the lagoon."

"Did you sleep okay after I left? No nightmares?" he asked.

"No nightmares, but it took me a long time to finally go to sleep. I'm going down with you today."

He looked at her in surprise. "I don't think that's a good idea. Besides, why would you want to go?"

"I'll be perfectly safe with the three of you men, and I think I need to go back to banish the memory of the bogeyman."

He raised a dark brow. "So, you did have nightmares."

"No, I just had a hard time getting things out of my mind. I need to go back down there one more time, Josh. I know I'll be safe with all of you there, and it will get last night out of my mind."

"Okay, if it will help, then you'll make us a four-man team." He took another drink of his coffee and sat up straighter in his chair. "I have to admit, I'm more than a little excited to see where all the tunnels lead. And we need to catch the guy responsible for the attack on you last night."

"What I don't understand is this. If he just wanted to scare me, he did that when he grabbed my arm. It was obvious I was terrified, and all I wanted to do was get away. Why did he grab my foot and try to drag me farther into that unknown tunnel?"

Josh's eyes darkened and narrowed. "That's the most important thing to figure out. Who else is using those tunnels and for what purpose? If we can find the answer to those questions then we'll know who attacked you."

"And then I want that tunnel entrance in the backyard filled in so that nobody can climb in or out of that hole ever again," she exclaimed fervently.

At that moment the doorbell rang. Savannah got up to answer. Ten minutes later she and the three men stood at the bush in her backyard. "It's about a three-foot drop, and then the tunnel descends quickly to allow a person to stand," she explained.

As she gazed down the hole where she had descended so many times in the past year, a shiver ran up her spine. She couldn't stop thinking of the night before.

Josh stepped closer to her, as if he'd felt her shiver and somehow wanted to banish it. Sheriff Trey Walker held several lengths of nylon rope, and Mayor Jim Burns had a box of sidewalk chalk in a variety of colors. They all carried high-beam flashlights.

Burns was dressed in a lightweight dark suit and a

white shirt. He had been mayor for less than a year, unseating Mayor Frank Kean, who had served the community in the position of mayor for twelve years.

Jim Burns was younger and had been responsible for the amusement park buying land and building in Lost Lagoon. He was also ambitious, high-strung and more than a little bit arrogant.

Savannah was surprised he hadn't brought his protégé and butt-kisser, city councilman Neil Sampson, with him. She was also surprised that Trey had come without his lapdog, Deputy Ray McClure, a creep who seemed to get away with as little work as possible.

Burns took off his jacket and carefully laid it on the ground, all the while nearly dancing with excitement. "I couldn't believe it when Trey told me about the tunnel system this morning. Let's get to it."

He was the first to descend, followed by Trey. Josh gestured for Savannah to go next, and then he brought up the rear. Instantly she felt a claustrophobia she'd never experienced before as more flashbacks from the night before ran through her head.

"You said this main tunnel runs straight to the lagoon?" Mayor Burns asked.

"Yes, but there are seven or so offshoots between here and there," Savannah replied. "The third one was where I was attacked."

Trey turned back to Josh. "But you checked that tunnel last night and didn't find anything?"

"I followed it until I came to a fork and then wasn't

sure which one to follow, so I came back," Josh explained.

"I think we need to proceed methodically," Burns replied. "We'll start with the first offshoot we come to."

Savannah bit back her disappointment. She'd hoped to follow the tunnel she'd been dragged into to see where it led. Even if there were forks, they could have explored where each one led.

They started down the first offshoot. Trey began to trail the thin rope as they walked, like leaving breadcrumbs for them to follow back home.

Flashlight beams danced on the walls, on the floor and ahead of them as they moved in silence. She had a feeling Trey and Jim were silent with awe. She couldn't help her own curiosity and was aware of the comfort of knowing that Josh had her back.

When they reached another tunnel on the left, Jim pulled out a piece of yellow chalk. As they walked down that way, he marked their path with bright yellow arrows.

Savannah had an unusually good sense of direction; it was what had guided her down the tunnel to the lagoon in the first place. She sensed that this new underpass was taking them someplace in the center of town.

They'd walked for quite some time, stopping every couple of yards for Jim to mark the wall, when they finally came to the end of the tunnel and a set of stairs that led upward.

Savannah's heart began to beat too fast as she wondered where the stairs would lead them. Was this where her attacker might have come from? Trey shoved the mayor behind him and pulled his gun. A glance backward showed her that Josh also had his gun out of his holster.

Had it been out the entire time he'd been walking behind her? Was he intent on protecting her from anyone who might come up behind them?

She chided herself. It wasn't about her. Certainly protecting the mayor of the city would be uppermost in Trey's and Josh's minds.

At the top of the stairs was an old wooden trap door in the ceiling. Trey shoved it open about an inch, just enough to allow in a faint glow of daylight.

"Where does it go?" Jim asked in a whisper.

"I'm not sure. I won't know where we are until we go up." He shoved the door open farther, but held it so that it wouldn't make any noise when it fell to whatever floor it was in.

Trey stepped up first and then the others followed. Savannah immediately suspected where they were...in the storeroom in the back of Mama Baptiste's Apothecary Shop. The smell of herbs and spices, of mysterious roots and such filled the air.

Trey closed the door quickly, and Savannah noted that it seemed to disappear as it fit so neatly into the dusty wood floor. It would be easy for nobody to know it was there.

Trey held up his finger to silence anyone from speaking while wild thoughts flew through Savannah's head. There was no way it had been Mama Baptiste down in the tunnel the night she'd been attacked.

But what about Mama Baptiste's son, thirty-three-year-old Eric? He and Shelly had shared a friendship of sorts before her death, but Savannah had always found the dark-haired, black-eyed man to radiate a dangerous energy.

Was it possible that he'd been the person to attack her? And if so, why? And if he had some reason to want to hurt her, would he come after her again?

Mama Baptiste squealed in surprise as the four of them came out of her storage room. She clasped a hand to her chest. "Most of my customers use the front door instead of the back, and they don't come in with guns drawn," she exclaimed.

Josh put his gun back in his holster, as did Trey. Mama's store held walls of tourist-type items for sale, but her main business was the herb and root concoctions she mixed and sold to people in town who suffered everything from an upset stomach to arthritis.

Strange herbs and roots hung drying from rafters in the ceiling, and Mama herself looked part gypsy with her long salt-and-pepper hair wild down her shoulders. She was clad in a bright red peasant-style blouse and a floor-length red-and-yellow floral skirt.

"We didn't use the back door," Jim said.

Mama Baptiste frowned in confusion. "Then how did you get in?"

"Through a tunnel that led to a trap door in the floor in your storage room," Trey said.

Josh watched Mama's face intently. She appeared genuinely shocked. "What are you talking about? A door in my floor?"

"Come on. I'll show you." Trey disappeared into the back room with Mama Baptiste as Mayor Burns wandered away from where Savannah and Josh stood near the counter.

"What about Eric?" Savannah asked softly.

"Have you and he had any problems?" Josh asked.

"None. I know he and Shelly were friendly, at least as much as Eric is friendly with anyone, but he and I have never had much interaction," Savannah replied.

"I swear I didn't know that hole in the floor was there," Mama Baptiste said as she and Trey returned from the back room.

"Maybe we should speak with Eric," Josh said. "Is he around?"

"I'm not sure where he is," Mama replied. She walked behind the counter and picked up a cell phone. "I can call him and get him here. But what does a tunnel have to do with Eric?"

"We'd just like to have a talk with him," Trey said with a sharp gaze at Josh.

Josh tamped down an edge of irritation. God forbid he attempt to do his job, especially when his boss was around. Mama made the call, and while they waited for Eric to arrive, Jim and Trey talked to her about business while Savannah and Josh wandered the aisles of the store.

Savannah said nothing, but Josh sensed a nervous

energy emanating from her, one that he didn't understand given the circumstances of the situation.

He finally took her by the arm and led her to a corner of the store, away from where the others stood waiting for Eric to arrive.

"What's going on? You seem unusually nervous."

Her dark chocolate-colored eyes gazed up at him, and in the depths of them he saw not just anxiety but also confusion. "I was just remembering back to the time before Shelly's murder. She and Eric were spending some time together, and Shelly had told me one night that she had a sticky situation on her hands, but she refused to be specific about what she was talking about."

Josh contemplated her words. "Do you think Eric had something to do with your sister's murder?"

"I don't know who killed Shelly, and I've really not had any interaction with Eric since Shelly's death. He just always made me feel uncomfortable."

"You haven't had much interaction with much of anyone since your sister's death," Josh replied.

"And that's the way I like it," she said firmly.

Josh wanted to tell her that it wasn't right for her to be such a recluse, that she was young and beautiful and deserved a life of happiness. Before he could say any of those things, Eric walked into the shop.

Eric Baptiste had the proverbial bad-boy aura. Clad in black jeans and a short-sleeved black T-shirt, he also had lean features and lips that looked as if they'd never smiled.

He was something of a mystery. He'd been born and raised in Lost Lagoon, but he was a loner who didn't appear to have friends and lived alone in one of the shanties on the swamp side of town.

"What's going on here?" he asked as his gaze went from Trey to Josh.

"Do you know about the tunnel under the floor in the storeroom?" Trey asked.

Eric's eyes narrowed slightly, so slightly that Josh wondered if anyone else noticed. It was a definite tell to Josh what the answer was to the question.

"Yeah, I know about the tunnels," Eric replied. His mother looked at him in surprise.

"Have you been down there?" Trey asked.

"I've used them." He looked at Savannah. "I use the same tunnel you do to get to the swamp."

"Why?" Trey asked.

"It's the easiest way to get to the swamp to gather the herbs and roots that Mama uses in her concoctions."

Savannah moved a bit closer to Josh. "Did you attack me? Did you try to drag me into another tunnel?"

Eric's features expressed genuine surprise. "I'd never hurt you, Savannah." His gaze on her was dark and intense, and Josh fought the impulse to place an arm around her and pull her tight against him.

A softness swept over Eric's face. "I can't believe how much you look like her." He frowned and turned back to face Trey.

"How well do you know the tunnel system?" Trey asked.

"I know there are lots of tunnels, and I also know Savannah and I aren't the only ones who have used them."

"Who else?" Jim asked. "And do you know the network well enough to map it out for us?"

Eric shook his head. "I don't know who else, but several times when I've been down there, I've heard male voices. I tried one night to figure out where they were coming from, but sound is distorted down there, and I never saw anyone else."

"What about mapping the network?" Jim repeated.

Once again Eric shook his head, his shaggy black hair shining in the light dancing through the store's window. "No way. I've only been in a couple of the tunnels. I mostly use the one in the back room to get to the tunnel that Savannah has been using to get to the lagoon."

"So you knew Savannah was using that tunnel," Josh said.

"I knew that she was mostly in the tunnel on Thursday or Friday nights, so I stayed away on those nights," Eric replied.

Once again he looked at Savannah. "If this is about somebody attacking you, then you all need to look someplace else. Shelly and I had become friends before her murder, and I would never hurt Savannah. When I look at her, she reminds me of how much I cared about Shelly."

"Where were you last night around midnight?" Trey asked.

Eric tensed and a knot appeared in his jaw, pulsing

in irritation. "I was at home at midnight last night. Was anyone with me? No, I don't have visitors. Did anyone call me? No, I don't chitchat on my phone at that time of night."

"Then nobody can corroborate your alibi," Trey said.

"My son would never hurt anyone," Mama exclaimed.

"Is this the part where you tell me not to leave town?" Eric asked wryly. "Is that it? Can I go now?"

Trey waved his hand dismissively. Eric nodded to his mother, then to Savannah, and then left the store.

"Everyone in town thinks Eric is just a no-count loner swamp rat who works for his mother in her store," Mama Baptiste said, her dark eyes lit with a fiery glow. "But he has a degree in botany. He could work anywhere he wanted, but he chooses to stay here in a town that gives him no respect, because he loves me. He would never hurt anyone."

"We're done here for now," Trey said.

"We're done for the day," Jim replied and gestured for them to follow him out the front door. "I've got a two-thirty meeting with Rod Nixon and Frank Kean about amusement park business," he said once they were outside in the hot afternoon sun. Rod Nixon was the owner of the amusement park.

Jim looked down at his white shirt that now had the tinge of brown dirt. "I need to get showered and changed. We'll work the tunnels again tomorrow, but in the meantime, I want this all kept quiet, and I don't want anyone down there without me." He turned to

Savannah. "I'll pick up my suit jacket from your place sometime tomorrow."

"I'll walk with you back to the station," Trey said to the mayor. City Hall was located right next door to the sheriff's station. "Josh, go home and get some sleep. Savannah, I'll be in touch if I learn anything new about the attack."

Together the two men headed down the street, and Josh turned to Savannah. "Come on, I'll walk you home."

"That's not necessary," she protested. "You need to get to bed so that you can be alert for your night shift."

"A few extra minutes won't matter, and besides, I insist," he replied.

They walked down the sidewalk that would take them to the side street that would eventually lead to her house. "I can't believe that Eric was using the same tunnel I've been using for so long and I never knew," she said.

"You know that makes him our number one suspect in the attack on you," Josh replied.

"But he said he'd heard other voices down there, which means somebody else is using the tunnels," she protested.

"That's what he said."

"You don't believe him?"

Josh released a tired sigh. "At this point I don't know what to believe. All I know is that I didn't like the way Eric looked at you or that he said you look so much like Shelly."

Somewhere in the back of his mind, Josh knew his feelings for Savannah weren't just professional. It was a touch of personal jealousy that had winged through him as he'd seen the soft look Eric had given her.

"Are you implying that Eric might have killed Shelly? I certainly didn't hear his name mentioned during the investigation." There was a touch of censure in her voice.

"We didn't know about any connection between Eric and Shelly at the time," he replied. A knot formed in his stomach, as it always did when he thought of the sloppy investigation into Shelly's murder.

They turned off onto the side street. "All I know is that I think it would be a good idea for you to keep your distance from Eric."

"I keep my distance from everyone," she replied wryly. "The only person I see on a regular basis is Chad Williams, who delivers groceries to me once a week, and my neighbor, who wishes I'd move out."

"Jeffrey Allen?"

She nodded. "I think he was thrilled when my parents left town, but he was upset that they left the house to Mac and me. He was hoping he would finally be able to buy it. He's rude and hateful and has made it clear that he thinks I should move out and sell the house."

"Has he given you any indication that he knows about the tunnels?"

"No, but I'm sure he probably knows about the one in my backyard now since we all went down it this morning. I imagine he was at his back window watching everything. There isn't much he misses in the neighborhood."

"Maybe you just gave me a second suspect to add to the short list," Josh said.

"I don't know. He's a creep but I can't imagine him going to such a length as attacking me to get me to move out."

By that time they'd reached her house. She pulled a small key ring from her back pocket and unlocked her front door, then turned back to face him. "Thanks for the company. Now go home and go to bed."

"You'd better do the same. You have a night shift to work tonight, too."

"True, but I can doze on my night shift. You have to be alert and ready to fight crime at any moment."

"If I don't see you before, I'll see you Thursday night at my place for dinner. Around six thirty?"

She hesitated, and he sensed she was about to cancel on him. He didn't want that to happen. He knew that she was forever changed by the murder of her sister and the basic destruction of her family, but he also knew she dwelt in a dark place that had become far too comfortable for her.

"I've already bought the best steaks in town and can't wait to get your opinion on my special seasoning," he said hurriedly.

She nodded, albeit with obvious reluctance. "Then I'll see you Thursday night."

"Great," he replied.

Minutes later as he headed toward home, pleasure

filled him at the anticipation of Thursday night, but it was tempered by concern about the attack on her.

Did Eric entertain some kind of sick obsession with Shelly that had now transferred to Savannah? Had he been the one who had attacked her? Or were there really other people using the tunnels? And for what purpose?

Was it possible that something evil was going on beneath the streets of Lost Lagoon?

Chapter Six

Josh felt as if he were preparing for the first date he'd ever had in his life. He awoke about noon and laid out the frozen steaks to thaw, then immediately set to cleaning the house as if a dignitary was coming to visit.

A nervous energy filled him, definitely because he would be spending time alone with Savannah. They wouldn't be traipsing through tunnels or talking to local officials. It would just be the two of them over dinner.

He desperately wanted the night to go well. He wanted the conversation to flow light and easy and for her to feel comfortable in his presence.

They would be eating in his kitchen rather than the formal dining room, which had become his home office. The top of the fine mahogany dining room table was currently covered with a large piece of poster board on which he'd been attempting to map the tunnels.

The kitchen was cozier anyway, he told himself. The round oak table would be conducive to a more intimate setting.

He was in the process of wrapping potatoes in aluminum foil to go into the oven when Daniel Carson opened his back door and walked in. "Don't you look domestic," he said in amusement. "All you're missing is a frilly apron."

"Just making sure I have everything under control," Josh replied. He gestured his fellow deputy and friend to a chair at the table. "Want something to drink?"

"I wouldn't turn down a cold beer," Daniel replied.

Josh snagged two bottles from the fridge and then sat across from Daniel. "So, what's the news of the day?"

"I had breakfast at the café this morning and heard that May Johnson's son is in the hospital from a dope overdose. It was apparently meth."

Josh raised a brow. "We don't get much of that around here. How's he doing?"

"He'll survive. How goes the underworld?"

"I'm not sure I understand why Jim decided to change courses and start in the tunnels closest to the swamp rather than those closest to Savannah's backyard, but we've been down there three times in the last week and have managed to map out a single branch with several forks."

"Anything exciting found?" Daniel asked and then took a swig of his beer.

"Dirt and more dirt. No gold coins, no rubies or diamonds or pirate treasure, just dirt and a couple of exits."

"Exits where?"

"One came up in the floor of one of the abandoned shanties on the swamp side of town, and another one opened up in a pile of brush just outside of town." Josh paused to sip his beer. "We haven't found any sign that those tunnels have been used in recent times."

"Shouldn't they call in some kind of expert for this?" Daniel asked.

"I imagine Mayor Burns eventually will, but I swear right now he's like a kid with a new adventure to explore. He doesn't seem inclined to share the information about the tunnels just yet."

"It is pretty amazing that they've been there all this time and nobody ever knew," Daniel replied. He leaned back in his chair and looked around the kitchen, then focused his attention back on Josh.

"You realize a steak dinner isn't going to make you feel less guilty about what happened two years ago," he said.

"That's not what tonight is about," Josh protested. "She fed me a gourmet meal last week, and so I'm just returning the favor."

"You know I feel guilty, too, about how the investigation into Shelly Sinclair's death went down, but we both knew we'd be risking our jobs if we tried to buck Trey's assessment of the murder. If we'd done anything differently we would have been fired and nothing would have been different anyway."

"I just wonder how different Savannah's life might have been for the last two years if we'd gotten the job done right," Josh admitted.

"I don't want you going all savior on me and try-

ing to save Savannah from herself and in the meantime getting hurt."

"I just think she needs a friend right now."

"Yeah, but the real question is, does she *want* a friend
right now?" Daniel countered.

The question hung in Josh's mind long after Daniel
had left. Was he trying to assuage his guilt by attempting to build a relationship with Savannah? Or was he
simply on a misguided quest to find the woman who
had once made his heart beat just a little bit faster, a
woman he'd wanted to pursue before tragedy struck?

It didn't matter that he wasn't sure of the answer.
All he knew was that he was looking forward to the
evening. By the time six twenty had arrived, he was
dressed in a pair of jeans and a button-up short-sleeved
blue-and-silver-striped shirt.

The table was set. The potatoes were cooking. The
steaks were seasoned, and a fresh salad was in the
fridge. The only thing missing was his date, and she
should be arriving within the next fifteen minutes.

He had called her last night to confirm tonight
but had gotten the impression that if there had been
a graceful way for her to back out, she would have
taken it. But he hadn't given her a chance.

He'd tucked in his shirt twice and opened a bottle
of wine when the doorbell rang. He hurried to answer,
and when he opened his door, he nearly lost his breath
to the beauty of the woman before him.

Clad in a peach-colored sundress that displayed her

beautiful shoulders, her small waistline and the length of her legs, she looked gorgeous.

It was obvious she'd taken extra time and trouble with her appearance. Her lashes looked longer and darker, a faint blush colored her cheeks and her hair fell in soft waves around her shoulders. The only things missing were a smile and a light of anything in her eyes.

"Are you going to invite me in?" she finally asked.

"Oh yeah, of course." He opened the door farther to allow her entry into his hallway. As she passed him, he smelled the floral scent that stirred him on every level.

"Your home is beautiful," she said as she entered the living room. It was furnished with modern but comfortable black-and-white furniture and glass-topped end and coffee tables.

"Let me give you the full tour," he said. She followed him down the hallway, where he showed her the two guest bedrooms, a guest bath and then the master suite complete with the bathroom with the oversized tub. He knew his pride was obvious, but he couldn't help it.

"You have wonderful taste," she said.

"You might change your mind when you see the formal dining room." He led her into the room filled with a desk, computer equipment, file cabinets and the table covered with the poster board of the mapped tunnels.

"You're mapping the tunnels," she said, stating the obvious.

"I'm doing the best I can with the information Trey gives to me. As you can see by the new red and green lines, they've fully explored two more tunnels in the last couple of days, although nothing extraordinary has been found. But we're not talking about that tonight." He gestured her to follow him into the kitchen.

She gasped in surprise as she saw the built-in double oven and an upscale microwave and convection oven. "Do you do a lot of cooking?" she asked as he gestured her to a chair at the table.

"Nah, I occasionally use one of the ovens, but the microwave and my barbecue pit are my real friends. The brick pit on the back patio even has a place for pizza baking. Wine?"

"Okay," she agreed. "Why would you go to the expense to put in such a kitchen when you don't cook?"

"Resale value," he replied. He set a crystal stem of red wine next to the red-and-black dishware that adorned the table. "I think my builder probably took advantage of me in adding all this stuff, especially since I have no desire to sell or move anywhere else."

"It's a dream kitchen," she replied, and for the first time since she'd arrived, her eyes lit with pleasure. "Is there anything I can do to help?" she asked when he took a salad from the refrigerator and placed it in the center of the table.

"Just tell me how you like your steak. Mooing, medium or well-done?"

She laughed. It was a brief noise like a wind chime musically dancing with a sudden breeze. It lasted only a mere second and appeared to surprise her as much as it pleased him.

"I'm sorry. I've never heard rare described as 'mooing' before," she said.

"Don't apologize for laughing, Savannah. If I had the ability, I'd make you laugh as often as possible."

Her eyes went dark. "Medium rare, that's how I like my steak." She focused on her wine and took a sip.

He'd stepped over the line. He picked up the plate with the seasoned steaks. "I'm going to throw these on the grill. I'll be right back." He stepped out the back door, where the elaborate brick grill was hot and ready to cook the meat.

He placed the steaks on the grill and then went back inside. "I'll need to go back out and turn them in just a few minutes."

"Tell me about the special steak rub you use," she said.

"Ah, it's an old family secret," he replied as he leaned a hip against the counter.

"But you're going to share that secret with me," she said with a small curve of her lips.

Hell, if he were a CIA agent, he'd spill every secret he knew for one of her rare, beautiful smiles. "I suppose I am. It's a little bit of molasses, a little bit of bacon and a pinch of cayenne pepper."

"Hmm, sweet with a little kick."

He grinned at her. "Reminds me of somebody I know."

That earned him a genuine smile. "I don't know how sweet I am, but I definitely have a kick."

All too quickly the steaks were done and the meal

was on the table. The conversation revolved around cooking as she shared some of her favorite recipes and he told her about his botched attempts to do any real cooking.

Those stories made her laugh several times. It was sweet music to his ears and confirmed to him that someplace inside the shell she presented to the world was a vibrant young woman who deserved a better life than the one she'd committed herself to.

"Let me help with the cleanup," she said when they finished the meal.

"Nonsense, I have all night to take care of it. How about we take a glass of wine into the living room and talk a little bit more?"

"Okay," she agreed.

He'd noticed her relaxing as the night had progressed, and the fact that she agreed to stay for another glass of wine and a little conversation pleased him.

He carried their wineglasses and followed her into the living room. Instead of sitting on the sofa, she walked over to the bookcase that held keepsakes and photos.

"These are your parents?" she asked and pointed to one of the framed pictures.

"Yeah, those are my folks. They live in Georgia."

"Are you close to them?"

"As close as I can be living this far away," he replied. "I talk to them about twice a week. They come and visit on their anniversary, and I always go home for Christmas."

She pointed to another photo and looked at him in surprise. "Is that you? And do you have a twin brother?"

"Yes, and I did have a twin brother. He died in a car accident when we were fifteen."

She picked up the photo and sank down on the sofa, and he noticed that her hands trembled slightly. She looked up at him, and her eyes were shiny with tears. "How did you manage to survive?"

He sat next to her. "I took his death hard, but I knew I had to go on if for no other reason than to honor him in my heart. That sports car I have is a car Jacob and I dreamed of owning when we were young. We both wanted to be cops when we grew up, and so here I am wearing a deputy's star. I survived, Savannah, and I went on to live my life because it was the only thing I knew how to do."

THE KNOWLEDGE THAT he'd lost a twin brother nearly stole her breath away. For just a moment she forgot about her own losses. She wanted to hold him, to comfort him for the tragedy in his own life.

"I'm so sorry." She didn't even realize she'd slipped her hand into his until she felt the warmth of his wrapping around hers.

"Thanks. It was a long time ago. Sometimes bad things happen to good people, but you already know that."

She set the picture on the coffee table. "Tell me about him."

He smiled. "Jacob was two minutes older than me,

and he never let me forget it. He was definitely the dominant twin. I was a bit shyer, and I idolized him." His smile drifted away.

"That's the way it was between me and Shelly," she replied. "She was only a year older than me, but she was more social and outgoing than me. I idolized her, too. But I was always Shelly's little sister to most of the people in town."

"Just like for the first fifteen years of my life I was Jacob's twin. It took me a while to figure out who I was without him."

She stood and took the picture and returned it to where it belonged. When she returned to the sofa, she took a sip of her wine and eyed him over the rim of the glass. "How did you do it, Josh?" she asked when she'd lowered the glass.

"I just figured the best way to honor Jacob was to live well. I had to find out who I was alone, and that meant just moving forward."

"I should get home," she said abruptly. The night had been too pleasant, his company both relaxing and exciting. Now knowing they shared common tragedies only pulled her emotionally closer to him, and she needed to get away from him.

"It's still early," he protested. "At least finish your wine."

She shook her head, stood and grabbed her purse next to her. "Thanks, but I've had enough wine." He jumped up off the sofa, and she headed for the front door. She turned back to him. "Thank you for a lovely meal, and I think that makes us even where dinner is concerned."

He stepped closer to her, and her heart jumped up in rhythm at his nearness. He smiled, that sexy expression that always pulled a pool of heat into her stomach.

"I don't think we should keep score on dinners," he said teasingly. The light in his eyes darkened, and he reached out and took hold of her chin. "I never saw you as Shelly's sister. You were always sweet, sexy Savannah to me."

Before she knew his intention, his lips captured hers. She wanted to pull away, but his mouth was oh so warm and inviting. Instead of stepping back, she found herself leaning into him, opening her mouth to allow him to deepen the kiss.

She'd once dreamed of what it might be like to be kissed by Josh Griffin, but now she knew her wildest dreams had simply been pale imitations of the real thing. There was no way she could have dreamed of the magic and the fire in his kiss.

She wanted to melt into his arms and stay there forever, and that was what made her break the kiss and step back from him. "I've got to go," she said, needing to escape before she fell into his arms again.

He stepped back from her. "Savannah, find yourself again. Find the person separate from Shelly."

She didn't tell him goodbye. She raced out the door

to escape not just her desire for him, but also his parting words.

She kept her mind carefully schooled to blankness as she drove the short distance home. It was only when she was in bed that she mulled over the night.

There was no question that she'd enjoyed his company. He'd made her laugh for the first time in years, and for the most part, their conversation had been relatively light and easy. He was still the man she'd found sexy and fun two years ago. He was still a man who drew her to him despite her desire to the contrary.

The fact that he'd lost somebody so close to him and had become the man he had spoke of his inner strength, a strength he didn't understand she didn't possess.

Shelly had been the strong one. Her parents had known it. Mac had known it. Everyone had known that Shelly was special, that she was a leader. Savannah had been happy to be in Shelly's shadow.

She tried to think about everything but that kiss. The kiss that had rocked her back on her heels and pulled forth a powerful emotion that had stunned her.

It was the thought of that kiss that finally got her out of bed around one. Sleep eluded her. She went into the kitchen and put the teapot on to boil water. Hopefully a cup of hot tea would relax her enough to sleep.

She pulled down a cup and readied a tea bag and then moved to the kitchen window and stared out into the night. Tomorrow night would be the first time in a long time that she wasn't going to make her ghost walk.

What on earth would she do instead with her night off? She started to move away from the window and then froze. She thought she saw some movement near the back of the yard, where several trees flanked the bush that hid the hole in the ground.

Was there somebody out there? Hiding behind the tree on the left and watching her? Was it Eric Baptiste? Had he been obsessed with Shelly and now had some sort of obsession with her?

She turned off the kitchen light and continued to watch the tree. Had she only imagined somebody out there? Was she just being paranoid?

The whistle from the copper teapot nearly sent her through the ceiling. She cast one more glance out the window and, still seeing nobody, she turned on the light and quickly moved the screeching teakettle off the burner.

Definitely paranoid, she told herself as she fixed her tea and then sat at the table to drink it. There was absolutely no reason to believe that she was somebody's specific target. The attack in the tunnel just might have been a case of being in the wrong place at the wrong time.

She finished her tea and went back to bed, where she finally fell into a deep sleep and dreamed of kissing Josh. When she awakened after noon the next day, her head was still filled with that kiss.

She spent Friday cooking and that evening had a meal of bourbon barbecue pork chops, cheesy corn and homemade biscuits with a touch of jalapeño peppers. She'd just finished eating when Josh called.

"I was wondering if you'd like a little company tonight," he said.

She knew what he was trying to do, fill the hours of the night when she'd normally be anticipating a ghost walk. "That's not necessary, Josh. I'm fine, and I'll be fine through the night."

"I just thought maybe…"

"Really, it isn't necessary," she said firmly. Dinner and done. That was what she had promised herself where he was concerned. "I've appreciated your support, Josh, but there's really no need for you to be worried about me anymore."

She could feel his disappointment even before he spoke. "Oh, okay then. You know I'll be in touch if we get a break in the attack on you in the tunnel."

"Thanks. Then I'll see you around." She hung up quickly, afraid that he might be able to talk her into letting him come over and hang out.

She spent the rest of the evening watching television and then at midnight headed to bed. She had to admit that there was a little bit of relief in not being able to pretend to be Shelly's ghost anymore.

For the first time in a long time, she was eager to go to work on Saturday night. At quarter 'til eleven she got into her car and drove toward the inn. She was grateful to have something to do besides think about her dead sister and a very much alive deputy.

She knocked on the locked front door, and Dorothy Abbott, the older woman who worked the shift before hers, hurried to unlock the door.

"Gonna have a hard time keeping your eyes open tonight," she said as she ushered Savannah inside. "Nobody is checked in. The place is quiet as a tomb." She handed the keys to Savannah. "And now I'm out of here."

The minute Dorothy was out of the door, Savannah relocked it and then headed for the reception desk and settled in for the long night.

She often wondered how Donnie Albright could keep the inn open with so few guests, but she assumed he must have family money and this place was just some sort of tax write-off for him.

She would never have managed to stay in her house if it hadn't been paid off when her parents moved away. Unlike Josh, who had maintained a close relationship with his parents, Savannah rarely heard from hers.

When she did call them, the conversation was strained and uncomfortable. It was as if she was a reminder of things they'd rather forget, a reminder of the daughter they had lost.

It was the same way with her brother, Mac. Since his marriage they'd had little interaction, and when they did it was usually because he wanted to take something out of the house.

Savannah had never been close to Mac and she had come to terms with the desertion of her family, but that didn't make it hurt any less. It only made her miss her sister more.

She pulled a notepad from the desk. It was a regular spiral notebook that she kept here to help her pass the long nights. She not only doodled mindlessly in it but also sometimes worked on recipes she'd like to try. She did this now, using the creative side of her brain to write down ingredients she thought might pair together well and then imagining how they might look on a plate.

The silence was broken only occasionally by thuds or thumps that she assumed were pipes expanding and contracting when the air conditioner turned on and off.

It was just after three when she got up to use the lobby restroom. She washed her hands and then wiped her face with a cold cloth in hopes of getting a second wind. She'd only been here four hours and already felt exhausted by doing nothing.

She stared at her reflection in the mirror over the sink and remembered that darned kiss from Josh. There was no question that he had been attempting to pursue something romantic with her. But she'd made it clear to him last night that she wasn't buying what he was selling.

She just wasn't ready to reenter life. There was still too much grief in her heart to allow in any other emotions. The problem was, Josh's kiss had shown her how to feel again.

Irritated that she was obsessing about a man she

wouldn't invite into her life, she left the bathroom and returned to her chair behind the desk.

She'd just sat down when the lights went out, plunging the inn into utter darkness.

Chapter Seven

Savannah remained frozen. This had never happened before. Had a fuse blown? She was sure the electrical wiring in the building was probably ancient, but she didn't even know where the fuse box was located.

She imagined it was someplace in the basement, but she didn't like to go down there. It was slightly dank and filled with supplies in boxes stacked with no rhyme or reason. Besides, the basement door was located in Donnie's private office.

Even if she found her way to the fuse box in the dark, she wouldn't know what to do when she got there. She knew nothing about electrical issues.

She was just about to reach for the phone to call Donnie when she heard a thump...thump...thump coming down the hallway upstairs. If she'd believed in ghosts, she would have assumed it was the spirit of old Peg Leg walking the hall.

But she didn't believe in ghosts. Whoever it was making the noise was very much human, and starting down the stairs.

"Hello? Who's there?" she asked.

There was no reply, but she could hear the person continuing down the stairs. If it was somebody not to fear, then why hadn't that somebody answered her?

Her heart banged in terror as she slid from her chair and beneath the desk. Who was in here? How had they gotten inside?

Was it possible somebody had sneaked in earlier in the day and had hidden in one of the guest rooms for this moment when she would be here all alone?

"Savannah." The sibilant, gruff, male whisper shot a new tremor of terror through her.

He knew her name. Whoever it was knew she was here, and he obviously wasn't interested in checking into a room for the night. The thumping stopped, and she had a feeling whoever it was had reached the bottom of the staircase.

"You bitch." The voice was guttural and impossible for her to identify. But one thing was clear…whoever he was, he was angry and she was in trouble.

She was a sitting duck under the desk. If he approached any closer she would have no way to escape, nowhere to run or hide.

At the moment the darkness was her friend. She had to assume if she couldn't see him, then he couldn't see her, either. Without making a sound, she scooted out from under the desk and headed in the direction of a large potted plant.

There were several plants in the lobby with pots

large enough for her to crouch behind. Her mind raced with options as she headed toward the closest plant.

She'd just reached the pot when a loud crash came from the direction of the chair she'd been seated in when the lights had first gone out.

She slammed a fist against her mouth in an effort to staunch the scream that begged to be released. She wondered if the noise she had heard when he'd walked across the upstairs had been a baseball bat or some other length of wood that he'd now used to slam into her chair.

Silence.

It was the ominous silence that occurred before an explosion, the proverbial calm before the storm. She tried to make herself as small as possible behind the planter and at the same time listened for any whisper of a sound that would let her know his location.

All of her senses were on fire as terror continued to beat her heart a million miles a minute. Was he close enough to hear her heart? Was he near enough to smell her perfume?

She couldn't smell him. She had no sense of anyone next to her or hovering nearby her. But the darkness of the room made her doubt her ability to sense anything correctly.

"Savannah, you can't hide from me forever." A small flashlight clicked on.

Although the beam of the light let her know he was across the lobby from her, it also shot her terror up a hundred notches. With that flashlight he could hunt her down.

He stood near the sitting area, but his beam of light shot back toward the desk, as if double-checking to make sure he hadn't missed her there.

She couldn't see him in any detail with the light he flashed before him. She couldn't even get a real sense of his height or weight.

Her mind whirled frantically. She couldn't slip into the bathroom. There were no windows, and eventually she'd be trapped in the two-stall room. Her cell phone was in her purse under the desk, so she couldn't call anyone for help. She couldn't even run for the door because it was locked and the keys were in the desk drawer.

The beam of light shone on the opposite side of the lobby, indicating to her that he was methodically checking anywhere that might be a hiding place.

Eventually he'd begin to work this side of the room, and she knew that if he found her, she would never leave the lobby alive. Why? What was this all about? Despite her fear, her brain worked to try to come up with a reason for this happening.

Twice he'd called her by name, making her certain that this wasn't just a random act of violence but rather a targeted attack on her.

She couldn't stay behind the plant pot forever. It was only a matter of minutes before he'd move to this side of the lobby and his light found her.

The effort to keep her screams inside was monumental. If she made any noise at all, he'd get her. She jumped as a crash of pottery splintered the silence.

"I'm going to find you, and you're going to pay for screwing things up." Unbridled rage filled the voice that she somehow knew she should be able to identify, but couldn't.

She was frozen with fear but knew she had to move and move fast. The question was, where? Where could she go where he'd never find her?

Should she try to double back to the desk, where he'd already searched? Could she silently follow him, staying behind where he was heading?

At seven Donnie would be arriving for the day, but that was still hours away. Her chest constricted, and for a moment she thought she couldn't breathe.

Think, her brain commanded. She had to do something before he found her and smashed her skull in with whatever weapon he wielded. The treasure chest! She was tall. She could reach the side and pull herself in. She could bury herself among the oversized jewels and maybe…just maybe he wouldn't think of looking for her in there.

The problem was, in order to reach the treasure chest she'd have to leave her hiding spot and creep across a large open area, where she would be exposed.

Die here behind the plant or die in the middle of the lobby floor? At least if she tried to get to the treasure chest, she'd know she'd done something in an attempt to stay alive.

Holding her breath, she scooted on her butt out from

behind the planter, careful not to make any noise that would draw attention.

As the flashlight beam shot across the other side of the lobby, she could see a faint glimpse of the person holding the light. Unfortunately, the person was dressed all in black and had on a ski mask, making him bleed into the surrounding darkness. She couldn't even begin to identify him.

She continued at a snail's pace across the floor, praying that his light wouldn't find her, that she wouldn't make a sound that would draw his attention.

There was another crash and the splintering sound of pottery shattering. He'd apparently smashed another plant pot. His destructive rage terrified her.

She finally made it to the side of the treasure chest where she could no longer see him, which meant he couldn't see her. If she climbed into the structure, would he find her there? If he did, she was aware that she was placing herself in a spot where there would be no escape.

She had no other choice. Within minutes or even seconds she would be out of options. She slid up to her feet and turned to grasp the top of the treasure chest.

Praying that she didn't grunt or groan, that she had the strength to pull herself up and into the chest, she drew a deep breath for courage and then pulled herself up.

The chest was filled with papier-mâché and Styrofoam rubies and emeralds, diamonds and coins. She managed to get into the chest and then burrowed down amid the fake jewels. She was grateful that when she buried herself, her attacker smashed another pot, hiding whatever sound she made as she covered herself with the large baubles.

"When I find you, I'm going to smash your head in," he growled.

She fought against a shiver and once again placed a hand over her mouth to staunch her need to cry, to scream out loud in horror. Why? Who was this man who wanted her dead, and what was his reason?

What time was it? How long would he carry on this attack? Aside from the abject terror that blazed through her, she felt claustrophobic as she burrowed deeper toward the bottom of the chest each time the intruder smashed something else.

A scream nearly released from her as he slammed whatever he carried on the top of the jewels above her head. The crunch of Styrofoam and papier-mâché made her heart stop. Thankfully she was deep enough in the chest that she didn't feel any real impact.

He cursed and screamed and Savannah remained still, praying for dawn. Even when he no longer made any noise and silence reigned, she remained where she was, afraid that he was still someplace in the lobby just waiting for her to show herself.

Time ticked by in agonizing seconds, in long, tormenting minutes. Savannah remained unmoving, afraid that even a deep breath might unsettle the "jewels" around her and give away her position.

Despite her fear, as time ticked by she must have

eventually fallen asleep, for the next voice she heard was Donnie's. "What in the hell happened in here? Savannah...Savannah, are you okay? Are you here?"

"I'm here," she replied, and as she dug herself out of the items around her, she saw the light of day drifting through the windows. She'd survived the horrible night, but the sight of daylight did nothing to ease the horror that still shot through her.

The tears she'd held in for what felt like a lifetime began to choke out of her as she fought her way to the top of the treasure chest and then climbed out and dropped to the floor.

Donnie ran to her, his wrinkled face and bushy salt-and-pepper eyebrows the most beautiful things she'd ever seen. He wrapped her in his arms. "Are you okay?" He looked around in shock. She followed his gaze and saw the damage that had been done in the darkness of the night.

"I'm sorry, Donnie," she cried. "I'm so sorry. Somebody got in here last night and tried to attack me. I'm so sorry about all the destruction."

"Hush," he said. "They're just things. They can easily be replaced. Are you sure you're okay?" He released his hold on her.

"No, I'm not okay," she replied with a barely suppressed sob. "I'm not okay at all. Please call Deputy Josh Griffin." She sank down to a sitting position with her back against the chest, shaking uncontrollably as she tried to process the night she'd just spent.

Donnie made the call to Josh, and Savannah remained where she was seated. At the moment all she wanted was Josh's arms around her. All she needed was the safety and security she knew she'd find there.

JOSH WAS JUST getting off duty when he got the call from Donnie telling him to get to the inn because something bad had happened overnight.

Donnie didn't waste time giving details, and Josh didn't waste time asking. All he knew was that Savannah had worked her shift last night, and the fact that anything bad had happened at the inn chilled his blood.

As he drove from his location toward the inn, he cursed himself for not asking questions. What exactly had happened? Was Savannah okay? Surely if she were seriously hurt Donnie would have called for an ambulance rather than calling him.

He stomped on the gas and wondered if he should call Trey or if Donnie had already done so. It didn't matter. If Trey hadn't been called, then Josh would assess the situation and decide whether the sheriff needed to be brought in.

He spun into the parking lot and saw only two vehicles, Savannah's navy sedan and Donnie's bright yellow pickup, indicating that there had probably been no overnight guests.

He parked and was out of the car in a shot. Donnie stood at the front door and opened it for him. The first thing that struck Josh was the utter devastation of the lobby. Pots were smashed, plants were overturned and even the coffee table in between the two sofas had a crack down the center.

The wooden chair behind the reception desk was in pieces, and his heart nearly stopped beating as he tried to process the destruction.

He took all this in in an instant. Then he saw Savannah seated by the huge gold treasure chest. The minute her gaze met his, she burst into tears, stumbled to her feet and raced into his arms.

"Are you all right?" he asked. He held her tight as she sobbed into the front of his shirt. What in the hell had happened in here? Who was responsible for all of this?

She nodded and continued to weep, her shoulders shaking and her body trembling against his. He kept his arms around her tightly, not asking any more questions and holding up a hand to stop Donnie from speaking.

It was obvious that at the moment, Savannah needed comfort, not questions. As he once again looked around at the damage, he tightened his arms around her, wishing he could take away the obvious trauma she'd suffered and pull it into himself.

She finally managed to gain some control and stepped away from him. She wiped her tears from her face but appeared unable to talk.

"I found this mess when I came in," Donnie said. "She was hiding in the treasure chest. She crawled out when I called her name. I was scared I'd find her dead somewhere."

It was the first time in all the years Josh had known

Donnie that the older man appeared shaken up. "Some-body made a mess in here. Thank God whoever it was didn't hurt Savannah."

"He wanted to kill me." Savannah finally found her voice. "I was at the desk, and it was about three fifteen or so and all the lights went out." She paused and vis-ibly trembled.

Donnie walked over to one of the light switches and turned it on. Nothing happened. "The electricity is still off."

"At first I thought it was a blown fuse or something like that. I was just about to call Donnie when I heard the thumping of somebody walking the upstairs hall-way."

"Old Peg Leg," Donnie said.

"It was no ghost," Savannah replied, her voice a little stronger now. "It was a living, breathing person, and he was definitely after me. He whispered my name and told me he was going to kill me."

A new chill worked through Josh. "He actually said your name?" he asked.

She nodded and wrapped her arms around herself as she began to tremble once again. Josh pulled out his cell phone and called Trey. This was definitely some-thing the sheriff needed to know about.

With the call completed, he dropped his phone back into his pocket, placed an arm around Savannah's shoulder and led her to one of the two sofas.

He pulled her down next to him as Donnie disap-peared into a back room and returned a few minutes later with a broom. "Donnie, you shouldn't do any cleanup yet. I'm sure the sheriff will want some of his men to process this as a crime scene," Josh said.

Donnie leaned the broom against a wall and sat on the sofa opposite them. "I can't figure out how anyone got inside. The front door was locked when I got here, and so was the back door. The only door that wasn't locked was the one in my office that leads down to the basement. And there are no windows to break into down there."

That didn't mean there wasn't another way into the inn. Josh thought of the tunnel system and wondered if there was some way into the basement that Donnie wasn't aware of.

He'd check it out once Trey arrived. "I'm not going to ask you questions now," he told Savannah. "Trey will want to question you, and there's no need for you to go through the details twice."

"I'll just say I've never been so grateful to hear Donnie's voice," she replied and looked at her boss fondly.

"After walking in and seeing the mess, I was just glad to see you alive and well," Donnie said gruffly.

The attacker had called her by name, Josh thought. There was no denying that whoever had been in here last night had been here specifically to hurt or kill Savannah.

Josh had thought the attack in the tunnel might have just been an accident of strange circumstances, but this changed everything. This attack had been personal, and she was the intended target.

It didn't take long for Trey and his favorite deputy, Ray McClure, to arrive, along with Deputy Daniel Carson, who said he'd heard the official dispatch and had decided to stop in at the end of his shift.

Josh was grateful to see his friend, who he knew was a better investigator than Trey and Ray put together.

"Jeez, it looks like a bomb exploded in here," Ray exclaimed. He walked around, shards of broken pottery crunching beneath his feet.

"Stand still," Trey said irritably to Ray as he sat next to Savannah on the sofa. "Let's hear what happened, and then we'll proceed from there."

Savannah recounted the night from the moment she arrived to when she went into the restroom and then returned to her desk and the lights went out.

As she spoke about the thumping noise and then the whisper of her name as the person came down the stairs, Josh wanted to wrap her in his arms once again and carry her far away from here.

She explained that she had hidden behind a plant pot and listened while the intruder had raged, smashing things and promising to kill her when he found her.

"And you didn't recognize his voice?" Trey asked.

"I felt like I should know it, but no, I couldn't identify it. It was gruff, like he was trying to disguise it," she said. She went on to talk about the flashlight he clicked on. She had known her hiding place behind a plant wouldn't keep her safe. That was when she decided to climb into the treasure chest and bury herself deep inside.

"Did you see him at all?" Trey asked in a concerned tone.

She shook her head. "He was just a dark shadow, and I think he was wearing a ski mask." She looked at Donnie and gave him a tense smile. "I've joked about that treasure chest being a monstrosity forever, but last night it definitely saved my life."

"It is a monstrosity, but I figure once the amusement park opens, tourists will want their pictures taken in front of it," Donnie replied.

"Unfortunately, if you want to try to pull fingerprints, I'm not sure he touched anything except with whatever bat or wooden stake he used to smash everything," she said to Trey.

"If he touched anything upstairs or the stairway itself, you should be able to pull some prints. I had Dorothy dust everything yesterday," Donnie added.

"Ray and Daniel, why don't you start in the guest rooms and see what prints you can pull off furniture or door frames?" Trey instructed. "I'll call in Deputies Bream and Stiller to help."

Trey got up from the sofa and took several steps away to make his calls. Donnie also got up and stood next to the treasure chest, surveying the surroundings.

Josh scooted closer to Savannah, his heart filled with the terror she must have felt through the long ordeal. "Thank God you were able to hide," he said softly.

"I don't understand why this happened," she said,

and he was grateful to see that her trembling had finally stopped, although her eyes still retained a depth of darkness that he knew was trauma.

"Let's talk about that," Trey said as he resumed his seat next to her. "You said you can't imagine why this happened? Can you think of anyone who might have a reason to want you dead?"

"No. I don't have anything to do with anyone. I haven't had any interaction, good or bad, with anyone for a long time. The only person I see on a regular basis is Chad Wilson, who delivers my groceries to me once a week."

"Has he ever had any issue with you?" Trey asked.

"No, although last time he came by, he asked me out and I turned him down, but he seemed to understand that the problem wasn't him, that I just didn't date at all. He stayed and visited for a while after that, so I thought everything was fine. I can't imagine Chad doing something like this."

Trey wrote for a moment in a small notepad he'd pulled from his pocket and then looked back at her. "We'll check Chad's whereabouts last night."

Deputy Derrick Bream and Deputy Wes Stiller arrived with their fingerprinting kits and were sent upstairs to join the other two deputies.

"What about Bo McBride? Have you had any interaction with him since he's been back in town?" Trey asked.

"No, but why would Bo want to hurt me?" she asked with a frown.

"Maybe he thinks you know something about your sister's death that could put him behind bars," Trey replied.

"So he's waited two years to attack me?" Savannah scoffed. "You know I don't believe Bo killed Shelly, and I'm sure he's not behind any plan to kill me now."

"I think a good question is how the perp got into the building," Josh said, knowing Bo McBride and the murder of Shelly was a touchy subject with Savannah. "According to Donnie, all of the outside doors were locked when he arrived this morning."

"You think a tunnel?" Trey asked.

"I think it's not only possible but probable," Josh replied.

"But Savannah said he came from upstairs," Trey said.

"And she was also in the restroom right before things went down. It's possible he came up from the basement and went upstairs while she was in the bathroom."

"Then how did he turn out the lights from upstairs?" Savannah asked.

"We'll figure out the answers, but right now I'd like to get a look in the basement," Trey said.

"I'm coming with you," Josh replied.

"And so am I." Savannah stood, a resolute expression on her face.

"Donnie," Trey called to the man who had remained standing next to the treasure chest. "Is there something strange in your basement?"

Donnie frowned. "I've got lots of what most people would consider strange down in the basement. I'm not sure what you're talking about."

"We need to go down there and check things out," Trey said.

Donnie shrugged. "Fine with me." He led them through the lobby to his private office, a small room with a desk, a computer and paperwork stacked on several file cabinets. He opened a door and turned on a light that illuminated a set of stairs leading down.

"I'm not sure what you're looking for, but feel free to snoop around," he said.

Trey led the way, with Savannah behind him and Josh following. The stairs were narrow, and once they reached the bottom, it was obvious Donnie had more than a few hoarding tendencies.

"I hope we don't have to move all these boxes and crap to find a tunnel in the floor," Trey said.

"If there is a tunnel and that's how the perp got in, then he wouldn't have had a way to stack anything back on top of the entrance once he left," Josh said. "We're going to find a place either in the wall or on the floor that's bare."

They fell silent as they searched. Josh was positive that there was a tunnel entrance somewhere that had allowed the perp to sneak in.

The fuse box showed nothing to indicate that the fuses had been blown, so the perp had obviously manipulated the electricity another way. They would have to call somebody from the electric company to find the issue and fix it.

The walls were made of concrete blocks, and it was Savannah who found the first loose one. She called the men over, and by the time five blocks had been removed, a tunnel entrance was revealed.

"So now we know how he got inside," Trey said. He pulled a flashlight from his belt and shone it down into the tunnel. "I'll have to get some equipment before I go in."

Josh nodded. He understood the reluctance of anyone to go into an unknown tunnel without the proper items to mark an exit out.

"If you've gotten all you need from Savannah, I'm going to follow her home," Josh said.

"Yeah, if I need to ask any more questions I know where she lives," Trey said absently, his light still focused into the darkness beyond the blocks.

"Oh, and if you don't mind, I'm officially taking vacation time as of right now," Josh said. "I have plenty of time coming to me."

Trey straightened up and looked at Savannah and then at Josh. "Are you planning on pulling some sort of private bodyguard duty?"

"Something like that," Josh replied. He touched Savannah's elbow. "I'd say your night here has been long enough. Let's head out."

He followed her up the stairs, his thoughts racing. When they reached the lobby, once again he was struck by the rage that had been unleashed…a killing rage.

The fact that it had been directed at Savannah chilled him to his very soul. There was only one way he knew to keep her safe, and that was why he intended to take charge of things whether she liked it or not.

"Donnie, Savannah is officially on an undetermined leave of absence as of right now," he said to the owner. Savannah looked at him in surprise but didn't argue with him.

Donnie nodded as if he'd expected it. "I'll call in some of my other gals to take up the slack. Besides, it's going to take me a couple of days to get things cleaned up."

"I hope you have insurance," Savannah said.

Donnie smiled gently at her. "Those pots were cheap enough, and I've probably got extra ones in the basement somewhere. I won't be making an insurance claim. A little elbow grease and things will be good as new. You just stay safe, Savannah."

"She will. I'm going to see to it," Josh replied. He turned to look at her. "I'll follow you home."

She nodded. "I just need to get my purse from the drawer in the desk." She retrieved her purse, and then together they left the inn.

The sun was up, and it was almost ten. Josh followed her car as they drove to her house. She had to be not only exhausted but also still experiencing some kind of posttraumatic stress from the horrifying night she'd just survived.

Making sure she got home safely from the inn was just the first part of his plan to assure her safety. She probably wasn't going to like the next stage of his plan, but he couldn't get past the knowledge that whoever had been in the inn last night had been filled with rage, and he'd named Savannah as his victim.

Josh had let down Savannah years ago when it came to pushing for an intensive, clean investigation into Shelly's death. He wasn't about to let her down now.

Chapter Eight

Savannah found herself alternately flashing with
warmth and shivering with chills as she drove home.
She tried not to replay the events of the night anymore
in her mind.

It was over. The sun was up and she'd survived the
long, terrifying night. As she glanced in her rearview
mirror, the sight of Josh's car just behind hers reassured
her. All she had to do was get home and lock the windows and doors and she'd be fine. Maybe she'd get a
security system installed, and then she'd never leave
her house again.

She had enough money saved up that would see her
through a couple of months jobless, and surely by then
Trey and his men would be able to figure out who was
after her and why.

She tightened her fingers on the steering wheel.
Who had been in the inn last night? Who wanted her
dead? Whoever it was had been so violently angry.
No matter how long she thought about it, she couldn't
come up with an answer.

Punching the button that would open her garage door, she tried to shove away any thoughts of the night, tried to reach the same level of numbness that had been such a constant friend of hers since Shelly's death.

She drove into the garage and got out of her car and then walked back to where Josh had parked in the driveway. "Get in," he said.

She frowned in confusion. "Why?"

"Because we're going to my place. I'm going to pack a bag, and you're going to have a houseguest until we get all this sorted out. So, get in."

Her initial reaction was to protest, but her lingering fear was greater than her pride or her desire to be alone. She got into his car.

"I expected an argument," he said as he backed out of her driveway.

"To be honest, I'm scared. I'll let you stay with me until I can get a security system installed. Then I'll be fine alone."

He cast her a doubtful glance. "Do you have any idea how easy it is to get around a security system if you know what you're doing?"

"Don't tell me," she replied. The idea of a houseguest wasn't particularly pleasant. The idea of Josh as a houseguest was even less desirable. He bothered her in ways she didn't like with just short contact with him. The idea of him living in her house felt very wrong.

But the idea of him being with her day and night also made her feel safe, and right now she needed that more than anything else. She didn't even want to acknowledge that a hint of excitement also filled her as she thought of spending time with him.

She could put her discomfort at sharing her space aside for a feeling of safety. She needed sleep after the long night, and she had a feeling that without Josh nearby, and knowing there was a tunnel entrance right in her own backyard, she'd never really sleep again.

They arrived at Josh's house, and he followed her to the front door. He unlocked it and they stepped inside. "Just hang tight. It shouldn't take me long." He disappeared down the hallway to the master bedroom.

Savannah knew that the tight control she'd had on her life had flown away. Things were happening spontaneously, without her control, and that was more than a little frightening in and of itself.

True to his word, Josh took only a few minutes and then reappeared with a large duffel bag in hand. Savannah frowned. "That looks like enough clothes to stay a long time."

"I intend to stay until the danger is over. Savannah, I know this isn't the way you want to live your life. I know the last thing you want is anyone staying in your house. But you have to face the fact that somebody wants you dead and this isn't the time for you to be alone."

"I know." She released a deep sigh. "Let's just get back to my place and you can get settled in."

"And hopefully you can get some sleep." They stepped back outside.

"I imagine you could use some of that yourself. You've been up working all night, too."

"I'll catch some snooze time. Don't worry about me."

Within minutes they were back at her house. She led him to Mac's old bedroom, the first one in the hallway. Josh set his duffel bag on the bed. "And you have the master suite?" he asked.

"No, I'm in the bedroom next door. The master suite has been empty since Mom and Dad moved away. I've stayed in the room I shared with Shelly since childhood."

"I need to see it," he said. "In fact, I need to see all the rooms."

She knew it wasn't mere curiosity but rather a need to check out windows and such for security purposes. She started the tour in the master suite, which held nothing but some storage boxes she'd gone through after her parents had left.

"Do you ever use this room for anything?" he asked. He was all business, his gaze sharp as he looked into the master bath and then returned to where she stood.

"No, not really. I use the bathroom in here, but I can always use the one in the hallway."

"Then I think the first thing we'll do is buy a doorknob with a lock so that nobody can come in through the windows and through the door into the main living area."

His words made her realize just how seriously he was taking her safety. They left the master suite, and she showed him a small bedroom across from hers. It was a guest room with just a double bed and a dresser.

"We'll do the same thing to this room," he said after checking to make sure the window was locked. "It's not used, and so we'll make access into the house a little more difficult."

A wave of shyness swept over Savannah as she led him into her room with its double bed, dresser and minishrine to Shelly on top of the desk.

He checked the window first to make sure it was locked and then paused by the desk, looking at the items. "A ceramic frog? There has to be a story behind that."

A bittersweet smile curved her lips. "Bo gave that to Shelly when he proposed to her. The ring was in the frog's mouth, and he told her she'd never kiss a frog because she'd spend the rest of her life kissing him."

Josh frowned. "We never found her engagement ring."

"You never found her real killer," she replied and immediately wanted to call the words back. "I'm sorry. I really don't want to talk about that now. All I want is to take a shower and fall into bed." At least the hallway bathroom was windowless, so she didn't have to worry about anyone coming inside.

"While you shower I'll get my things unpacked," Josh replied. "And we need to keep your bedroom door open at all times so that I can hear if you might be in trouble."

"Okay," she agreed. She didn't particularly like it,

but she'd like it even less if somebody managed to get through her window and attempted to get to her. She wanted Josh to be able to hear everything, even if she snored.

She grabbed a clean nightgown from a drawer and headed for the bathroom. It was only when she stood beneath the hot spray of the shower that she began to weep as the trauma of the night gripped her once again.

Leaning weakly against the shower stall, she wept with fear not only for what she had experienced but also for what the future held. If somebody wanted her dead and that person wasn't identified, he would probably eventually succeed.

There was only so much Josh could do to keep her safe. He could stay here, but it would take only a single shot through the kitchen window, a sniper's bullet, to find her while she had her morning coffee.

Somebody had wanted her sister dead and had succeeded. Why should Savannah be any different? She just hoped that before she died, she'd know who was responsible and why they had wanted her dead.

JOSH PLACED HIS gun on the coffee table, stretched out on the sofa and closed his eyes. Savannah had showered and was now sleeping soundly in bed. He hadn't wanted to go to Mac's room and crawl into bed, for he feared his sleep would be too deep.

He figured he'd sleep lightly on the sofa and awaken easily at any alien noise that might mean danger, although he was expecting a quiet afternoon. The attacker had been up all night and had expended a lot of energy. Even the bad guys had to rest sometime.

Josh needed to catch some shut-eye, but his brain raced, making it impossible for sleep to break through the chaos. Who had been in that inn last night, and who on earth would want to kill Savannah?

She'd lived like a virtual recluse for the last two years, so the odds seemed slim that she'd done something to somebody that would warrant this kind of reaction.

Could the attack be related to Shelly's death? He just couldn't believe that a murder that had taken place two years before had anything to do with the threat to Savannah now. Had Chad Wilson taken her rejection of him more seriously than she'd thought? Was Eric Baptiste involved?

He finally drifted off to sleep and was shocked to realize it was nearing dusk when he awakened. The first thing he did was jump up off the sofa and check on Savannah, who was still sound asleep.

He checked the rest of the house and then went into the kitchen and raided the cabinets until he found the coffee and cups and then put on a pot to brew and sat at the kitchen table.

He pulled out his cell phone and dialed Daniel, assuming he'd probably be up and around by now after his night shift and work at the inn that morning.

"Did I wake you?" he asked when Daniel answered.

"Nah, I was just getting ready to make me a sandwich."

"How did things go after we left this morning?"

"No fingerprints found, no sign of forced entry, so we are sure the perp came in through the tunnel."

"Did you all check out the tunnel?" Josh asked. He got up to pour himself a cup of coffee.

"Trey called Mayor Burns, and the two of them and Ray went in, but I haven't heard what they found. Trey sent me home to get some sleep. You might check with him. How is Savannah doing?"

"She's still asleep. I've moved into her place for the time being. I swear, Daniel, I can't figure out who might have a beef with her."

"I don't know. It all started with that attack in the tunnel," Daniel said. "And the only person we've learned about so far who knew about the tunnel system is Eric Baptiste."

"Who supposedly had become friends with Shelly just before her murder." Josh heaved a sigh of frustration.

"If Eric knows anything about Shelly's murder, he's not talking," Daniel said.

"I still can't figure out a connection between Shelly's murder and what's happening now. It's been two years. Maybe since Eric knew about the tunnel network, it's possible that somebody else knows and thinks Savannah is a threat to whatever is going on down there."

"We've got to figure out if something is going on in the tunnels, something worth killing for," Daniel replied.

"Eat your sandwich. You've given me plenty of food

for thought," Josh said. The two men disconnected, and Josh carried his coffee cup back to the table and sat.

He called Trey to get an update and was still seated at the table thirty minutes later when Savannah entered the kitchen. Her hair was sleep-tousled, and a pink robe wrapped around her and was belted at her slender waist.

"Sleep well?" he asked and tried not to notice how sexy she looked with her sleepy eyes and bedhead.

"Like a log," she replied. "What about you? Did you get in some shut-eye?" She walked across the room to the coffeepot.

"I just woke up about an hour ago," he replied. "I think it would be a good thing if we could work into twisting our hours to normal ones so we sleep at night and are awake during the day."

She joined him at the table and wrapped her hands around her coffee mug. "Why?"

"Because I think we need to spend our days out and about and doing a little investigating of our own."

Her eyes widened as if he'd just asked her to walk a tightrope between two skyscrapers. "I really don't like the idea of being out and about."

"I know I'm asking you to leave your comfort zone, but to be honest, I think Trey is more interested in investigating the tunnels than he is in investigating who might be after you. I just think we need to be proactive."

She took a sip of the coffee, her eyes dark and

fathomless over the rim of her cup as she stared at him. "Proactive, how?"

"We need to talk to Bo, and I want to check out this Chad guy who delivers your groceries every week. You should be seen in town, and we can gauge people's reactions to you."

She lowered her cup slowly and stared past his shoulder and out the window, where the last gasp of twilight painted the scenery in deep purple shades. "You have no idea what you're asking of me." She looked back at him.

"I think I do," he countered. "You've hidden out here for two years, and I'm asking you to leave your safe haven because I don't think it's necessarily safe anymore." He was asking her to rejoin life again, and he hoped in doing so he wasn't putting her more at risk of death.

"I'm safe with you here," she protested.

"I don't want us to be sitting ducks here. I want to find out who is behind the attacks on you, and we can't do that just by hanging out here."

"Okay. We'll do it your way," she said, but he could tell the idea didn't sit well with her. "In the meantime, I don't know about you, but I'm starving."

She jumped up from the table and went to the refrigerator. "How about cheese and mushroom omelets with toast? Usually when I wake up at this time of night, I'm ready for breakfast food."

"Sounds good to me," he agreed. He had a feeling

her sudden starvation came from her need to change the subject. "What can I do to help?" he asked.

"Just sit there and stay out of my way," she replied.

He figured what she'd really like to do is pretend he wasn't there. But he was here, and he wasn't going anywhere until the danger to her had been neutralized.

She worked silently, cutting up mushrooms and whisking eggs in a mixing bowl. He watched her, enjoying the sight of her as she bustled around, a look of fierce concentration on her face.

She deserved so much better than what she'd given herself over the last two years. She should be having lunch out with girlfriends, enjoying drinks and dinner at Jimmy's Place.

It was ironic that he was pulling her back into life because somebody wanted her dead. The truth was, he remembered the rush to judgment in Shelly's murder, and he didn't trust Trey to investigate the attempts on Savannah's life adequately.

When Josh had spoken to Trey on the phone earlier, Trey had even implied that perhaps Savannah had done all the damage to the inn herself the night before, that she was seeking new attention since she was no longer doing her ghost walks. Josh had only just managed to tamp down his outrage at his boss.

"I spoke to Trey just before you woke up," he now said.

Savannah poured the egg mixture into an awaiting omelet pan and then looked at him expectantly. "Did they find anything? Fingerprints or any useful evidence?"

"No, nothing like that. Mayor Burns showed up, and he and Trey and Ray went into the tunnel and followed it until they reached a three-pronged fork. They remained in the main tunnel and found an exit at the edge of the swamp shanties but didn't get a chance to complete their exploration of the other two forks. They plan to do that tomorrow."

She placed four slices of bread in the toaster and pressed down on the knob. "So, it's possible that whoever came out into the inn came from that entrance near the swamp. Both Eric and Chad would know that area."

"Chad is from the swamp side of town?" Josh asked. "I don't think I've ever met him."

She nodded and flipped the omelet pan to the other side. "He's four or five years younger than us. He's Sharon's son and mostly works in the back of Sharon's grocery store, so you probably haven't seen him there. Sharon lived in one of the shanties when Chad was growing up. He told me he was fifteen when his mother finally moved them to a house near the store. He doesn't strike me as the type who would get into trouble."

"That's what we thought about Coach Cantor, and he wound up being a sick stalker bent on killing Claire Silver," Josh reminded her. "Just because he's nice when he delivers your groceries doesn't mean he shouldn't be looked at more closely."

"All I know is that I want whoever is after me behind bars sooner rather than later." She moved the pan off the burner and turned toward the counter as the toast popped up.

It wasn't long before they were seated at the table and eating. The silence between them grew to an uncomfortable level as Josh tried to think of a topic that might be neutral and pleasant.

She didn't appear bothered by the silence, but then she probably wouldn't be. He imagined she was accustomed to it. But he found it odd to sit at a table with another person and not have any conversation at all.

"What do you do when you're here in the house all day?" he finally asked.

She looked up from her plate and frowned thoughtfully. "I spend a lot of the day sleeping, and then when I'm up, I watch television or clean house. Sometimes I work on creating new recipes or read. What do you do during your spare time?"

"Like you, I sleep during part of the day, and then I sometimes meet Daniel for a late lunch or I hang out at Jimmy's Place and socialize."

"I still think of Jimmy's Place as Bo's Place," she replied. "I haven't been in there since Bo sold it to Jimmy and left town."

"Maybe we'll have a late lunch there tomorrow."

"Why would we do that? I can make lunch here," she protested.

"Because I've often seen Bo and Claire there in the afternoons, and talking to them is as good a place as any to start our own investigation."

"I can't imagine that they'd have any information that might tell us who is after me," she replied.

"They've been stirring up things about Shelly's murder. Who knows what they might know or what other gossip we might hear while there that will move us forward."

She shook her head. "I hate this. I hate all of it. I was perfectly content with living life on my terms, and now I feel like I'm being forced out of my comfort zone."

"Taking steps out of your comfort zone isn't always a bad thing," he countered softly.

She looked at him dubiously. "And when was the last time you stepped out of your comfort zone?"

"The night I had you over for dinner," he replied easily. "You were the first woman I've ever invited to dinner at my house. I can't remember the last time I was so nervous, except when I heard there'd been trouble at the inn."

"You were nervous to have me to dinner?" A tiny smile danced at the corner of her lips.

"Terrified," he replied. "I wanted the night to go perfectly, and I was afraid I'd accidentally stick a fork in my eye or catch my pants on fire while I was grilling the steaks."

She giggled. "You're silly."

"Maybe you need a little silly in your life right now," he replied.

Her giggle instantly died. "Josh, don't push me. The fact that you're here in my house, the idea of going out and mingling with other people and the knowledge that somebody wants to kill me are more than enough for me to handle right now."

"I just remember the young woman who used to flirt with me, the one who laughed so easily and made me want to be around her," he said.

Her eyes darkened once again. "That woman is gone and she's never coming back."

"You have no idea how much I mourn her passing," he said with more emotion than he'd intended.

Her cheeks flushed with a faint pink tone, and she glanced away from him. She started to rise from the table and then sat once again, her eyes huge. "Josh, I just saw somebody at the window."

Chapter Nine

Adrenaline flushed through him. "Act normal," he instructed her. "Clear the table and pretend that nothing is wrong. Don't look toward the window again. I'm going to grab my gun and go out the front door. I'll lock it behind me. Don't open it again for anyone except me."

He got up from the table and sauntered out of the room with a forced ease. The minute he left the kitchen, he raced for his gun and was out the front door.

The hot July night smacked him in the face but didn't slow him down. He ran to one side of the house and peeked around the corner. Seeing nobody there, he ran to the next corner that would show him the backyard.

Thankfully the moon was three-quarters full, spilling down enough illumination for him to see without any artificial light. He gazed around the corner and saw a figure clad in black moving across the yard.

"Halt," Josh cried and then cursed as the person took off running. He wasn't about to shoot an unknown person in the back for window peeping. "Stop or I'll shoot," he bluffed.

Apparently, the man knew it was a bluff because he didn't slow down. With another curse Josh took off after him. Whoever it was appeared physically fit, and Josh had to push himself in order to make any gain on him.

The window peeper ran across the backyards of several houses and jumped a chain link fence, which started a dog barking frantically. Josh reached the fence as the perp flew over the opposite side of the fence and cut between two houses, disappearing from Josh's view.

Instead of jumping the fence, Josh raced along the edge of it to the front of the house, but the perp had disappeared. Josh crept as silently as possible, his gun still in his hand as he passed the house with the fence, and spun around the corner to see if the "Peeping Tom" might be hunkered down there.

Nobody was there. There wasn't even a shed or outbuilding for him to have hidden in. Josh looked across the street, where there was also no sign of the person.

He had no idea where to go next. The hunt was over and the man had gotten away. He turned to head back to Savannah's house. Dammit, if he'd just been a little faster he might have caught the man and solved the mystery of the attacks on Savannah.

There was no way he really believed that some teenager or creep was trying to get a cheap thrill by peeking into a window. This felt far more ominous, considering what Savannah had been through the night before.

Josh's car was in the driveway, so whoever it was had to know that she wasn't alone in the house.

Had he just looked in to make sure Josh was really there? Was he trying to get an idea of the floor plan of the home? Or was he obsessed enough that he'd just needed to catch a glimpse of Savannah?

It was the last possibility that worried him. Who could be obsessed with a woman who had been nothing more than a ghost in the past two years? And why would that obsession be fed by a killing rage against her?

A new thought struck him, one that had him racing back to Savannah's house as quickly as physically possible. Had the person in the backyard simply been a ruse to get him out of the house, leaving Savannah alone with the real threat?

His heart pounded with new anxiety. He reached Savannah's front door and knocked a frantic rhythm. "Savannah, it's me."

She opened the door to allow him inside, and he breathed a sigh of relief. "I'm assuming you didn't catch him," she said as they walked back to the kitchen.

"He had too much of a head start, and then I lost him." Josh placed his gun on the table and flopped down in a chair at the table, still slightly winded by his unsuccessful race.

"You think it was my attacker?" she asked and sat across from him, worry evident on her features.

"I think we'd be foolish to believe it wasn't," he replied.

"He told me I screwed things up," she said more to herself than to him.

Josh sat up straighter in his chair. "You didn't mention that before."

"I just remembered it. He said he was going to kill me because I screwed everything up." She gazed at him in confusion. "How could I possibly have screwed up anything for anyone?"

"You said Chad Wilson asked you out and you turned him down. Maybe you screwed things up for him because you didn't indicate any romantic interest in him. Or maybe Eric Baptiste is using the tunnels for something other than finding plants and roots for his mother's shop."

Josh got up and poured himself a cup of the coffee and returned to the table. "Daniel reminded me that the first attack on you took place in the tunnel, and after that, the tunnel network was no longer a secret."

"I ruined things because it's my fault the tunnel network was no longer a secret?"

"It's a theory, but not the only one," he replied. "It's possible this has nothing to do with the tunnels, and it's also possible it has everything to do with the tunnels."

"Jeez, thanks for making me feel better," she replied drily.

"I just don't want us to have tunnel vision, no pun intended," he replied. When he was involved in the investigation into Shelly's death, Trey had suffered from tunnel vision, focusing on one suspect to the exclusion of any others. Josh wasn't going to let that happen again. "I should probably call Trey and tell him about this latest event."

"Why? What's the point of bothering him? I'm assuming you couldn't identify the person at the window. I only got a quick glance at him, and he was wearing a ski mask."

"You're right," Josh replied in frustration. "I just wish I had caught him. Then we might have all the answers we need. Case closed."

She glanced toward the window and then looked back at him. "Why don't we go into the living room? I feel like I'm on stage sitting here in front of these windows."

He took a last sip of his coffee and then placed the cup in the dishwasher. He followed her into the living room, where she sat on one side of the sofa and he sat on the opposite and placed his gun on the coffee table in easy reach.

"I still don't understand why I was attacked in the tunnel," she said. "And you already knew about them when I was attacked."

"Yeah, but nobody else knew that I knew about them," he reminded her. He grimaced. "If I'd told somebody instead of agreeing to let you make that final walk, then you wouldn't have been attacked."

"If Shelly hadn't gone alone to the stone bench down by the lagoon the night that she did, then she wouldn't have been murdered," she countered. "We can't go back and change things."

"I know, but I wish I could," he replied.

She looked at him curiously. "What would you change?"

He leaned back against the sofa cushion. "I would

have insisted Jacob not get into a car with a bunch of his friends and a driver I knew liked to speed and drive recklessly. I would have fought to get Trey to do a more thorough investigation into your sister's death, and I definitely would have asked you out over two years ago instead of being afraid you'd turn me down."

She gazed at him in surprise. "You were afraid I'd turn you down?" He nodded. A wistful smile curved her lips. "And at that time, I was afraid you'd never ask me out. Then Shelly was murdered and everything changed, and now there's no going back."

There was such finality to her words. While he believed she was still attracted to him and he certainly was still attracted to her, she intimated that there was no chance for them to ever act on that attraction.

He was here not because she wanted him here but because she needed his protection. She'd made it clear that she had no desire to change the isolation she'd crawled into in this house.

He might be able to change things for an investigation. He could force her out of the house, make her interact with other people, but ultimately he had a feeling that once she was no longer in danger, she would return to the isolation that seemed to bring her comfort but no happiness.

SAVANNAH AWAKENED AT ten the next morning, dreading the day to come. She and Josh had stayed up until three and then had agreed to head to bed and get up earlier than usual for both of them this morning to start their foray into the public arena of Lost Lagoon.

She didn't want to go out. She didn't want to talk to other people, but she did want answers, and if Josh thought they might find some by going out, then she'd just suck it up and go along with his plan.

Hopefully this would all resolve itself quickly. She glanced toward the desk that held Shelly's memorabilia. She knew it was grief that drove her to remain disconnected from anything and everyone. But the grief had become familiar. It felt so safe and comfortable.

She dragged herself out of bed and pulled on her robe. Though filled with dread, she moved her feet down the hallway toward the bathroom. The scent of coffee let her know that Josh was already up.

She opened the bathroom door and gasped. Josh stood at the sink clad only in a white towel wrapped around his slim hips. Half of his face was covered in shaving cream, and his eyes widened in the mirror at the sight of her.

"Oh, sorry," she exclaimed and told her feet to move backward and out the door. Her feet weren't listening. In fact, she was brain-dead. The only thing working in her head was the visual feast of his broad, muscled chest, his lean waist, his slim hips and the length of his athletic legs.

Heat rushed through her, the heat of fierce desire. He was gorgeous with his clothes on, but with just a towel around his waist, he was sex with shaving cream.

"Uh…do you want to help me finish shaving?" he asked with a touch of amusement.

His voice snapped her brain back into control. She grabbed the doorknob, stumbled backward and slammed the door closed.

She went back into her bedroom and sat on the edge of the bed, trying to erase the vision of Josh from her mind. It was impossible. It was stuck in her brain like Spanish moss in a cypress tree.

As if the day wasn't going to be difficult enough, she thought. Now she had to deal with the vision of a very hot, very sexy man in her head.

It was eleven when they left the house. Thankfully neither of them had mentioned that moment in the bathroom. He'd been fully dressed when he'd peeked into her bedroom and told her the bathroom was all hers.

She couldn't remember the last time she'd been outside the house during the day. She had dressed in a pair of white capris, a gold-tone sleeveless top and sandals, and as Josh backed out of the driveway her nerves roared to life.

Josh was dressed casually in a pair of jeans with a navy-blue T-shirt tucked in. Around his waist he wore his gun and holster, letting her know that while he chatted about driving around town and stopping in at Jimmy's Place for lunch, he hadn't forgotten their real purpose and his self-proclaimed duty to keep her safe.

"It's a beautiful day," he said as they left her neighborhood and headed for Main Street.

"It's hot and sticky," she replied.

He pointed up to the ridge where the construction of the new amusement park was happening. "It looks like they're making good progress."

"It's just going to ruin the town with all the commercialism."

He shot her an amused glance. "Do you intend to be perverse all day?"

"Maybe. I haven't decided yet." She shot him a small smile. "Actually I'm not trying to be perverse. I'm just nervous," she admitted.

"You don't have to be nervous. As long as I'm by your side, I swear nothing bad is going to happen to you."

"I know that," she replied and turned her head to look out the passenger window. What he didn't understand was that a threat to her physical being was only part of her anxiety.

She had been pleasantly numb for almost two years, caring about nobody and fine with the fact that nobody cared about her. She was afraid that somehow this entire experience was going to make her care again, feel again.

They passed the Pirate's Inn, and she fought against a shiver as she remembered the night of terror she'd spent there. She wondered if she'd ever be able to go back to work there when this was all over.

"Where are we going first?" she asked.

"Hardware store to get locks for the spare room and master suite," he replied. "And after that, since it's still early, I thought we'd stop by Claire Silver's place and talk to her and Bo. Maybe their unofficial investigation into Shelly's death has stirred up something that has to do with what's happening to you now."

"I just can't imagine the two things being tied together," she replied.

"To be honest, neither can I, but I intend to leave no stone unturned. If nothing else, we can exclude that possibility and move on to the next."

"Do you have a definite next?" she asked.

He cast her a quick grin. "I'm working on it as we speak."

She looked out the passenger window again as a vision of Josh in that darned towel flashed in her head. Even now she could smell the lingering scent of shaving lotion coupled with minty soap and the spice of his cologne.

She was grateful to get out of the car when they arrived at the hardware store. It took only minutes to buy the locks and then return to the car that smelled of him. When he pulled up in front of Claire Silver's house, Savannah was grateful to get away from his evocative scent.

Claire lived on the shanty side of town. The swamp came precariously close to the backyards of the row of shanties that lined this particular street.

Some of the shanty-like structures were little more than abandoned lean-tos that had once served as homes to poverty-stricken families. Others, like Claire's, had been renovated into cute, neat homes.

"Mayor Burns is probably going to have all the

abandoned shanties pulled down before the amusement park opens," Josh said as he parked in front of Claire's place. "He'll consider them a blight on the town and a detriment to the tourist trade."

"Those shanties were the first structures to make the town. It's kind of sad to tear down the history just because it isn't pretty," she said.

They got out of the car and walked toward Claire's front door. Savannah steeled herself for talking to Bo for the first time in two years. He'd dated Shelly since high school and for ten years after that. He had been the big brother to Savannah that Mac had never been.

She'd also been friendly with Claire and now considered her a good partner for Bo. She had no resentment that Bo had moved on. She wanted only happiness for him.

Josh knocked and Bo opened the door. He looked at her and flew out the door and pulled her into a hug. "Sweet Savannah," he whispered in her ear.

He smelled just like he had when he'd been dating Shelly, like clean male and a faint woodsy cologne. She hugged him back and fought back tears. He finally released her and stepped back. "I can't tell you how much I've wanted to contact you since I've been back in town. Come on, let's go inside where it's cool."

Claire stood from the sofa as they all came inside. Greetings were exchanged all around, and they landed at Claire's kitchen table to talk.

"We heard about what happened at the inn," Claire said. "I'm so glad you're okay."

"I plan to keep her okay despite the fact that somebody wants her dead," Josh said.

Claire's blue eyes darkened, and she reached across the table and captured Savannah's hand in hers. "I know exactly what you're going through. I know the fear of not knowing who you can trust." She released Savannah's hand and narrowed her gaze at Josh. "Don't tell me you're here because you think Bo had anything to do with the attack on Savannah."

"Quite the contrary. We're here to see if, during your investigation into what happened two years ago, you might have stumbled on something that put Savannah at risk," Josh replied.

Bo frowned. "Nothing that I can think of, but we haven't managed to dig up much of anything new about that night. Our investigation got sidetracked when Roger Cantor, the high school coach who turned into an obsessed stalker, came after Claire."

"Did you know that before her death, Shelly had become friends with Eric Baptiste?" Josh asked.

Bo nodded. "Yeah, I knew about their friendship." He looked at Savannah, his gaze soft with caring. "You and I both know that Shelly probably wasn't ever going to marry me. As much as we loved each other, she wanted out of this town. I wondered if she saw Eric as her ticket out of town."

"How so?" Savannah asked.

"I know Eric has a degree. He could probably go anywhere in the country and get a job teaching. Maybe she thought she could talk him into leaving Lost Lagoon and taking her with him," Bo said.

"Do you think he's the person who met Shelly that night? Do you think he murdered her?" Savannah asked, a jumble of emotions rushing through her.

"I don't know," Bo said. Once again his gaze went to Josh. "All I know for sure is that I didn't kill Shelly."

"And you have no clue who might be after Savannah," Josh asked.

"None, but I want you to see to it that she stays safe." Once again Bo looked at her, and in his eyes she saw the caring, the tenderness that spoke of old days and bittersweet memories.

It was too much for her. Those memories of carefree days and laughter with Shelly and Bo cascaded over her, bringing a pain that pierced through her.

She stood from the table. "We need to go now." Josh looked at her in surprise. "They've said they have nothing for us." She swallowed against the pain she'd refused to feel for two long years. "Thank you for letting us talk to you. Bo, I'm glad you've found happiness."

She didn't wait for Josh to follow. She raced out of the door and headed for his car, stuffing down the agony that seeing Bo had created.

She was already in the passenger seat when Josh came out of the front door. He got behind the steering wheel and turned to look at her. "Are you all right?"

"No, I'm not. I want to go home. Please just take me home."

"But we'd planned lunch at Jimmy's Place," he protested.

She opened her car door. "Either drive me back to my house or I'll walk. I don't want to see or talk to anyone else today."

"Get in. We'll go back to your place."

She slammed the car door and buckled up. Irrational anger toward Josh combined with the aching grief of loss. It was his fault that she had lost her cocoon of numbness that had served her so well.

Seeing Bo had hurt and reminded her of all she had lost. She didn't want to feel that hurt. She wanted to crawl back into her detachment from people and life.

Chapter Ten

The next day at noon, Josh and Savannah headed for Jimmy's Place for lunch. Savannah had spent much of her time the day before holed up in her bedroom while Josh called Trey to make sure the sheriff checked out not only Eric's alibi for Saturday night but also Chad Wilson. After that he had restlessly roamed the house.

He hadn't considered how difficult it might be for Savannah to see Bo again, but when she did appear for dinner, she seemed angry at Josh. While they'd eaten he'd tried to talk to her about her feelings, but she was having nothing to do with any deep conversations.

She answered him tersely and refused to make eye contact with him. When the kitchen was clean she returned to her bedroom for the remainder of the night.

This morning it had been as if yesterday had never happened. She'd greeted him pleasantly and they'd shared coffee talking about nonthreatening, nonsensical things.

Things had remained light and easy between them until it was time to leave the house. Only then did he feel the tension that rolled off her and knew this outing would be another difficult one for her.

Part of him wanted to coddle her. If she felt most comfortable at home, then that was where she should be. But the stronger part of him believed she needed to get out of the house, start rebuilding a real life for herself.

Josh knew that grief could be a crippling thing, but he also knew she'd carried hers long enough. It was time for her let go and move into acceptance. Shelly was dead, but Savannah was still very much alive.

Each time he saw a spark of the woman she'd once been, he wanted more. He wanted her. No woman had ever stirred him like Savannah did. He'd believed she could be the woman for him two years ago, and he still felt the same way.

"Are you hungry?" he asked as he pulled into the parking area next to Jimmy's Place.

"I can't tell if it's nerves or hunger that's making my stomach jump and kick," she replied.

"Probably a little bit of both." He shut off the engine and turned to look at her. "There's nothing to be afraid of, Savannah. We're in a public place and I've got your back."

"I know. I'm just not used to being around so many people. But let's do this," she said with a tone of resolve and opened her car door.

Jimmy's Place had once been Bo's Place, but when Bo had been accused of Shelly's murder, the patrons of the hugely popular upscale bar and grill had stopped coming. Bo had left town and sold the place to his best friend, Jimmy Tambor.

It was Jimmy who greeted them as they walked in the door. Lanky and slightly awkward, the sandy-haired man smiled even wider as he saw Savannah. "Gosh, Savannah, I haven't seen you in forever. You look terrific. It's great to have you here."

"Thanks, Jimmy."

"Table for two?" he asked and looked at Josh.

Josh nodded, and Jimmy led them away from the bar area and into a dining area, where Josh immediately spied a table full of town officials.

Mayor Jim Burns, former mayor Frank Kean, councilman Neil Sampson and Trey Walker all sat at a long table. With them was Rod Nixon from the amusement park. Trey motioned them over, and Josh immediately felt Savannah stiffen.

Still, she walked next to Josh as he headed for the men. "Savannah," Neil said with a smile. "What a surprise. I've heard you've had a rough time lately."

"I'm fine," she replied tersely.

"I wanted to let you know that I checked out Eric's and Chad's alibis for Saturday night," Trey said to Josh. "Unfortunately both of them claim that they were at home alone all night, and nobody can corroborate their alibis."

"The exciting news is that we've mapped out miles of tunnels," Jim Burns said.

"And they all appear to be solid. We're talking about how to capitalize on the find when we've finished mapping the rest and they all prove safe," Frank Kean added.

"The tunnels add a great feature to the amusement park," Rod added.

Josh nodded. "I'd like to get a copy of whatever map you have," he said to Trey. "I've started my own map, but obviously you all have done a lot more exploring in the last couple of days."

"Stop by my office later this afternoon and I'll give you a copy of what I have," Trey said.

"Will do," Josh replied.

Moments later he and Savannah were seated at a table some distance away from the group. Jimmy took their drink orders and then disappeared.

"Okay, tell me which of those men you don't like or don't trust," Josh said.

She hesitated and unfolded her napkin in her lap. "It's not a matter of trust. I just don't like Neil Sampson. He's an arrogant jerk."

"Does he know you think he's a jerk?" Josh asked.

"Probably, although I've had nothing to do with him for a long time. We dated briefly about three years ago." Her cheeks flushed with a faint pink hue. "He was my first real grown-up relationship." It was easy for Josh to read between the lines. Neil Sampson had been Savannah's first lover.

The conversation halted as Jimmy arrived with their drinks and took their food orders. After he'd left, Savannah continued, the blush still riding her cheeks.

"We'd only dated for about a month when he decided

it was time to get intimate. I didn't really feel ready to take that step with him, but it happened, it wasn't pleasant and after that I stopped seeing him."

"Did he rape you?" Josh asked in a low whisper, his blood starting to boil.

"No," she assured him quickly. "More like coerced, but I didn't tell him no."

It didn't matter. Josh still wanted to smash Neil's handsome face in. "I know he dated Claire for a while, but apparently she didn't find him to her taste, either," Savannah added.

Once again they both fell silent as Jimmy arrived with their food orders. "Neil is very ambitious," Josh said once Jimmy had departed. "I think he's grooming himself to be the next mayor. I wonder if he sees you as a threat to his reputation."

"I wouldn't hurt his reputation by telling anyone that he was a crummy lover who pressured me into having sex with him when I wasn't ready."

"You know that, but does he?" Josh looked across the room at the subject of their discussion. Neil was a good-looking guy who had become Jim Burns's right-hand man. He was also arrogant and gave off an aura of entitlement.

Josh shifted his gaze to the other diners in the place, seeking anyone who appeared to be paying too much attention to Savannah, anyone who seemed to radiate any animus. While the place was fairly filled with lunch diners, Josh didn't notice anyone or anything odd.

Josh attacked his burger. "Did you know that Shelly was having doubts about marrying Bo?" he asked after a couple of bites.

Savannah frowned with a french fry in her fingers. "I know that Shelly loved Bo, but she wanted out of Lost Lagoon so badly, and Bo had built up his business and had his mother here. He wasn't going to leave, and if she hadn't died I think she wouldn't have stayed here and married Bo."

She popped the fry into her mouth and then took a drink of her soda. "She told me before her death that she had a sticky situation to deal with and even though she wouldn't go into any details with me, I think that situation had to do with the decision she had to make where Bo was concerned. I still don't see how what happened to Shelly has anything to do with what is going on with me."

"I agree," Josh replied. "I think we can put that piece of the puzzle behind us. It just doesn't fit."

He looked again at the table of town bigwigs, his focus yet again on Neil Sampson. Had Savannah downplayed what had happened between them years ago? Had their intimate encounter been more of a rape than she'd indicated?

If so, then Neil could potentially see Savannah as a risk to his grand ambitions. Rumor was that he not only wanted to become mayor but also had intentions of eventually entering politics in a bigger way.

The fact that she had been a virtual recluse for the past two years might have lulled him into a sense of safety.

He had certainly learned of the attack on her in the tunnels, and that might have made him realize if she left her isolated lifestyle, if she started to talk to people, then she might tell somebody about what had happened between them.

That would definitely besmirch the stellar reputation he'd worked so hard to build for himself over the past couple of years.

It smelled like a potential motive to Josh.

FIVE DAYS LATER, on Sunday afternoon, Savannah worked in the kitchen preparing a mandarin orange, bacon and spinach salad, beef Wellington and new potatoes in a garlic butter sauce.

She had talked Josh into spending the day in after the past week of socializing and visiting nearly every storefront and person in Lost Lagoon.

He now sat at the kitchen table with the newest tunnel map that Trey had provided him the day before. "If these tunnels were really made by pirates, then they made sure they had plenty of escape routes."

Savannah left her work at the counter and moved to the table to peer over his shoulder. "It looks like a colorful mess to me."

She was acutely aware of the scent of him that had become so familiar in the last week. It was a fragrance that evoked memories of the kiss they had shared and that moment when she'd seen him in the bathroom clad only in a white towel.

She stepped back and returned to the counter and

her cooking. She was becoming far too comfortable in Josh's company. He made her laugh and he made her think. He fascinated her with his stories of his childhood and what it was like to be a twin.

With each day that passed, she felt him getting beneath her defenses. They had developed a domestic intimacy that had her thinking about how things could be if she would only allow him into her heart.

She'd been half in love with him before Shelly's murder. She was walking that same path now, trying to fight against it but feeling she was losing the battle.

It had even become easier each day for her to leave the house and interact with other people in town.

She'd forgotten how many friends Shelly had before her death, friends who had also been Savannah's. As she met up with them, she was fascinated to learn who was dating whom, who had gotten engaged and all the girl gossip she'd missed for the past two years.

Seeing those people again hadn't been as painful as she'd expected. In fact, there had been a lot of laughter and warmth.

She knew Josh was keeping in close phone contact with Trey concerning the attacks on her, but the official investigation had come to a screeching halt, as had Josh and her unofficial investigation.

Josh had made it clear that he had three potential suspects on his short list: Eric Baptiste, Chad Wilson and Neil Sampson.

He believed Eric might be involved in something

illegal in the tunnels and was now angry that Savannah had told about the tunnels.

He also believed it possible that Chad had some crazy crush on her and now wanted some revenge because she hadn't shown any romantic interest in him.

Finally, he believed it was possible Neil just wanted to silence Savannah forever so she wouldn't be a threat to any future political ambitions he might entertain.

She found it difficult to believe any of those men had been behind the attacks on her, but she also believed that Shelly's killer had walked the streets of the small town for two long years and probably appeared to be a nice, pleasant man that nobody would ever suspect of being capable of murder.

She was particularly aware of Josh this evening. She found comfort in him seated at her table, a sense that he belonged there for every dinner and for every morning cup of coffee. Dangerous thoughts, she reminded herself as she crushed garlic that filled the air with its pungent odor.

Josh was here to protect her from a threat she was beginning to believe might already be over. Nothing had happened over the past week to shake her up. Nobody had acted odd or displayed anything but delight at seeing her out and around town.

Equally dangerous thoughts, she told herself. She shouldn't be lulled into a false sense of safety just because it had been a quiet week.

"There are a couple of tunnels off the main one that you used that still haven't been explored," he said, breaking into her thoughts. "Maybe you and I should go down and check them out."

She turned once again to look at him. God, he was so handsome with his dark hair slightly mussed and a gleam of intelligent concentration in his eyes. He was dressed in a pair of jeans and a light blue T-shirt that hugged the breadth of his shoulders.

"I'll be honest with you. I don't think I can go down in the tunnels again," she confessed. "Even the thought of it closes off my throat and makes me feel like I might have a panic attack."

"That's okay," he replied with an easy smile. "It was just a thought, but we can leave it up to the others to finish mapping the pathways."

He folded the map and shoved it to the side. "What's for dinner? You've been working on it for a while now." She told him her menu and he released a low whistle. "If you keep feeding me this great food each night, I might never want to leave."

And that was the problem. She was beginning to think she didn't want him to ever leave. The silence of the house that she'd once found so comforting had been banished by Josh's presence.

They spent each evening after dinner with a glass of wine in the living room, where they talked about the little things that built a relationship.

She knew his favorite color was blue, that he loved his work here but would eventually like to get on the day shift. She learned his mother's name was Rose and his father was Rick, and she had shared some of her pain over the desertion of her own parents after her sister's death. That had become her favorite time of their day together, when they sat on the sofa and shared pieces of themselves.

She jumped as the doorbell rang.

Josh was on his feet with his gun in his hand in a second. "I'm assuming you aren't expecting anyone," he said.

"Definitely not," she replied.

"I'll answer the door. You stay here," he instructed her. He disappeared from the kitchen. A moment later he returned with Savannah's brother trailing behind him. Mac Sinclair was a big man with an imposing build. He had the Sinclair dark hair and brown eyes and always radiated irritation that bordered on an explosion of anger.

"Mac," Savannah said in surprise. "What are you doing here?"

"Sheila thinks the lamp in my old bedroom will look perfect in our bedroom, so I've come to get it."

This had been a common occurrence since their parents had left the house and Mac had married and set up his own home. He'd already taken the gas grill, a recliner and sundry other items. It was as if when he needed to shop for something he just came here and took what he wanted.

"But it looks nice where it is," she protested and trailed after him as he headed down the hallway. "And Josh is using that room right now." Josh remained in the living room, obviously deciding not to get involved in a sibling argument. "Why don't you just go buy your own lamp?"

They entered the bedroom where the pretty silver lamp sat on one of the nightstands. "Everything in this house is half mine," he replied. "You're lucky I'm just taking a lamp and not the sofa or something else. Besides, I doubt if Josh is doing any reading at night."

He yanked the plug from the wall and picked up the lamp. Savannah wanted to protest but decided an argument with her hot-headed, mean-tempered brother over a lamp wasn't worth it. There was another lamp in the small locked spare room if Josh needed it.

She followed him back down to the living room, where Josh stood waiting. "Josh," Mac said as if noticing him for the first time.

"Mac," Josh returned coolly.

"I heard through the grapevine that you were on babysitting duty," Mac said.

"Your sister is hardly a baby," Josh replied evenly, but his jaw bunched in a ticking knot.

"Just take the lamp and go, Mac," Savannah said. She didn't want to hear her brother degrade her or Josh defend her. She just wanted to get back to the peace she'd felt before her brother had shown up for one of his occasional raids.

Once Mac had left, she and Josh returned to the kitchen. She went back to the counter to continue her dinner preparations, and Josh sat back at the table.

Dinner was a success. The beef Wellington came out perfectly, as did everything else she had prepared.

The conversation flowed easily, and it was just after seven when the kitchen was cleaned up and they each carried a glass of wine to the living room.

As usual, he sat on one side of the sofa and she sat on the other. Now that they were out of the kitchen with the cooking smells, she could smell him, that heady scent of clean male and spice-laden cologne.

"I'm probably going to gain a hundred pounds during my time here," he said and patted his flat abdomen.

"You'll gain way more weight eating George's greasy burgers or all that fried food at Jimmy's Place," she replied, but his words had pulled forth that erotic picture of him in the towel, the sculptured bulk of his magnificent body on display.

They sipped their wine in a comfortable silence for a few moments. "Does Mac come by often and just take what he wants from here?" he asked.

"Often enough," she admitted.

"Do you always let him take what he wants so easily?"

A knot twisted in her stomach as she thought of her older brother. "Most of the time. To be fair, the house was left to both of us when Mom and Dad left town. He could have forced me to sell and split the cash, but thankfully he's let me stay here, so if he wants to take some things from here, I don't argue with him much. There's an extra lamp in the spare room if you need one next to your bed."

"Nah, I'm fine with just the overhead light," he replied.

She took another sip of her wine, the knot in her

stomach twisting tighter. "Sometimes I wonder…" she let her voice trail off, unsure she could speak aloud the haunting thoughts she'd entertained for the last two years.

"You wonder about what?" Josh placed his wine-glass on the coffee table and moved closer to her on the sofa.

Savannah set her wineglass down as well, gazing at Josh intently. "Sometimes I wonder if it was Mac who killed Shelly." The knot inside her eased as she finally spoke of the secret thought she'd held inside for so long.

Chapter Eleven

Josh stared at her in surprise. "Why on earth would you think that?"

Her eyes misted with sudden emotion. "I don't want to believe it. You're the first person I've ever told, but for the last two years I've often wondered."

"Why would Mac kill Shelly?" Mac's name had never come up in the initial investigation. He'd appeared nothing more than a grieving brother at the time.

"Mac hated Bo. He didn't think Bo was good enough for Shelly. He didn't say too much when Bo and Shelly were dating in high school, but as their relationship continued on, Mac was on Shelly's back all the time to break up with Bo. When they finally got engaged, Mac was livid. He tried every way possible to get Shelly to break off the engagement, to get her away from Bo."

The mist in her eyes had become pools as she continued, "I don't think he meant to kill her, but Shelly gave as good as she got from Mac. When he yelled at her, she'd yell louder. While I was always a little bit afraid of Mac and his temper, Shelly never was."

"And so you think it was Mac she met that night at the stone bench down by the swamp?"

"If Mac had asked her to meet him there at that time of night, she probably wouldn't have thought twice about it. I believe it's possible Mac tried to talk Shelly into breaking up with Bo, and things got out of hand between them. It's possible Mac's temper got the best of him. I don't believe he killed her on purpose, but maybe they got into a tussle and Shelly wound up dead, and Mac stole the engagement ring as if to have the final say."

Twin tears trekked down her cheeks and she shook her head and gave a forced laugh. "I must sound crazy. Sometimes I feel like I'm crazy even to consider such a scenario. Most days I don't believe it's possible that he had anything to do with the murder, but other days I can't help but wonder."

Josh's heart squeezed tight at the sight of her tears. "Do you really believe that your brother is capable of killing your sister?"

"That's just it. I don't know. All I know for sure is that the wrong man was accused and that the killer is still walking free." She waved her hand as if to dismiss the topic, but tears ran faster down her face, and Josh could stand it no longer.

He reached out to her, and she came into his arms. She cried only a brief time and then raised her head to gaze at him. "I don't want to believe that Mac is capable of such a thing. I just wish I knew who killed Shelly and who wants me dead."

Josh swept several strands of her silken hair away from her face. "I wish I could give you the answers to all of your questions," he said softly. Then he did what he'd desperately wanted to do for the past week. He kissed her.

Rather than shying away from him, she leaned into him, opening her mouth to allow him to kiss her deeply, soulfully. Just feeling the heat, the softness of her lips, turned him on full force.

However, he had no intention of taking it any further unless she initiated it. He knew what he wanted, but he cared enough about her that it had to be on her terms or not at all.

As she continued to cling to him, as the kiss deepened and went on, he was conscious of every soft curve pressed against him, the heady scent of her that swirled in his head and increased his want.

She finally broke the kiss, her eyes dark and glazed with a desire that fed his own. "Make love to me, Josh."

He looked deep into her beautiful eyes, seeking any doubt she might have after what she'd just asked of him. He saw none, and when she stood and pulled him up off the sofa, his heart pounded with sweet anticipation.

He'd wanted her two years ago, and spending this past week with her had been more than a little bit of torture as he fought against his desire for her. That desire now roared through him as she led him to her bedroom. The bed was neatly made, and he scarcely got inside the door before she wrapped her arms around his neck and pulled him tightly against her as she sought his lips for another kiss.

He didn't hesitate to comply. He took possession of her mouth as he tangled his hands in her long silky hair. She molded her body to his and moved her hips just enough to set him on fire.

The spill of illumination from the hallway was the only light in the room, but it was enough for him to see her beautiful features as she broke the kiss and stepped away from him.

He stood perfectly still, watching her walk to the opposite side of the bed and pull down the spread to display pale pink sheets.

He stopped breathing as she reached down, grabbed the bottom of her T-shirt and pulled it up and over her head, revealing bare skin and a lacy bra. He still didn't breathe when she kicked off her sandals, unzipped and stepped out of her capris and then got into bed and covered up with a sheet.

"Aren't you going to join me?" she asked, a sexy huskiness in her voice.

He finally breathed, drawing in a deep gulp of air as he sprang into action. He yanked off his T-shirt and stepped out of his shoes. His socks followed, and he nearly fell over getting out of his jeans.

The minute he got into bed and under the sheet, he was surrounded by the scent of her, a fragrance he never wanted to get out of his head.

Their bodies came together at the same time they

kissed once again. He marveled at the softness of her skin, the fire in her kiss.

He'd wanted her to come alive, to feel, to be more present, and she was definitely present in this moment. She stroked down his bare back, and at the same time he reached beneath her to unfasten her bra.

When he had it unhooked, she moved her shoulders to allow him to pluck it off her. He pulled his mouth from hers and instead began to blaze a trail of kisses down the length of her neck.

She grabbed his hair, and a gasp escaped her as he covered one of her nipples with his mouth and used his tongue to lick it into a hard pebble.

She moaned his name. He moved to her other breast, taking his time to give her the most pleasure. He wanted this to be an experience she would never forget, a gentle, tender loving that would banish whatever Neil Sampson might have done to her.

He wanted to brand her as his, to make it impossible for her ever to want to make love to any other man. It was with this thought that he recognized the depth of his love for Savannah Sinclair.

A HAZE OF pleasure swept over Savannah, a pleasure she had never known before. His hands and mouth moved over her body in a languid fashion, as if he were in no hurry to finish.

He held his weight on his elbows as he slowly kissed down her stomach to the edge of her panties and then back up again. Her entire body pulsed with need, a new feeling for her.

She'd wanted him since they'd shared their first kiss, since she'd seen him in that low-slung towel, but she couldn't believe she'd made the brazen request that he follow through on giving her what she wanted.

She'd known he wouldn't deny her. She'd felt his desire for her almost every moment they had spent together. She was thirty years old and had experienced sex only once before, with Neil Sampson. And what she'd gone through with him wasn't even remotely close to what was happening now with Josh.

Josh was focused solely on her pleasure, and oh, what pleasure he brought her. When one of his hands slid down her stomach and over the silk of her panties, she instinctively moved her hips up to meet his touch.

Her silk panties became hot, an irritating barrier she wanted gone. As if he read her mind, his thumbs hooked on either side and he slowly pulled them down, moving his body as he tugged them down her legs and off her feet.

Her heart pounded and her breathing became even more rapid as he crawled back up and captured her lips with his. At the same time, his hand slipped down to touch her where her panties no longer shielded her.

His fingers found her most sensitive spot and began to rub back and forth in a rhythm that swelled up sensations inside her, sensations that climbed higher and higher, until she could stand no more.

Her release crashed through her, along with an

uninhibited gasp of laughter and a surprising sob. She gazed up at him in wonder, having never experienced that kind of sexual fever and overwhelming loss of control before.

"Can you do that to me again?" she asked breathlessly.

He laughed and kissed her cheek. "I can definitely try."

And he did. Twice more she rode the waves of intense climaxes, and after the last one, while she was still gasping and boneless, he slid off his boxers and positioned himself between her thighs and entered her.

He remained unmoving, as if making sure she was comfortable. She was more than comfortable. Her entire body was on fire. She wrapped her arms around his back, wanting to keep him that close to her forever. He began to move his hips against hers, and they quickly found a rhythm that stole her breath away and forced all thoughts out of her head.

There was just Josh, filling her, surrounding her and kissing her with a tender passion as their bodies moved in unison.

She was shocked when the waves of sensation began to build yet again, sweeping her up in an intense sensual haze that washed over her. At the same time she felt him stiffen and moan her name as he found his own release.

They remained interlocked for several long minutes, too breathless to move, neither willing to break their intimate connection. "That was better than amazing," he finally said.

"That was better than awesome," she replied with a smile.

"I don't even think there's a word in the English language to describe what it was." He stroked her cheek with his thumb, and for a brief moment, in the faint light of the room, she saw a raw, vulnerable emotion in his eyes.

It was there only a moment and then gone. She tried to convince herself she'd just imagined it. It had just been a trick of the light. That look of pure love had been nothing but her imagination.

He leaned down and kissed the tip of her nose, then rolled from the bed and to his feet. "I'll be right back," he said.

He padded naked out of the room, and Savannah stared up at the ceiling, thinking about what had just happened. She'd never known that making love could be such exquisite pleasure.

The night she'd spent with Neil had been filled with pain and shame. Josh had given her something far different. Josh had given her pure and unadulterated pleasure. He'd gifted her with sweetness and gentleness that had touched not only her body but also her soul. Her body still hummed with a contented relaxation she hadn't felt in years, perhaps had never felt before.

He returned to the room, smelling of soap, with his gun in hand. It was obvious he meant to sleep with her for the rest of the night.

"My turn," she said and slid from the bed. She hurried into the bathroom. She knew it was a bad idea to allow him to sleep with her, but the idea of having him right next to her in bed for the entire night was both provocative and comforting.

One night, she told herself as she left the bathroom and headed back to her bedroom. One night of lovemaking and one night of sleeping together and that would be the end of it.

She couldn't afford to let it happen again. She didn't have the desire or the strength to love anyone again. But for just this single night, she'd let go of her fear and allow herself to feel. Then tomorrow she could crawl back into her cocoon of isolation and self-protection.

She was grateful that when she got back into bed, he didn't seem inclined to talk. He just pulled her close to him, close enough that she thought she could feel his heartbeat against her own.

When she was almost asleep, she turned over with Josh spooned around her back, his breath warming the back of her neck. Nice, she thought. So nice…and that was her last thought.

When she awakened the next morning, she was in bed alone.

The smell of frying bacon and fresh brewed coffee drifted down the hallway from the kitchen. She rolled onto her back and stared up at the ceiling, where the morning sunshine danced through a slit in the curtains.

Instead of stretching like a satisfied cat, she turned back on her side and curled into a fetal ball. Mistake…

As magnificent as last night had been, it had been a huge mistake.

She knew that Josh had a romantic interest in her, and last night had to have given him all the wrong impressions. She thought of that moment when she'd believed she'd seen raw love pouring from his eyes.

It had awed her. It had frightened her. She didn't want him to love her, and she definitely didn't want to love him. He'd already forced her out of her home and into town, something she hadn't wanted to do. She'd been like a snail, perfectly happy and safe in her little shell, but he'd pushed and pulled her out into the dangerous world of emotional vulnerability once again.

It had been over a week since the attack on her at the inn, and nothing more dangerous had happened to her than a hangnail. There were long periods of time as she and Josh were just walking the streets of Lost Lagoon when she forgot that somebody wanted her dead.

In fact, there were long periods when she was with Josh that she forgot to be unhappy and didn't think about her grief or the loss of her sister.

It felt like a betrayal to Shelly, as if she were on the verge of forgetting one of the most important, most beloved persons in her life.

She finally unfurled and got out of bed. She grabbed her nightgown, pulled it over her head, topped it with her robe and headed for the bathroom, where she brushed her teeth, washed her face and pulled a brush through her hair.

She felt unaccountably shy about seeing Josh this

morning. He'd not only given her sexual pleasure she'd never known existed but also been like a warm, comforting blanket she'd snuggled into as she'd fallen asleep.

With a final flick of the brush through her hair, she set the brush down and left the bathroom. She heard him before she reached the kitchen. He was singing a popular tune slightly off-key but with cheerful enthusiasm.

He stood at the oven, using a spatula to stir scrambled eggs in her iron skillet. He was clad only in a pair of jeans, looking hot with his bare torso and totally at ease and at home with his bare feet.

"Good morning," she said.

He jumped and turned around with dismay creasing his forehead. "Shoot, I was going to serve you breakfast in bed this morning."

"That's sweet, but I'm up now." She walked over to the counter with the coffeemaker and poured herself a cup. "But you can serve me at the table."

"It's just not the same," he replied with a pretend pout. He whirled back around as the toaster popped. She sat at the table and watched in amusement as he tried to juggle buttering the toast and taking the eggs from the skillet and getting it all, along with the bacon, on two plates.

He set her plate in front of her and then sat down across the table with his own. "I was going to make you pancakes, but I didn't see any pancake mix in your pantry."

"I don't use a mix when I make pancakes," she replied. She was grateful that, other than his breakfast-making, things appeared normal between them.

She just hoped she could make him understand without hurting him that last night was a one-time deal and wasn't going to be repeated.

As they ate, he talked about the different kinds of pancakes his mother used to make when he was young. Once again Savannah was struck by the domesticity of the scene.

What scared her was that she'd grown accustomed to sharing breakfast with him, eating lunch out and returning home to cook him a good dinner. They had been living like a married couple, and it was all too easy for her to fantasize about it continuing on forever.

It was time to pull away from him, to distance herself from the life she knew he could...he might offer to her. She knew he was here to protect her, but the lines had become blurred between them.

She was no longer a victim waiting for an attack. She felt as if she were a woman who'd already been attacked...by a love she refused to acknowledge, a love she didn't want to embrace.

It was definitely time to withdraw, to crawl back into her shell of safety where she didn't feel, where grief and heartache could never touch her again.

Chapter Twelve

By Tuesday afternoon, Josh knew that Savannah had gone back to the woman she had been when he'd first caught her crawling out of the hole in her backyard.

Throughout the day before, as they'd gone into town and eaten lunch at Jimmy's Place, she had been quiet and withdrawn, as if she wanted to be anyplace else but out with him.

He'd tried to start several conversations but had finally given up when she hadn't responded to any of his attempts. He could only guess that their lovemaking had scared her, while it had emboldened him.

He was in love with her, and that night had only solidified what he already knew. He wanted to build a life with her, have children with her and have her embrace life and happiness once again. He'd thought their night together had been the beginning of all of that happening.

But it had become obvious that for her, that night had been the end of anything between them. Fear and grief once again clung to her, and this fed his frustration.

Over the last two weeks, he'd seen her laughter. He'd felt love flowing from her. He'd seen the potential future with her in it, and he'd liked what he saw.

But this morning, she'd stayed in bed during the time they normally shared breakfast. Then, when she'd finally gotten up and he'd mentioned heading out into town for the afternoon, she'd refused to go. Instead she'd returned to her bedroom and he hadn't seen her since.

He'd made several phone calls, talking to Daniel for a while to get his take on the investigation into the attacks on Savannah, and then calling Trey to get an update.

An hour ago, Ray McClure had run by a copy of the most recent map of the tunnels. Josh had pored over the map, finding it interesting that Trey, the mayor and whoever else was involved had been working backward from the swamp, leaving several of the tunnels closest to Savannah's house still unexplored.

Once again his concern was that Trey was far more interested in the tunnels than he was in solving any crime or helping to protect Savannah.

He'd finally rolled up the map and carried it into the guest room where he'd been staying. He returned to the kitchen, surprised to find Savannah there, rummaging in the refrigerator.

"I had a ham and cheese sandwich for lunch," he said. "There's still plenty left if you want one."

"Thanks." She pulled out the packages of ham and cheese and a jar of mayo. He sat at the table and watched as she made her sandwich, wondering if she intended to take it back to her bedroom to eat.

He was ridiculously pleased when she carried her plate to the table and sat across from him. She took several bites and chased them with drinks of sweet tea.

She didn't speak, nor did she look at him. She kept her gaze focused on her plate as if he wasn't in the room at all. His frustration grew. He felt as if she was punishing him for a decision that had been her own.

He hadn't taken her down the hallway to the bedroom to make love to her. She'd been in charge of the whole thing, and now she acted like he was the one at fault.

"Nice day," he said, breaking the silence.

"Who cares?" she replied.

He leaned back in his chair and released a deep sigh. "What's going on, Savannah?"

She finally looked at him, her eyes dark and fathomless. "This isn't working for me." She pushed away her plate with her half-eaten sandwich.

"What isn't working?" he asked, wondering if she wanted something else to eat.

"This…" She pointed to herself and then to him. "You being here. We haven't learned anything worthwhile about who attacked me. Nothing else has happened to make me think I'm in imminent danger."

"That's because I'm here," he countered.

"I'll call Buck Ranier this afternoon and have him install a security system that rings right into the sheriff's station. I'll be safe here alone, and you can go back to your own life and work."

Josh stared at her in disbelief. "Is this because of what happened between us the other night?"

She looked away from him. "No...yes, partly," she replied. She released a sigh and looked at him once again. "I know you care about me, Josh."

"I'm in love with you, Savannah." He hadn't meant to tell her like this, not under these circumstances, but now that he'd spoken the words aloud, the depth of his love for her filled his heart.

Her eyes were huge. "I don't want you to be in love with me."

He released a dry laugh. "You don't get to be in charge of how I feel about you. I love you and I want to build a future with you. I want you to have my babies and sleep in my arms every night for the rest of our lives."

She raised her chin and her lips trembled slightly. "I might not be in charge of what you want, but I get to be in charge of whether you're welcome here or not, and you're no longer welcome here."

"So, you're kicking me out?" He stared at her in stunned shock.

"That's exactly what I'm doing," she replied.

Josh's frustration exploded. "Why? So you can crawl back into the hole of darkness you've been in for the past two years? So you can wallow in your grief forever instead of accepting that a terrible thing happened to your sister, but you're still very much alive? You staying miserable and isolated won't change anything, Savannah. Shelly is dead, and you've been her ghost for too long."

She got up from her chair and stepped back from the table. "Shelly was murdered, and you and all the rest of your buddies didn't do anything to find her real killer. You pinned it on Bo because it was the easy thing to do, but you didn't conduct a real investigation."

Her words pierced through Josh's very soul. He wanted to deny them, to protest her assessment violently, but he couldn't. She was right. Dammit, she was right, and he couldn't do anything to change what had happened two years ago.

"Maybe you don't love me at all," she continued. "Maybe you just feel guilty about what you didn't do for Shelly."

This brought him up out of his chair. "Trust me, Savannah. I know the difference between guilt and love, and while I will always regret not pursuing the investigation into Shelly's death more thoroughly at the time, guilt has nothing to do with me loving you."

He took a step toward her, but she backed away from him. "I don't want you to love me, and I don't want to love you," she replied, her voice louder than usual. "And you're wrong that I've been stuck in grief for the past two years. I've been in a safe place where I've felt nothing, and that's the way I like it."

"What about happiness? Don't you want to be happy, Savannah? Don't you want to feel and give love, to have children and build a life of happiness?"

He gazed at her and knew his heart was in his eyes for her to see.

She looked away from him. "I'm happy alone, and that's why it's time for you to leave. I told you I'd call Buck and arrange for security. That's all I need." She looked at him once again, and tears shone in her eyes. "I don't need you and I don't want you here anymore. Please just go."

He stared at her, stunned by what she was saying and unable to do anything except what she asked. He wasn't here in any legal capacity. Officially he was on vacation, making him just a guest in her home… apparently an unwanted guest.

"Okay, I'll go," he finally said, because he couldn't legally do anything else.

He'd leave for a couple of hours, give her some time to be alone and maybe cool down. Then he'd come back, and hopefully they could have a rational discussion instead of the emotionally charged one that had just taken place.

He already had his gun around his waist, but he refused to go into the bedroom and pack his things. He refused to accept that this was the end of things. He didn't want to believe that she didn't love him and that love wouldn't eventually win.

He left the kitchen and headed for the front door, aware of her following him. When he reached the door he turned to look at her. "Are you positive this is what you want?"

She hesitated a moment and then nodded. "It's exactly what I want."

"Shelly's funeral should have been a double one," he said. "Because when she was buried, you gave up on life. You're a dead woman walking."

He didn't wait for her response but turned and walked out of the front door. Myriad thoughts flew through his head as he went to his car.

He looked around the neighborhood to see if anything or anyone appeared unusual but saw nothing. It wouldn't be unusual for Josh's car to leave Savannah's driveway in the middle of the day, either. There was no reason for anyone to believe she was in the house alone. Everyone would just assume she was with him in the car someplace in town.

He didn't even want to think about the ache that resounded in his heart over the heated words they'd exchanged, words in which she'd denied any love for him in her heart.

He believed in his heart that she did love him, but he couldn't make her admit it, and he certainly couldn't make her act on it. She was determined to stay in a state of limbo between life and death, and until she decided to make a change, his efforts on her behalf would be fruitless.

He'd give her a couple of hours to cool down. In the meantime, he decided he might do a little tunnel exploration on his own. When he returned, he had to convince her somehow that he could be her bodyguard and nothing more, because the most important thing to him, no matter how she chose to live her life, was that she had a life to live.

THE MINUTE HE walked out the door, Savannah crumpled on the sofa in tears. Agonizing waves of emotion
swept over her, the very emotions she'd spent two years
attempting not to feel.

He was in love with her. He wanted to build a future
with her, and she'd just told him to get out of her life.
She was in love with him, but she was afraid to invite
him into her heart.

And for several tormenting moments, she wondered
what she truly was afraid of. After Shelly's death, she
had never wanted to feel again, to love or care about
anything or anyone again.

But for the last couple of weeks, Josh had pulled her
back to life, had forced her to find her laughter and a
joy she hadn't experienced since Shelly's murder.

She had a feeling it would be impossible for her to
go back to the ghost she had been. Josh had breathed
life and love into her heart, which was why she had to
send him away. She was afraid of everything he held
out in a tantalizingly close hand.

She finally wiped away her tears and got up from
the sofa. She grabbed her cell phone and looked up
the number for Buck's Security Systems. She hoped
he could come right over and get something installed
by nightfall.

She knew eventually Josh would be back, if for no
other reason than to pick up the clothes he had left
behind. But she'd accused him of slacking in Shelly's
murder investigation, which was hitting below the belt.

She couldn't blame Josh for what she considered a

shoddy investigation into Shelly's murder. He'd had to follow the orders of Trey, and Trey had truly believed Bo guilty.

Still, she had no idea how angry she might have made Josh by blaming him. Maybe it was good if she made him angry. Then he'd want to keep his distance from her.

Thankfully the phone call to Buck resulted in the older man telling her he'd arrive within the hour to get her set up with the most updated security system he installed.

While she waited for Buck to arrive, she threw away her half-eaten sandwich and placed the plate in the dishwasher. She then scrubbed down the countertops and shone the wood of the cabinet fronts, needing the physical activity to keep her from thinking.

She didn't want to think anymore. She didn't want to replay Josh's words of love in her head. She didn't want to worry about some creep trying to kill her. She just wished for mindlessness.

She was grateful when Buck finally arrived with his utility truck filled with goodies to keep her safe and sound in the house. She unlocked the doors to the master suite and the extra bedroom that she and Josh had locked up on the first day he'd arrived.

"I'm assuming you want every window and every door covered," Buck said as he walked around the house to check it out.

"And security cameras at the front and back doors," she replied.

"Then I'd better get started." He walked out to his truck, and Savannah sat in a chair in the living room. He returned with all kinds of wire and items Savannah didn't recognize. She only knew they would keep her safe from harm while she was alone in the house.

She wasn't really concerned about being safe during the daytime hours. She just wanted the added protection for when night fell. It was in the dark of night when she'd been attacked at the inn and when she'd seen somebody peeking in her window. It was in the darkness that she felt most vulnerable.

By four o'clock, Buck had every window and every door in the house wired not only to sound an alarm that would awaken the entire neighborhood but also to ring dispatch at the sheriff's station.

He'd also shown her how to monitor her front and back cameras from her computer, allowing her to see about a three-foot radius around both doors.

It was just after four thirty when he left, and Savannah told herself she felt as safe as if Josh was sitting next to her with his gun.

She fixed herself an omelet for dinner and sat at the kitchen table to eat it, pretending to herself that she liked the silence of the house without Josh's presence.

She'd gotten halfway through the omelet when she saw Trey Walker at her back door. She got up from the table, wondering what the sheriff would be doing here. His updates, what few there had been, had always come through Josh.

Maybe he finally had news for her. Maybe he'd discovered the identity of the attacker and was here to tell her the danger was over.

She punched in the numbers to disarm the security system and then opened the door to allow him inside. "Trey, what's going on?"

His eyes shone with excitement. "You've got to come with me. I think I've figured out the answer to everything, but there is something you need to see."

"What?" she asked eagerly.

"I can't explain it. I have to show it to you." He took her by the arm and led her out the door. When she realized they were headed to the bush...to the hole in the ground that led to the tunnel, she dug in her heels.

"Trey, I don't want to go into the tunnels," she protested. "Just tell me what you found."

"It will just be for a minute," he assured her and pulled her forward at the same time he turned on a flashlight.

"Really, Trey, I never want to go down in the tunnels again." She yanked her arm free from his grasp.

Trey pulled his gun and pointed it at her. "I'm afraid I must insist, Savannah."

She stared at the sheriff, her heart pounding with fear. "What are you doing, Trey?"

"I'm taking care of business," he replied. "And if you get down there and think about running, I'll shoot you in the back." There was no hesitation, no emotion in the flatness of his cold eyes. "Now let's go." He gestured to the hole.

With her mind reeling and her heart beating so fast she was half breathless, Savannah started down the three stairs that led into the tunnel.

Chapter Thirteen

When Josh left Savannah's place, he didn't go home. He called Trey and got his answering message. Josh left a message telling him he was taking a break from Savannah's house and would be back there before dark.

Instead he drove into town and to Mama Baptiste's shop. From his trunk he grabbed a flashlight. Once inside the shop, he bought a package of colored chalk.

"I'm using your tunnel entrance," he said to the older woman as he paid for the chalk. "Where is Eric? I don't want any surprises when I go in."

Mama Baptiste's dark eyes flashed with irritation. "My son would never hurt you or anyone else. But you don't have to worry about him being down in the tunnels. He's at home sick today."

"Do you mind?" Josh pointed toward the back room where the tunnel entrance was located.

"Who am I to mind? I'm just a shopkeeper. You're the law," she replied.

Within minutes Josh was in the tunnel and headed for the main passageway Savannah had always used for her ghost walks. He had a mental picture of the latest map Trey had provided him in his head.

Trey and his cohorts had been working from the swamp toward town to map the maze of tunnels, but Josh wanted to check out the last two that were branches from the main path that Savannah had used.

Savannah. His heart ached with thoughts of her. It was obvious his love wasn't enough to make her want to embrace life once again. He'd seen so many glimmers of vibrancy from her, when her eyes had shone with passion and caring, when her laughter had filled the air. He'd had such hope for her, for them, but now that hope was gone.

There was no way he intended to leave her in the house alone at night even if she did have a security system installed. It had been his experience that it was in the dark of night that bad things happened, when neighbors were asleep and couldn't witness, when shadows hid the coming and going of criminals.

He felt she'd be safe this afternoon. People would believe she was out with him and not at home. They had established habits over the last two weeks that would make anyone assume that they were together.

He finally reached the main passage and the steps that would lead up to Savannah's backyard. He turned and passed the first two branches that he knew had been explored and mapped thoroughly.

The third branch was the one where Savannah had been attacked. It had been explored until it forked, and then only the left fork had been followed to the end.

When he came to the fork he went right and began to mark his passage with a bright purple piece of chalk.

It appeared to be just another hole in the earth, no secrets, no hidden gold and no reason for somebody to protect this passageway by attacking Savannah.

He hesitated when he reached a second fork. Left or right? If his internal direction was right, the left fork would take him closer to the swamp while the right one would take him more toward the center of town.

He took the right one, continuing to mark his progress with the chalk. The last thing he wanted was to be down here alone and somehow get lost.

Shining the light on his watch, he saw that it was just after four. He wanted to make sure he was up and out of here long before dark. Even if Savannah wanted him out of the house, if necessary he'd stay in his car in her driveway to assure her safety through the days and nights.

He could have sworn she was in love with him. He'd seen it in her eyes, felt it in her touch. But he'd never considered that she might hold such resentment toward him about Shelly's murder investigation, that maybe her resentment might be bigger, deeper than any love.

He quickened his pace, the only sound the echo of his footsteps. He paused only occasionally to mark his path. What he hoped was that by the time he returned to Savannah's, she would have cooled down and realized that, with or without a security system, him being there was the best way to keep her safe.

Although it would be difficult for him, he'd promise her bodyguard behavior and nothing more personal. The rage that had been expended the night she'd been in the inn confused him. Normally a person holding on to that kind of rage wouldn't be able to contain it for over a week.

He was surprised that something else hadn't happened, that the person had managed to keep control for so long. He wasn't sure if his presence in her home was thwarting another attack or if the person was just patiently waiting it out.

Josh couldn't spend the rest of his life on vacation and protecting Savannah. In fact, the last time he'd spoken to Trey, his boss had asked him when he'd be back on regular duty, and Josh hadn't had a definitive answer.

As he'd walked, he'd felt the descent of the ground taking him deeper and deeper. His heart began to pound when he came to the end of the passageway and saw a set of wooden steps built to take somebody upside. The stairs looked relatively new and solid.

Somebody had gone to a lot of trouble to make this tunnel entrance easily accessible. At the top of the stairs was an ordinary door.

He pulled his gun, as always wary as to what he might be walking into. He placed his flashlight on the top stair and then grabbed the doorknob, surprised when it turned easily beneath his grip.

The door opened without a groan or a creak, and he grabbed his flashlight once again as he walked into total darkness. A quick sweep of the light made him guess that he was in somebody's garage, and the utter silence told him he was alone.

He found a light switch on the wall and turned it on. The space felt oddly familiar, with a seed spreader hung on a rack on the wall and a red riding lawnmower parked on one side.

It was only when he looked at the shelves on the opposite side of the space that his breath caught in his throat. Stacks of plastic-wrapped white substance filled the shelves, and next to one of the stacks was a miner's helmet with a light.

Josh moved closer to inspect the sacks of white. If he had to guess, it was meth. Had Savannah interrupted a drug ring using the tunnels to transport their product? It would appear so.

He frowned and looked around again. Who did this garage belong to? He had a feeling of déjà vu, as if he'd seen this place before, although certainly not with the drugs on the shelves.

He headed for the door that obviously led from the garage into the main house. He held his gun steady in his hand, his heart beating a frantic rhythm.

Was anybody home? He didn't hear any movement or noise coming from the other side of the door. Once again he set his flashlight down and grabbed the door-knob, hoping that the room he was about to enter was as empty as this one.

He opened the door and winced as it gave a faint groan. The door led into a kitchen and he instantly recognized it. The plain beige walls, the white blinds at the window above the sink, and the clock on the wall shaped like a gator…it was intimately familiar.

He'd sat on one of the stools at the island and eaten pizza for a Christmas party. He'd drunk many a beer on the black leather sofa in the next room.

He was in Sheriff Trey Walker's house. Those drugs were in Trey Walker's garage. No wonder the sheriff had steered the team exploring the tunnels to the ones nearest the swamp. He'd had to protect the one that would lead them here.

Fear sliced through the shock of discovery. He'd told Trey he was leaving Savannah alone. He had to get out of here. He had to get to Savannah.

He made a call to Daniel and told him to get to Trey's house and sit on it, that there was evidence that needed to be protected. After the call, he ran the way he had come, leaving through the tunnel and racing as fast as he could to get to Savannah.

He followed his purple marks until he exploded out of the exit in Mama Baptiste's shop. He didn't speak to the startled woman as he ran by her and out the front door where his car was parked.

All he could think about was that he'd not only left Savannah alone but also given her attacker a heads-up that she would be home alone.

He would process his shock at Trey's disgusting corruption later. Right now he needed to get to Savannah's house as soon as possible.

His mind was blank other than with need to protect

the woman he loved. It didn't matter that she didn't love him back. He could live with that. What he couldn't live with was being even partially responsible for anything bad that might happen to her.

His heart dropped to his feet as he saw Trey's car parked two doors down from Savannah's house. Nobody was in the car. He was with her, Josh thought. He was with her right then, and she was nothing but the person who ruined whatever drug business Trey had been conducting through the tunnels.

You ruined everything. That was what the attacker had said to her that night at the inn. Now Josh understood what she'd ruined.

Josh squealed into her driveway and was out of the car before the engine had completely shut down. As he knocked on the front door, he noted the wiring that indicated to him she'd done as she'd told him she was going to do. She'd called Buck.

But no security system would stop her from opening the door to the sheriff. She would have no fear of letting him inside. She'd have no idea that the danger to her wore the uniform of authority.

He knocked twice, and when nobody answered, he ran around to the back of the house. The back door was open, and he peeked inside and saw a half-eaten omelet on a plate on the table.

He stepped inside, and it took him only minutes to clear the entire house. Nobody was home. He stepped out the back door and looked around. Trey's car was here. He couldn't have taken her anyplace far.

He stared at the bush and knew with a heart-stopping certainty that Trey had taken her underground to kill her.

TREY HADN'T TAKEN her far before he tied her hands behind her back. "Why are you doing this? What have I done to you?" Savannah asked in tears as they went deeper and deeper into the maze of passageways. Trey remained silent, his gun shoved hard against her back.

"Please, Trey, just let me go. I don't know anything about anything. I don't know what I've done. I don't know what you've done. If you'll just let me go, I'll forget all about this. I swear I won't tell anyone."

"Shut up." Trey finally spoke, his voice harsh. "I don't want to hear your sniveling another minute."

They continued to walk the earthen burrow, and as they did, thoughts flew through Savannah's head. She knew she was never going to leave these tunnels alive. She didn't understand why, but she'd been marked for death, and these were her final minutes on earth.

For the first time in two years, she realized she didn't want to die. She wanted to live, and not just the way she'd been living. Josh had been right. She'd been going through her life like Shelly's ghost, but she wasn't a ghost, and Shelly would have wanted far better for her.

She'd been foolish to believe that she could go through the rest of her life only holding on to memories and not realizing she needed to love and be loved, to build new memories and live life to the fullest.

Shelly would have wanted that for her, and instead

of the silly ghost walks to pay tribute to her sister, her tribute should have been to live well and find happiness. Like Josh had done...he'd lived his life as a tribute to his brother.

Now it was too late. Trey had taken her down so many tunnels she was utterly lost, her sense of direction had abandoned her and if he shot her now she suspected nobody would hear the blast of his gun.

"Was it you who attacked me at the inn?" she finally asked, needing some answers before the horrible end she knew awaited her.

Trey didn't reply.

"At least tell me what I've done before you kill me," she exclaimed. She stopped walking and turned to face him, his flashlight a blinding beam in her eye. "Don't I have a right to know?"

"Your stupid walks pretending to be your sister's ghost got in the way of a lucrative business."

"What kind of business?"

"I guess it doesn't matter what you know now. Occasionally a fishing boat comes into the lagoon carrying packets of crystal meth. This often happens on a Thursday or Friday night...the same nights you were in the tunnels. We unloaded the packets and carried them through the tunnel to a holding area, where eventually it was distributed to a handful of drug runners."

She stared at him in shock. Drug trafficking? "Who else is involved in this besides you?" She was stunned at his words, at his utter lawlessness, but she wanted all the answers before she died.

"Enough talk. Keep walking," he snarled.

They didn't walk too much farther before they reached a deep alcove set back in the tunnel wall. "Inside, against the back," he instructed her.

She wanted to balk, especially when she saw wires that indicated the entrance of the alcove was rigged with explosives. So, he didn't intend to shoot her. He was going to blast the explosives and bury her alive.

She turned and tried to rush him, hoping to push him aside and run, but he easily shoved her backward, his gun leveled at her center. "Doesn't matter to me how this gets done," he said. "I can either shoot you or blow you up. Now get to the back like I told you."

A bullet would end things immediately. As Savannah walked to the back of alcove, she realized she still entertained a modicum of hope that she'd be saved.

"Sit down with your legs out in front of you," Trey commanded.

She did as he asked, and while he tied her ankles together with rope, any thought of escaping on foot disappeared. She'd thrown Josh out of her house and had said some terrible things to him. This was all her fault. If she hadn't been so afraid to embrace Josh's love, he would still have been at the house when Trey had shown up at the back door.

The only hope she had now was that Josh would have cooled down enough to return to pack his clothes. He'd realize she was gone and go hunting for her. She didn't know if he'd figure out she was down in the tunnels or not.

All she could do now was pray that he'd somehow find her before Trey set off the explosives that would bury her forever.

"How could you be a part of this, Trey? As a law enforcement official, was the money good enough to twist you?" she asked.

"Better than good enough," he replied and leaned against the wall as if he had all the time in the world. "I now own part interest in the amusement park that's going to make me a very wealthy man. I sure as hell wouldn't have been able to do that on my sheriff's salary."

"So this was all about money." As long as she kept him talking, she gave Josh more time to find her. "Was it worth it to sell your soul?"

He laughed. "What makes you think I had a soul to start with?"

"Did you kill my sister? Did she somehow find out something that put your operation at risk?"

"No way," he replied. "I still believe Bo McBride killed your sister, but I had nothing to do with her death. The deal with the amusement park wasn't even a thought then."

With each moment that ticked by, Savannah's hope of rescue diminished. "What are you waiting for?" she finally asked. Just sitting here, waiting for death, filled with regrets, felt like a particular form of torture.

"The boss to arrive," he replied.

"Who is the boss?"

"It doesn't matter to you. You'll be dead in a matter of minutes."

A dark figure appeared behind Trey. Savannah assumed it was the boss, come to witness or make sure that the explosives rigged were appropriately set.

"Put the gun down, Trey." Trey stiffened, and Savannah rejoiced as she heard the deep, familiar sound of Josh's voice. He'd found her. She didn't know how, and at the moment she didn't care. All she knew was that she was saved.

"You wouldn't shoot a man in the back, would you, Josh?" Trey asked.

"Try me," Josh replied in a harsh voice. "Besides, you aren't a man. You're vermin preying on the town and on the woman I love. Try me, Trey. I'm more than itching to put a bullet in your back."

Trey slowly lowered his gun and set it on the ground. Josh turned on a flashlight and shone it on Savannah. "You okay?"

"I am now," she replied with a sob of relief.

Before they could exchange another word, Josh was hit in the back of the head and fell to the ground, his flashlight falling from his hand. Mayor Jim Burns stepped over Josh's body and looked at Trey in disgust.

"Good thing I came along when I did," he said.

"I just want to get this done," Trey replied and picked up his gun from the ground. "I never had the stomach for this kind of thing, and now we have two to kill instead of one."

Savannah was in a state of shock. Jim Burns was the

boss man? Josh had found her, but now he was going to die along with her. She wished he'd never found her.

"You knew the risks," Jim replied. "This has to be done to protect our investments."

Jim moved to what appeared to be a timing device connected to the wires. "I'll give us ninety seconds to get far enough away before the blast."

"How about two minutes?" Trey replied. "Just in case we've miscalculated the distance to safety or we stumble on the way out."

Savannah watched in horror as Jim nodded and set the timer. The two men went running out of the alcove and down the tunnel to the left.

She looked at the unconscious Josh.

They had two minutes to live.

Chapter Fourteen

The minute the two men ran, Josh jumped to his feet. The blow to his head hadn't knocked him out, but he'd played possum, knowing he stood no chance against two armed men.

Savannah gasped as he grabbed his flashlight and then raced to her and scooped her up in his arms. He ran down the tunnel to the right, unsure where he was going but knowing he needed to get as much distance as possible between themselves and the alcove that was about to explode.

He had no idea how much explosive they might have set, but if it was enough it might take down not just the alcove but the entire tunnel system. The explosion would shoot out and the force would follow the tunnels, potentially bringing with it fire and total destruction.

Josh tried to hold Savannah while at the same time wielding a flashlight so he didn't run face first into a wall. His heart pounded with the tick-tock of a countdown to detonation.

Savannah didn't say a word, nor did he attempt any

conversation. All he cared about was getting away from the alcove, as far and as fast as possible.

The deep rumble of the explosion erupted from someplace behind them, but instantly he felt the force of displaced air at his back. He immediately set Savannah on the ground and shielded her with his body, unsure what else to expect.

The earth shook around them, and dirt and rock fell from the ceiling, pummeling Josh on his back. Dust filled the air, choking them both. Then silence.

He remained on top of her, trying to catch his breath and waiting to make sure no more earth would shift. He finally sat up. He first looked down at Savannah, who appeared to be all right, and then shone his light ahead and through the dust-filled air. He was grateful to see that the tunnel hadn't caved in.

"We've got to get out of here," he said, unsure how solid the tunnel structure really was now. Once again he scooped her up in his arms and continued forward, seeking any exit that would take them up and out.

It felt as if he walked forever before he realized that somehow they had wound around and were now in the main tunnel that ran between Savannah's house and the swamp.

He carried her up and out by the bush in her backyard and hurried into her back door. He set her on the edge of a kitchen chair and then rummaged in the drawer for a knife to cut the ropes that tied her wrists and ankles.

She was covered in dust, including her face, making

her brown eyes appear even larger than usual. When he freed her, she jumped up off the chair and wrapped her arms around his neck.

He held her tight, thanking every deity he could think of that he'd found her in time, that she was safe and sound. While he would have liked to stand and hold her forever, he was aware that this wasn't done yet.

He released her and stepped back. "I've got bad guys to get in jail. You lock yourself in here and stay hidden so nobody knows you're home. Don't show your face until you hear me calling to you."

"Do you think anyone heard the blast?" she asked.

"Doubtful, but I'll know when I talk to Daniel. If anyone heard it somebody would have reported it by now."

He pulled his cell phone out of his pocket. Right now he had an advantage since Jim Burns and Trey Walker believed he was dead. As long as they continued to believe that, he had some time to get things into place for a takedown of the two top authority figures of the town.

He called Daniel, and for the next fifteen minutes the two men set into place what needed to be done. "Come by Savannah's when you have things in place," he said and then hung up.

"I'm going to change clothes," he said to Savannah. "You make sure the alarm is set and then stay away from any windows, and Daniel told me there's been no report of an explosion."

He first went into the bathroom and used a wash-cloth to clean away any dirt that was present on his face, neck and chest. He left the bathroom and entered the spare room, where he quickly changed into a clean pair of jeans and a button-down white dress shirt.

When he left the bedroom, he found Savannah sitting on the edge of the tub in the bathroom, still covered with dirt. "Are you going to be okay here alone?" he asked.

She nodded. "As long as the bad guys believe I'm dead. Jim Burns and Trey Walker are influential people. Are you going to be able to have them charged and arrested?"

"Trey has a garage full of evidence, and I have a feeling once he's under arrest he'll turn on Jim like a gator twirling to catch a fish."

"You'll come back here when it's all over?" She looked achingly vulnerable, and he wanted nothing more than to take her in his arms once again.

But he had no right. She'd made it clear to him where they stood with each other before he'd left her house earlier. When he'd taken care of Jim Burns and Trey Walker and the danger was gone, he'd return here to pack his bags and leave her life forever. "I'll be back," he replied.

She stood. "I'm going to take a long, hot bath."

"If I'm gone when you get out, you'll know Daniel picked me up."

She gave him the alarm code to leave the house and rearm the system when he did.

He left the bathroom and closed the door behind

him. She'd be fine without him now. She would choose whatever life she wanted without him in it.

He went into the living room and stood next to the window, where he could peer out but couldn't be seen by anyone. He was still shocked to learn that his boss and the mayor of the town had been in cahoots in a drug trafficking ring. Who else might be involved?

He was eternally grateful that when he'd gone down into the tunnels in search of Savannah, he'd managed to follow the sound of Trey's voice to find and save her. And his heart ached with the knowledge that his time with her had come to an end.

He would never again see her smile at him across the breakfast table. He would never hear her laugh again as he regaled her with one of his stories from his youth.

He'd never know what might have been if she'd loved him.

He hadn't loved Savannah just for the past two weeks. He felt as if he'd loved her for his whole life. He shook his head as if the motion could dislodge the pang in his heart.

Daniel had been equally shocked when Josh had shared with him what had happened and what he had learned. Hopefully he had managed to do what Josh had asked, and by the time darkness fell, the town would be rid of two nefarious characters who had abused their positions of power.

Daniel pulled up, and Josh quickly punched the numbers in to allow him to leave without setting off the alarm. He made sure it was secure again and then raced to jump into the passenger seat of Daniel's car. Daniel roared away from the curb.

"Did you get what I wanted?" he asked his friend and coworker.

"You're lucky I'm good friends with Judge Bolton. He was a bit reluctant to issue a search warrant, but he was more ticked off by the idea of a corrupt cop and mayor, so he signed off on it."

"They aren't just corrupt. They tried to kill Savannah and me," Josh said tersely. "My greatest pleasure will be getting handcuffs on both of them."

Daniel cast Josh a grin. "I knew you didn't have your cuffs with you, so I brought a spare pair. I also know that Trey left the station about twenty minutes ago, so he should be home by now, enjoying a cold beer and dreaming of his future wealth."

"That's just the way I want him, feeling safe and secure until I show up and destroy his world." Josh thought of the vision of Savannah huddled at the back of the alcove, waiting for death to come to her, and his anger at the two men responsible grew.

"Let's just hope he isn't moving the product you saw in his garage as we speak," Daniel said.

"I doubt it. With him believing that Savannah and I are dead, he has no reason to be in a hurry." Josh sat forward in his seat as they turned onto the block where Trey's home was located.

The only car parked in front of the sheriff's house was his patrol car. A light shone from the living room window, and all looked peaceful and normal.

"I want to be the first person he sees when he opens his door," Josh said. "You back me up."

"Got it."

They pulled into the driveway and walked to the front door. Josh knocked, and when his boss answered, Trey's eyes opened wide and then narrowed. "You can't prove anything," he said immediately. "It's your word against mine. I'm the sheriff of this town, and you're just a disgruntled employee I've been having problems with lately."

Daniel cleared his voice and stepped into view. He held out a piece of paper. "We're here to serve a search warrant for these premises."

"And we're going to start our search in your garage," Josh added.

Trey tried to push past the two men, but Josh grabbed him by the arm, twirled him around and snapped handcuffs on his wrists.

"Now let's take a look in your garage." Josh grabbed Trey's elbow and led him to the evidence that would be the end of life as Trey knew it.

IT WAS AFTER TEN when Daniel finally dropped Josh back at Savannah's house. The place was dark and looked as if nobody was home. Apparently Savannah had taken his advice to heart and hadn't turned on lights to indicate that anyone was there.

"Savannah," he yelled through the door.

She immediately opened the door and let him inside. "Is it done?"

He nodded and turned on the end table lamp in the living room. "It's over. Trey and Jim are both behind bars and will face a judge sometime tomorrow. We also arrested Ray McClure on suspicion of conspiracy."

She sat on the sofa and motioned for him to join her. Dressed only in a short gold-colored nightgown and matching robe, with her hair shiny and her brown eyes sparkling with gold flecks, she broke his heart all over again.

"We don't know for sure what Ray's involvement might be. He swears he knew nothing about the drugs, but he was Trey's right-hand man, so the jury is out on whether he was part of the crime," he continued.

"Trey started singing like a bird once we had him in custody. Apparently both he and Jim were investing heavily in the amusement park, and he told us it was Jim who attacked you at the inn. Jim wanted revenge on you because you brought attention to the tunnels."

"Did he say who grabbed me in the tunnels?" she asked.

"Apparently that was Trey. He wanted to scare you enough that you'd stay out of the tunnels forever. Apparently he didn't intend to hurt you."

"I wish he'd told me that. So, what happens now at the sheriff's office? With the mayor? Who is going to be in charge?" she asked.

"Daniel will probably step in since he's the chief deputy sheriff, but to be honest, I'm not sure what's going to happen. It's possible that because nobody knows the depth of corruption, the department of justice or attorney general will have to come in to sort things out."

He forced a smile at her. "So, it's done. You're finally safe now, and I'll just get my things and let you have your life back."

He started to stand, but she grabbed him by the forearm and pulled him back down on the sofa. "It's not over yet." Her eyes simmered with an emotion he couldn't read, but a small fist of anxiety curled in the pit of his stomach.

She tucked a strand of hair behind her ear and stared at a point just above his shoulder, nervous tension rocketing through her. "I said some terrible things to get you out of the house. I didn't mean them. I know you weren't responsible for the investigation into Shelly's death. I wanted you out because you scared me, Josh." She looked at him. "Everything about you scared me."

"Why?" he asked in obvious confusion.

"Because you are vibrant with energy and a love of life. Because you forced me out and back into the world I thought had betrayed me by taking Shelly away."

"As I recall, I said some pretty rough things as I made my exit from here," he replied.

She smiled ruefully. "You spoke the truth. I had become a ghost. I'd given up on life and on any idea of finding happiness. It just felt like a betrayal of Shelly."

"I remember the first time I went out with friends after Jacob died. A bunch of our friends were going to a horror movie, and I decided to go after weeks of just hanging around in the house. I felt guilty the minute I got into the car. I shouldn't have been doing anything without Jacob. Then the movie started, and it was the kind of gory horror movie that Jacob loved. At that moment I felt his presence inside me, and I knew he was glad I was going on with my life."

He gazed at Savannah, knowing that his love for her shone from his eyes. "She will always be alive," he said softly. "Just like Jacob will always be alive to me. He lives on in my memories and in my heart."

"When Trey took me down in the tunnel and I knew I was probably going to die down there, I suddenly realized how much I wanted to live, how disappointed Shelly would be in me because of the choices I've made since her death. Shelly loved life. She embraced it like a favorite teddy bear, and that is what she would want me to do."

Savannah could tell by Josh's expression that he wasn't sure where this conversation was going, but she did, and she only hoped she wasn't too late.

"I shed my ghost while facing death," she continued. "I found the real Savannah again, the woman who wants to open a restaurant and laugh at silly stories. I'm the woman who loves to sit on the patio in front of the ice cream parlor and eat a waffle cone."

She moved closer to him on the sofa and saw by the look in his eyes that it wasn't too late for her, for them. "Josh, I'm the woman who was crazy about you two years ago, and now I'm the woman who is crazy in love with you."

He remained unmoving, his blue eyes shimmering. "Say it again," he demanded.

"I love you, Jo..." She didn't get the whole sentence out of her mouth before his lips claimed hers in a fiery kiss that stirred her from head to toe.

When the kiss finally ended he laughed, the sound one of pure joy. "I got the bad guys in jail and I got the girl. Life doesn't get any better than this."

"Yes, it does," she replied and snuggled against his side. "There's building a restaurant and being together and making babies."

His arm tightened around her. "I like the sound of that, especially the last part."

She smiled up at him. "The restaurant is going to take some time. But we're together now, so we could start working on the last part."

She laughed as he jumped up off the sofa and held his hand out to her. She grabbed his hand, and as he led her down the hallway toward her bedroom, she knew he was really leading her into her future...a future of happiness and laughter and love.

Epilogue

It was the beginning of a new month, and for Savannah it was the beginning of her new life. August had arrived and with it big changes not only for the town of Lost Lagoon but also for Savannah.

Although it had only been a week since she and Josh had professed their love for each other, Savannah was moving into Josh's house. Mac was thrilled that she was selling out, rubbing his hands together at the prospect of the money from the sale of the house.

Jeffrey Allen had already contacted the Realtor she'd hired to handle the sale, and negotiations were in the works even though she had yet to put a For Sale sign in the yard.

Both Trey Walker and Jim Burns were in jail, facing a variety of charges. Both men had been denied bail by the judge they had faced, despite the arguments by their lawyers.

For now Daniel was working as acting sheriff, but rumor had it that the attorney general was sending somebody in to take over and clean up any lingering corruption.

At the moment, the last thing on Savannah's mind was evildoers and town business. As she filled a box with her clothing, all she could think about was Josh and the happiness that filled her heart.

Over the past week, her love for him had only grown stronger. Once she'd truly let down her defenses, she'd allowed his love to flow over her, into her, and she'd never known that kind of joy before.

Some people might accuse her and Josh of rushing things by her selling the house and moving in with him, but she'd never been so sure of anything in her entire life.

She checked her watch. After two. She needed to leave here by three so she could get to Josh's house and have dinner waiting for him when he got home just after five.

He was on day shift now, but Savannah had already warned him not to get used to her cooking dinner for him every night. Just as she'd embraced loving Josh, she'd re-embraced her old dream of opening a fine-dining restaurant in town.

She was going to have it all, a love to last a lifetime, a successful business and eventually a family. She walked over to the desk and picked up the ceramic frog that had belonged to Shelly.

She cradled it in her hands. She would always feel grief and loss when she thought of Shelly, but with Josh's help, she'd finally moved into acceptance.

Just like Josh had told her, Shelly would always be with her, in her memories and in her heart. Even now, as the ceramic frog warmed in her hands, she felt Shelly smiling down from heaven at her.

Shelly would sing with the angels at Savannah's wedding. She'd shine down with her smile when Savannah opened her restaurant, and she'd be with her in spirit when she gave birth to her first child.

Savannah hoped someday the murder of her sister would be solved and the guilty put behind bars. But even if that never happened, she was determined to get on with her own life.

Savannah jumped as she heard the sound of the front door opening. She set the frog down in the box of clothing she had packed and hurried down the hall to see Josh.

"Hey, what are you doing here?" she asked.

As he walked toward her, his lips formed that sexy smile that she knew would warm her heart for the rest of her life. "I was in the neighborhood and decided I needed a kiss." He pulled her into his arms.

She smiled up at him. "Do you always just stop in at some random house when you're on duty and feel the need for a kiss?"

"Nah, I'm very picky. I only stop to get a kiss from the woman I'm going to marry."

"Good answer, Deputy Griffin," she said just before his mouth slanted to hers in a kiss that told her everything she needed to know about her future…and it was going to be magnificent.

* * * * *

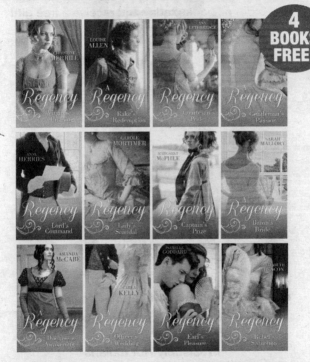

  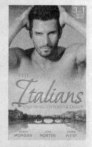